THE DREAM OF FAIR WOMEN

BOOKS BY HENRY WILLIAMSON

NATURE BOOKS

TARKA THE OTTER
THE OLD STAG
THE LONE SWALLOWS
THE PEREGRINE'S SAGA

NOVELS

THE BEAUTIFUL YEARS
DANDELION DAYS
THE DREAM OF FAIR WOMEN
THE PATHWAY

With the pendent
THE STAR-BORN
(*now being amended and prepared for publication*)

The above make the tetralogy called
THE FLAX OF DREAM

THE PATRIOT'S PROGRESS
In collaboration with Mr. William Kermode

OTHER BOOKS

THE WET FLANDERS PLAIN
THE VILLAGE BOOK

THE DREAM OF FAIR WOMEN

BY

HENRY WILLIAMSON

WITH
A VALEDICTION TO
THE FLAX OF DREAM

'Save his own soul he hath no star'
SWINBURNE

LONDON
FABER & FABER LIMITED
24 RUSSELL SQUARE

FIRST PUBLISHED IN JUNE MCMXXXI
BY FABER AND FABER LIMITED
24 RUSSELL SQUARE LONDON W.C.I
PRINTED IN GREAT BRITAIN
BY TREND AND COMPANY PLYMOUTH

TO

J. D. BERESFORD, who helped the
young writer much; coupled with
the name of WALTER DE LA MARE
—friends seldom seen, but well
beloved

CONTENTS

'THE POLICY OF RECONSTRUCTION,
OR,
TRUE RESURRECTION'

Chapter 1

FAR below, at the bottom of the coombe where the sea glimmered with the grey-purple of after-sunset, they saw the smoke rising straight above the cottage. 'Yes, Maddison's at home,' declared the girl, and walked on rapidly, followed by her silent, as if reluctant, companion. The path was narrow and uncertain, broken by the feet of cattle among the furze and bracken and brambles of the coombe-side, and frequently the young man muttered curses when the spines pricked through the stockings he wore with his golfing suit of Harris tweed. Halfway down they heard the noise of the fast-falling stream; the path wound through a thicket of blackthorn, and she half turned to give him her hand, as though playfully frightened at the dark still maze of spines and branches around and above them; but at his firm clasp, and the beginning of an appealing expression on his face, she slipped her fingers out of his retaining hand, and continued down the path. The young man stared bleakly after the girl; then, scowling, he followed slowly.

He came up to her silently, standing on the single slab of rock thrown across the narrow stream about fifty yards above the cottage; he stood behind her, neither speaking nor appearing to take interest in her nearness. Suddenly she pointed, and shared a swift eager glance with him, for a light, as of a candle, was moving across the lower window. A large white bird beat slowly and silently past them, and flew in through the open casement.

'It's exciting! Come on, Pat.'

Bluish smoke from the cottage rose wavering, almost straight; the waves mumbled on the beach below. As they walked beside the walled-in garden between the path and stream gulley, the light within the room ceased to shine; then it was winking again, and they were near enough to see the flickering candle-flame and to hear the thin whining of a dog or dogs within the cottage. The door was beside the window; she knocked with her knuckles. The whining changed instantly to the furious barking of two dogs, in which could be heard other noises, like the cawing of a crow and the flutter of wings. Through the casement floated the owl, two dark eyes in a white face, yellow-ish wings wafting it the way it had come. After an interval of listening, and glances exchanged with her companion, the girl smiled, and rapped on the door again. The barking increased, near the shut door.

They waited; and the barking went on.

She picked up a stone and struck twice sharply on the door, like a postman's knock. The barking increased to a frenzy of snarling.

Going to the open window, she called out:

'Are you there, Captain Maddison?' in a tone of voice that caused the man beside her to give a half sigh, half sneer, and turn his back on her.

'Lie down, dogs. You're only spaniel pups; you can't do the heavy faithful hound on me. Captain Maddison?'

She peered over the window sill, and saw a black and white kitten staring fixedly at her from its squatting place on some books on a single shelf nailed to the opposite wall. At the other end of the shelf a bird like a seagull was perched on one leg, also staring at her.

'Pat, I must leave the message,' she called out loudly. 'I'm going in to see if I can find a pencil and paper.'

'All right. I'll wait here.'

'He's probably round at the back. You'd better come in with me.' In a lower, more intimate voice, she said, close to him, 'I'm feeling rather nervous, darling. Don't let me go in alone.'

At the intimacy of her voice he adjusted his Old Etonian tie with a quick movement, rapped on the door, and lifting the latch, opened it. The spaniel puppies ran back, barking less decidedly.

'You naughty little things,' she cried; and stooping, held out her hand. The smaller of the two dogs, with white patches on its brown coat, wriggled towards her, drawing a thin wet line of nervousness after it on the stone floor. Just before its tongue licked her outstretched hand it rolled over on its back and lay there, fluttering its tail.

'The darling, it's still got its baby-teeth!' she cried, as though in rapture, and glanced up as though expecting to see the inner door opening. 'I wonder where he can be?' she whispered to her companion.

'Urgent private affairs, perhaps'; he shrugged his shoulders.

The other spaniel slunk about at the far end of the room, sometimes sniffing at the crack under the inner door, whining and growling. The eyes of the man and the girl began to rove about the room and its contents. The cat stretched and jumped down from the bookshelf, and rubbed itself against his stocking.

'Puss, puss,' he said, and seemed to forget it.

A wood fire burned in an open brick hearth, warming their legs. Many sheets of paper were roughly piled on the small three-legged round table, with a fountain pen and several books, illumined by the candlelight.

'Better shut the door, Pat. The candle's "leaking", as Jonquil would say.'

There were no chairs in the room: only the table, a couple of boxes, the bookshelf, some sacks on the floor, a jar of water, a worn-out broom with barnacle-bored handle, and several odd boots, probably for burning, for obviously they had been washed up by the sea.

'Not exactly a luxurious place, what?' drawled the young man.

'Hush!' she said.

They listened. The dog growled. The salt-wood in the fire hissed.

' "The Policy of Reconstruction, or, True Resurrection",' she read aloud, softly, peering over the table. 'H'm.'

'A long letter to *The Times*, what?'

'Don't keep saying "what", my dear,' she said serenely. 'Be yourself.'

'I am,' he replied; and she detected the uneasiness in his voice.

'Poor old Pat,' she said.

She began reading.

'And the term went on, preparing us for "the conflict of a mature life", stealing the wind and the sun which make the genius of man. On the tower of the school floated the national flag, frayed and bleached in the white air passing over all lands with the secret gifts of heaven, the white wind fraying and bleaching all flags. And the term went on in the shadowed classrooms, the last term for me and Jack, Bony and Rupert, Fitzaucher and Burrell, all the friends who had swatted and played together—the summer of 1914, which was to see the apotheosis of ideas and methods which everywhere had crushed the imaginative tissues of childhood, as the young leaves of dandelions on the Gadarene slopes.'

'What does apo—the—o—sis mean, Pat?'

'Lord, I don't know.'

'Thought you were at Eton.'

'So I was. But I've forgotten my Lat—my Gree—my damned classics. Why?'

'Nothing. Listen!'

They listened.

'Perhaps the candlelight was invisible until we got to the right angle,' she said. 'Perhaps no one was in here, after all. I wonder where that door over there leads to.'

They looked at the inner door. The other spaniel pup was sitting against it.

She lifted the latch and opened it. The puppy slunk upstairs.

'Captain Maddison!' she called up into the darkness.

They heard the tap of dog-claws on the wooden floor above; then silence. She closed the door softly.

'He may be upstairs,' she whispered. 'If so, it will pay him out if we remain here until he comes down! I wonder where the puppy went to?'

'Sleeping on the bed, if there is a bed,' said the man.

'Listen, Pat, what do you make of this?' She read aloud what she had read to herself a few moments before.

'Seems religious,' commented her companion. 'Is it all like that?'

'I don't know yet. I wonder what school he went to. Anyhow, I know it wasn't Eton, so you're quite safe when we do find him, my dear Pat.'

'You seem to be in a very amiable mood,' drawled the man. 'But still, I suppose it's inevitable,' he added bitterly. 'What about writing out the message; or haven't you thought of it yet?'

'Oh, yes, I've been thinking of it for a long time,' she replied evenly as she turned over the sheets. 'But I do think it is such a pity you aren't truthful, my dear Pat. To me, I mean.'

'But, Lina, I am,' he replied appealingly. 'Good. I thought I'd lost them on the way down.'

While she had been speaking, with her back turned to him, he had been searching assiduously in his pockets, muttering an occasional 'Blast!' or 'Damn!'; now, as she turned over the sheets on the table, he held out a yellow packet of cigarettes over her shoulder. 'I say, have a gasper?'

'Naps Spreycombe was at Eton,' she said musingly, ignoring the yellow packet, 'and he said you were not at Eton. Why swank, Pat?'

'Spreycombe, pooh! He was sacked for stealing!'

'Yes, I told you that, didn't I?'

'As a matter of fact I was sacked, too; that's why I went to Canada.'

'Oh, yes? My dear Pat, swank is so silly. Besides, you don't need to. It isn't everyone who's got the D.S.O. and a bar, and the M.C., and those other pretty ribbons you wear with them.'

He replied as though scornfully: 'I suppose you think they're just swank, too?'

'Certainly not, my dear Patrick Colyer. I've looked them up.'

'Well, next time you see Spreycombe, ask him for a list of O.E.'s,' he said more easily; and leaning over her, with his hand on her shoulder, he rubbed his cheek against her own. 'Darling, have I done anything?'

'Darling Pat,' she murmured, 'of course not'; and she went on reading.

After a moment passive beside her, he left the table, and standing with his back to the fireplace, lit a cigarette.

He blew on the glowing end repeatedly; then: 'You seem to find great interest in another person's private papers.'

'I do. Great interest. Listen to this, Pat.'

'From the very earliest times I have been struggling to be myself. Before I knew good from evil—at least, the good and the evil of those standards which made the Great War—I was having the value and the practice of these abstract qualities rammed into my un-understanding consciousness.

'I was often condemned and punished for the manifestations of my growing instincts, including that of the most valuable in human life—the social instinct. For instance, if at school something of great interest occurred to my mind (something of the free natural life) and I communicated it to another—the will to share a joy—I was invariably discouraged, if not punished. Any instinctive protective devices to guard the mental and imaginative tissue were not recognized as such: they were condemned as vices, and I was made to double my body, and to shut my eyes, and await the strokes of pain; for I was helpless.'

'In other words, he was swished for being a bloody little liar,' said the man, and laughed to himself.

She glanced around the room, at its bareness, at the cobwebs along the broken ceiling, from the cracks of which hung old straw fragments and the husks of seeds scattered by the mice of long ago. On the bookshelf stood a pot of paint, a brush stuck to the wood beside it: the shelf was crudely painted with yellow stripes, on which were the marks of cat-feet. She turned over a page, then another page.

'Once there were crowds of cheering men in London and Paris, Berlin, St. Petersburg, Vienna, and New York; and following the cheering was activity and an unusual friendliness in each of those places, while the rulers of nations became solemn and earnest, all praying to God, all believing in their national righteousness. And *because of the praying*, men continued to die and to be maimed, until for many men death and wounds were reliefs from the desolation and despair of war. In that war my body suffered and sweated, and was tempted to destroy itself; but Hope for wounds made me, in common with millions of other men, keep on. O Great Earth Spirit, to which my thought rises in the sunlight of the hills, and when the stars are faithful and bright over the wide ocean, the sunset-sunken sea, no man wanted to die, yet the bones of murdered men girdle the earth, and the footsteps of women follow in pride and grief and prayer to the wildernesses where they lie. And so it was in ancient Rome, in Babylon, in Assyria, in Egypt—in all the civilizations that have been. Pride; and prayer to God. Their Gods are dead; the sand hides the skulls of their priests, and hawks nest in the walls of the ruined temples, to which the sunlight has returned. The sunlight! Truth pours down in the sunlight! The sun pours its beams on the worn stone of the cathedrals—Canterbury, Cologne——'

She turned over the page, looking for writing more personal.

'How about supper?' asked the man behind her. 'We told old Fatface in the pub we would be back by nine o'clock.'

'Just let me read this.'

When, after a minute, she continued her search among the papers, he said,

'Why not come down to-morrow and finish the serial? Fatface said the hermit is out walking all day; so you'll have all day for it.'

'You have no soul, my dear Pat.'

'None at all; merely a foolish sense of reticence about another man's private papers.'

'Once an Old Etonian, always an Old Etonian, what? Well, I suppose it's no good waiting any more for him to come in. But I'd like to know where that puppy went to, all the same.'

She crossed swiftly on her toes to the door leading to the bed-room, opened it slightly, and listened. The other spaniel slipped through the space, and pattered up the bare wooden stairs. She turned towards the fireplace, and pointed upstairs. There was an expression of smiling excitement on her face that further depressed the young man watching her.

'Pat,' her voice called clearly, 'Captain Maddison may be ill upstairs. Don't you think we'd better go up and see?'

The man called Pat shrugged his shoulders. 'I don't know.'

'I'd better take the candle, I think.'

She went slowly up the stairs, holding the candle above the level of her eyes. The stairs creaked. She stopped halfway up, listening to the whining of the dogs; she heard the noise of bumping. Hot grease fell on her hand from the crooked candle-flame. She climbed to the top of the stairs.

'Is anyone there?'

The space upstairs was divided by a lath-and-plaster partition, and a doorway between the two small limewashed bed-rooms. The first room was empty, except for three cardboard texts hanging from rusty nails on the walls.

'God Bless Our Home, Fear The Lord,' and 'Seek And Ye Shall Find,' she said aloud. The texts looked as if they had been there a long time.

The puppies were whining in the next room. Overcoming a thrilling feeling of fear in the eerie light, she looked round the doorway, smiling.

'Anyone there? May I come in?'

Still smiling, she pushed open the door. The room was empty. She put down the candle on the washstand. The pup-pies, crouching on the recessed window-seat, looked at her over their trembling shoulders. The air moved past her towards the window, flattening the candle-flame. She shivered.

'Pat!' she called out. 'Pat, come here!'

He leapt up the stairs. 'Hell! Damn the place! It's all right: I only cracked my napper on that bloody beam.' He came up slowly, rubbing his head.

'Poor old Pat; never mind. I say, I believe he jumped out of the window!'

'I don't wonder at it. He's got you taped, my dear. No, honestly, was he really hiding up here? I thought I heard a thud outside, too. Extraordinary chap.'

She was looking about the room. On a camp bed, broken at the foot end, was heaped a pile of bracken over which two army blankets were spread. There was a wooden washstand, with pitcher and basin. Dust and a drowned beetle lay on the sunken surface of the water. A candle-end was guttered in a bottle-top on an upright sugar box by the bed. In one corner of the room was an old khaki field-valise, with 'W. Maddison, Reserve Cavalry' printed thereon in letters of cracked white paint.

'I bet he pinched those army blankets,' remarked the man.

'Quite right, too! Poor dear, he doesn't seem to be very comfortable. My God, look there!'

She pointed at a large black bird hunched at the end of a whitewashed beam crossing the ceiling. It blinked a sulky eye at them.

'Jesus Christ, what next?' exclaimed the man.

'What is it, Pat, a crow?'

'Looks like a young raven. God, what an existence. Fatface at the pub said he was queer. Fatface was certainly right!'

'Poor old Pat—the conventional Etonian.'

'But dash it all, it's unhealthy!' he replied, putting his hand on her shoulder and fondling her neck with the back of his fingers. She moved away, and he scowled at the jumping shadow on the white wall behind her.

'Shut up, you beastly curs! I say, we ought to be getting back, Lina. Seriously, I didn't leave the lamps of the bus on, either.'

'Square the bobby with a drink when we get back. I'm enjoying this adventure! Listen!'

The girl, the man, the crow, the puppies, all listened.

'Look!' she whispered, pointing to the candle-flame, which was now bent away from the window.

'Did you leave the outside door open?'

'No!'

'Then he's downstairs!'

They heard stealthy movements below. She clutched his arm. 'My God, Pat, supposing he's mad!'

Yes, someone was shuffling the papers on the table. They stared at each other.

'Keep still!' he whispered.

For about half a minute they remained unmoving, listening intently. They started violently, and the man swore, as the puppies jumped or rather fell down behind them, and made a whining rush for the door. They heard them tumbling downstairs. She laughed with relief.

'Come on, Pat,' she said loudly, as one of the puppies barked happily.

'Nothing worth pinching up here!' And taking the candle, with her arm in her companion's, she led him downstairs. The door was wide open; most of the sheets of *The Policy of Reconstruction* were gone from the table; the room was empty; and outside the faintly starry night was silent beyond the sounds of the stream and the waves, and the distant bleat of a goat tethered somewhere on the dark hillside.

Chapter 2

The landlord of the Nightcrow Inn, coat and collar and waist-coat off, was leaning over the bar, reflectively prodding one of his ruinous molar teeth with the burnt and pointed end of a matchstick. He was a short, sturdy man, with a round face and small clipped moustache; his face and elbows were brown with the sun, while the forepart of his head was bald and shiny as a new chestnut. 'Yes,' he was saying in the intervals of absorbed probing, 'us wants a bit of rain to bring on the pays and the tetties, and my cabbages be running up to spill.' The peas and the potatoes lacked rain; and the cabbages were sending up the branched stalks of yellow flower-clusters, which took the goodness of the green hearts, and made them not worth the cutting. The lack of rain was being widely discussed in the village, and indeed all over England at that time, for no rain had fallen since March, and it was now the third week of June.

About a dozen men were seated on wooden benches round the polished table, relaxing after the day's work in the fields. It was a Thursday night, and only the quiet men were there: the others had spent their beer money earlier in the week. The nightly game of whist in the corner was over; the worn and grubby cards were piled on the table. The room, with its dark beam and joists and smoke-yellow ceiling, was lit by a paraffin lamp hung on a bent nail beside the small American wall clock. A man entered and closed the door.

'Pint of fivepenny, please, Albert.'

'Yes, sir,' replied the landlord, and went to take the pot. He came back from the barrel-room with the ale, and placing it on

24

the table, took up the money with a word of thanks, and leaned as before over the bar.

'Be the lady and gennulman in t'other room?' enquired the newcomer in a whisper, jerking his head towards the sitting-room through the wall. His ragged coat was spotted and splashed with mortar; he was a mason working on the first cottage to be built in the district following the Great War.

The landlord nodded.

'Be'm biding yurr the night? What be'm, honeymooning?'

'Not so far as I know,' said the landlord. 'What makes you ask that?'

' 'Tes what they be telling,' replied the mason; and he took a long pull at his beer.

' 'Tes a master great motor-car they came in,' remarked another man.

'Aiy,' said the landlord quietly. 'The gennulman be a famous flyer, so the young lady was telling me. He shot down nigh on fifty German flyers. 'Tes true, for she showed me the photos of his airyplane. Very nice couple, they be.'

'Friends of the young chap down by the mines, ban't 'em?'

'Aiy, that's it!' spoke an old man in the corner. 'I was walking along wi' me basket on me arm, slowly like, for it were turrible hot in the lane, when I heard a roarin' and a bawlin', and a motor-car passed in a cloud of dust, and stopped in front of me, and was as quiet as you please, a-mumblin' away like a ole drummle-drane in a cowflop.'

They laughed at the reference to a wild bee in a foxglove flower; but he held up his hand, and went on:

'A young lady turns round, as pretty a maid as ever I zeed, and says, "Please can you tell us where Captain Maddiz'n lives?"

' "If you please, young lady, the gennulman you'm enquiring for resides to Rat's Castle," ' I said. 'That's as true as I'm sitting here!'

Shouts of laughter bestirred the air. He was the village wit:

he had told the same tale thrice in the last hour, sitting on the same seat under the clock. The old man held up his hand again. From the corner, his face, shiny like an old apple, glanced in a semi-circle to gather in their attention. He wore an old tweed fishing cap, a black shirt, a crumpled collar and a frayed tartan tie knotted as though it were a bootlace.

' "And what be his occupation, if you please?" her zays.

' "Looking after sick birds and beasts of the fields, miss," I zays, "and also studying of many books."

' "A pity he hasn't studied his face in the glass," her says, 'that's as true as I be sitting yurr.'

They laughed again; but the raised hand checked them.

'Listen, please, to what I be telling. The young lady asks me if I'd like a ride in the motor-car, and I zays: "Thank you very much, young lady; it be a hot day, and if you'm going my way I'll give you instructions how to reach the gennulman's cottage, which us calls Rat's Castle hereabouts, if you'll excuse me telling ee." Then almost before a flea could hop across from my hat to your hat, us had cut through a gale o' wind and I was getting out of the seat by the churchyard gate. 'Tes true what I be telling, mind! Yes, 'tes!'

'Aiy, 'tes true enough,' said a soft melancholy voice. It came from a man sitting in shadow: a man with a long black moustache, a decayed hat, and eyes that looked in different directions.

' 'Tes true what Muggy Smith have just been telling, for I spoke to the young lady when the car stopped, and although I've got one glassen eye, I can see just as well out of t' other booger!'

They bellowed with laughter, except the old man in the corner, who was preparing to continue along his own line of humour.

'Just a minute, chaps,' interrupted the landlord, who had put the matchstick into his waistcoat pocket, and was now fingering his pipe. His voice dropped, and he jerked the pipe-stem over his shoulder. 'They'm in the next room, so be careful what you'm saying. I'm only just telling 'ee, if you understand my meaning.'

Nobody spoke for an interval; and the man in the corner was about to say something, when the door opened and a complete silence came over the room until the young gennulman they were all watching murmured to the landlord: 'I'd like a double whiskey and soda, please.'

'I'm sorry, I've no soda, sir.'

'Then I'll have water, please.'

'Thank you, sir. Was the supper to your liking, sir?'

'Quite.'

'And the lady, sir, I hope was satisfied?'

'Yes, thank you. And I'd like some cigarettes.'

'Thank you, sir.'

Absorbedly they watched him swallow the glass of whiskey; then, pouring a little water into the empty glass, swallow the water.

'Another, please.'

'A double, sir?'

'If you please.'

'Thank you, sir. Excuse me asking, zur, but be you going far to-night? I was only asking because you said something about the lights, and these lanes be narrow for anyone not used to them, if you understand what I'm saying.'

'I understand perfectly.' He swallowed the fresh glass of whiskey as before. 'How far off is Ilfracombe?'

'Eight mile, zur, as near as makes no odds.'

'Can I get any carbide anywhere near, d'you know?'

'Not that I know of, zur. Branton's about the nearest place for that sort of stuff. Us'v got oil, zur, if that be any good.'

'I'll have to risk driving in the dark, that's all. Damn it! Another whiskey, please. And have a drink yourself. And everyone else, too.'

A chorus of 'Thank 'ee, zur's' arose gratefully from around the table.

' 'Tes a bit risky, zur, with the fog about now at night, zur, if you'll excuse me telling 'ee. And Mullacott hill, zur, be dangerous, with several bends.'

The stranger drank again.

'I didn't want to come to see the blasted idiot, anyhow,' the landlord heard him mutter, before he went to collect the glasses being rapidly emptied.

When all were served, and murmurs of 'Here's your very good health, zur'—'My best respects, zur', were arising, the gennulman said: 'Is there anywhere here in the village where one can get accommodation for the night.'

The landlord thought a while before replying.

'Yes, sir. I don't know whether it would be very grand, zur, but us might be able to oblige you, zur. I'll ask my wife, if you'll excuse me a minute. How many bedrooms would you be wanting?'

The visitor stared at the floor; then he lit a cigarette, deliberately, avoiding the landlord's eyes.

'I ought to try and get back,' he muttered. 'Just a minute, I'll ask—er—damned nuisance—blast the fellow—rotten lamps—pre-war German car, you know.'

'Not much good, a German car, I expect, zur?' remarked the landlord, trying to make an apt remark.

'On the contrary, my dear fellow, it's a Mercèdes.'

'Yes, yes,' muttered the landlord.

'If you'll pardon me, zur,' spoke the old man in the corner, 'I've never been so fast in my life before as I went this evening, zur. And I'll thank you again, zur, for your kindness, zur!'

'Don't mention it,' replied the young man, shortly.

'A German motor-car, zur, I think I heard you say,' said the mason in the spotted coat.

'Oh, really.'

The mason began to puff his fag-end violently.

'I suppose you won that one, zur?'

'Won it? What do you mean?'

'Ah s'pose you won thaccy in—i' th' war, zur,' declared the mason, swallowing smoke. He began coughing violently. The young gennulman waited with a scowl on his face; and after the bout of coughing the mason perceived, unhappily, that he would have to speak again in order to break the terrible silence. But——

'He means, zur,' said the landlord, 'that you obtained the car from the Germans, after we won the war, zur. Ban't that your meaning, Tam?'

'Aiy,' mumbled Tom.

'No,' replied the visitor. 'I had it before the war.'

'Thankee, zur,' murmured Tom gratefully, and swallowed the rest of his pint of beer.

'Beg pardon, zur, but what horse-power would that one be?' asked the landlord, who was feeling that his conversation was being appreciated by the gennulman.

'Ninety.'

'Ninety!' echoed the mason.

'Develops over three hundred,' murmured the visitor. 'I'll be back in a minute.' Puffing at his cigarette in a quick attempt to overcome the smell of whiskey, he went through the door and closed it.

'A very nice gennulman,' observed the soft-voiced man in the decayed hat, wagging his head slowly several times.

'Plenty of money, must have,' said the mason.

'He's got it all right,' continued the soft almost sing-song voice, 'you can allus tell a proper gennulman, midear. Aiy, you can. Proper gennulman. Aiy, I reckon he could spend five pound and not miss it. Proper gennulman.'

'I bet he don't live in a Rat's Castle,' chuckled another.

'Noomye! He's got it! I can allus tell a gennulman. Not that I'd say a word against Mr. Maddz'n. As quiet a little chap as you'd find anywhere; don't interfere with nobody, and

29

keeps himself to himself. When his hat's on his head his house is thatched, an' he can come and go when he likes,' said the glass-eyed man in the decayed hat.

'Aiy, but living like that a man gets nought to eat; he's zo thin as a rasher of wind.'

The conversation returned to the absence of rain, the good bullock-grass and the fine fields of wheat, but 'us wants a gude drap o' rain to put more heart into the garden'. While the quiet mid-week evening talk was going on, the door opened again, and there was immediate silence.

'Good evening,' said the newcomer quietly, looking on the floor, conscious of the break in the talk, and of the eyes of everyone in the room upon him.

'Good evening, zur,' replied everyone.

After a pause the old man in the corner said importantly: 'Mr. Maddz'n, zur, if you'll please to listen, I have something to say to you.'

'Aiy,' cried the man with the glass eye, lifting his head and glancing around as if to centre attention upon his equally important news. 'Mr. Maddz'n, if you will excuse me telling 'ee, there be a lady and gennulman waiting vor zee 'ee.'

'One moment, Billy Brown, if you please. Mr. Maddz'n, zur, if you'll please to listen to me——'

'They'm in t'other room, having zupper!' cried the voice of the mason in the lime-spotted coat.

'Thank you, Tom Brown, but I can tell the gennulman myself, midear. Please to listen to me, zur——'

'Friends of yours, I fancy, sir,' said the landlord confidentially, leaning over the bar. 'A lady and gennulman. They've been down to your place——'

'Mr. Maddz'n, if you please! I daresay you noticed a motor-car outside in the lane, zur? I had the pleasure of ridin' in 'n back along, and of directing the lady and gennulman to your place. I did what was right, I hope, zur, and no man can't do no better. He can't! Beggin' your pardon, sir.'

'Thank you,' murmured Maddison. He leant against the wall, and took a book out of his pocket. 'A glass of beer, please.'

'Thank you, zur. Fivepenny, or sixpenny?'

'Oh, any. Fivepenny, thanks.' He opened the book, and began to read.

'Certainly, zur. Shall I tell the lady and gennulman you'm arrived, if you please?'

'Oh, don't bother, thanks all the same,' murmured Maddison, not looking up from the book.

'Very good, zur.' The landlord, a retired corporal of yeomanry, went through a low doorway into the barrel-room, returning with a small glass of beer, which he put down beside the visitor, saying courteously: 'Thank you, zur.'

Maddison stood unmoving, reading. Four men under the clock began to play whist. The man called Billy Brown was watching Maddison earnestly, intently, as though with concern that his information had not been appreciated. At last Maddison looked up from the book, and the expression on his face was familiar to the one-eyed man. The young gennulman seemed excited by his 'studying', and was staring far away. Some thought him mazed, but he, William Brown, thought him as good a little chap as ever walked in the parish, paying his way and interfering in no man's business. He came once a week to the village to buy the simplest and cheapest foods; why he chose to live in a Rat's Castle with only dogs and cats, where he came from, whether he had parents or wife, no one in the parish knew. Many had seen him by day on the hills, lying on his back with his face to the sky. He avoided most men, but whenever he met them he had a smile and a friendly word for them, so that Brownie considered him 'a proper gennulman', even if he didn't have much money to spend. Billy Brown's eye stared straightly at the gennulman's. He beckoned him mysteriously, rose off the bench, craned over the table, and whispered hoarsely into his ear:

'The young lady spoke to me confirmationally when I told

THE DREAM OF FAIR WOMEN

her I knowed 'ee fairish well—beggin' your pardon, zur.'

'Have a drink, Brownie?'

'Thank 'ee, zur,' replied Brownie, promptly, swallowing what was left in his glass. 'Mis'r Maddison, you weren't o-ffended at what I told 'ee, were 'ee?'

'I am very interested, Brownie.'

Brownie made a cawing whisper over the table. 'Her were a most bootiful maid, and her told me confirmationally that her wanted vor to meet 'ee, midear. 'Tes all right! Her's out t'other room now, with t'other gennulman. You go in, midear, and take a bit o' supper along with her, while you can. I reckon the gennulman have got plenty o' money, and he can pay for it, I reckon!'

'Thanks.'

'You ban't o-ffended, be 'ee, Mis'r Maddison, at what I did tell 'ee?'

'Of course not.'

'Did 'm go down to your place? Did 'm, sure enough?'

'Yes.'

'Didn't 'ee zee 'm, tho?'

'I left the spaniel pups locked up,' said Maddison in a differ-ent voice, for he had seen, without removing his eyes from the other's face, that the door had opened. 'They were howling and trying to get through the window. I must be getting back to them.'

For answer Brownie began to nod his head and wink his eye and point with his nose; but before he could whisper the gennulman had turned away and opened his book.

'Your ale, sir?' said the landlord quietly, moving the glass nearer.

'Thanks. Also the pint for Brownie. How much?'

'Eightpence ha'penny, if you please. Thank you, zur. Any-thing for you, sir?'

'A whiskey, please—as before. And drinks all round.'

'Certainly, zur, thanking you very much.'

32

'Quite welcome.'

Conscious of the newcomer's scrutiny upon him, Maddison opened the book and began to read: he took a drink of his ale. He tried to read, but his mind was unfixed from his imagination. He finished the glass of ale. The landlord awaited him.

'This gennulman has invited all to partake of a drink with him——' began the landlord, looking at Maddison.

'Partake of liquid refreshment,' interrupted the gennulman, putting down the empty whiskey glass.

'Beggin' your pardon, zur——'

'Joke, m' dear fellow, joke!'

Maddison hesitated, meeting the other's glance. 'It's very kind of you, but I seldom drink more than a glass of beer, if you'll excuse me. I suppose I drank too much during the war!'

'Beer, my God, I don't blame you. Why not try whiskey?'

Again Maddison hesitated. 'Thank you, but I daren't touch it.'

'Bloody good stuff, my opinion. As you wish. Fatface, another double for me, anyhow!'

'Very good, zur.'

Maddison closed the book and slowly put it in his pocket. Both men watched the landlord pouring the spirit from an earthenware jar into a pewter noggin, thence to a glass.

'There you are, Captain,' said the landlord, looking slightly scared at the boldness of his address.

'Chin chin, likewise cheerio,' cried the captain, draining the glass. A murmur of amazement arose in the room. Never had such rapid drinking of spirits been seen in the Nightcrow Inn since the death of Squire Priddle.

'Have you read Jefferies?' said Maddison suddenly, when the 'Best respects' and 'Here's your very good health, zur' were over. 'Richard Jefferies. A most marvellous writer and thinker. Look, I'll show you.'

He drew the book from his pocket, and opened it at a place worn with much opening. 'Look, read that!'

C
33

The other man took the book, and stared at the print; then muttering that his eyes were so bloody weak after his last crash, he moved towards the lamp on the wall beside the clock, nearly falling headlong because one foot slid on an iron spittoon. On recovering his balance, he kicked it away violently. Holding the book under the lamp he stared at the print, frowning and muttering to himself.

' "O beautiful human life!" ' he read aloud, slowly. ' "Tears come into my eyes as I think of it." '

A man laughed, and another followed him.

' "So beautiful, so inexpressibly beautiful!" Well, that's that. It's nice to know that somebody thinks so.'

Again they laughed. 'Bloody fools,' he muttered, giving the book to Maddison. 'They understand nothing.' He laughed to himself, as though bitterly. 'God—world a bloody place— have another drink—God's sake. You were a soldier, weren't you?'

'Yes,' replied Maddison.

'Been demobilized long?'

'About ten weeks. Are you still serving?'

'Yes. My name's Colyer.'

'I'm Maddison.'

They shook hands, Maddison smiling, Colyer with downcast eyes.

'Looked you up earlier in evening,' drawled Colyer. 'Toppin' little pups you've got, what? 'Fraid they bunked off somewhere. Hope you won't lose 'em.'

Maddison did not reply. While he was trying to think what he should say, he became aware that he was being watched.

The two men were lounging against the bar counter, Colyer with his back half-turned to the open door leading into the barrel-room, so that only Maddison saw, in the dark space beyond the other man's shoulder, a woman's eyes gazing intently at him. He looked away; glanced up again. The eyes were so bright and steady that they held his glance and caused Colyer to turn his head. Still with her smiling gaze upon Maddison, she walked through the door-space, and putting her hand on Colyer's shoulder, said: 'So you're found at last, Captain Maddison! We were just in time to save the puppies from dashing themselves to death from the bedroom window. What darlings they are! What are their names?'

'One's Billjohn, the other's called Tatters. I got them from Brownie over there.'

'Aiy,' cried the one-eyed man. 'Proper li'l dogs they be, and will serve 'ee well, zur, if you'll excuse my telling 'ee.'

The old man with the knotted tartan tie and black shirt, sitting in the corner, cried out: 'Beggin' your pardon, young lady and gennulman, but I be real pleased that you have met one another at last. Don't heed what I say, young lady, I don't mean no harm to nobody, but I thought I'd just say, if you'll excuse me telling 'ee, how pleased I be vor Mr. Maddz'n to meet with such nice company. That be all, thank you, midears.'

'Aren't they sweet?' said the girl softly to Maddison. And turning her head she said, exactly mimicking their burring speech: 'Beggin' your pardon, old sir in the corner, if you'll excuse me tellin' 'ee, midear, but I'd be plaized if you and all t'other gennulman will have a li'l drink along o' me.'

They stamped their feet on the lime-ash floor, thumped fists and slapped hands on the table, rolled their heads, shut their eyes, and opened their mouths with laughter. She spoke, as Brownie said many times afterwards, 'as though her'd been born and reared in th' parish'. All the men in the room stared at her face, except Colyer, who stood with his back to the long table, slightly swaying, supporting himself with one hand on the bar counter, the other rubbing his forehead.

'Proper, proper!' yelled Brownie.

Then she was by Maddison's side, and he was talking with her, scarcely knowing what he or she was saying in the exhilaration and strength he felt coming upon himself from the frank amity of her eyes. Their voices were low.

'I wanted to call you Willie Maddison, for your cousin Phil always speaks of you as Willie, but that beard simply terrified me.'

'Oh, Willie is such a soppy name.'

'It is a good name, and just suits the boy who threw all the jay-traps away, and tried to blow down the tower of Colham School with a blunderbuss! Ah, I know all about you, Willie Maddison!'

'Who told you? How much do you know? What's your name?'

'Ah! I have several. I started life with Evie; then Eva; then it was Eve; then Eveline, and now it is E-v-e-l-y-n.'

'Lovely names, all of them.'

'After that I must buy you a drink! Well, Captain Maddison, what are you going to have? It's my round.'

'Would you think me very rude if I just talked to you?' replied Maddison. 'I——'

'Drink to me only with thine eyes,' said Colyer, holding up a glass of neat whiskey. His half-closed eyes looked at no one. 'Cheerio, everybody. Here's to 's all!'

He spoke through his teeth; then raising the glass, poured the spirit into his mouth, without appearing to have swallowed, and banged the glass on the counter. He laughed quietly, as though with memory, as he swayed slightly on his feet. ' "O beau-ti-ful human life". Jesus Christ.' He laughed bitterly. ' "Tears come into my eyes when I think of it"—just like Mr. Bloody Warbeck when he mouths Swinburne. Hell, I'm blotto. Landlord, where's landlord? Christ' sake, give me another whiskey.'

Maddison noticed, without appearing to notice, that there were tears in Colyer's eyes.

'Pat, you've had enough,' said the girl, close by his side. 'You know you mustn't drink, since your crash.'

36

'Crash 'gain to-morrow,' he muttered, smiling wryly at the glass clutched hard in his right hand. 'All best pals—gone west. Beautiful—human—life. Christ. Bloody peace!'

The girl turned away from him, and said softly to Maddison: 'Poor Pat, but if he will drink——' She paused, then looked at Maddison standing above her. 'You're very tall; and your beard makes you appear taller. You must be taller than your cousin Phillip?'

'Phillip's six feet; I'm an inch more, I think.'

'I'm glad you don't drink. I admire people who remain themselves—but it's very difficult sometimes.' She sighed. 'I read part of your manuscript. It's startlingly beautiful. I'd love to hear you read it, but——' She stopped.

'I must apologize for hiding when you came,' said Maddison, after a pause. 'But to be frank, I went upstairs to spy on you while you were approaching; then I thought I'd wait and see what would happen if I didn't answer; then I felt an absolute fool, and, as you know, I had no alternative but to jump out of the window!'

'It was quite an adventure. Phillip has the same sense of fun, too. He sent his love to you, by the way.'

'Is that the message?'

She laughed. 'Yes. We heard quite by chance that you were here—from someone getting crabs and prawns on the rocks of the bay.'

'How is Phillip? Is he still at Folkestone? I saw him last in March when I passed through the Dispersal Unit for demobilization.'

'He's left the Dispersal Unit at Shorncliffe, and gone to No. 6 Rest Camp on the Leas. At least, he's supposed to be there; but actually he's never there, nor are any of the other officers, so far as I can make out.'

'Truly a Rest Camp! It's a mike! Now you're for it!'

The last remark referred to the noisy apparition of Billy Brown, on his feet, waving a stump of a pipe in one hand as he beat time to a song which consisted of a series of semi-connected bellowings. His one dark eye stared earnestly at Maddison, while his arms waved as though he would embrace him. The song was prolonged for some time, in spite of the shouts and laughter of the other men. By now the room was full of smoke, through which the lamp shone with a soft yellow light upon the dark beam and joists of the ceiling.

'Drinks all round for everyone,' said Maddison. 'I say, Evelyn, have you seen the new moon? It's like a gold curlew's bill. Come out in the lane: we can see it from there.'

They went through the door-space, and through the sitting-room to the lane, and the clear night air and the distant drone of the Atlantic. 'Look, there is Venus, too. Soon they will sink together beyond the sea.' He heard her sigh beside him. They went back into the Nightcrow.

Time slipped away, and during the noise and hilarious confusion, she said to Maddison, who was bending down to hear, 'When may I hear the rest of the "Policy of Reconstruction"?'

He said nervously: 'Did you really like it?'

'My dear, it made my heart ache.'

He stood upright, taking a deep breath, and breathing out again slowly, imperceptibly, not daring to look at her, but awaiting. She glanced away; and a moment later he heard her say: 'I think your friend is trying to speak to you.'

The friend, Brownie, was on his feet again, craning over the table, waving a pint glass full of beer in one hand, and staring earnestly with his one eye in Maddison's direction. Brownie was trying to make a speech.

'I allus said,' he declared, slowly and with long pauses, waving the glass and spilling the beer, amidst shouts of merriment, 'that Mis'r Mass'n was allus a proper gennulman—interfering with nobody's business—and now I'm very glad vor to see—he'm chummed up with another leddy and gennulman—like himself——'

'Christ!' muttered Colyer. 'Tears come into my eyes.' He

gulped down another glass of whiskey. His eyes were blood-shot, and he made a wry face as he jerked the glass from his mouth.

The landlord's daughter, leaning on the bar and staring at the lady, said: 'It be ten minutes after ten, feyther!'

'Drink up, chaps!' cried the landlord, in apprehension of the constable who every evening was known to be standing outside in the lane. 'Come on, boys. Ten minutes after ten.'

Hilariously they got on their legs and crowded to the door-way, each man politely bidding the strangers good-night.

Maddison lingered, hesitating; and as the room cleared, the girl said softly: 'I am staying here for a few days; may I come sometime, when you're not busy? Or shall I be a nuisance and bother you? I have a lot to tell you about Phillip.'

'Thank you!' He hesitated. 'When——?'

'Come up and see me in the morning.' She added in a louder voice: 'Well, good-night, Captain Maddison. I enjoyed our talk immensely. I'll get Jefferies's books and read them as soon as I can. Au revoir!'

Colyer was leaning over the bar, his back to them. 'Good-night,' said Maddison, but he did not appear to hear. Then the fresh air of night was cold on his face.

The lane led westwards to the coombe and the sea. As he went gaily in the keen air he felt an exaltation at the thought of his free life. He joyed in the night beauty. Like a gold cur-lew's bill the new moon curved in a violet sky, the murmur of the sea suddenly increased to a noise like the rumble of a distant barrage, and the coombe opened before him. He quitted the cart-track and followed a path through furze and rising brake fern to the cove below. His way was lit by a globe of silver, Venus reluming the pale evening vapours over the sea. By his side the stream murmured round the stones and its bubbles glimmered in the little pools. Rabbits fled from quiet nibbling at his swift descent, and somewhere a roosting bird twittered a drowsy alarm. 'O beautiful human life!'

Chapter 3

RAT's CASTLE, as the villagers called the half-ruined cottage where Maddison had come to live five months after the Armistice, was originally a lime-burner's cottage. A limekiln overgrown with brambles and elderberry trees was built into the hillside above it. For nearly half a century no fire had been kindled in its well, to roast the chalk brought in French ships, which used to beach in the sandy cove on the ebb and sail away on the rising tide. Kiln and cottage were deserted.

Then, at the beginning of the twentieth century, the lord of the manor, wishing to increase his revenues so diminished by taxes, tithes, betting, drinking and gambling, had installed machinery in the valley for the mining of iron. Miners had tunnelled into the hillside, using only pick, bar, and blasting-powder. The hillside was rich in iron ore, and deposits of tin, silver, copper, and manganese were found, but in such small quantities as to be commercially worthless. When the crushing and washing and hand-furnace processes had been working a year, it was found that the wages paid, the cost of haulage, and the freight charges to Swansea over the Severn Sea, were far greater than the money received for the ore. The squire, who had mortgaged his property in order to work the mines, continued the hillside borings for a further eighteen months, hoping to find some of the gold rumoured immemorially to be lying in that district of North Devon adjoining Exmoor. The complete failure to find anything but iron and negligible amounts of other metals was responsible for his complete abandonment to whiskey and his death a year later. For many years afterwards the failure of the mining was discussed in the

Nightcrow Inn; they shook their heads and lamented the death of the old squire. The farmers who had bought the land were not liked: there was nothing like a gennulman. Every spring-time more borage, docks, nettle, hemlock, and other tall weeds flourished round the machinery-shed; the iron roof grew more rusty and took on the hue of the red stone heaps. Brambles and wild roses formed a natural screen for the holes gaping in the hillside. To this solitary place, Maddison, walking round the coast, his pack on his back heavy with books, unshaven for many days, wearing his soldier's uniform with regimental and rank badges and medal ribbons removed, arrived one April evening, and made a fire, and cooked a meal, and rested, tranced with a reverie of stars shining in the pool by his feet, the flicker of flames, the murmur of stream and wave, the owls crying about the ruins. The sea gleamed, the air was still, the mice ran by his silent form. Here at last was peace, he thought; here he would dwell, and await the revelation. All night he lay by the fire, between sleeping and waking, arising when the stars were paling to watch the dawn over the Exmoor hills.

From the landlord of the Nightcrow Inn—who for a few pounds had bought the coombe, together with the derelict buildings, for the rabbits which abounded there—Maddison learnt that the place was called Shelley Cove. The name was the crown of enchantment. Eagerly he offered to rent the cottage immediately on the owner's terms, which was four pounds a year. Maddison paid for a year in advance, and returning immediately by train to his father's house in Rookhurst, he packed his army valise with some spare clothes and blankets, and borrowing a book on conchology from his father, went back to Rat's Castle, elated with his vision of the future. He began *The Policy of Reconstruction* in a state of extraordinary excitement, which lasted from the sunset of a Friday night until the sunrise of the following Sunday, during which time he wrote 44,000 words and ate nothing and drank two pitchers of spring-water, and never walked more than half a dozen paces from the cottage door.

In the intervals of pacing round the table he read the chapters aloud to himself, inducing therefrom an emotion which he thought was Truth, which inspired him further and annihilated fatigue. He recited to himself poems from *Songs of Experience* and *Songs of Innocence* of Blake; read passages of Jefferies's *Story of My Heart*, Thompson's *Mistress of Vision*, Barbusse's *Under Fire*, Conrad's *Youth*, where the ship was burning, Masefield's *Old Front Line*. But Blake and Jefferies were glanced at most: a few lines were sufficient for a foothold from which his mind might spring into space where was neither sound nor form nor colour, where like a White Bird in a shining void it spread its wings and was free. The White Bird perceived Truth in a timeless flash, Light within light, but the intellect could not understand or interpret the vision. Pacing the floor, he perceived the earth as something small and swung in space, something which moved for a while only. He saw the material ideas of mankind as a corrosion on the surface of the moonlike earth, a corrosion which marred the planetary gleam, on which the Light of the shining void gleamed vain and faithful and sad.

He slept all that Sunday, and on the Monday morning he awakened with a feeling of deep and luxurious contentment, never known since the days of lying naked in the sun on Heron's Island, so long ago—nearly five years. And now he was quite old—twenty-two—and had no more illusions about Love: he was old, and henceforward would be serene, for he had found salvation in Nature. The mood of contentment had remained with him during the days and weeks that followed, while he revised his manuscript, and walked many miles every day, arising with the sun and sleeping dreamlessly. He bought the spaniel pups from Brownie, and carried home two kittens with them; and finding a seagull with a broken wing, on the shore, he took that, too. Very soon he had an otter cub, and various fledgeling birds, a buzzard hawk, carrion crow, jay, magpie, and jackdaw.

On the morning after his visit to the Nightcrow Inn, Maddison lay on his bracken bed in the upper room of the cottage, listening to a trickle of happiness falling in the dim room. Two swallows were talking to one another in the mud nest just outside the casement, under the thatch. Other birds were singing in the coombe. He lay drowsy and at rest, his mind dim as the dawnlight, for an hour, when various noises began to arise outside the cottage. There was the noise of scolding, as of linen torn; immediately afterwards a grey and plum-coloured bird, with blue eyes and black cheeks, flew to the window-sill, raised its crest, expanded and contracted the irides of its eyes, and screamed again. Seeing the open eyes of the man who fed it, the jay hopped to the bed, and standing on Maddison's head, began its morning search in his hair. This action caused one of the spaniel pups, who had been lying all night as though dead at the foot of the bed, to lift its head and growl. Seeing Maddison's eyes, it seemed to leer at him sideways, showing its little white teeth, while its tail-stump bumped violently on the head of another animal lying curled beside it.

This animal was dark brown in colour, like the spaniel, but its head was smaller and flatter, apparently without ears. It was an otter cub. Awakened and disturbed by the beating on its head, the cub rolled over on its back, yawned, clutched the tail-stump between its short forepaws, and bit it in play. While Maddison watched with relaxed contentment, other birds alighted on the window-sill—a young carrion-crow, and a big brown hawk with a hooked bill and large yellow legs and feet. Then came a jackdaw, which alighted on the sack of sun-dried grass which was the pillow, and squabbled with the jay on Maddison's head. The kittens stretched luxuriously, disturbed by play of pup and cub, and curled to sleep again.

'Well, I suppose it's time to get up,' said Maddison aloud; and hearing his voice, the young birds opened their beaks and

43

screeched, fluttering their wings for food. With supple swiftness the otter cub unrolled from his play and ran to Maddison's head, staring at him with dark eyes; while the two pups stretched themselves, yawned and yowled, and with wagging tail-stumps thrust themselves to his face and licked his chin until hurled away. Only the kittens did not care. They settled more comfortably into the warm communal sleep-hole in the bracken.

'Up we all get!' Maddison shouted suddenly, for a yellow glow, like the wan spectre of a moth, had lit on the wall opposite. The sun was rising.

He seized the two brown blankets, and dragging the scampering and upset animals, went down the stairs. In the lower room he was greeted by the seagull, making raucous noises and dragging its broken wing. Pups and cub avoided the seagull, which was old and unfriendly. The cub moved swiftly around the room on its low legs, turning nervously with a sweep of its long tapered tail. Then like a brown ripple it was gone through the round cat-hole in the lower part of the door, followed by the pups. Maddison lit some sticks in the hearth, filled the iron kettle from a pitcher, set it on the crook, and opening the door, was in the cold air of morning.

While he was shaking the blankets before hanging them to air on the garden wall, the puppies tried to pull them out of his hands; afterwards they ran into the cottage, to reappear dragging an old pair of Maddison's trousers which was supposed to be their bed in the coal cellar under the stairs.

'Billjohn! Izaak Walton! Tatters! Come on!' he called, going down the path to the cove below. The otter cub ran after him, but the puppies, who did not like being dragged into the water, slunk behind, whining.

Leaving the trees and bushes of the coombe, the stream flowed into a little pool, and thence through wave-worn grey boulders it rushed, before sinking into the shell beach of the cove. The otter cub slid into the fresh water, rolling and swirling, biting the bubbles as it played on its back, while the jay, the crow, the hawk, and the jackdaw, flew round Maddison's head, screaming for their breakfast.

He waded out until the water was over his knees, then plunged into a wave, and struck out for the Cormorant Rock beyond the cove's widening, followed by the otter cub who dived and rolled around him.

The agonized barks of the puppies on shore awoke echoes in the cliffs that towered above the green water, and a score of daws glided from their nesting ledges with sharp ejaculations. He turned on his back and floated, watching them. Two gulls flew overhead, their wings gleaming with the sun. It was lovely to float in the water, to feel yourself a spirit that was beyond grief or joy, but tranquil and—— 'Get away, damn you!' he spluttered, for Izaak, the otter cub, had crawled on his chest, causing Maddison's head to sink under water. Together they swam to the Cormorant Rock, and crawled out of the sea. While the cub slipped back into the water to hunt for fish around the rock, Maddison climbed to a flat ledge above, and sat in the rays of the sun. His skin was a golden brown. Exhilarated by swimming and the glow of the sea, he closed his eyes, sighing with deep contentment. Here he would live forever, sufficient to himself, having done with all unhappy things. So he dreamed with the sun hot beyond the yellow-red of his closed eyes . . . until the noise of crunching and flapping made him aware of the otter cub with a fish.

'A bass! A two-pounder! Now don't you eat it, Izaak! Come on!'

He stepped down and dived into the sea, then put his head under water and commenced to beat along with the crawl-stroke. This was exhausting, and soon he ceased and swam in on his side, the beady eyes in the bewhiskered head of Izaak often near his own with the great fish in its mouth.

'Here I am, my faithfuls,' he said to the prancing pups as he emerged dripping and flushed. They sprang up to him, they grovelled before him, they entangled themselves round his feet, they picked up dried seaweed and killed a dozen imaginary rabbits for him.

When he had put on shirt and khaki trousers, he milked the goat tethered on the hillside above the cottage. The milking was hindered by the pup Tatters, who attempted alternately to pull the beard of the goat and to drink the milk in the pail. He was not agile enough to avoid the ill-humour of the goat, however, and after a butt in the ribs fled tail down and yelping, pursued by the pup Billjohn, who tugged at his ear and rolled him over. A snarly fight ensued, which was terminated by a rush for home lest the others should eat all the breakfast.

'Outside,' he yelled, and all except the seagull made for the door. They returned immediately, and recommenced their requests for food. He opened the door of the coal cupboard, taking out a big black pot, in which was their food, consisting of stale crusts of bread, rabbits, bones, hedgehogs, laver seaweed, potatoes and fish, all boiled up together. Into a large dish he poured the cold stew; there was a commingling of wings, heads, and feet, and noises of sucking, munching, cracking and pecking. The birds squawked, the cats hissed and spat and boxed with their paws, the dogs growled and bristled to each other, the otter cub ate unmolested.

While they were eating, Maddison broiled the bass, and threw what he could not eat into the black pot, for the next meal of his dependents.

After the meal he cleaned his teeth with a green willow stick, one end of which he had frayed by beating on a stone. Then he went on the beach, and lying on his back, looked up at the sky through his hands till he felt himself tenuous and impersonal as the blue space over him. He felt a peace, a concordance with all things.

The strand was deep with brittle shells. Many hours had he rested there, trying to identify them from the hand-coloured plates of the Conchology book. The shells were so empty and

quiet: the sunshine alone knew of their ancient dreaming—
broad sunset shells, washed with the western summer sky-hues;
tiger scallops, and pod razors; little milky arcs, and wentle-
traps like the conical hats of mediæval women; the pelican's
foot and the tiny reddish pheasant shells; tusk shells—horns for
fairy winding—and the cowries, wherein murmured a per-
petual sea-chafing; pearl-like tellins and lovely fragile bubble
shells. There were caps of liberty—like those worn with the
tricolour, but shaped before man tipped his arrows with flint.
And turret shells, and the lime-built house of the rare violet
snail. Spring tides had left an irregular riband at the top of the
beach near the broken lumps of grassy earth, a litter of driftwood bored by worm and barnacle, the bark of pine spars from
distant shipyards, grey gull-feathers and the blue and scarlet
claws of fiddler crabs, rusty tins and dried corpses of spined
sea-urchins. The sun shone on them all, alone knowing of
their ancient dreaming; and he would dream with them,
holding them in the palm of his hand, even as Jefferies had
done.

Every morning Maddison had lain here in the sun while the
wavelets broke on Shelley Beach, and the stream lost itself
murmuring in the sea. There were elvers under the slatey
stones, and many hours he had spent in trying to catch them
as they wriggled away when their hiding-places were lifted. It
was a simple joy to watch them, like the pleasure of finding
strange wildflowers on the hillside. For he was convalescent
after the consumption of spirit which had ravaged Youth
during the days of war, when nothing assumed definite form
in the hectic mists hiding a world of painted quicksands ever
shifting and changing, and ever sucking down human life. On
these painted quicksands he had seen only the crude colours of
ephemeral excitement, where the standards and codes of
rational and matured men were meaningless, for they were
applicable only to the firm ground of civic life. Like many
another youth, he had been blown by every wind, a feather on

47

the shore of the world, with but one thing constant in his mind, an intense yearning to be loved by the girl he had loved since he was eight years old. Elsie Norman had not cared, yet he always hoped; and the sick hopelessness of his desire had caused him to make a refuge in imagination. Whenever he saw her during infrequent visits to Rookhurst he became dry-throated and trembling, but so great was his need and desire that he never lost hope.

There had been moments, in the desolation of loneliness, when he had wanted to assoil himself, as a hunted stag soils in its pit; except for one lapse he had been too fearful and dis-inclined. Often he had sought relief in drunken revelry with the comrades of his mess, always being the last to go to bed—unless indeed he were 'completely blotto' early in the night, a state which was frequent. Drink made him brilliant and excited, or violently unhappy, but never quarrelsome—until the inevitable:—

'Where's Mad Willie? Let's rag his cubicle—put coals in's bed?'

'No, he's blotto—catting his heart up. Mixing drinks 's what does it.'

Had the roar of the ante-room on guest nights ceased for ever? Had the squadron horses neighed their last on the picket lines, while the night-horizon flickered and bubbled with gun-fire, and the men on picket duty sat around their coke braziers? Had they ever tried to make a Gap at Monchy, to be jammed and broken on the wire of the Hindenburg Line? Never again to have such friendships? Or to see the white flares beyond the parapet at night and hear the mournful wailing of gas-horns over the wastes of the Somme battlefields? Gone, gone forever. His heart ached: the splendid, bitter days of the war dimmed the sunlight as he lay on the beach of shells, among the dried weed and black brittle cases of dogfish eggs cast up during old storms, and corks and rusty tins, all the littered drift of the sea. He wandered the twilight tracts of the lost generation, a dead man with dead men, with aching breast, for he was living. Yet even as life arises out of death, even as light arises out of darkness . . . he arose and hurried into the cottage, scarcely seeing the boulders before his feet. His under-lip was thrust over the upper-lip; his eyes were hard and bright with inner strength. He sat down before the table, and began to write rapidly; the eighteenth chapter of *The Policy of Reconstruction, or, True Resurrection.*

Chapter 4

THE sun had passed over Shelley Cove when he rose from the
table, took his stick, called the pups, closed the door, and set
out for a walk. It was pleasant to rest on the sward of the
terrace halfway up the hillside, seeing the cove a long way
below with its grey boulders washed by the green waves. The
coombe of thorn bushes and trees narrowed as it rose for half a
mile inland, and near the sky he could see the first cottages of
the village. There was no sound except that of the waves
saying *aa-aa, aa!* on the rocks below, the whisper of a passing
linnet, and the distant cries of nesting gulls.

'I am so happy,' he thought, pressing his fingers into the
sward. 'O God, the world is a lovely place.' The puppies,
watching his face, wagged their tails violently.

On the top of the down he felt he was walking on the top
of the world. The fields fell away under his feet, to the western
sky and the Atlantic blue beneath a sun that had flamed since
April without a cloud to shield the earth from its fire. Sea and
sky were fused by the heat till there was no horizon, and distant sailing-ships seemed to be making skyey voyages. Into
this still prospect of sky and ocean the headland was thrust like
a great golden tiger-shaped beast, striped with dark hedge-
banks, lying dead and shrunken in the azure calm of the sea.
For centuries the headland had been a haunt of wreckers, who
tied lanthorns to cows grazing there, to deceive the sailors into
thinking they were riding lights of ships at anchor. Many a
wooden vessel had had her back broken by the rocky paws of
the Leap. A buoy now swung in the racing tide, but sometimes
in winter a tramp or fishing trawler, lost in fog or driven by

storm, had her plates ripped out by the black claws of Bag
Leap. It is a dream country, he thought, and joy made him
shout aloud, and hurl his stick and run with all his strength
across a field, followed by the panting spaniels. For an hour he
walked on, joying greatly in the sun and the wind. Over the
remote tranquillity of landscape rose the blue hills of Dartmoor,
forty miles southwards. The wild bees sang as they burred
past to the thyme: the wind in the tufts of thrift stirred the
pink flowers; somewhere a titlark was singing as it dived from
the sky. Stonechats in summery vesture of brown and black
perched on springs of furze and made their stone-chipping cries
of alarm as he passed with the dogs.

He was approaching the headland, when his musings were
interrupted by the behaviour of the puppies, some yards in
front of him. They were standing still, pointing, their backs
stiff, their tails stuck out. Billjohn gave a querulous growl and
turned to see his master's face, and reassured, he trotted
forward.

Maddison saw a girl walking along the stone wall of the
forty-acre field called, inexplicably, Fourteen Acres. She was
a quarter of a mile away, and the blouse she wore was very
white in the sunlight. He sat down and watched her slow progress among the sheep on the brown pasturage. The rising
heat caused the fields and hedges to quiver brilliantly, and the
thin cries of the flock rose with the torrid air. Sometimes she
stopped; sheep were following her, and their thin bleats
streaked the quivering glassy brilliance of day. He saw her
clamber over a gate, until she was hidden from him behind a
further wall. Was this the girl he had promised to meet in the
village that morning? If so, he must avoid an awkward
explanation. He sat down and waited until he thought she
would be out of sight, then he walked on towards the headland.

After crossing many fields he saw the wide bay below, with
lines of waves breaking regularly on the sand. He jumped
down into a sunken lane, which was thick with dust, deep

under its hedges of thorn, bramble, and dogwood, but not cool. There were many flies here, and baby rabbits crouching under the leaves of dock and cow-parsley. He called the pups to heel, forbidding them to touch or chase. The lane bent to the right at the top, so that the sun was in his face; there was no shade, except where the shadows of telegraph-poles were thrown obliquely across the lane. The single wire, connecting the coastguard lookouts, made no humming; it was a thin line in the intense blue. A yellowhammer sat on the wire near a bleached pole, singing.

The lane led to another bay south of the headland; on the crest he turned right-handed, climbing a gate, and walked along a rocky cart track. The puppies, glad to be off the heated dust of the lane, rushed away over the brown sward. He walked on; his direction was now westwards, with the southern sun on his left cheek. A sheep track led past furze bushes curiously stunted and rounded like green puffballs, in the roots of which rabbits had made their buries. Stonechats scolded him and the dogs, and a sparrowhawk dashed away from a stone wall on which it had been plucking a linnet. Larks were above, raining down their joy. Constantly daws called *jack, jack,* the sound mingling with the scambling cries of gulls which had their nests far below the slope of green bracken and gorse, where the land ended in ragged cliffs that dropped sheer to the rocks and the yellow sands. The air straying past him was fresh and sweet, murmuring with the wave-lines scarcely breaking so far below.

The stony track rose gradually to its highest point, and he was able to see the north side of the headland for nearly two miles. Sound of iron on iron, a faint *clenk*, made him look down the bend of the path. With surprise he perceived that the girl was just in front of him. He crouched immediately, wondering if she had seen him, for at the questioning yaps of the spaniels she had glanced round. Her blouse in the intense sunlight was a brilliant white against the yellow charlock of the oat-field. Her hair was a reddish brown. She swung a sun-bonnet on her wrist.

He watched her, then sat down and looked across three miles of azure water to Morte headland like a great lizard lying in the sea, with the coast of Wales beyond and faintly far away. He was uncertain what to do. Blue sea and yellow sands below would mean a cool and sparkling swim, and afterwards a sunbath and a lovely dream, lying on Vention sands while the young kestrels chattered in their eyrie in the cliff, and the pipits dived singing to their nests in the tussocks behind the grey boulders. It was so lovely to wander, naked and alone, on vast sands where only the footprints of gulls were pressed besides his own and those of the dogs. A feeling of disintegration came to him, and he despised himself for having gone up to the inn the previous night, because of a charming voice. He determined to go down to the sands, and jumped to his feet, but took a last glance at the girl. She was no longer to be seen.

Where had she gone? Again he saw her steady eyes, saw her red lips, her slow smile, heard her words, *My dear, it made my heart ache*. He hesitated, and decided not to go down to the sands. The pups followed him towards the gate and the oat-field choked with charlock.

Just beyond the corner of the field a swarded cart track led through a brake of blackthorn to a disused quarry, where once he had flushed a tiny and rare falcon called a merlin. It was a small quarry where grew wild ivy and stonecrop, and, earlier in the year, bluebells and primroses. Brambles of blackberry and wild rose, no longer crushed by cartwheel, stretched across the path. He had a kettle hidden in a thorn in this quarry; often he had made a fire here, and brewed nettle tea. As he crept over the briars silently, holding the neck-skin of the tugging puppies, he felt a thrill as though he were trespassing with Jack in those days of long ago. He had an extraordinary feeling that Jack was near him in the sunshine, laughing with him. 'Jack,' he said aloud, so sharp was the impression that

53

Jack was there. 'Jack, this is like old times, isn't it? Remember when we stalked old Norman as he was painting in Hangman's Mash, and chucked clay bullets at his easel?' Then with a start he realized the girl was just beside him, sitting in the shade of an overhanging rock, her chin rested on her hand. She looked at him, neither welcome nor resentment in her eyes which seemed to hold a wild gentleness and an absence of personal regard that made him feel ashamed.

Out of the rock just below her feet hart's-tongue ferns were growing, and realizing where she was sitting he cried, pointing with his stick: 'I say, don't move suddenly, will you? There's a nest of robins under that arch of ferns. Be awfully careful!'

'I know,' she answered with a swift sidelong smile. 'The mother is on the nest now. Don't be so worried! But, to ease your mind, I'll come down.'

She rose upright, and he noticed the grace of her poise as she prepared to jump. She leapt from a height of five feet, alighting with her hands on his shoulders, and falling against him, so that he put his arms round her and held her.

'I say, have you hurt yourself?' he enquired, with false anxiety, still holding her. He felt very bold at his action.

'Not really,' she replied. 'I was trying to show off, I suppose.' She sat down, and began to play with the smaller spaniel.

'This little doggie is a sweet thing. What do you call him?'

'Oh, that's Billjohn. He was the nestledraff.'

'The nestledraff?'

'The baby of the litter, you know. The Devon folk pronounce it "nissledraff". It is usually the most affectionate.'

'Oh, I love Billjohn,' she replied, picking up the puppy and resting her cheek on its head. Billjohn tried to show his affection by licking her ear.

'You can have him,' said Maddison, contemplating her curve of cheek. She was holding the puppy against her throat and chin, regarding him all the time with glances of friendly eyes.

'That's very kind of you,' she replied, 'but I am certain that you must be very fond of him, Captain Maddison.'

'I am,' he said, 'but——'

'But what?'

He hesitated.

'I think he'd like you just as much as anyone.'

She laughed. 'How quaint you are, giving away your dogs and your enthusiastic compliments to strangers. Do you give many away like this? There, you see, Billjohn would miss you very much if you betrayed him by giving him away!'

Billjohn struggled away, and bounded to his master, who now had the whole upward regard of the blue-grey eyes. He could think of nothing to say: there was no need to say anything. Under the frank amity of her gaze he felt irradiated; he did not know he was smiling too, as he glanced shyly at the lovely face of the girl who sat opposite him. Her nose was straight, and her lashes were long and dark, and curved in profile as he saw when she turned to look where he pointed at a lizard on a rock in the sun. Her lower lip was full, and red like a wild raspberry set in a complexion sea-tinged and scarcely freckled. She rested the weight of her turned shoulder on an arm uncovered to past the elbow; even as he noticed this she rolled higher the white silken sleeve.

'I love warmth,' she smiled. 'Your arms are brown, aren't they? I can see the sun glinting on the little gold hairs of your forearm. Somehow mine will not get deeply tanned like yours.'

She held her arm towards him. He took her wrist, holding it with his fingertips, pretending to be looking at her arm, while he murmured: 'The Greeks made their youths and maidens run races in the sun, for it was their ideal to have perfect bodies as well as lofty minds.'

'The sun is my god.'

'He is mine, too. Rather! May I take my shirt off?'

She laughed. 'You are the quaintest child!'

Again he felt a glow as of irradiation, and was shy of taking off his shirt.

'Aren't you going to take off your shirt?'

'I feel a fool.'

'Because I laughed. You are as sensitive as a child. Now what can I do to persuade you that I was laughing *for* you, not *at* you? Please, *please* take off your shirt, Captain Maddison.'

'You are laughing at me!'

She touched his cheek. 'So bearded, and so very young! How can I help laughing at you. So very serious a young man!'

To her surprise she saw that his face had become sad. He was staring on the ground. She took his hand in her hand. 'Don't think me callous because I laugh, my dear. When I read parts of your book I felt I could have wept. I couldn't say what I felt last night, because I dreaded that Pat would not have understood. That's why I wanted to see you this morning, to tell you that before I went away.'

In the silence he heard a pipit singing in the sky.

'O, that bird! I—I—Are you going away?'

She laughed, squeezing his hand. 'Sometime—maybe.'

Watching the expression on his face, with the downcast eyes, she smiled.

'But I may come back here, and bring Jonquil.'

'Who is Jonquil?'

'My little daughter.'

He said nothing; he moved a piece of stone with his finger, sitting cross-legged before her, brown and slim, his glance fixed on the ground.

'You walk most of the day, don't you, Captain Maddison?'

'Yes.'

'Do you often come here?'

'Yes. I like the headland, and the peregrine falcons lording it over the whole bird world.'

'Hawks are cruel things, I think.'

'They kill to live, like everything else. Except, perhaps, some men who live to eat.'

'You look as though a good square meal wouldn't be amiss, anyhow! Have you got anyone who cooks for you?'

He shook his head.

'I believe you must be half starved.'

'No, I'm not.'

He stared skywards at a gannet, a great fishing bird from Lundy.

'Do take off your shirt, won't you? Isn't the sun glorious? Doesn't it make you feel that you would like enormous teeth to bite into it? How about that for the subject of a rhyme?'

He smiled, and she smiled into his eyes; but his smile was so sad, she thought.

They both looked up at the gannet, which had made a harsh cry.

'Will you come and see me when I return? I'm thinking of taking rooms at Cryde Bay.'

'Yes, thank you very much. Look! Quick!'

He leapt up, pointing at the gannet, which had dived with a splash, transfixing a fish with its beak. She stood beside him. 'My dear, it's the most thrilling place I ever knew. No wonder you like being by yourself.'

He did not answer.

'Perhaps I'm in the way? I'd better go.' She paused, her eyes downcast. 'Only—I—I—couldn't help wanting—to be friends.'

'Don't go, please! I—I—if you only knew——'

They sat down again. He felt as though one of his ribs were aching. The puppies were stretched out on the sward burnt and parched by the droughty heat. Jackdaws winged by over-head, and she looked up while he stared at her blue-grey eyes, radiant and mirthful and fringed with dark lashes. Her teeth were white as a young terrier's; how soft was her throat, how vivid her hair; and she would no longer look at him. She was staring over the ocean, where the fishing boats in the Severn

Sea seemed to be hanging in mist and sky. Becalmed on the windless blue, the sails looked as though the faintest breeze would lift them as brown butterflies adance on airy nothingness.

'It has occurred to me,' she said whimsically, suddenly looking straight in his eyes, 'that a child of your years—let me see, I should imagine you to be about twenty-two—wearing a beard—a beard curiously uneven, let me tell you—it occurs to me, that, like every other child in the world, you need someone to look after you. I think I shall assume the responsibility of a foster-mother, and darn your socks, and make you shave your beard—your uneven beard.' She regarded him intently. His eyes fell before her gaze.

'I know I must look rather terrible.'

'No, I do not mean that exactly. What I think, however, is that you should shave it off at the earliest opportunity. I am sure you would look much nicer.'

He felt a fool, and said so.

'Oh, don't feel a fool, Captain Maddison. It is only a pose, isn't it?' she suggested.

'I hoped it was a beard,' he replied.

She laughed. 'Tell me, are you going to live like that, always?'

'Yes, I hope so. Except for my birds and animals.'

'Where did you get them?'

'I abducted them from their parents. Except the gull and the owl, which I found in iron traps, and mended.'

'Oh, you dear thing. Do you have any visitors there?'

'A few rats at night, sometimes.'

'Be serious, Mr. Maddison! Haven't you friends or relatives?'

'I have a father somewhere, I think.'

'What a vague young man it is! Do tell me some more.'

He was enjoying her interest in himself, and felt thrilled by her gaze.

'Have you any brothers or sisters, or a mother?'

'My mother died when I was born.'

'Poor child,' she murmured. In the quiet they heard the cries of sheep, pitiful cries for water which quavered into the heated air. The hill springs had long dried up, the ponds were hard mud. The rattle of cloven feet on rock came near. Several sheep, panting, were coming down to the quarry.

'The sky does not care whether they live or die,' said Maddison, in a wild and bitter voice. 'And the same indifference is shown to mankind. How much longer will mankind believe in a God directing all human endeavour? The only thing that cares for us is ourselves.'

'Yes, that is true——'

'And when a man of vision does appear, he is either destroyed or neglected. Listen, I will read you something! This is Jefferies, who lived very near my own home.'

He pulled a book from his pocket, and read with a wild fervour.

'My heart looks back and sympathizes with all the joy and life of ancient time. With the circling dance burned in still attitude on the vase; with the chase and the hunter eagerly pursuing, whose javelin trembles to be thrown; with the extreme fury of feeling, the whirl of joy in the warriors from Marathon to the last battle of Rome, not with the slaughter, but with the passion —the life in the passion; with the garlands and the flowers; with all the breathing busts that have panted beneath the sun. O beautiful human life! Tears come in my eyes as I think of it. So beautiful, so inexpressibly beautiful!'

He finished reading, and turned away.

'There are tears in your eyes, too,' she said.

'He was one of the greatest men that ever lived!' he declared. 'Look, I'll show you his portrait.'

'Is that why you wear a beard?' she enquired, looking at the photograph he turned to at the beginning of the book. 'But that's a beastly thing to say, isn't it? Are you hurt?'

He shook his head. They walked out of the quarry in silence.

She despises me, was his thought, as he stopped to watch the sheep whose cloven feet rattled on the hard ground. They were scraggy, gasping in the heat, fixing their eyes upon him as though beseeching green grass. He saw that the flanks of several were crawling with maggots, that even now heavy-winged flies were laying the eggs which shortly would hatch. The sheep showed no fear of the dogs; they had come to him, who appeared as a godhead, for relief: while overhead in a sky blue and hard as a sapphire burned the sun. One lay down, a froth on its nostrils. Its sides were red and raw. Its woolly skin flapped on its side like stiff leather. Maggots had eaten it loose. He contemplated the agony of the dying animal. Was there a beneficent deity directing all earthly endeavour—caring for the things it had created? Six months since, and half the world was a shambles, men destroying one another.

She clung to his arm.

'My God, what can we do? Can't we tell anyone?'

'The farmer may be miles away. The maggots hatch in a few hours, and by to-morrow the sheep will be mad, if not dead.'

'Come away! Oh, how can you stand there and look at them?' She hid her eyes with her hand. 'Do come. It can't be good for you to think about it——'

'It's the law of life; yet there must be some purpose in life other than reproduction.'

'Oh, I can't understand how you can bear it!' she cried, and slipping her arm out of his, she ran up the path. He watched her going away. At the top of the track she turned, and stood waiting. He walked slowly to her.

'You didn't feel the sun on your body after all, and it was my fault! Listen, I've an idea. Come with me to Cryde Bay, and help me look for rooms. Then we'll swim. Those poor sheep . . . but it doesn't do to think about them. The sun that is cruel to them and to the grass is kind to us, anyhow.'

'You should read Jefferies!'

'I want to, very much!'

'Did you like what I read of *The Story of My Heart*?'

'My dear, it was beautiful. Just like your own "Policy of Reconstruction".' She gave him a sidelong smile. ' "The Policy of Reconstructing the Story of my Heart." Ah, it is good to see you laugh. But I do understand, really I do.'

'You know, I feel rather a scarecrow to go to Cryde Bay with a lady.'

'No one of the slightest importance to you or me lives at Cryde Bay. And I'm not a lady.'

'Well, I shall have to swim in my clothes.'

'That will ruin the excellent crease in your trousers, won't it?'

'Haw, haw! Good joke! I say, why not come down to Vention Sands?'

'I told Pat Colyer I'd be at Cryde.'

They walked on not so swiftly because Maddison's pace had slowed. 'I don't think I'd better come,' he said.

'But why not?'

'I think I'd better go back to the cottage.'

'But I don't even know the way to Cryde Bay.'

'Oh, it's quite easy, if you follow the path round.'

She hesitated. She said calmly,

'Very well, Captain Maddison. Good-bye!'

She ignored his dismayed glance, and waving her arm, walked on alone, watched by the whining puppies. He wanted to see if she would turn round; but no, she did not turn round. Farther and farther away she walked, until she was a small white spot against the green slope of the headland. Why had he made such a damned fool of himself before her? Gripping his stick, he walked rapidly back along the way he had come. Reaching the dusty lane, he paused irresolute, then turned north towards Shelley Cove. He must write another chapter of *The Policy of Reconstruction, or, True Resurrection*, which was to be dedicated to Richard Jefferies, his only friend.

Chapter 5

HE was greeted with a mixture of movements and cries as he approached Rat's Castle. The seagull had been asleep in the oven, the kittens were on the bookshelf, the owl on the ceiling-beam, the daw and jay on the roof. Maddison emptied the rest of the stock-pot on the grass outside, and left them to fight over the food, while he wondered which book he would read. There were the volumes of Richard Jefferies—*The Amateur Poacher*, *Bevis*, *Field and Hedgerow*, *Amaryllis at the Fair*, and *The Dewy Morn*; there were books by Thomas Hardy and Joseph Conrad, and John Masefield's *Gallipoli*; beside these there were the poets, Thompson, Keats, Blake, Shelley, and a living poet named de la Mare, whose verses he had come upon in a shell-hole near Passchendaele—sodden, yellow, and rat-gnawn, but how the thoughts of a brother man had consoled him!

The works of the other authors, with the exception of *Bevis*, had been sold to him by an old second-hand bookseller in Dover, into whose shop he had strolled after he had passed through the Dispersal Unit at the neighbouring camp of Shorncliffe. That day had been the crystallization point of his life.

Now he tried to read Thompson's *Hound of Heaven*, which he understood only partly; but his mind would wander, so he put the book back on the shelf, and went outside. The golden tranquillity of the cove no longer sufficed him. He saw the peregrine falcons—larger female falcon and smaller male tiercel—sweeping at great speed from over the sea. He watched them until the falcon dived, and the tiercel swung still, a mere speck, above. The waiting bird fell, and Maddison wondered as they disappeared behind the line of the hill what life had been shattered; then his thought returned to the girl. He threw aimlessly a few pebbles into the water, and although the puppies waited bright-eyed for more, he disregarded them. He stared unseeing at the water, then decided to go over to Cryde Bay. He must see her before it was too late; she might be leaving even at that moment. A dozen gentle glances and soft words arose dreamlike beside the path as he leapt up the hill. He was impatient of his tardy progress, and longed for a horse to carry him at a gallop across the headland. An hour shone away, and at last he was going down the sunken track on the south side of the headland, seeing the sandhills and the few houses of the bay below.

From the track he came to the lane, and so to the fork which led to the headland path by one way and to the bay by the other. At the fork he saw a long low grey motor-car standing with two wheels in the ditch. A row of poppies grew on top of the wall behind it. Out of the side of its bonnet four exhaust-pipes emerged like brass-bound snakes, which became a single fatter snake stretching the length of the car to the rear. It was obviously the racing car he had seen the night before, standing outside the Nightcrow Inn. He recalled how many young R.F.C. officers had bought second-hand high-powered racing cars for a few pounds in 1915, and had them fitted with great tanks holding fifty and sometimes a hundred gallons of petrol. The work had cost nothing, since it was done by the aerodrome mechanics, and the petrol had cost nothing, since it belonged to the Government. His cousin Phillip had told him of a friend, a flying-officer named Julian Warbeck, who had had such a car, which in the early days of the war was never washed in anything but petrol. Now, with petrol at four shillings a gallon these ninety horse-power cars must be expensive things to run. He noticed that two suitcases and a bearskin flying coat were thrown into the rear seats of the Mercèdes.

Taking the left lane, Maddison came to the sands. He passed

under the whitewashed sea-wall of the cottages on his right. He began, as though casually, to look around. The sands were empty except for gulls standing on the broad shining wetness where the stream through the dunes was spreading itself, and a horse and cart getting seaweed by the rocks of the low tide half a mile distant. He wandered towards the water, thinking that the sea was blue-grey as the eyes steadfastly watching him from the air. An aerial voice chanted: *I started life with Evie; then Eva; then it was Eve; then Eveline; and now it is E-v-e-l-y-n,* and he stopped still and stared into a tide-pool at his feet. Perhaps she was in one of the cottages over his right shoulder—he must not glance around—watching him from behind the curtains: she would be eagerly combing her hair, then she would add an alluring and deliberate poppy-smear to her lips, and then stroll towards him, affecting surprise at the encounter. Ah-ha; he, Maddison, knew about women! But—what was Colyer? And she was married; at least she had said she had a little girl. She was so young to be married! Perhaps Colyer was her brother.

Perhaps she was having tea in the cottage. He would wait until she appeared. He went down to the rocks to pass the time, watching the myriad life there—the shrimps and prawns, the crustaceans, anemones and sea plants. Idly he plucked horse-winkles and pitched them in a pool, continuing this until a sharp sting on his ankle made him aware of a sand-flea prospecting for blood. He killed it, and arose from the sharp pinnacle of rock that was slowly numbing him.

The shore was still empty, except for the gulls like many seed-pearls scattered on the sands. Watching them, he felt a loneliness, and a return of sadness akin to that felt after the Armistice, when the spirit of comradeship was changed in the squadron mess; when friends who had carelessly and happily been such, had returned to civilian life, and there had been nothing to take their place. The happy circle round the stove in the ante-room after mess dinner was broken up; nobody seemed to want to drink any more hot whiskey and water, with lemon in it: the wassailous spirit of comradeship had gone for ever. He had never been so lonely as when he left to be demobilized, and gone home to his village to brood on the bitter changes that war had wrought; and finding nothing left for him, he had set out with a pack on his back, meaning never to return. Had he not, like Jefferies, entirely and utterly rejected civilization—civilization that was worse than barbarism— since it chained a man to slavery in its factories and towns, and as compensation, released him so that he might mutilate or be mutilated in order to save that civilization. Then he saw her.

Billjohn and Tatters, who had been chasing footprints round the rocks, rushed towards her: she was bending down to caress them; she was looking his way; she was waving her hand. Maddison cleared his throat, and hitched up his trousers. He wished they were not so shabby, or khaki, for Colyer was dressed in a dark blue flannel coat with brass buttons, with white trousers, and brown buckskin shoes that only Guardees wore. And he wore the black, pale-blue striped Old Etonian tie. 'O, why did I come here,' thought Maddison.

'Hullo, I thought I saw you. You've met, haven't you? Captain Colyer—Captain Maddison.'

They shook hands, both saying: 'How do you do.' Colyer drawled: 'Hot, what?'

'Yes, isn't it?' replied Maddison.

'Don't be formal, you two.'

They both made a mirthless exclamation, and waited for her to speak. She played with the puppies.

'I saw your car in the lane, Colyer.'

'That doesn't altogether surprise me,' replied Colyer, 'for I left it there.'

'Haw, joke!' scoffed the girl, and Maddison smiled to hide his discomfiture.

Captain Patrick Colyer continued to say nothing, and to avoid looking at Maddison. Easily he sauntered along, hatless, hands in trouser-pockets. His forehead was high, with golden hair rippling back in waves; he had the blue eyes of a girl, a feminine mouth, and a delicate complexion; he looked slightly sulky, as one always accustomed to attention and a little wearied by it. Maddison imagined that he danced perfectly, that he drove his car at great speed and steered with one negligently gloved hand, and that under no circumstances would he appear ill at ease.

'We had a perfectly priceless bathe this afternoon, Captain Maddison. I say, I refuse to call you Captain Maddison, beard or no beard. I shall call you Maddison, or Bill.'

'Thank you, Evelyn!'

'Heartily reciprocated, Bill. Isn't it a pity, this is Pat's last day of leave. He has to go back to-morrow.'

'Are you driving far?' asked Maddison.

'Cranwell.'

'Oh, yes, I know. I was stationed at Grantham in Lincolnshire, at the Machine Gun School, for a few weeks in 1916. Your face is familiar, somehow.'

'Oh, really.'

They strolled along in silence. Maddison poked at the sand with his stick. Then he said:

'Your bus looks as though it could move. Is it hot?'

Captain Colyer continued to look on the sand. Maddison envied his air of nonchalance as he drawled,

'Fairly hot.'

'What is it?'

'What make, you mean? Oh, a Merc.'

'Has it a powerful engine?'

'Useful. Ninety horse. She'd lap at about a hundred and twenty on Brooklands, I expect. I've never tried her out properly.'

'You'll come and have tea with me?' asked Evelyn, turning to Maddison.

'I must get back, thank you,' he replied.

'Oh, n-no. Please, you'll have tea with me?'

'Yes, I would l-like to,' he stammered, and she laughed delightedly, thinking that he was mocking her.

Captain Colyer strolled on in front. His face showed a languid indifference. They went up some steps to the grass enclosure before the two cottages. A ship's figurehead of a wooden woman was nailed to the gable of a shed beyond.

'She decided me to stay here,' said the girl. 'She looks so sulky, so I thought I'd remain and laugh at her. She wants reconstructing!'

They laughed; but Maddison felt the Jefferies book in his pocket. Jefferies understood.

'Pat, tell Bill about Shiggles.'

'My dear Lina!'

Captain Colyer raised his eyebrows and stared at her.

'Shiggles is the most curious servant in the world, Bill. He is over seventy, and has a face like a bull moose. Pat saved him from a bear in Canada, and ever since Shiggles has devoted his life to him. When Pat was shot down over his own 'drome Shiggles wanted to go up and meet the Hun himself. Tell him about it, Pat.'

'My dear lady, why bore him?'

'Well, if you won't tell him, I will. Pat, I may tell you, Billy, has brought down forty-seven Huns. He got the second bar to his D.S.O. for——'

'Oh, I say, really, Lina, it's hard on a fellow to have his past raked up.'

'I shall say what I like about you. Oh, all right, if you would rather I didn't. I'm glad someone is sociable. Well, Billy—oh, here's Mrs. Shrake. I'll order tea.'

'Have you heard from Lionel lately?' he heard Colyer drawling; and he wondered who Lionel was.

'Not lately,' she answered immediately. 'The mail is not due till next Wednesday, and I rather expect to hear about his leave. He is expecting it, I know. Lionel is my husband,' she said to Maddison. 'I didn't tell you I was married, did I?'

'You said you had a daughter.'

'Oh, did I? I don't wear a ring, you see. Sea water, you know, makes the fingers shrink.'

'Yes, blame sea water,' drawled Captain Colyer.

'You satirical beast!'

'Ambiguity, not satire, Lina. My wit, like your temperament, is essentially adaptable.'

'Subtle man! But are you shocked at me for not displaying my badge of conjugality, Bill?'

'Why should anyone be shocked in an age when we all please ourselves?'

'Oh, do we? You seem to be worldly-wise all of a sudden!'

Maddison assumed what he hoped was a flippant air in order to hide the depression that he felt coming in him. He felt himself a stranger; he was ill at ease, and he had to suppress a desire to say something startling, anything in order to break the constraint. How he envied Colyer's easy manner! He spoke to Colyer about his journey; and Colyer answered so curtly that the depression changed to an inner contortion. That tie, that blue coat, those buckskin shoes, the Distinguished Service Order and bar—of course Colyer was contemptuous of him! Dare he go away? Then he saw that Evelyn was contemplating him with a frank wistfulness; she half closed her eyes, tilted her head slightly, and gave him a deliberately tender glance.

'Let's have a bathe before tea,' she suggested, 'only, Pat, you mustn't be reckless.'

'I am *never* reckless,' Captain Colyer protested as they went out.

'I want you to notice the wooden woman,' said Evelyn to Maddison, and she led him round the corner. At once her voice changed, and she said tensely: 'What's the matter?'

'Nothing is the matter.'

'Why are you so strange? You bewilder me. One moment

you are gentle and like a sweet child, and then you become cold and distant. Why is it? What have I done?'

'You have done nothing.'

'Is it because Pat is here?'

He did not know what to answer, and stared on the ground.

'I thought so! Oh, you child, do you know what that implies? Listen. There is no time now to tell you the whole circumstances, but Pat is one of the nicest boys in the world. Poor fellow, he was expelled from Eton, and had to go to Canada just before the war. That manner of his is just a mask to the world. You would think to look at him that he was effeminate and a useless creature, wouldn't you? Yet he is one of the bravest of men, one who has had to restrain all his feelings, otherwise he never would have come through the war alive. That's why he appears without emotion. When he drinks he's pathetic, as you saw last night.'

He nodded sympathetically.

'And, Billy, why did you behave so to me this morning? It wasn't good form, was it, my dear? You made me miserable.'

'I'm sorry, but——'

'What?'

She waited.

'Tell me, my dear. I do so want to be your friend.'

'Well——'

'Tell me.'

'Well, I—oh damn—you'll think me a fool, but—well, you see, I didn't—er—know you were—oh damn—married.'

She laughed. Then she sighed. She kicked a piece of wood softly. She seemed to be remembering something far away. Looking at him, she observed in a voice of reflective resignation: 'I was married when I was sixteen.'

'And are you unhappy?' he asked earnestly, grasping her arm.

'I am not very happy,' she said, her eyes on the ground.

'I am sorry I was beastly to you.'

69

'Dear boy, I understand. Pat will go back shortly, I expect, and then you must take me to your cottage, and we will have some lovely long talks.'

'Will you really come?'

'My dear, I am so looking forward to it. You must show me those peregrine falcons of yours, and the seal, and Izaak the otter, and all your birds. And you must read me some of Jefferies.'

'You haven't forgotten him, then?'

'Why, no! I've been thinking of you every minute since we met, thinking of you alone with your old birds! And Jefferies! I wrote a long letter, too. . . .'

'I say, give it to me.'

'No, it is such a foolish letter. I wrote it because I could not sleep. Oh, when you spoke to me last night my heart was aching for you. I could understand so well how the war hurt you, the mental suffering, I mean, in addition to the physical suffering. You make me feel so shallow and useless, and although I want to help you, I don't see ——'

She pointed to the wooden figurehead. 'Look at her, scowling at me, the old fool. That's the world; but we are young, my dear, and—don't worry, or be so sad—things will come all right in time.'

'I'm very happy,' declared Maddison.

She squeezed his arm. 'Of course you are, my dear.'

'Evelyn—if I may call you Evelyn.'

She said softly: 'I've been wanting to hear you say my name ever since I saw you.'

He fumbled in his pocket.

'Evelyn, may I read what I wrote this morning?'

'Yes, do! I'd love to hear it. But here's Pat. Be nice to him, Bill. It's his last evening in this lovely Devon. He's a tragic person. He and I are very close friends. The girl he loved has just married someone else, and he was so terribly miserable that I persuaded him to bring me down here in the Merc—for

70

he loves his old Merc more than anything on earth, I think. Listen, quick. Will you lunch with me here to-morrow? All right. Hullo, Pat. Bill and I have been telling the wooden hag what we think of her.'

'Oh really.'

'Yes, really.'

'I've been thinking,' said Colyer, through teeth nearly closed, 'I had better be clearing off now.'

He held out his hand. 'Good-bye, Lina. Good-bye, Maddison.'

She went to him, exclaiming in a voice of self-reproach: 'Pat, darling, you simply cannot go to-night. Fatface is preparing a simply gorgeous supper—prunes, cold pork, sardines, and tinned salmon, just like last night! Pat, my dear, why this thusness?'

She squeezed his arm. Seeing this, Maddison made an excuse to find his dogs, and went away. By the sea-wall gate he glanced round to see her still talking to Colyer. How hurt he must have been, seeing a friend, on his last afternoon, desire to be with someone else. Poor Colyer, to be chucked by a girl, and then to feel that he wasn't wanted by his friend, either.

'God, I know that feeling,' he muttered to himself, and touching the book in his pocket to assure himself of his companion, he climbed over the sea-wall by the limekiln, and set off at a rapid pace across the fields towards Shelley Cove.

Chapter 6

'I DIDN'T think you'd come,' she said, meeting him on the sands of Cryde Bay next morning. 'Did you get my note? We looked for you in the Nightcrow last night. Pat went off happily this morning.'

He wore a pair of trousers less ragged, and a clean shirt. His hair was brushed and his nails were cut. He noticed that she had powdered almost imperceptibly her face, and her lips were touched with a suggestion of scarlet. A dark blue bathing dress was slung over her shoulder.

They sat on the rocks, while she kicked off her shoes and began to remove her stockings. Deliberately he watched the gulls patrolling the surf till she had finished, and when the white flesh of her knees was covered by her skirt, he turned his head and asked if she would like him to stow stockings and shoes in his pocket.

'I like to feel my toes pressing into the sand as I walk, don't you? I feel I can love everything then, even hawks—but not old men who live to eat!'

They exchanged smiles.

She held one foot up for his inspection, extending the toes. The first toe of each foot was slightly longer than the big toe.

'They are lovely feet,' he said gravely.

'Is that why you wrinkle your forehead?'

He made no reply, and she said:

'But, of course, I know—to a man like you the idea is more vivid than reality.'

Slowly he said: 'It isn't really, but, you see, when one has——'

72

'Life is cruel to the beauty it creates,' she interrupted. 'I've been haunted by those poor sheep.'

Her words, and the suggestion of an impersonal sadness in her charming voice drew his glance to her profile, but she appeared unconscious of his regard. A wave of the rising tide swilled into the pool in the sand by which they stood. A sodden bundle of black and white feathers was rolled over. It was a guillemot, one of many killed by the tar-like oil-fuel which ships in the Severn Sea dumped overboard when cleaning their tanks. She touched the corpse with her foot, with seeming carelessness.

'Well, what are you thinking?'

'I was thinking of what you said about life being cruel. Has it been cruel to you?'

'Oh, no. I am resigned, that is all. To the cage of life, maybe. But do not let me worry you with my troubles.'

'Have you any?' he asked. 'You won't worry me, really. I would try and understand—O, you will laugh at me.'

'No, of course I will not,' she replied, touching his hand. 'One does not laugh at sincerity.'

'You are like a lark that sings for joy,' he said in a low voice. 'I can only stand below and watch you, and listen.'

'How many women have you said that to?' she enquired, and walked away. He stood still. He looked at the few people on the sands, and then realized that perhaps he had given offence. Why had she spoken in such a different, almost a cynical, voice? Was it slighting, or rude, to say she was a lark? O God, he was a damned fool to have come over. He was weak: when would he learn that only by being alone could he be himself. Well, he would apologize for his gauche remark, and then say good-bye.

She was paddling. He called her name, but she did not turn round. Disregarding his trousers, he waded in a foot of water, and said hurriedly that he had brought her stockings.

'Your dogs are looking for you,' she answered, turning to

73

look at the puppies who dared not follow him. 'Don't distress them. Besides, your best trousers are getting wetter every second. Can't you roll them up? I say, you didn't mean that about the lark, did you?'

'No, I didn't. I'm sorry.'

'You didn't mean it?'

He stared at her. 'I like larks,' he said.

Her look gave him an exquisite feeling. 'Billy,' she whispered, 'I thought you were laughing at me.'

'No, I wasn't.'

'I think you are the most innocent thing I ever encountered.'

Her mouth is sad, he thought, staring at her. He felt a little fear; deep within himself he trembled. He was overcome by a surge of happiness which made him incoherent. Here was one who believed as he did, one whose freedom of spirit was probably inherited from some far ancestress, one who was not a type crushed into inanity by civilization. How sublime was the adventure, how the gleaming wavelets washed her feet: he could cry aloud for the happiness that was in his life. Ah, but she had said something about the cage of life. Because she was married? Feeling bold, he said,

'Evelyn, do you really feel caged?'

She said 'Oh, no'; but immediately his mind conceived her to be a tragic figure; and seeing his serious face, she flipped him lightly on the cheek with her bathing dress, and said: 'You won't run away, will you, Willie Maddison? Shall we bathe? Didn't you get a bathing suit at the store in Cryde village as you came through?'

He told her that he had no money with him. Immediately the smile went from her face.

'Oh, why didn't you ask me for money, dear boy? I had no idea that you might be hard up. Look here, can I help you in any way? I haven't got much with me, but in the cottage——'

His heart was warmed by her generosity. He told her that he had never expected to bathe at Cryde Bay. In Shelley Cove, he

74

said, he did not need any garment, since no one ever came near it in the early morning or at dusk.

'How shocking!'

'But I can bathe in my trousers,' he said; 'they dry afterwards in a very few minutes.'

'Can you swim? There's a pretty dangerous current at half tide. It drowned two people during the war. The Claw, you know.'

'I know,' said Maddison. 'I was here with Cousin Phillip in 1916; we spent a fortnight's leave together. Dear old Phil. I haven't heard from him for ages. The last time, he was in love with a girl whom he'd known since boyhood, and unhappy. God, I hardly know anyone who hasn't been unhappy! But coming generations won't suffer as we did!'

She watched his face: the under lip was thrust out: his eyes lost the childlike candour which had first attracted her, and moved her deeply; the eyes were strong and intent; his chin was thrust forward as though at an invisible enemy which he knew he could master. He is a child, and he is a man, she thought.

'I met Phillip first at a dance given by his regiment; he had just "got the bird", to use the slang phrase, from that girl you mentioned. He was awfully disconsolate, poor old boy, and standing about all by himself in his new blue uniform which he had just bought, he told me, at Moss Brothers! All dressed up, and no girl to love him! I say, Billy, do let's bathe!'

'Rather, Evelyn!'

'See you in a minute,' and waving her hand, she went towards the rocks.

At first he was apprehensive in trousers, but immediately she made him forget it by envying the tan of his arms and shoulders.

'I must hold my arms to the sun,' she said, 'the sun that is the giver of joy. I wish I was big enough to bite chunks out of that great gold orb! Tell me, Billy, is any of my unruly hair coming out under the cap?'

'No,' he answered, not daring to do more than glance. 'I say —I wonder if you would do me a favour?'

'What is it?'

'Will you let your hair down? I think a woman's hair is so glorious. Let me see it shining and free.'

'It's very ordinary hair,' she said, 'and perhaps you would be disappointed.'

'Please do!'

'No, Mr. Maddison, I am afraid I cannot. What would that elderly gentleman who lives in that house above the rocks over there think of me? For I have noticed that he passes most of his morning at an open window with a pair of glasses. No, I shall not let you see my womanhood's crowning glory, and I think that if you had used original epithets for its description it would have been more sincere: although I know that Rupert Brooke is a pretty good poet.'

She spoke in such a droll way, and with such suppressed radiance in her face that he put his arms round her shoulders and kissed her cheek. Alarmed by the unbreathing stillness of her during the embrace, he ran into the shallows and plunged into a curling green breaker. He swam submerged as far as possible, and then came up, shaking water from his eyes. She was just behind him, and swimming with easy over-arm stroke, breasting the waves and laughing among the silver sunpoints of the foam.

The salt water darkened her lashes and gave a maiden purity to her eyes; two curls of auburn hair were damp against her cheeks, and her arms were smooth and slim and white.

'Billy, it's marvellous!'

'God, I'm happy! Do you see Lundy on the horizon? I feel that I could leap like a salmon into the air and dive right under the sea, and come up alongside in a second, fling my arm over it and haul myself into the sky.'

'I love to see you happy,' she said, touching his cheek as she swam past him.

76

'I say, we're out of our depth. The current of the Claw sets in at this tide!'

'Now is the supreme moment to die! To be drowned together! Are you a good swimmer?'

'Yes, fairly.'

'Well, then, let's swim out and risk being drowned. Are you game?'

'Yes,' said Maddison. 'Come on!' as he turned and took a few strokes seawards.

'Oh, come back,' she cried; 'I didn't mean it.'

'Funk!' he answered, by her side.

'If you mock me,' she jested, 'I will bite you.'

'When you've bitten the sun into small pieces?'

'Bearded beast,' she snorted, swimming away from him.

He pursued her, and caught her by the shoulder, when she pleaded for grace, immediately afterwards telling him in a mocking voice that she liked him to frown.

'Drown me with your firm brown hands round my neck, strong man. Bow wow! No, no, I didn't mean it. Oh, you are a great rough thing! First you kiss me, then you run away like a startled deer, then you push me under water. Really, you know, Mr. Maddison, it is not done, to duck a lady—I should say an imperfect lady. For how long have you known me?'

She dived, caught his leg, threw him under water, and swam away laughing. He chased her, and splashed her, amid entreaties for mercy; and so they went on, thinking nothing, hardly realizing how they spoke, or what they were saying. They wandered three hours on the sands before dressing. Stilly in sunny air floated the June hours, and somehow they were in a cottage parlour, and Evelyn was pouring out tea, and her eyes in the shade were lovely and meditating as those of a child who sits in a meadow singing to the blue crane's-bill flowers it has gathered. Then their glance would soften and go out to him as his heart beat proudly for the company of her beauty. No mortal was near them: the cottage wife was a smiling face that appeared and faded. Again they were on the sands, wandering by the pools, and standing on the rocks, maintaining by warm handclasps a steady balance while the tide crept in. A flow of birdsong was come into the air, and a golden highway was opened across the sea; the foam was tinged with purple as though along that western ocean road the carousing sun was spewing the wine he had quaffed all that day at the tavern of the drouthy earth. Venus shone in the luminous lower air, a chaste wife watching his return, with her the virginal and breastless moon, her daughter.

She looked over his shoulder as he wrote down the image in his notebook, murmuring that he would use it in the *Policy of Reconstruction*, and might he dedicate the book to her? She pressed his hand to her lips, and held it against her heart, saying that she was not worthy of such friendship and trust. Long was the parting on the hillside, the dread severance delayed till all the stars were shining in the tranquil night of summer. At last, at last, it had to be; one more good-bye breathed in the dewfall, one more lingering wait, and up the hill he went with his dogs, in his head held so high a sweet mazeful wonder of loveliness.

Swiftly he climbed the hill, and crossed the lane and the fields, and so came to the down. Somewhere in the towns and cities the clocks ticked off tame hours of an artificial life, but here no time existed. He strode on, treading fields of starved oats that waged a continual war with thistles, fern, vetch, and bindweed. Sometimes he paused to hear the sounds of the quiet night: the hum of a beetle, the purring rattle of a far eve-jar perched on a dead stump in the bracken, the snuffling of the puppies and sometimes a thin whine of enquiry at a rabbit bury. In the west over a steely sea the horizon lifted with sunset-dark hoverings, the glow of some great conflagration beyond the world. His heart felt great as the sunset, which he watched, for the first time in his life, with an equal mind. Overhead the stars kept their ancient ways, the faithful stars which he had watched from the fields of Rookhurst, from the London streets, from Gallipoli, from the downlands of the Somme. Here nothing was between himself and the wheeling stars, no smoke or fog, no snarling night-bombers or angry-red fireprick of shrapnel. There over the sea were Castor and Pollux, the heavenly twins, and yellow Capella. There, too, was Spica Virginis the maiden, his own bright star, near Corvus the raven and Regulus the lion. He remembered the night five years ago when he had stood at the edge of Crowstarver's Spinney and through his tears bidden farewell to the village where the long years of childhood and boyhood had passed so happily.

A short-eared owl beat with slow flight over his head and cut short his retrospection. Suddenly he realized that his pets in the cottage had not been fed since sunrise that morning. He regarded them with remorseful impatience; for to-morrow, as early as possible, he was going over to Cryde Bay. The last cornfield, a rock-strewn patch sown with corn and growing with charlock, was left behind, and the lane leading to the village was dark before him.

Sunday night talk in the Nightcrow Inn was, as usual, quiet. Brownie, wearing his special Sunday night garb of a khaki tunic with a deciduous bowler, was regarding with dolour the pint pot before him, and smoking a short cutty. Under the lamp the old man with the knotted tartan tie was sitting, smoking a cigarette in a long tube.

Maddison ordered a pint of beer, smiling round the company of men who wore their best clothes and hats. The faces of the landlord's two daughters, leaning over the bar and joking with some youths drinking lemonade, were like flowers in the smoke. Everyone was happy, himself happiest of all. Landlord was smiling and asking what he would have, no scowling faces anywhere: boots stamped on the stone floor, ancient granfers sitting muffler-wrapped and silent in the corners, dogs and puppies playing and chasing one another and squirming

under everybody's legs, Brownie crying: 'Will'um Jan—
Will'um Jan—look 'ee at the dogs; fine li'l boys they be, Mis'r
Meddlesome, midear! Zo 'ee went to Cryde Bay s'marnin and
zeed li'l ruddle maid!'

Maddison sat beside him and shouted in his ear that he
didn't want everybody to know where he had been, and would
Brownie keep the secret? Brownie replied: 'That's right, midear. It bant no one else's bizniz! Don't 'ee be afear'd, no
one'll know!'

He drank from Brownie's pot, and Brownie drank from his.

'Doan't 'ee go yet, Mis'r Meddlesome, zur, doan't 'ee go yet,
midear. Zstop along o'me and have a li'l confirmational conversation. Bide awhile, midear, wi' ol' Broonie.'

'No, I must go, Brownie. I've got to get my bread and
potatoes and other things. I've got a guest coming to lunch
to-morrow! Drink up, and have another.'

'Thank 'ee, Master,' replied Brownie, draining his pot.
'Willum Jan, Tattery, stop it! Praper li'l dogs they be, aiy,
aiy! Bread and tetties for dinner! Corbooger! Mis'r Meddlesome, will 'ee do me the honour of accepting a li'l bootiful
small sweet li'l rabbit my dog picked up to-night? 'Tes a
bootiful sweet flavoured li'l rabbit, I'll guarantee!'

'Thank you,' he answered, flattered by the invitation.

'Did you go zwimmun to Cryde Bay to-day, zur?' asked the
landlord in a low confidential voice, as he took Brownie's mug.

'Yes, I strolled that way to-day.'

'Aiy, I heard tell-on you were zeen over there,' volunteered
the landlord, disappearing through the doorway to the barrel-
room. Coming back with the ale, Maddison whispered for the
loan of a razor. Secretly and with a smile he was given it; he
departed to go to the farmhouse for his bread and half a pound
of butter.

'That's a lovely bit o' butter, zur,' said the farmer. 'Two
shillun, zur; butter be scarce. They be charging six shillun a
pound in Ilfracombe, too, and the same for cream. 'Tis the

drought, zur, and the war. Well, and what do you think of Cryde Bay, zur? Hot on the sands, weren't it?'

'Oh, were you there to-day?' enquired Maddison.

'No, zur. Us poor men have to work all the day. Anything else, zur?'

'No, thank you.'

'Can't I zell you a nice li'l chicken? I killed a couple only last night. Bootiful white meat, for I hanged 'n upsidown for two hours before pricking the throat.'

'I have a rabbit, thank you.'

'Yes, zur,' said the farmer. 'I expect you'll be dining over to Cryde Bay, zur, now you've got a bit of company? Mrs. Fairfax is a very nice lady, zur, if you will pardon me zaying so.'

'Good-night,' said Maddison; and he hastened out of the village, lest he meet the policeman, the parson, the schoolmaster, the Rate-collector, etc.

The stream rested in a little pool, before losing itself in the shingle, and as he passed he heard a faint whistle. He turned towards it, calling *tikkytikkytuck*. There came to him a noise like the scrupeting of an ungreased axle, and the stars that shone in the black water quivered and went out. A splash, and Izaak greeted him with a low *tikkytuck*. The cub sniffed, then turned and went into the water, with its alarm cry—a mewing chatter. It must be Evelyn's scent, he thought.

'Tikkytikkytuck,' called Maddison, and the cub appeared and followed him swiftly into the cottage.

He felt remorse at the frenzied greetings given him by his pets. The kittens mewed, the birds squawked, the gull hopped in and out of his feet, dragging its broken wing. Fortunately there was some stew remaining in the stock-pot, and this they were given. He skinned the rabbit and put it on to boil with some potatoes, carrots and barley. In the starlight the goat was milked; Izaak drew comfort from a bottle, the kittens and the puppies lapped from a dish. While the driftwood crackled and the flames flapped around the pot, he shaved his beard with

F

many groans, and then sat and surveyed the hearth, thinking how he could pass the time until the morrow.

He did not want to go to bed: he was not tired; nor could he read. *The Policy of Reconstruction* seemed false. As he stared unseeing, it was borne upon him how lonely and purposeless had been his life in the cottage: a mere existence. *The Policy of Reconstruction!* He was living his own reconstruction, since he had met Evelyn! Heart-ache was really rib-ache, or the ache of the scar whence the rib had been taken. Quickly he wrote the thought on a piece of paper. God, he was happy. He shivered and hugged his knees. What would happen in the future? His mind, busy with beauty, cast aside the speculation. The present only mattered. One might be dead on the morrow. That was the philosophy during the war, and it applied equally to civilian life.

He sat there, and heaved more wood on the fire when the flames lessened. Through the window a star shone steadily. The puppies slept on the old trousers. One kitten was washing the other upon the bookshelf. No sound came save the wash of the sea, ceasing never, the dry whisper of the beetles exploring the floor for scraps of food, the hoot of an owl, the squeak and scuffle of rats inside the walls. He yawned many times, but his brain was never so active—how the star was like a dancing kingfisher! While others slept, he would cherish the wonder in his heart.

With his long thin Arab-like foot—for he had removed his shoes—he stroked and smoothed the heads of Izaak and the pups. Then rising, he took a pencil and paper and began to write rapidly. The sound of the waves ringing a phantom carillon on the drowned shells died away in the night, the tide reached its lowest ebb, the last ember ceased to tinkle in the grate, but still he wrote on. At last, suddenly weary, he threw down the pages, and turning into a comfortable position in the chair, drowsed into sleep: to waken as the puppies barked frantically at the apparition of an old ragged man at the door, holding a crab in his hand. It was only Jack o' Rags, a half-witted hermit who had been injured in the mines years before, and who lived in the machine-shed.

'Thanks,' cried Maddison. The idiot laid his offering on the doorstone, and slouched away without speaking. Immediately Izaak seized the crab and broke off a leg, but Maddison took it from him.

'Evelyn said she liked crab,' he said aloud. He hesitated. 'But I'm not going to boil the poor brute.' Should he return it to the sea? The otter cub whined. 'O, here you are, Izaak; God will tell you what to do with it.' He hurled the crab on the stone floor, and watched the fight over the fragments.

Chapter 7

THEY met again the next morning, and went down to the deserted Vention sands. To his embarrassment and pleasure she said that he looked absurdly young without his beard, and very good-looking. The sun shone brightly for them, and a white mist lay over an unmoving sea. They bathed, afterwards lying among the big blue and grey boulders at the edge of the land till the sun was high above them. Reluctantly they arose and scrambled up the little footpath through the thistles and brambles of the cliff. He went first, helping her over rough places. Once she nearly slipped or seemed to: he caught her round the waist, and exerted an unnecessary amount of strength in assuring himself that she would not fall. Reaching the top, they passed along the path through the barley. The girl led the way; occasionally she turned, and each time he dwelt on the glowing cheeks, the bright eyes, the ardent hair, the white neck. How proud was her bearing, and yet when he looked again it was that of an eager maiden. The spirit of the wild was within her young body, the beauty of the sea within her eyes.

'Why so silent, Billy?'

He was just thinking, he said. She waited a moment for him to draw level with her, and linked her arm in his, looking into his face.

'Tell me what you were thinking!'

They passed through the corn and sat down, while the heated air in the barley made a dry dissonance with the summer wavelets on the sands below. Their shoulders touched; his left hand, pressed on the grass, lay against her smaller one.

He did not speak, and she linked her little finger with his.

'Tell me what you were thinking!'

'Oh, but I cannot,' he exclaimed, looking on the ground.

'Go on,' she whispered; 'don't be shy with me, Willy.'

A bird made its incessant stoneclacking cry. After several hesitant beginnings he said:

'I can't tell you!'

'But do!'

He looked towards a coombe grooved between the hills, where the heather was growing purple. After a while she murmured: 'You haven't told me.'

Two black birds passed over from the mainland, croaking down the blue sky. They were ravens sailing to their nest on the headland.

'I believe you want to humiliate me,' she complained.

'No,' he said, anguish in his voice. Then: 'May I read you something? I wrote it to you last night.'

'Give it to me!'

'I daren't.'

'I'll take it. It's mine!'

'Oh, please. It's so silly.'

'Very well, but I think you're a cheat. You read it to me.'

He began, after much hesitation and frowning, to read tonelessly, then stopped. 'No, that's nothing. That's only about you. Here's the part. Promise you won't laugh?'

'I promise.'

After an effort he began:

'I see the Spirit which has been unchanging since the first life stirred on the cooling crust of the great fireball of the earth. I seem to glimpse it as something too beautiful for words, and that the spirit of mankind is one with it—one in a luminous realm of beauty. And then I think that this is only an illusion, that it is a function of the mind that is self-induced. Terrible thought! That all is illusion! But even if it be untrue, I can see the mind of mankind built up of impressions throughout the centuries, from the blue sea and the sun-sparkle on it, from the blown hair of the wind, from the odour of the flower. And from impressions also the bird has got its song, and the dandelion its colour. Sometimes at night I lie and watch the stars and then I feel how much greater I am than those suns hurtling and roaring through space—because they are but matter, and I am a mind! And then, suddenly, my ecstacy goes as I think of all the hunger and disease on this little cooling fireball which we call the world—there should be no hunger, no slum-consumption, no wars! Night and day I thinks of these things —wars, and consumption, wasting disease, and strife! All caused by man's desire of happiness—because he follows false ideals. I can sympathize with all men, for I am a man who wants natural happiness—someone to love, and'—'God, it's rot! Rot! No, no, give it back to me, Evelyn, please, it's silly stuff, and I ought never—very well, don't forget I asked you not to read——'

Evelyn read slowly, quietly:

'. . . Someone to love me, to live with me in my cottage, to guard the well of my spirit where I draw Truth which is also my life.'

She quietly folded the letter.

'I don't care what you think,' muttered Maddison, 'I haven't spoken—the real me hasn't spoken—to anyone since the summer of 1914. I had a friend then, only I didn't appreciate him until it was too late.'

Gently, very gently, she covered his hand with her own, and said nothing. The summer stir of the sea was soothing like a whisper. She waited, her eyes gentle and sweet, and she said softly: 'Read on.'

After more persuasion he finished the letter.

'The day after I met you I sat here, and loved the sun, the sea, and the sky. Suddenly I was afraid: for I can love all these things, but they do not respond. I realized that I should grow old, that I should die, and still the wind would shake the poppy, the blue butterfly seek the harebell, and the trefoil be yellow on the hillside. I shall be gone—dead—and nothing I can do now can avert that. Nothing that we can do can stay death. And yet we hasten it—think of the war—the dead men at Suvla Bay, in the burning scrub—or drowned in the waters of Third Ypres. . . .'

He was genuinely moved by his own writing; and he hoped, with a desperate subconscious hope, that she would be moved, too. She made no sign that she had heard; he dared not look at her directly, but he waited, concealing his dread and longing by an expressionless face. He longed to bow his head on her lap, and find rest there.

'I knew I ought not to have read that awful rubbish to you,' he muttered, after a silence of nearly a minute. 'I suppose I was trying to impress you with my marvellous style. "Foxy, sir, foxy! Come along, sir, I'll give you that cane!"'

'Don't! I do understand. You awaken things in me I thought dead. Trust me; I swear to God I will never hurt you. But, dear child, I'm not worth thinking about. I am a mindless clod.' Impulsively she held his coat and leaned forward. 'Lovely smell your coat has. Wood smoke and salt wind, and wild thyme. Poor, lonely, dreaming youth—I wish I could help you.'

He did not move, and she turned away: the pain in his heart seemed to be echoed by a curlew crying over the wasted uplands.

'You are like those fields,' she said. 'You are parched and overburdened. All you boys who went into the war from school are the same—there's your cousin Phil, and Julian Warbeck—but Julian's terrible, a fine mind wasting itself with drink—and Pat Colyer, and many others. But how can I help them? I can give them friendship, but they never remain content with that. Of course people talk about me in Folkestone—people like the wooden woman, dead people, without feeling, sheep-eyed old women—God, how I hate them. Now you see what a shame-less creature I am.'

The pain in his heart grew. Did he love Evelyn? Yes, yes, and it was too late. She was married, she was a mother: *I can give them friendship, but they never remain content with that.* O God, he must go away.

Beside them a poppy droiled in the sun, a bloom of scarlet from the dried earth. It was the only wild flower that he could see, and, while other plants were withered, it seemed to find nurture for its untamed bloom.

'A solitary poppy,' said Evelyn, 'a single poppy in all the desert of the world. Wear it for me,' and she snapped the flower from its stalk, and leaned over him to place it in his buttonhole.

'Poor flower,' he murmured; and his eyes filled, for he was thinking how Jefferies, wasted with disease, had loved the pagan poppies. Jefferies, with his bearded face hiding the deep lines of his suffering; friendless almost, misunderstood; but the pale ray from heaven had touched his brow . . . Jefferies would always be with him!

'I'm sorry,' she said.

He felt tired. The sunlight was harsh and unreal. He got up and followed her up the hill. She was sitting on the grass, looking at the sea. He stopped beside her, but she did not heed him.

'I think I must go back to the cottage now,' he said. Why had he said that? O, he had longed and longed for her to swim with him to the Cormorant Rock: to read her *The Policy of Reconstruction*; and Jefferies, and Shelley, and Thompson.

'Very well. Good-bye. Don't let me detain you.'

He waited. Her face was expressionless, except for the eyes, which were filled with hurt gentleness. With his stick he swiped at the tops of thistles, knocking them off.

'Not poor thistles?' she said in an icy voice, with scornful

pride in her glance. 'Only poor poppy because *you* didn't pick
it? O, it is sad.' Her beauty anguished him.

'Good-bye,' he said, casually.

'Good-bye. Shall I see you again?'

He longed to abandon himself to her. But he shook his head.

'You mean that?'

'Yes.'

'That is a plain answer, anyway.'

The suffering was heavier within him. She looked at him
levelly, with widened nostrils.

'You are just trying to annoy me, I believe. You say you
want friendship, but you just humiliate me all the time. I was
fool enough to believe you; but now I know you are just selfish
and conceited. Very well, you can bloody well go to hell!'

And springing up, with averted head and biting her lower
lip—that full red lip—she walked away.

The next afternoon when he went over to Cryde Bay he was
told that Mrs. Fairfax had left that morning for her home in
Folkestone.

Chapter 8

THE moon that had been like the gold bill of a curlew grew fuller, and Maddison watched it rising later every evening. It was quiet above the valley as the roistering sun rolled home, and wearily the earth put up its shutters. No one came near him, wandering on the down, finding a melancholy interest in the song of evejars, the far high scream of racing swifts, and the antics of dogs and otter cub. Soon the moon was a gold hulk adrift in the reefless night sky, dismasted and rudderless, yet its ghostly crew forever netting the stars. By the thorns and the stunted holly bushes on his way down to Shelley Cove a swarm of chafers boomed and flipped, and moths whirred in the still air of the empty summer evenings. 'You'm luking woebegone, midear,' said Brownie, when one night, unable to contain his melancholy, he went to the Nightcrow Inn. ' 'Tis the hottish weather, zur. It be pressing on all things. What, be homewards a-ready to Rat's Castle, midear? Surenuff?' and the one eye regarded him tenderly. 'Gude-night, zur, gude-night!'

Children ceased their clamouring play of hide-and-seek in the drangs and gardens as he passed, murmuring tinily, 'Mis'r Ma'sson'; cottage wives smiled and said: 'You'm a proper zstranger'; and there was a silence after he passed. He felt himself to be a stranger, an outcast, his heart to be derelict like the gold hulk sky-logged in the Exmoor vapours. The western sea and sky smouldered with the last of the sunset. A sad dusk brimmed the valley. The wavelets of the cove no longer chimed the elfin bells of the cowries and tellin shells: there was only the dirge of the sea. He read the third volume of *Bevis*, while it seemed that his spirit was trying to tear itself from his

body to join that of Jefferies which had wandered round the
shores of the New Sea, and had fished near the island Seren-
dib, and had sailed the blue boat *Pinta*, and tacked into the
wind while the ripples went *sock sock* against its bows.

How Jack and I used to pore over this book, he thought. We
too made a hut on Heron's Island; we too had a catamaran,
and caught perch in the Longpond. There was Bony, too, and
Rupert—they had been the original members of the Owl Club.
Now these were gone—whither? Jack—part of the sour Flem-
ish earth at the edge of Ploegsteert wood. Bony? Shot down in
flames over Havrincourt Wood in the Hindenburg Line.
Rupert was in the sand on the edge of the dry salt-lake of
Suvla Bay. Well, they were happy: for they were of sun, air,
water, earth—which were not sad.

The printed page became blurred, and the book slid to the
floor. Billjohn whined at his knees. Tatters and Izaak were out
hunting, but hearing their mate's whine, back they came,
tumbling through the circular hole at the bottom of the door.
Around Maddison they leapt, rolling with him on the floor,
whining and gurgling, licking his face, his bare ankles, his
hands—they liked the mild and personal salt of his wet cheeks.

And when the morning came they were around his pillow,
snoring, on their backs with legs askew, but very warm and
comforting. He threw off the blanket, and with it the five
animals. He jumped down the stairs, and at the open door
drank the cold sweet air of morning. A grass-green wave
curled and crashed on the shingle: the sound awoke in him an
ecstacy of living. Into the foamy water he plunged, and swam
to Cormorant Rock. When the sun first filled the valley with
light he swam in, and gave the animals their meal. They
snarled and chattered, and stole food from one another's
mouths. When all was finished the puppies returned to the
trousers and slept, Becky washed Pie, Izaak went off on a
secret business, and the daw caught flies at the window. Lying
on the beach, Maddison read aloud how the dying Jefferies had

remembered the summers of his youth when he had been in love.

'A sweet breath on the air, a soft warm hand in the touch of the sunshine, a glance in the gleam of the rippled waters, a whisper in the dance of the shadows.'

'There can never be summers again like those at home, when Big Will'um and Jim Holloman were in the mowing meadows,' he sighed.

'The ethereal haze lifted the heavy oaks and they were buoyant on the mead, the rugged bark was chastened and no longer rough, each slender flower beneath them again refined. There was a presence everywhere, though unseen: on the open hills, and not shut out under the dark pines.'

And there was Dolly, turning the swathes with the other girls, who went at evening to the pool in the brook to dip.

'Let not the eyes grow dim, look not back but forward: the soul must uphold itself like the sun.'

'Yes, uphold itself like the sun; but Jefferies, like me, upheld himself in ancient sunlight. From the memories of those taintless days I draw my strength; by the past, man's mind is made strong with beauty.'

'In the blackbird's melody one note is mine: in the dance of the leaf shadows the formed maze is for me, though the motion is theirs; the flowers with a thousand faces have collected the kisses of the morning.'

'I suppose Evelyn has forgotten me,' he said to the jackdaw; 'I cannot read, I cannot think, I only want to be with her. She was so sweet, and she understands. Captain Colyer must be much more companionable than myself. I have known her but a week, and yet everything is changed. I wish Jack o' Rags could speak.'

The idiot was emerging from his underground home in the hillside opposite the cottage, yawning and stretching his arms. Maddison walked over to him, calling out a greeting. He did not answer, but stared at him dazedly. Bits of his brackeny bed were in his hair and beard, and the mouldy coat he wore was fastened by thorns; the hair on his face and chest was tumbled and black as a shot crow's wing.

'Have you been sleeping?' asked Maddison in a loud voice. The man made some unintelligible reply. A green luminous moss grew on the side of the tunnel, and a cow's skull lay at the entrance. Then Maddison noticed that he had a wound on his foot, as though he had trodden on a rabbit gin.

'How did you do that?' he asked, but received no coherent reply. The puppies were barking furiously from beyond the tunnel mouth.

'Get away!' cried Maddison. 'Shut that damned row! Outside!'

They slunk away, and played on the shingle.

'Come with me,' said Maddison. 'I'll clean your sore for you. Fortunately my dogs aren't so hungry as those dogs that licked Lazarus, otherwise you might get the eggs of a tapeworm into your blood. Poor Tatters was very sick last night: I shall have to get some dope for him.'

The conversation, or monologue, continued while Maddison poured some warm water from the kettle into a basin, and tore an old clean shirt into strips. Jack o' Rags sat on the threshold.

'Not there, if you don't mind,' suggested Maddison. 'On the grass. Or better still, on the beach. Preferably below the line of high water. Thank you. God, you stink. Why don't you take a swim now and again?'

93

While he was washing the wound a musical cry like that of a Tyrolean goatherd echoed in the coombe.

Maddison breathed deeply; his heart beat violently.

'Hullo,' was all he said when she was near.

'Hullo,' she called as she crossed the shell beach.

He dared not look at her. How could he get rid of Jack o' Rags?

'I've been so worried. My poor little Jonquil has had influenza. I went home to nurse her. She's better now. Did you get my letter?'

'What letter?'

'I wrote to you five days ago. Now I remember, for I've been so busy, I don't think I posted it.'

'Oh.'

'Anyhow, it only said I might be returning with Jonquil, and my maid. At the last moment I came alone. And who's your friend?'

'This is my father. Father, stand up and meet Mrs. Fairfax. He's been dancing too hard at the Band of Hope socials in the village and his shoes were too small. He's badly blistered.'

'Seriously, who is he? My dear, his foot is bad.'

Maddison explained. 'He's quite harmless, and deaf, so he won't be insulted. I'm just going to bathe his foot.'

'Can he understand what one is saying?'

'No.'

'Billy, you amaze me more every minute. What an extraordinary child you are! You never mentioned that you had a lodger.'

'I haven't. Jack o' Rags lives in the mine over there.'

'Good heavings—heavens! My village childhood coming out in my speech. I say, let me dress his leg for him. I know all about nursing. I was a V.A.D. during the war, in a casualty clearing-station, too, so I know all about it. You can't use that rag—it would give him blood poisoning. Have you any iodine?'

'No, but I've got some boric powder.'

'That's better than nothing. I'll wash it for him, if he won't object. Doesn't he stare at me? Poor old fellow, he ought to be in hospital. How does he live?'

'On berries and rabbits, raw!'

'Robinson Crusoe and his man Friday! Hullo, is that Izaak? He doesn't like me—hark at that snarling chatter. What a lovely creature—look at his brown tail! Oh, the darling's only got three paws. How sweet of you to nurse these poor broken things.' She gazed at him; and suddenly turned away.

'Sorry, I'm gushing again. May I go inside and see your cottage, please?'

'Do, please.'

'Oh, what a mess everything is in! Never mind, I'll set to work in a moment.'

She spoke as though the sight of disarrangement within was hurtful to her. He felt that her compassion was for himself, as she moved quickly round the room, gazing at his books, reading the titles aloud, touching them, putting them in order.

'My dear, how damp they are. Look at the mildew.'

'I know, Evelyn. I mean Lina. May I call you that please?'

'Why, certainly. And yet—I like your grave pronunciation of my name. No, you must not call me Lina—everyone calls me that. Call me Eve.'

'Eve, I am so glad you have come to see my cottage.'

'Are you, really?'

'I cannot tell you how glad. I have missed you—but I should not say that. But, you know, it is a poor place to invite anyone to.'

'It isn't—it's—your socks, my dear: they are not mended. Don't you get blisters?' She looked into his face. 'But first we must attend to your father's foot. See how he stares at me.'

'You must forgive his lack of polish, Eve. He is a self-made man. Poor Jack o' Rags, I hope I'm not being too callous about him.'

'My dear, I had no idea you were such a wit! Billy, it's lovely to see you so happy and gay!'

A wit? But he wasn't a wit. Could it be possible that he was a wit?

He was sent upstairs for the boric powder, while with sleeves rolled up she scoured the basin with sand, and washed the linen. All the while she spoke to him, her lips dewy with a smile, her glance tender. She knelt before Jack o' Rags, and with firm hands bathed the sores, then frowningly inspected them, after which she asked for a knife. At her bidding he purified the blade in the ember flames of the wood fire, and when it was cooled she with swift gentleness cleansed the hurt. The water became stained, but Jack o' Rags did not wince. Now she was laving the bony leg, and the idiot was touching her auburn hair in wonderment and gratitude.

'Mind, he's got fleas,' said Maddison.

'So have I,' replied Evelyn.

She smiled, and he realized with pain that all men must surely be drawn to her, because she was gracious to even the least among them.

'And now I must attend to you,' she told Maddison. 'You must work under my command. And before I can issue orders I must inspect the entire place.'

'Upstairs?'

'Yes.'

'But it is so untidy.'

'I am prepared for disorder.'

'You will get a shock.'

'That will be stimulating.'

He lifted the latch and she went up the stairs. The first room was small; a tiny window permitted light to enter. One corner of the ceiling had fallen in, or rather on a previous occasion, Maddison, crawling over the laths in order to find swifts' nests, had suddenly fallen through the plaster, to the surprise of himself and two rats who had been exploring his kit during his absence. Spiders' webs were spun in the corners and ruined with wood-dust which trickled from the holes of death-watch beetles. Evelyn made many exclamations when she saw the state of his bedroom, and immediately ordered the bracken to be burned. She said that his coats hanging upon nails around the walls were damp, and the delight of moths. She exclaimed at the swallow's nest under the thatch, and took the broom, pretending to knock it down, but with a cry he restrained her, explaining afterwards he was of course foolish, but that he loved the swallows. Looking at him, she said that it was unhealthy to have animals and birds sleeping in the same room, although in other and less intimate ways they might compensate for lack of human friends. He flung the coats through the window with such force that she stopped sweeping and laughed at him.

She worked hard, scrubbing the floor when it had been swept. 'You must strip off all those newspapers, and get some whitewash,' she suggested, pausing to read the date of a sheet that was stuck over a crack. '*The North Devon Herald*, 17th December, 1899—they talk about the war. That must be the Boer War. It has been stuck there a long time. You must tear all this down.' He protested that he liked it there, as it belonged to a past age and gave him a feeling of awe whenever he glanced at it. She laughed again, and said he was a proper old granfer, but said it so softly that he touched her cheek.

She threatened him with the scrubbing-brush, then knelt to continue her work.

'At any rate I am some good,' she reflected, when the bedroom was clean and tidy.

'What do you think of me as a skivvy, Billy? Not very much. Well, I used to be one in a castle, once! You don't believe me? It's true. Now, if you give me your socks I will go downstairs and darn them. Come on, take 'em off. Well, what does that matter? While I am darning you can change your trousers and I will patch that little rent in them. How surprised you look!

G   97

Didn't you know that they were torn in two places? Now I've made the sensitive child go quite red in the face. And that reminds me, I saw a rare flower this morning that will interest you: the Scarlet Crane's-bill. It was growing by a stone heap near the Bay. I remembered it from an illustration in a little book I used to love when I was a child; a sort of wild geranium. I thought that you would like to hear of it. Such a sweet flower. I didn't pick it, as it might have been one of your friends. Was that correct? You don't think it improper of me to sit on the bed of a young bachelor's establishment? And what a bed! I don't wonder you need bracken! Excuse this tomfoolery, but I feel that I must bubble on in my nonsense. I want to laugh and dance and sing and shout. Now tell me what you have been doing with yourself. Meanwhile, come here, and I'll sew a button on your shirt for you.'

He shifted on the creaking wooden framework.

'Come on!'

As he did not answer, she asked him if he felt shy.

'Oh, no. But the bed might collapse at any moment!'

'Yes, you are!'

On the ceiling of that small room were gliding the yellow ripples thrown up from the sea. He had a feeling of delightful fear, because her voice was altered, and she was looking at his eyes, and he did not turn to her gaze. A leisured song of blackbird came down the valley, and the summer wavelets shook the shells of the cove.

'Why do you mock me?' she breathed.

He looked on the floor and tried to think of an answer.

'I don't, really.'

'You do. Often there is dislike in your eyes.'

'But I like you!'

'Oh, you like me, do you? All-men-are-brothers-sort-of-idea, I suppose? I believe you care more for a swallow than for a human being.'

He did not know what to reply.

'I believe in your heart you despise me for coming over. Ever since I saw you last I have been thinking of you—you who care not if you never see me again.' She seized his left hand, and said that she wanted to hurt him, to be cruel to him, to make him suffer, because he scorned her for trying to help him. His thumb was bent back, and although the pain was sharp he did not move, but said:

'Break my thumb, if you want to; I don't care.'

She flung away his hand and told him to leave her, that she despised and hated him. He got up and went to the stairs, but she called his name, and he waited.

'Oh, I am sorry; truly I am. I am half wanton, you see, and I did want to try to be decent.'

At this confession he remained silent, waiting with a feeling of fascination to hear what she would say next.

When after a while she said nothing he returned slowly to her side, and touched her hair. She looked up at him, and he saw that her eyes were wet.

He tried to force himself to kiss her; but he could not move. O, she would despise him.

'I'm sorry,' he managed to say.

'Billy dear, I'm crazy. I won't misbehave again. Forgive me.'

'Nothing to forgive,' he muttered.

Without looking at him she went past him, downstairs. 'I am going to cook your lunch for you,' she said. 'Hullo, your father, I see, has installed himself by the hearth.'

'Good-bye,' cried Maddison, coming down the stairs rapidly. 'Good-bye, Father. Good-bye, good-bye, good-bye!'

The idiot arose and shuffled out through the doorway.

'Well, that's one way of treating the prodigal father,' laughed Evelyn.

Afterwards they collected the coats and blankets. It was necessary first to shake off the animals who were comfortably stretched out on them in the sun. He suggested a walk to the

pine woods beyond the village. In a dream of soft valley sunshine he walked with her, while magpies scolded their approach
from afar, and the voice of a turtle-dove throbbed with love in
the thorn brakes. But a moment seemed the walk up the path,
and then they were in the thatched and limewashed village
street, stroking every grimalkin on garden wall, and speaking
to housewives who craned round doorways and greeted them
while covertly wiping hands on aprons. Proudly he walked by
her side through the shadowed street, and so to the lane deep
under hedges, passing gates through which were seen poppy-
red cornfields and meadows of tall grasses, and talking inti-
mately of things light as the wings of honey-flies darting about
the taller flowers of scabious.

'Lord, it's hot,' he exclaimed. 'These damned trousers are
too long.' He took a knife out of his pocket, and opening an
enormous blade, proceeded to slit them down the hem, from
above the knee, while she looked on in amazement.

'But, my dear, you can't walk about like that!' she laughed.

'Yes, I can. Come on. No, you're right; they flap too much.
I'll convert them into shorts.' With the blade he cut them off
above the knee, and then flung the pieces into the hedge.
'That's cooler.'

'Billy, you're quite mad!' She laughed at the ragged fringe
of his trousers. 'You are the queerest creature I ever met.'

They wandered over parched fields to a quiet valley of sap-
ling oak and cone-bearing trees, over which in sunny wind
three buzzards were soaring. Pigeons clattered away through
dense larch twigs, as they walked beside a stream. A herd of
wild red deer trotted up the steep hill as soon as the wind
brought human scent to their nostrils; there was a stag with
growing antlers, and three hinds, each with a tiny calf and a
pricket, which he explained was the last year's calf. Hand in
hand they watched them bounding among the pines, and then
went on till they came to cool beech-trees where in dancing
light and shade they rested beside a well fringed with water-

hemlock and brooklime. Coloured chips of stones were clear in the light-laden water.

'This is the well of St. Flammea,' he told her, 'and it is legend that a knight crept here when wounded and his blood dripped into the pool. His lady found him as he was dying, and he told her that his spirit would go into the ground and rise with the spring. He was a poet, and her brother had waylaid him in the wood and stabbed him. So this water never ceases to flow, like the poetry of the earth.'

'And what did his lady do?'

'When he died she held her face under the water and was found drowned with him. That is the story of Saint Flammea, as afterwards the knight was called.'

'I wonder if it is true?' she said, meditatively.

'I shouldn't think so,' he replied, 'for I have just made it up.'

'Billy, you imp! Your voice was so sad that I believed you. You're lying?'

'I may be. I was always a bloody little liar, you know.'

'Ah, you heard what Pat said!'

'Yes; but it's true.'

'I don't care if it is; *I* believe you. Do you think that any-one's spirit could be in water?'

'Who knows? Why shouldn't it be?'

'But you assume that there is a spirit? A friend of mine, "Naps" Spreycombe, once told me that religion was based upon fable. How do you know you have a soul?'

'It is your spirit that shines in you now. I cannot see it. But because I cannot see it is no proof that it isn't there. Reason tells me I am a spirit, just as reason tells me that one of those little coloured stones on the bed of the well is matter. The two are utterly apart. My body is matter. My body and my spirit are different things, blended temporarily.'

'I wonder if this water would ever cease to well,' murmured Evelyn, regarding her own image.

'Not even in the longest drought. It flows for ever, coming

from the purity of the earth. As this water, the life-giving water, wells up, so does the goodness or the poetry, or the desire to be beautiful and to be calm—whichever term you prefer—rise in man's soul. If this well be choked, the water will rise elsewhere. Keats knew that when he said that "the poetry of the earth is ceasing never".'

She turned away.

'What's the matter, Eve?'

She said with flippant tenderness, in order not to hurt him: 'I don't want you to talk about Keats. It's not good for you to think too much about poetry. Look what it did to Julian Warbeck.'

'What did it do to Julian Warbeck?'

'Made him a drunkard.'

'Oh, Eve, are you serious?'

'My dear, you'd be serious if you had to deal with Julian Warbeck very long! But I don't want to talk about him. I can see your eyes in the water, so big and solemn. W-will-yum!'

'And I can see yours.'

'What are those sweet blue flowers?'

'Brooklime.'

'They are like the wondering eyes of a child. My Jonquil has eyes like that.'

'And Jonquil's mother has eyes that are the colour of the little wild grey wood dove.'

He was quoting what he had written about her the previous evening.

'You're mocking me,' she pretended, looking into his eyes.

'Not altogether, Lina. "My wit, like your temperament, is essentially adaptable," as Colyer said.'

A willow wren sang of summer among the cones, and afar but distinctly heard, a pheasant was disturbing the afternoon calm with his crowing. The hum of insects formed a slumbrous undertone in the tranquil larch forest, while goldcrests flitted along their verdant roadways above.

A gossamer drifted towards them, which touched his face. A slight contact; she brushed it away. Another gleaming thread floated by.

'Did you feel it?' she asked.

'Yes.'

'I feel that I am being bound by a million such threads. The glance of an eye, a shy smile, a thought of beauty that echoes in my heart, a kindness done to me.'

Her hand sought his, and clasped it. The willow wren still piped away golden minutes. He felt her hair against his cheek, and wanted to put his lips to it.

'Billy.'

'Yes.'

'Do you like me?'

'Yes.'

'How much?'

'Twenty-five per cent.'

'What does that mean?'

'Nothing—a feeble joke.'

'Billy, do you know, you are unique? I never met anyone faintly resembling you. That is the truth. Do you hate me?'

'How could I do that?' he said, looking into her eyes, and feeling very bold.

'You are sweet to me,' she whispered, her eyes falling under his glance. 'Ah, but I am bad.'

'You are good,' he said, his cheek against hers. 'You are beautiful, Eve.'

'No, I am bad. Just fancy, I've got a child who's five years old. Darling, darling Quillie! She's got a rotter for a mother.'

A tear trilled down her cheek, and fell into the water and was lost, and tiny ripples spread across to the petals of the brooklime.

'You are good, Eve. You are only a child yourself.'

' "Child!" I'm older than you are. Why, you're only

twenty-two, but I'm twenty-three! And I've been married since I was sixteen. Who are you calling "child"?'

He put his arm round her shoulders and hugged her, whispering that she was good, and laying his cheek against the cold tears. Soon she was smiling at him with misted eyes, and confessing that she was an idiotic person to weep, because it made her eyes red.

Chapter 9

SINCE swallow-time of that year the sunlight had pressed upon the land, drying up by midsummer most of the hill springs and many of the village wells. As the drought increased so was more misery made for the sheep. Old Voley the shepherd began to look haggard; not only was the loss to his master heavy, but he had a love for the animals at whose birth he had watched. All day long their pitiful cries quavered into the heated air. Whenever he appeared on the down, a gaunt grey-beard riding bareback and bridleless his tamed Exmoor pony, they greeted him with thin bleats and came towards him. On the hard brown ground their feet made a dry rattle. Voley grunted as he surveyed them. He and his mate worked from the first light, dipping them in wash troughs to kill the maggots.

Winged insects increased as the sun scored its highest arcs across heaven. In the sunken lanes hid the horse-flies that rose silently to draw blood whenever man or beast passed by. Evelyn and Maddison each carried a whisk of leaves to beat them away. They came unbeknown and settled on the neck or the wrist, until a sharp sting betrayed them. Often they pretended that one was on the other's legs or back, and giving each other very many unnecessary swishes. His eyes were merry, he was strong and lithe; they talked quickly and bubbles of humour and laughter rose all day to their lips. He sang songs and played the buffoon. He delighted in seeing her eyes, and often would ask her to look at him, so that he could dwell upon their brightness. He told her how he had pined throughout the war for love; and how he had longed to go to his village; and being there, how restless and miserable he had been. 'All done with now, thank God.'

'Where is your home?'

'Near Colham—a place called Rookhurst.'

She seemed astonished, looked intently at him, laughed quietly to herself, seemed about to say something, hesitated, then changed the subject and asked him to tell about the girl he had loved.

'I only thought I loved her. I remember that she used to insist that I had an unhealthy mind, because I felt most deeply the things that never troubled her—the migration of birds, for instance. Of course, I see now how fatal any union between us would have been. For me it was an attraction of like for unlike; and that is a very strong one. But it cannot last. Perhaps unions were not meant by Nature to be permanent. Marriage is only made durable by links of taste—if one has enthusiasms in common, they usually last, whereas the links of mutual attraction don't. If only Keats could have outgrown his love for Fanny Brawne—if only he had been well—what things he would have done!'

She asked to be told about Fanny Brawne, and he told her.

'I believe I must be a sort of Fanny Brawne,' she meditated aloud, 'although Julian Warbeck once called me Dolores. So I read it—you know Swinburne's poem? I didn't know whether to feel pleased, or not. Poor Julian!'

'You like Fanny Brawne, or Dolores!' he scoffed. 'Why, you're like——'

'What am I like?'

She wooed him to tell her, but he dared not say she was like Mary Magdalene, lest she laugh.

They walked on, coming to the snout of the headland, pink with sea-thrift, and sat at the brink of the precipice, on the wild thyme and among the trembling feathers of sea birds. Lundy was half dissolved by an azurine mist lying over the calm sea that seemed after the sweltry light of day to have been bleached of its deep colour.

'What's that thing down there like a big black bottle?' she asked.

'That's a seal!' he cried.

A black head was thrust up in the water five hundred feet away. He stood up and shouted, but it did not stir. When its lungs were filled with air, it turned, showing a sun-spash on its dark body, and disappeared. He turned to the south. From here could be seen the Santon Burrows behind a shallow coast which was broken by the wide estuary of the Taw, confluent near its mouth with the swift Torridge. Under his hand he gazed at the estuary glistering like the track of a snail, seeing across it the waterside houses of Appledore nearly resolved into golden vapour and the sky.

'It is very beautiful here,' her voice said dreamily. 'Come and sit beside me, Billy. Tell me a nice story.'

A titlark in corant dive of joy fell behind them, in its bill a song-straw pulled from the sun.

'We are living like Immortals,' he said.

'What is this little bone in the grass, Billy?'

She held out a tiny white fragment.

'It is the leg bone of a small bird, probably a titlark.'

'Poor little thing,' said Evelyn, 'I wonder how it died?'

'Probably one of the peregrines caught it.'

'Doesn't it seem sad that only this bone remains of a beautiful living thing, that used to sing and to flutter its wings, and love its mate? Isn't it a terrible thought that everything goes to dust: eyes, lips, smile—all, all to dust—blown by the wind anywhere. O, I will not be buried in the ground.'

' "With the carrion worm mining in the seat of intellect," ' he quoted.

'I cannot bear that thought.'

' "Even if there be no immortality, at least I shall have had the glory of that thought," ' he quoted again. 'O, Jefferies, my Jefferies!'

'Is that from the book you showed me?'

'Yes.'

'It also said that to-day is everything.'

'It is easy to believe, in this loveliness of air and sea and sky that to-day is everything,' he said.

'It is more than that to me.'

'What do you mean?'

'Don't you feel that anything wonderful has come into your life?'

'Yes,' he said, looking at the sun sinking behind Lundy vague in the Atlantic horizon.

She said gently: 'That means no. No, of course, you don't regard me as I regard you. Why should you? Look at me, look at me, don't turn away.' She was almost sad. As he would not look at her she stood up, and stared across the sea to the Santon Burrows.

He did not move; and soon, as though tired of inaction, she rose and stood on the lip of the precipice.

'Be careful,' he cried aloud in his anxiety.

'Oh, don't worry about me,' she declared, walking away. He watched her disappear round the hunch of the promontory.

Afterwards he followed along the stony path to Cryde Bay, watching the packs of swifts which wheeled in the air, aloof from all other birds. They fled screaming, hunting their prey as they played. Martins flew in happy parties just above the cliff-line, but there were no swallows. For years their numbers had been lessening. During April he had lamented the dwindled swallows; now he thought of them hardly at all.

She sat by a hill stream, on a patch of yellow trefoil, snapping the yellow flowers from their stalks.

'Ah, no,' he begged, 'they are as beautiful and happy as yourself, Eve.' She pulled a handful and flung it at him; there were tears in her eyes. He took her hand, pleading forgiveness.

Her yielding humility made sweeter the reconciliation. The rich light of evening slipped away into dusk and moonlit peace. Till half past eleven they wandered over quiet sands where ring-plovers called *tu-lip tulip* as they sped by the sea.

'To-morrow will be a full moon,' she said as she bade him good-bye outside the sea-wall of the cottage. 'O Willie Maddison, think what the sea will look like from the down!'

'Just ordinary, I'm afraid. The moon rises in the east, and it won't be over the west until nearly dawn.'

'Then we'll stay out all night! Shall we? Won't it be fun! Let's be naughty, and stay out all night! Doesn't it thrill you?'

'Yes! We'll make a fire and boil a kettle! Eve, it will be beautiful.'

He gently kissed her cheek.

'Good-night,' she breathed in the midnight dusk, and slipped from his half-embrace, and was gone.

All the next day, as though overcome by the sun's furnace that seemed to fuse sea and sky into a candent blue puddle, they and the dogs lolled on the Vention sands, bathed in the pools and the sea. A swooning wind blew from the land. They could hear the rattle of sheep's feet on the hard turf of the hills as if they were near them, so distinct was sound in the shimmering air. From the valley miles inland the puffs of the London train were audible.

She wore her dark blue bathing dress, and her face and neck seemed untouched by the light and fire which burnt to a deep hue his face and limbs, and burnished his brown hair. He touched her knees and shoulders, asking her why they were brown and not her face. She replied: 'That's a secret, William!' but afterwards showed him a bottle which she said contained an old country recipe against sunburn, a lotion made from the blossom of elderberry, rose, and an essence of a cornfield wild flower called fumitory.

'My grannie told me years ago how to make it.'

They sat with their backs to a grey rock on the hot, loose,

white sand. Yellow flags were in bloom on a shelf of land twenty yards in front of them, where the path led to the barley above the cliff. A band of swallows came down to the sands and sped twittering for a while before returning to their nests under the sheds of the inland village. Tall green reeds on their left gave forth a gentle rustle as they moved their plumes and pennons. A steady roar came from the returning spring tide, but through the roar they could hear the cries of sheep on the hills above, and the petulant chattering wails of young kestrels from their eyrie in the thorn brake. Beyond the reeds and the short slope above them an intense blue met the white barley-hail stirring on the edge of the sky. Spires of sorrel stretched up with thin grasses, where butterflies clung and rested.

It was time for tea, and she left him to get driftwood for the fire. Her bare feet on the loose sand made a musical, purring sound, and so bright was the light from the sky that her grey sun-shadow seemed to shrink into the glistening specks. He observed her stooping to gather sticks, singing, happily absorbed in her task. She moved in simplicity as though passion and thought had never come to her, untroubled like the white gull gliding over the sea. He became eager to see her knees as she bent down, so rounded and smooth, and unlike his own, which were hard and bony. Her loose auburn hair fell over her shoulders and the powder-blue stuff of her dress. She smiled at him, and he saw her white teeth as she tossed back the tresses. He watched her, feeling suspended in the clear air whose colour was so pure and unsoiled.

A flock of daws and rooks flew high over the beach, wheeling in the warm air, ascending, and circling, and twirling and slipping past each other with cries of joy, and as he looked up they veered into the sun and were hid in blinding light. In roll and agitation they were through the radiance, and sailing down to their nesting ledges in the cliffs.

She came back with twigs and bits of fir-bark, a broken basket and several lumps of sea-coal. He made a fire between two boulders, and boiled a kettle filled from a trickle of spring water among the rocks. She made tea in the kettle, and they drank out of the same cup, declaring that it was the nicest tea in the world. Scalded cream and raspberries they ate with a crusty cottage-loaf, using flat stones for plates. They spoke in broken sentences, with nods and single words. Their thoughts were conveyed by a glance, a smile, a look.

After tea they dressed and sauntered to the line of the tide, climbing a rock and sitting together while the sea came swiftly over the sands and the waves broke below them. The sun was high in the west, the sea azure at the end of the headland, and in silver glitters spread across to Lundy, which was consumed in shining mist. Five black spurs of rock were in the western silver path a quarter of a mile in front of them, the jagged out-lines brazen as though heated almost to melting. Slowly the burning sea reduced the points, the waves threw spray over them, and a mist of steam arose. Against their own rock the rollers were crashing and seething, pouring off in cascade and waterfall. The air was cool and fresh. She was splashed by a big ninth wave and pressed herself against him. A sunbow came out of the broken wave, gave them delight, and fled. He put his arm round her, and left it there long after the breaker had beaten its strength away on the sands behind them. The lobe of her ear showed through her hair so loosely coiled, and he had a desire to fondle it with his teeth. But as though antici-pating the desire she looked at him, and he could not bear her gaze.

At sunset they scrambled along the rock and jumped off above the tide. Slowly they went along the sands and up through the dunes and over a waste land where grew vipers' bugloss and tall mulleins among brambles and tufts of burnet rose, and so through the heather and ling to the down, often turning in enchantment of the ocean seen from the high ground. On the horizon Lundy now was grape-coloured, and rising baseless in a golden fume between sea and sky. Two mated buzzards were soaring in tranquil circles a mile above the world. In silence they sat and looked across the sea. They were alone with the wandering air and its birds. His heart yearned for the meaning of beauty, wild emotion rushed to him as he thought of the everlasting loveliness that one day he must leave. His spirit said that it was immortal, that freed of earthly thrall It became merged into a glory which forever irradiated matter, manifesting Itself in bird and flower, in animal and man. From the germ or the seed It built Itself in the form of an intellect or a blossom, a soft coloured wing or a reedy note of song. She cared nothing for the abstract. Her heart desired a perfection of life for herself, for a love completed and lasting; and these were only to be found in what to herself she called the ideal lover, whose every embrace would be as sweet as the first. Then the joy of service would ever be fresh, her beauty would ever be a wonder to bind him, so that in being supreme she would, and how joyously, make herself the slave.

Both felt a sadness because in thought they faced the unknown, the inapprehensible. He thought with wild sadness, I want to go out to this beauty, to lose myself in the sky, so that I can be myself. She thought as tears brimmed in her eyes, I want something for myself in this beauty; I want to grasp it for myself, to take it into my heart. It will always elude me.

'Darling Eve.'

'Darling Billy.'

No other words were spoken as they turned from the luminous sea and walked through the heather and bracken. Ghost moths of summer drifted over the path as they brushed the ferns, and grasshoppers were singing on the ground. The moon would not lift its rim above the hills till the evejars had been reeling a long time. Slowly and in silence they crossed the down. In the dusk the lighthouses upon Lundy were flashing their first white warning to mariners. Along the path they went, down the hill track, and to Shelley Cove. Their entry was greeted by frenzied cries for food.

'It's time the birds found their own food,' said Maddison, irritably. 'However, I must in common decency milk the blinking goat.'

'I'll do it,' said Eve, 'while you light the fire.'

'Will boiled eggs and toast and marmalade be enough?'

'Rather!'

At owl-light they left the cottage, and loitered on the beach, smoking and watching the phosphorescence in the waves. She smoked her cigarette quickly, so that her cheek was frequently fired by the glow. Abruptly she flung it into the water: it hissed and died.

'The moon will be rising soon,' said Maddison. 'Come to the top of the down.' Hand in hand they went up the path, followed by Izaak and the two spaniels.

Chapter 10

Above the coombe the stars were watchful and pale. Into the quiet night from the tower of St. Flammea's Church were rolled the passing hours. The afterglow of sunset was over the western ocean. From the hill they could see the dark spread of water that flowed round the headland, and regularly from Harty Point came a prick of fire, which increased to a glare of red, then shrank to an ember which went out and was followed by a white-gold beam flashing across Bideford Bay. Curlew and wading birds flighted from the estuary were calling in the night, and somewhere in the heather wastes near them a rabbit screamed in a snapped gin. As they listened with the echo of pain in their hearts the cry ceased, there was a grunting noise, and the rattle of a chain.

Evelyn clutched his arm, and they remained still. Something was scratching at the ground, and the chain of the gin was rattled. Then something was pushing clumsily through the undergrowth.

'It's probably Jack o' Rags,' he whispered.

'I'm afraid.'

'Don't move.'

They peered in the direction of the movement; something was crawling over the low heather and tufts of moorland grass. It was grey, like a shadow, and hard to discern. It moved nearer and nearer to them. The pups growled.

It smelt them, and stopped. Evelyn made a slight exclamation; it rustled away swiftly, with the chain of the trap knocking against stones.

'It's only a badger.'

114

'But did you really think it was Jack o' Rags?'

'No. I knew it was a badger.'

'You beast, to scare me like that!'

'The badger was more scared than you were.'

'I like that badger,' said Evelyn, laughing with relief, 'he is a very decided person. If he's going to do anything wrong he does it thoroughly. Fancy tearing up the trap as well! The height of impertinence! It's like eloping with another man's wife and taking his dog and kennel at the same time.'

And now the east was distained by a yellow mist that floated before the moon, and the bended ash-trees against the sky formed a dark filigree. Although the golden arch was not yet risen, the duskiness grew less and was like a myriad grey and black atoms whirling silently and sparking lightlessly under the stars.

His mind was wandering again. He was thinking of one of his grooms, whose face had been bisected by a splinter of shell while he had been talking to him. Maddison had gone to see the dead man's wife after the war in a Waterloo slum. He remembered her sad eyes, and the dog who still waited in its kennel outside in the squalid yard. He sighed involuntarily.

Evelyn unlinked her arm. The arch of the moon was above the earth, and stirred by its gleam a blackcap roosting in a bramble began to sing. The low notes were soft in the night lit by moon and stars and quenchless afterglow.

'I've made another coarse remark,' she said desperately, 'but it slipped out before I could check myself. I saw humour in that animal's escapade, and as usual said the wrong thing. However, I am myself, as you once said of yourself. I wish I were not, sometimes. I feel your cold disapproval.'

'Eve, what are you saying? I haven't the least idea what you mean.'

'Forgotten all about me?'

'Only for a second. How cool your hand is, Eve. I love your slender fingers. It's like holding an otter cub's paw.'

THE DREAM OF FAIR WOMEN

'W-warm heart, Billy. Your hand is cool, too.'

'Your dulcet voice has the tone and stammer of a nightingale,' he quoted from what he had written about her in *The Policy of Reconstruction.*

'Darling Billy. But you do not care for me.'

'I do, Eve.'

'Your heart is cold.'

'It isn't, really.'

'Oh, yes, it is. But it will grow warm when you meet someone good.'

'I've met you, Eve.'

They sat in the heather and watched the moon. Their shoulders and cheeks were near together. He drew away from her, so that he might watch the light on her face.

'Billy, what does it all mean—life, and emotions, and impulses? What does it lead to? Why do I seek love and never find it? What is it all for? What is God? O, we on earth are just wandering in darkness.'

I will light a torch that all shall see, he thought, inspiring deeply the white breath of the moon, and feeling the strength of the earth in his heart. He felt an impatience for the feebleness of her feeling, as she centred all things upon her own intimate sensations.

'You say all human ideas are vain, all hope is illusion, so what have we left to hold on to? Only love. Love is always sad—passion, I mean. Why do men fall in love with me, why do they say things that stir me and draw me to them? Many men have said they loved me, but not one of them has loved the real *me.* They have loved, or thought they loved, my beauty. But to them I can give nothing. Billy, I feel crazy in this moonlight. I am being frank with you, because I feel that never again shall I meet one like yourself.'

He was thrilled by her words; he said in a childlike voice, pointing,

'Look at the moon, how swiftly it rises.'

116

The moon was free of the earth and floating in the sky.

'It is like an old spade guinea.'

She clasped her knees with her hands, and hid her face. An evejar reeled its song on a dead elderberry near them, flew away, returned, sang again, and flew away; the moon rose up. At last he asked her if she were cold.

'No,' her muffled voice replied.

'Dear Eve,' he said, tender at her silence.

'Unhappy,' she whispered.

He put his left arm round her shoulder, hugging her close, feeling as though they were two moon-beings. Her white wool jersey was very thin, and the shoulder was soft. He lifted her face and turned it to him. The gleam from the thin worn coin was reflected in a tear as it rolled down her cheek.

The bubbling songs of many evejars were now linked around them. An owl quavered on the slopes below. The sea rippled away to the night's infinity.

Above them the night breeze shook the dry frame of an elderberry long since ruined by the salt sea winds. One barkless branch rubbed against another, causing a weary squeaking, as though in ghostly derision of life with its toil and ineffectual striving to form leaf and blossom forever. The air was quiet again, and the tree—a musician unheeded and ancient—ceased its dreary scraping.

'Dear child,' she murmured, touching his cheek, 'I believe you are beginning to like me.'

The air moved again more gently, drawing from the gorse bushes a faint sighing, and shivering in the heather where they sat with the stars hung over them like little lamps on the white branches of the dead elderberry tree. A moth fluttered round their heads, its wings touching them.

'Your cheek is so soft, Eve.'

'Yours is like sandpaper, Billy. No, come back. I like it. It feels strong.'

'I'm weak.'

THE DREAM OF FAIR WOMEN

'Silly, you're full of strength, if only you'd trust yourself. I'm weak, Billy.'

She leaned upon him, placing an arm on his shoulder like one whose strength is spent. She murmured something, but he did not hear any word. A feeling of remoteness came over him, everything seemed unreal in the quiet moonlight. The feeling of remoteness and unreality increased when she began to murmur deep in her throat, and closed her eyes, and pulled down his head. She fondled his cheek with her mouth, and turned her head slowly so that her mouth touched his lips. Her arm tightened round his neck, and she pressed her mouth to his mouth, while with a feeling of confusion still far away from him he tried to make himself return her kiss, lest she should feel scorned. He could not move. His brain felt white and remote as the moonlight.

She dropped away from him and hid her face in the heather. She lay still, and he heard her groan.

'I've dug my own grave,' she cried, sitting up with her back to him. The moon made a halo round her head. What could he say? He strove to speak to her, but no words would arise out of his acute feeling of shame. She would despise him.

'I'm going away, Billy. Good-bye.'

'No—no—don't.'

'Can't you realize how I hate myself?' she asked desperately. 'You must despise me.'

'Despise you? *You?* You must despise *me!*'

She moved closer to him.

'Billy, haven't you ever kissed any woman before?'

He did not answer.

'Then you haven't kissed anyone?'

'I don't know.'

'You haven't! Tell the truth, Billy. Have you?'

'No.'

She looked at him intently. She was a different Eve: the Eve

118

he had seen looking at him over Colyer's shoulder in the Night-crow Inn. She looked so young, so innocent.

'Don't go, Eve. I think I should not want to live if you went away.'

She bowed her head.

'Eve, don't cry.'

He clasped her head on his shoulder and stroked her hair. All his body felt warm and happy. Poor Eve, she was only a child. He cherished her head. She lay still in his arms.

He felt her tears dropping silently on his knees, and cherished her the more.

'Look at me,' he said, and she turned in his arms so that the moon shone on her face. With his hand he smoothed the hair from her forehead. White brow, soft throat, maiden lips, her virginal moon beauty stirred a pain in him that was a delirious sensation.

'You look like the Madonna,' he said, and laid his cheek on her cheek, while his clasp tightened around her body.

'Your body seems very slight. And very soft, too.'

After a while he said: 'I want to take down your hair.'

'Yes,' she said. She helped him shake the tresses free. Their softness covered his head. She took him in her arms.

'You're my little boy,' she whispered.

Clearly in the white night rolled the hours from the church clock.

'Midnight,' they whispered together.

The moon shone stark and white before them. Sometime later she murmured: 'I ought to be going back home.'

'No, you mustn't go. Your hair is beautiful. It has netted the stars. It's Titian.'

'So I'm told.'

'By whom?' he asked, moving apart from her.

'By you, Billy.'

He hugged her. 'Eve, I love you.'

'Ah, but you don't.'

'I do.'

She began to stroke his hair. 'Kiss me very, very gently, Billy.'

'Your lips are soft, Eve. Eve, I won't let you go home. Damn, the furze pricked my knee.'

'Yes, it's been sticking into me all the time! But I didn't care.'

'Let's go to Shelley Cove and make a fire, shall we? And swim?'

'Lovely!'

She bit his ear playfully.

'Billy, you are such a liar, but do tell me the truth. Honestly, am I the first woman you've kissed?' she asked, as they wandered down the hill, arm in arm.

'Yes, kissed properly.'

'What do you call properly?'

'Well, I wanted to kiss you.'

'You didn't want to kiss the others?'

'There was only one.'

'Tell me about her.'

'You'd be shocked.'

'No, I wouldn't. Did you sleep with her?'

After a pause he said: 'Yes.'

She walked silently by his side, her arm loose in his.

'I don't believe you.

'Quite true.'

'Who was she?'

'She was a prostitute,' he said, distinctly. He felt himself in uniform, belted, booted and spurred. He felt so much stronger than the little girl with long hair over her shoulders walking by his side.

'Billy, it isn't true, is it?'

'Perfectly true. I'll tell you about it. I was drunk. On leave with Phillip and another man. We drank nine bottles of claret between the three of us in the Piccadilly Grill. I was so drunk

I thought I was sober. Strangely, I wasn't sick. Going back to the Somme next day. It was October, '16. Thought I'd be killed; very merry evening. Somehow I got off with a bird in the Piccadilly tube. How I got there I don't know: oh, yes, I think I was looking for a lavatory. Anyhow, I'd lost Phil and the other fellow. "You're awfully drunk," she said to me. I'd seen her in the grillroom dining there with a man. Then I found myself walking with her in Torrington Square. Walking upstairs. In a room. I wanted to clear off, but daren't. She was hard; and I didn't know what to do.'

'Did she kiss you?'

'She tried to.'

'What did you do?'

'Nothing.'

Her arm was withdrawn.

'She behaved just like myself, in fact.'

'Not quite.'

'How horribly cynical you appear all of a sudden. I don't like it.'

'Sorry. Where's Izaak? Tikkytuck! Tikkytikkytikkytuck!'

The cub whistled in front; the pups ran back to him.

'Well, to finish my bit of autobiography. It was horrible. I couldn't speak to her or look at her in the morning. Luckily I met Phillip at my tailor's in Conduit Street, and my tailor told me of a chemist in Vigo Street who would stop any possible after-effects. Twenty grains of mercury subchloride—one minute—one guinea. So I was all right.'

They reached the cove in silence. In the cottage he gripped her and kissed her on the mouth. She tried to struggle free.

'No, you're just laughing at me.'

'I told you the truth, and you don't like it.'

'It doesn't seem you, somehow. I don't understand, that's all.'

'Well, don't tell me to bloody well go to hell, anyhow. God, why am I talking like this? I feel so strange, as though dead

121

and animated by the phosphorescence of decay. It's the moon-light in my skull.'

He put a match to the mass of dried driftwood, and the resin-ous wood spluttered with flame. Rapidly she rubbed a crimson salve on her lips, looking in a little hand mirror. 'The salt water sometimes hurts my lips.'

'Darling Jezebel, I'm sorry I was hard coming down the hill. I do love you, really.'

She looked at him with sorrowful eyes. 'You frighten me,' she said. 'I'm not Jezebel.'

'I know you're not. You are really a somewhat pathetic little girl, and a very beautiful one.'

'No, be serious. I'm afraid of the future. I l—love you Billy. And I didn't want to love anyone ever again.'

He held her and kissed her.

'No, not now, dear. I want to be alone for a while. Let's swim!'

'Yes. Let's undress on the beach.'

They went out into the moonlight, to the beach white with shells. He pulled off shoes and shirt and trousers, and stood naked, waiting for her, sometimes glancing at the movement, insubstantial and silent, of limbs and garments on the sward beyond the pool. Then a moon-maiden was gliding over wet sands, calling his name as she merged into the hissing snow-white surf. He waded after her, in water glittering with broken moons. She was waiting for him, a mermaid to her waist. With a sweet shock he knew the beauty and mystery of a woman's breasts, and the white flesh of her ribs. As he came near to her she shook her hair over her shoulder, so that it hid her breasts, and clasped her arms, and leant forward so that he could look only at her shadowy eyes, and at her mouth dark and luring.

'I've got to twist up my hair, or it will get salt and sticky. I'll swim after you,' she said; and the moon-maiden had fled. The otter's flat and silvery head looked up and whistled with delight.

With the otter beside him, he swam towards the Cormorant Rock, feeling the unreality, the timelessness of the summer night. He had no body, no senses, no instincts, no thoughts: he was a dream of moon and water. Sitting on the shining sea-weed of the Cormorant Rock, while the otter shook the water from the rough hair of its coat, and then rolled on its back on the slippery weed, he watched her swimming to him, part of himself, the rib that had been striving to grow again to cover his heart. She climbed out, and sat below him, an arm support-ing her body half-turned towards the moon. She sat tranquil a while, before lying on her belly and slowly drawing herself over the seaweed until she was clasping his feet with her hands, thrusting her head between his ankles, to kiss one foot, then the other, until his being shed its dream of moonlight, and his blood was thrilling with her warm wet mouth; he must turn away, sit with his back to the moon, concealing his desire in shadow. 'O beautiful human life!'

Chapter 11

BRIGHT wood-flames made faint thunder in the chimney. Surrounded by birds and animals, watchful or drowsy, they sat side by side, staring at the light beating on their faces, while the kettle hummed its small tunes in the symphony of fire and water. She nursed two kittens, while a spaniel slept with its head across her ankle. She watched him making cocoa. They must drink from the same cup, he said; and while she sipped the steaming liquid, she looked at him with eyes that no longer challenged, but were humble.

'Why so sad, my sea-maiden?'

'I was thinking of the future. I'm afraid.'

'Of what?'

'Of everything, but chiefly of you.'

'Of me?'

He knelt before her, clasping her face in his hands, and smiling into her eyes, and touching with his lips her cheeks, her eyelids, her brow, her mouth, murmuring: 'I love you, darling Eve', till his ardour made her yield.

'It is foolish to think,' she murmured; 'only love counts. We may be dead in a week's time.'

'But do you love Li—your husband?'

'No. He is the average cold Englishman. O, I cannot bear to think of his coming home on leave so soon!'

'So soon?'

'Yes. I've been trying to tell you all day. He's coming home next week. There, now, I shouldn't have told you. I've upset you.'

'No, you haven't.'

124

He drew away from her, and stared at the fire.

'I don't love him,' she repeated, 'but I tell you honestly that I like him. And I've told him that, too; only like a man, he won't accept it.'

'It's late,' he said curtly. 'Hadn't we better be going back to Cryde Bay?'

'Do you want me to go?'

'Perhaps you had better.'

'Billy darling, don't be so cruel. Come here and sit quiet with me. There, now, don't you be a naughty little boy!'

He hid his head on her lap, while she stroked his head; but she knew he was not yielding to her. When he looked up, therefore, and asked if she would like to hear a chapter of *The Policy of Reconstruction*, she replied:

'Yes, do read it to me. Only I don't want you to get upset.'

He got up with a look in his eyes that was not for her; a strained look that made her feel uneasy and slightly irritable. He returned with the manuscript sheets, and sat down by her side on the sacks.

'Would you be more comfortable lying down, dear? Lay your head on my lap, if you like.'

'No, thanks. This was written while you were in Folkestone. It's about you. I don't know if it would interest you.'

'I'm sure it would.'

'Tell me if I bore you!'

'Yes. But you won't.'

He begun, after several false starts and pauses, to read:

'When I was a boy my friend and I used to go into the woods, and every year we waited for the nightingale to return with the swallow. The journeys the little frail winged ones made across the sea filled our minds with glamour. All the winter we waited, until the time came for the birds to return: and then the joy of the first swallow, the first cuckoo, the early sweet-violet and the willow-wren perched on the withies by the stream. Could I but tell you of the glamour of those fled springtimes, when the meadow grasses waved their plumes in the wind, among the ox-eye daisies and the sorrel. Of the nightingale singing in the copse at night! Many people on hearing the nightingale for the first time are disappointed: the bird's song is perfection of spirit; if it were a little less than perfection, it would move all human hearts at once. I pray for power to bring back that awareness into the human mind; I feel in my mind all the flowers and the songs of boyhood are stored, and I must pour them out, giving them shape and form in sentences which will ring in the hearts of all who read, and soften them, and bring back to them the simplicity and clarity of the child-heart. For the hope of the world, of the human race, is in the child. Its young mind must be impressed with natural beauty, not dreary, dead facts of what kings died and when, and what $a^2 + b^2$ equals. The tissue of the child-mind must be free as a dove's breast-feather drifting in sunlit air. But what do they do to the imaginative tissue of little children? They blench and wither it by forcing it to apprehend unintelligible facts. They strip the petals of its young blossom! And certain idealists—is this boring you?'

'Not at all.'

'You seem doubtful.'

'I was only wondering what it had to do with me.'

He flung down the manuscript.

'Billy, darling, forgive my stupid remark, but you did say—'

'You come in later.'

'Do read on, there's a dear. Yes, I really want to hear. I agree with every word of it, and I love you for it.'

'And certain idealists, whom men call fanatics and lunatics and criminals, try to break down the old civilization, hoping to recreate a better world of men, but all is foredoomed to failure until the extra wisdom has come into men's minds. They neglect the secret of the woods and fields, and how they expand man's spirit if he knows them when little.

'So dear to me are these things that words are clumsy to express them by. Sometimes I have the power, when my thought soars like a White Bird above the world, and I am absorbed in the core of Life, where is no emotion or fret, struggle or longing. Then the nightingale sings in ancient moonlight, and I listen with Keats, for I have the vision of Keats; but for words I strive in vain. For domination over them I will pace the night from sun to sun, under the stars which shine steadfastly over a world of men tired after the day's labour. My labour is eternal—for thus are some men born, and by it are born again of the virgin soul. My brain is a forge of fire wherefrom the precious metal of those taintless days I hammer out my images. Sometimes under the stars I feel that my love is with me, my love lost forever, and misery quenches my mind-fire, and the images are corroded, and all is illusion; and I am alone, terribly alone, on an alien planet. The same voice that Keats heard I hear now—it sings in the celestial stream of star-dust from everlasting to everlasting—the bird whose heart is breaking, even as Keat's heart was broken—O, it's bloody rot!'

He leapt up, and flung a wicker basket of driftwood into the hearth. The puppies barked at the suddenness of noise, and Izaak sprang up, hissing through his teeth. Maddison sat down dejected.

'Darling.' She clasped him. 'Darling, did you really feel like that about me?'

'I suppose I did. God, what a fool I am.'

'Hush, don't be so sad. I love you from everlasting to ever-lasting.'

His eyes as he looked at her caught and held the rambling light of the candle, and smouldered in the gloom of the sink-ing fire. They were upbrimming with a deep warm brown, mysterious, translucent, and tender.

'You are as young and innocent as Jonquil. Come, my dear, and sit beside me, and rest yourself. Don't think any more of your old Policy of Self-destruction. No, no, no, I didn't mean it. Billy, Billy, I love you; can't you see, and want you to be happy. O God, I'm not clever like you, and I don't want to be. O, I can't stand it any more: I'm going home. Let me go. I'm not good enough for you. Really, I mean it. Let me go.'

He put his arms round her body, clinging to her, pressing her down on the sacks. She accepted but did not respond to his kisses. With his free hand he gathered her hair and pressed his face into the thick masses, twisting a tress round his throat, binding himself to her.

'How lovely and warm you are, Mrs. Fairfax. Much nicer than the prostitute. Poor prostitute. Kiss me!'

His hand sought and fondled her breast.

'You don't love me, Billy. Do you?'

'That's no reason why I shouldn't kiss you. Only you are such a little ruddle devil. Ruddle is the red colour of the clay in the iron-stone quarries. Your darling hair is ruddle-red. Brownie calls you the ruddle maid.'

She smiled sadly to herself.

'My dear,' she whispered. 'I love you so much that you make me feel about fifteen, when—but I won't tell you.'

'What? Tell me!'

She would not tell him; she would not respond to his caresses, so he drew apart again. He wanted to be free, but he could not leave her; he did not want to be free, he would have her, by God!

'Come on, then, we'll go to Cryde Bay.'

She rose on an elbow, staring into the fire; then kneeling to shake her hair from her shoulders, she smiled at him with such tender gravity in her eyes that a savage wish to make her unhappy came over him; and when she held her arms for him he flung them by her side, so that she fell over, to lie with her face hidden in the sacks, weeping.

'Are you ready?'

He went to the door, opened it, and looked at the sky. The night was white and blank, with the ancient moon shining vacantly over the hill. A child was lying on the floor, weeping, because he had hurt her; Eva, a child of the sun, a child whose personal sunrise he had denied. *I started life with Evie; then Eva; then it was Eve . . .*

He leant against the doorpost. It were better that a mill-stone . . . his book was illusion. 'Eve!' he cried, the tears streaming down his cheeks.

The puppies watched lest master try and slip away from them. He had endeavoured to do this several times recently when going swiftly up the hillside, but as he always took his own particular scent with him he was easily tracked. They watched him alertly, because the moon was full, and master's movements might mean another fine hunt after rabbits. Master waited by the open door. When their kind friend, his companion, whispered, he shut the door and went to her. He spoke in a strange voice, and knelt on Billjohn, on whom tears were falling, without apparently noticing that he was there. No pat or ear-fondle was given Billjohn, who slunk away, followed by Tatters and Izaak, to the pair of trousers in the corner which was despised now that they no longer seemed a part of master. And to their amazement they had to remain there all night, for in the strange voice master bade them go downstairs when later they attempted to follow to their usual rest.

As the moon passed over the valley, its light came shyly into the room, and the darkness stole softly away. The bookshelf became silver, with a silver-and-jet cat curled on the poets' volumes. Gradually a kettle on the table became silver-lustred. Upon the handle of the kettle was perched a silver headless bird. The pale visitant explored the dim corners of the room and revealed a mass of brown and white hair that sometimes quivered and emitted little barks and yelps.

Izaak stirred in the wood cupboard, and a blunt nose and silver whiskers peeped underneath the door; an eye was silver-glinting. As it rippled to the round hole in the cottage door the seagull emerged from behind a pile of boots. Billjohn rose and yawned, then realizing where he was, he went to the closed staircase door, and whined. Tatters heard him, and soon there was a duet. But master did not come. So after a shivering doze on the trousers they all squeezed through the round hole into the cold dawn, just as the owl drifting whitely down the coombe came to rest on the sill. He flapped to his beam and as he folded his wings a strange face looked up and stared at him sleepily. One skirl of dismay the owl gave, then flapped out of the window again.

They saw master hours after the sun had risen; he did not feed them; and at noon went up the hillpath with his companion, after untethering the goat. He deserted them all that day, and the next day, and the next day, and the next day.

The carrion-crow went off, after vainly cawing for the human figure which used to feed it. The crow found plenty to eat in the coombe; birds in their nests, young rabbits that sat still with filmy eyes and drooping heads after the weasels had drunk their blood, yellow snails by the brook, sun-beetles, and strange woolly things that never moved but smelled sweetly in the heat.

The jay and the jackdaw kept together until the fourth day, when they too went off into the world of trees and bushes and things that moved on the ground.

The moon that had been the austere luminary of human passion fell into ruin and its gleam was dulled. Becky was playing with Pie one evening near the bleating, suffering goat when something ran past her. She caught it, held it in her mouth and growled. Pie came near and she spat at him, so he tripped away to catch one for himself. Thereafter they did not care very much whether they were given milk or stew. Mice were plentiful. The seagull suffered the pain of hunger until it drove him to hunt on the beach for dead fish and in the bracken for beetles, moths, and everything small that flew and walked. Once he discovered two greyish creatures squatting on the ground, looking like feathered toads. They hissed, and a bird like a hawk dashed at him, clapping its wings over its back and trying to knock him over. When he saw that it could do him no harm, he killed the nestlings with two blows of his beak, and swallowed them as they were. The parent evejars chattered in anguish, but the gull did not care. Thereafter he explored the coombe more thoroughly, and managed to find plenty to eat, including frogs and small rabbits. He forgot about the tall wingless food-giver, and became agile and a quick walker in spite of webbed feet. The gull was not, however, quick enough to avoid a white grinning snap in the dense undergrowth by a hawthorn; but the fox, disliking the taste of his flesh, left him for the ants and the brown sexton-beetles.

After whining and whistling about the cove, swimming to the Cormorant Rock, running up the path and down again, through the round hole in the door into the coal house and out again and over the chairs and round the floor, raising his little flat head and sniffing and crying, Izaak the otter cub set off on a journey up the stream, catching small trout and eels and playing alone under the waterfalls. Brownie in the Nightcrow Inn one evening said he had seen the otter crossing the lane at the top of the valley.

'Her were terrible fast on her legs, her were. Her disappeared through the hedge by my garden, her did, surenuff, and so to the brook in Varmer Galsworthy's water-meadow. Mis'r Mass'n doan't care, I reckon. Him be full of love for the ruddle maid, and she'm wedded a'ready, they do tell. But the gentry don't worry about morals, do they, Albert, midear?'

'Some do and some don't, in a manner of speaking,' replied the landlord, meditatively probing his teeth with a burnt matchstick. ' 'Tes human nature to some people, if you understand my meaning.'

'Mis'r Mass'n be proper in love. Her's a neat little person, too. Aiy.'

'Took two rooms down to Cryde Bay, ban't 'm?' enquired the mason with the spotted coat.

'It be none of my business,' said the old man in the corner. 'It be none of my business, midears. And it ban't anyone else's business neither, if you will kindly listen to what I be telling. I say it ban't none of nobody's business but the lady and gennulman concerned. Do ye hear what I be saying? It ban't none of my business.'

The conversation was continued at intervals for several days: the lady and gennulman were seen in many places, among the rocks and swimming in the sea, playing and laughing: on the headland and on Vention sands, playing leap-frog, splashing one another while the dogs barked and played: in Barum town on market days, and many other places, while the sun blazed in the July sky.

One evening the gennulman reappeared in the Nightcrow Inn, and drank two pints of ale in five minutes. Then he asked for a third pint. Brownie, who had been eyeing him with affectionate pride, amazement, curiosity and delight, remarked that he must be thirsty.

'Turrible hot weather, measter.'

The gennulman nodded and fondled his dogs; and suddenly left the Inn without a word. Reflectively Brownie drank the gennulman's pint. Nor did the gennulman go over to the Bay the following day, but walked about alone, rarely speaking to anyone.

'I did zee un in the churchyard reading the tombstones,' Brownie told the Nightcrow Inn. ' "What, be 'ee choosing 'ees grave, midear?" I asks un. He did zigh and zay: "Noomye, Broonie," he zays, "I be here to think," he says. "Company o' dead men," I told un, "be unlucky, Mis'r Mass'n." "The faithful dead," he repeats, "the faithful dead." "Faithful," just like that he spoke; "faithful," he zays—he'm full of words and eddication! "You'm thinking on the war," I zays. "Forget it," I zays, "asking your pardon, Mis'r Mass'n," I zays. "Broonie," he zays, catching my arm, "Broonie, you've got a kind heart, Broonie." I did tell the gennulman that I tried to do my best to help others, that be all, though I couldn't afford to put money into the conviction bag of Zundays, for I have nigh on a score of childer.'

Tom Vissik, a jovial farmer of seventy-one years, saw the gennulman meet the postman the next morning. He received a letter, and went in the direction of the Bay.

'But us knew her'd went,' recounted Tom that evening. 'Because a master great yellow motor-car drove up with a tall dark gennulman, and her packed her bags, and went off wi'n. "Naps," her call'n, so Mrs. Shrake did say. A proper gennulman, plenty of money, I reckon.'

Chapter 12

Aɴ hour after receiving his letter, Maddison was sitting on the sandhills of the Bay. The sun glared on him, but he was not conscious of heat or light. He noticed the people below on the beach, wondering how they could look so happy. Their laughter mocked at reality. He moved about from one place to another aimlessly, and by the stream that lost itself in the sands of the bay he took her letter from his pocket.

'9A, THE PARAGON, FOLKESTONE.

'Oh, Billy, my dear, if my writing is incoherent forgive me, because it is long past midnight and I am distrakted. Billy, we must not meet again: I'm not worthy, but I have been praying for the strenght to do the only right thing, and that is not to interfere with your life any more. I know it means never seeing your face again. You will think me callous. Think that I am. Then you will forget me sooner.

'Billy, to think I shall not see you again. The room is cold, and like a grave. I can't sleep, so I'm waiting for the dawn. I can hear the tide, just as in Shelley Cove. If you had only come to say good-bye. I didn't mean what I said about your believing yourself to be a saviour of mankind. I was fretting about things, that's why I was so horrid. You were so sweet. But I must not write like this. I must be strong, or I shall be coming back to you right away.

'In case you are lonely, I will write sometimes. Don't be angry, Billy darling, because I'm inclosing ten pounds. It is part of a present Lionel gave to me. Get something useful with it, some new clothes and socks. Now it's too late, I remember

134

I never mended yours. A fine woman I am! Still, remorse is cheap, as you may have realized.

'I am back in a false life, but thank God one can't think if one is always doing something. I shall never forget you. One day you will find a true woman to love you, and look after you; but, Billy, don't be hurt, but you mustn't expect her to live in Rat's Castle! I am laughing now, old fellow, but I can't see properly to write. No, I didn't shake some water out of the rose bole over the letter; they are my own genuine tears. I can see you laughing when you read this, and then growing sad at once. Or don't you give a hoot for Eve?

'Billy, dear, do not worry about Life. It is very distressing to witness your pain, believe me. But things will come all right. You are a brave old fellow. So I end my letter to you, most tender of men, with the request that you think only of your vision, and no more of

EVA.'

The letter, scrawly and with misspelled words, and smudged as though with tears, was re-read several times. He was recalled to reality by the sound of footfalls beside him. Looking up, he saw a small and slender girl wearing a green jersey. She was about eighteen years old. He watched her with anguished intentness; the girl had a resemblance to Evelyn. He noticed her smooth and freckled brow; her fingers were frail, like the feet of the goldfinches sipping by the water. Her locks, short and curling, were tawny like a squirrel.

She stood and watched the goldfinches. She whistled, as though she would speak to them. They splashed and ruffled in the stream, dipping their crimson faces, and twittering in the cool water. He watched the girl, imagining that she was Eve. She appeared unembarrassed by his stare. When the finches had flown, she turned and said:

'Isn't your name Maddison?'

'Yes.'

'I thought it must be. You probably think I'm mad to speak to you like this?'

'No, I don't. But I'm curious to know why you ask.'

'Do you know Mary Ogilvie?'

'I used to, when I was a boy.'

'She wrote from Folkestone, where she's staying with an aunt, and said you were living near here, and we've been trying to find where, to look you up.'

'Oh, thank you,' he murmured.

'Where are you living? No one here seems to know.'

He told her, and she said that her name was Diana Shelley. Regarding her finger-nails, the slim little creature added: 'Are you fond of music?'

She spoke with hardly a movement of her lips, with a lack of animation; her eyes were of the intense blue of the wild chicory flowers growing at the waterside.

'I would walk miles to hear music.'

'Then walk to Speering Folliot church next Sunday after evensong. I'm playing for an hour. Half past seven. Come to tea, if you're not doing anything particular. You know the place? Monks' Orchard. Anyone'll tell you. Come to lunch, if you like, or come over in the morning. Mother will be glad to see you. And you might meet Mrs. Ogilvie. That's Jean Ogilvie over there, with the long plaits.'

'Thank you very much.'

'Bring them, if you like,' pointing with one foot to the puppies.

She acknowledged his bow with a slight inclination of her head, and strolled away to some girls on the sand who had been looking at her. One of them turned a 'cart-wheel' on her hands. Alone once more he read his letter twice, and then went to the rock where Evelyn had sat and removed her shoes and stockings. Happy family parties passed him, children with pails and spades and large straw hats, cheerful mothers and brown-faced fathers. He sat with bent head, staring at nothing. More people came by, glancing at him curiously.

Children came to stroke timidly the panting dogs, then they too passed on nearer the sea, and their cries came with the plaints of gulls. He sat there for nearly an hour, cross-legged, unmoving, while beside him a skipjack beetle, seemingly terrified by the immense journey, commenced to traverse the desert of the hot sand with tiny movements that were almost severed, so laboured it to reach protection. It left behind it a braided track in the sand.

He covered it with a little sand, and watched it struggling free. Laboriously it walked up the crater he had put it in, the sand grains falling under its feet. As it reached the edge he pushed it back, and buried it again, watching with a feeling of poignancy increasing as the movements of the tired insect grew more feeble. *I started life with Evie; then Eva; then it was Eve*—and here the tiny beetle, and here an immense and devilish instinct to torture. God so loved the world that he tortured Jesus Christ: perhaps God and Devil were one: of course they were, for man made both god and devil out of his own feelings. A discovery! He felt Jefferies near him in the sunshine. Jefferies would never fail. The thought gave him an ephemeral joy.

Tenderly, remorsefully, he picked up the beetle, and put it to safety among the marram grasses. Unable to bear the terrible emptiness of the sands, he set off up the lane, crossing the base of the headland till he reached the familiar heathland of the Down. He stopped many times to look at Vention sands, which bore now such an aspect of desolation. The sward was brittle, and his leather shoes slipped on it. While he was climbing in puissant sunlight he longed to attain the down's height where he might cast off the burden of his anguish. Above the heather line of the down the sky burned with a fiercer blue, and the upright stalks of the brake fern gave it a ragged fringe. At the summit he flung himself down on the sward disverdured so cruelly of its summer flowers, but here there was no relief, no assuagement. He must walk on. The dogs walked at his heels, panting.

Two hours after leaving the Bay he arrived at the cottage, but when he opened the door he wondered why he had hurried there. Already the place brooded upon its desertion. A web had been spun by a spider between the table and the bookshelf, and the insect was hanging in the centre of its snare. A gnat was glued to one of the support-lines, moving wearily its legs, conveying along the line too small a vibration to warrant its seizure. The ashes of the driftwood fire were flat on the hearth, the plain interior of the cottage was gloomy and quiet with an absence of sound.

He realized that an escape was not to be made by a contemplation of the sacks whereon she had knelt and looked at him as he stood by the open door. He went out into the sunshine, and crossed the wringing shell beach whence the high tide had just ebbed; again he felt the anguished need to be up by the sky. The way lay past the rusty machinery shed in whose shade flourished the rank growths of hemlock and nettle. A chiffchaff piped higher up the coombe, its unvaried song borne on the stir of hot heather wind. The dogs followed patiently, but immediately he sat down they seemed to collapse, and lay on their flanks, panting, with red tongues lolling over white fangs.

A pair of ravens, surfeited after their meal on a dead sheep, passed over at a great height, and the sound of their croaking floated lazily down the shimmering sky. The sun scorched his cheeks; the dogs sought the little human shadow, but groaningly crept away again to seek coolness. Butterflies went by in the sunshine, a scent of wild thyme mingled with the scent of the sapless grasses; endurance was without avail, and he returned to the Cove.

Inside the doorless machinery shed there was a sad green tranquil shade. The glass of the window frames was missing, and the woodwork rotten, the red mortar crumbling between the blocks of ironstone. A wren had its nest in a hole in one vall, and four tiny faces peeped forth, awaiting the parents. Their black eyes showed no fear of him, nor of the dogs that immediately flopped down on the rubble and slept. No birds came with caterpillar or spider, and the little drowsy eyes of the nestlings narrowed and closed with their heartbeats. He watched them, his thoughts straying back to the days of his boyhood at Rookhurst, when such a simple thing would have made him happy.

The forge, with its dilapidated chimney, stood near the shed, nearly hidden by elderberry, gorse, and bramble. A carrion-crow's skeleton now rested upon the bellows, with a gold ant lurking within the shadowed cave of its skull. At the base of the stonework was a heap of jagged iron ore, with creepers of bramble wandering over it. He pulled at one, and saw that it had put down a root over a foot into the pile, searching for ground wherein to obtain lodgment. Thus did the creeping plants of the earth care for the derelict works of man who by power and flame once crushed the iron heart of the rock. All hope, all endeavour, all was unavailing.

He saw the dragonish flowers of viper's bugloss growing, and was reminded of the stoneheaps on the Colham road along which in far-away years he had been wont to make such lagging progress to school. Brown flowers of hounds-tongue, with their mousey smell, grew with them, the underside of their leaves a resting place for yellow trumpet-snails that would put forth their horns in the dewy twilight; when the glow-worm should seek to numb them with its poison. The plants were food for snails, the snails were food for glow-worms, the glow-worms were food for birds, and the birds were food for hawks and animals of prey. The human race was preyed upon by disease. And a taking-back into the earth was inevitable for the humblest weed under his feet.

It would seem, therefore, that all endeavour was futile: the species might have its guardian, its godhead; but there was no heavenly protection for the individual: from dust it came,

139

whether man or weed, and to dust it returned, its life like a
spark struck by steel from flint. In the light of fact, how feebl
and frighteningly baseless seemed the imagined creeds and
religions of mankind, of black man, of brown man, of whit
man—all so certain of eternal happiness after death.

In vain man's spiritual fire tried to fuse the titanic iceberg o
Truth, floating everlasting in the bitter sea of life. He hastened
into the cottage to write down the image for *The Policy o
Reconstruction*.

At nine o'clock that night he was playing whist at the Night
crow Inn, partially drunk. His partner was the bowler-hatte
Brownie, who under the influence of ale sang snatches of som
fuddled song about a man visiting another man's wife durin
her man's absence, and owing to an unexpected return the in
truder was forced to hide up the chimney, perched on the bar
The owner of the cottage lit a fire, and the intruder was soo
smoked out. This folksong had over twelve verses and wa
called *Will the Weaver*.

A man began to tell him about his climb of Raven Rock som
time in the past, when his wrist was sprained and he had bee
hauled up by his teeth. He tried to force himself to listen, bu
his thoughts were not in the Nightcrow Inn. In his mind h
heard a whispering in the night, felt hot breath against h
mouth, caressed her smooth body that in the darkness, unseen
was so smooth and white to the touch. Every thought of he
wounded his mind the more; wildly he wondered how the pai
was to be endured for the rest of his life.

'Another whiskey, please.'

'A double, sir?'

'If you please. And have one yourself. Beer for bloody Ol
Brownie, too.'

'Hi—i! Mis'r Mass'n!' cried Brownie, waving his glass.

The minute hand of the clock was approaching the hour o
ten when the door of the Inn opened, and a ragged ma
seemed to creep shamefully into the room. Immediately he wa

houted at, and one youth pushed him over. The newsvendor, or such he was, sprawled on his hands and knees. The laughter that was given to the sight of this comic play provoked a ploughboy to seize his bag and empty the papers on the stone oor. Maddison noticed that the ragged man's ankles were aw, for he wore big boots without socks. His head was ropped, his jaws toothless with brown stumps, his skin the olour of a worn copper coin. An old shirt, from which the ollar band had been ripped, was visible because the lapels of is frock coat which dragged on the roadway when he walked apped open. He had tied up the bottom of his coat with ring, in order to prevent the wastepaper he collected in the ning from falling out of these improvised sacks.

Somebody seized his boot and tugged amid laughter; the ploughboy pulled the oddmedoddery frock coat, the rotten itches gave way, and hundreds of paper, cardboard, cigarette nd wrapper fragments fell out of the pockets.

'Stop,' said Maddison, his lower lip over the upper lip, his res set. He remembered the skipjack beetle; the lower lip ftened. 'He's trying to earn his living, like all of us,' he said, nd kneeling down began to collect the scattered papers. rownie helped him, and others, while the ploughboy looked olish. 'It's only a game, I know, but the poor old chap looked red,' said Maddison to him. 'So perhaps you'll forgive my terfering. Let's all have a drink on it in a moment.'

The beer was brought by the landlord, helped by his two aughters.

'Good health, zur!' said the ploughboy, earnestly.

'Thanks!' smiled Maddison, offering him a cigarette.

'What be you taking, zur?'

'Whiskey, please.'

'A double, sir?'

'No, a quadruple.'

'A noggin?'

'Two noggins, for God's sake.'

'That will be eight altogether, sir?' asked the landlord incredulously.

'If you please.'

'Very good, sir.'

Maddison continued to turn the pages of a torn and grim book he had picked up. The newsvendor was whining in his ear that it was a railway book, a very good railway book, sixpence he would take for it. Maddison replied curtly that he did not want it for sixpence: for a moment he was hurt that gratitude should express itself in this manner. Then he noticed that it was a Bradshaw's *Railway Guide*. He thought that he would look at Folkestone because she lived there. The seed of the idea sprouted and grew rapidly in the imaginative soil so richly fertilized by the whiskey he had drunk. He would damn well go to Folkestone!

He purchased the tattered copy for the sum asked, and tried to find the town of Folkestone.

'Looking for a train, zur?' enquired the landlord, after five minutes' search.

'Aiy aiy, Corporal.'

'There be none now till Monday.'

'Hard to find the place, Captain?' he next heard him say.

'Yes, I can't read it,' he replied, as he flung the book violently on to the floor, amidst laughter. 'Bloody old Bradshaw, only Einstein could understand it!'

'Here's a local time table, Captain,' said the landlord, handing him a small blue book. He found a list of the trains, studied them without being able to concentrate, and glanced listlessly at the advertisements. These included, for some reason, a short essay on the rare wild flowers of the district.

The name of the scarlet crane's-bill seemed to stand out upon the flimsy paper, for he remembered that Eve had told how she had found a plant by a stoneheap near the Bay, how she had said that its name was remembered from childhood days. He realized that the name of the flower must have held her idle fancy as she was looking at the very same railway time table. With a piercing anguish he joined the labourers stamping out of the smoky inn.

He fell over a prostrate form outside: it was Brownie. They took half an hour to reach Brownie's cottage a quarter of a mile away, both singing while they dragged each other in arcs and parallelograms down the lane.

Mrs. Brown, attracted by the dreary moaning of some song, opened the door of the cottage just as Maddison, lying on the roadway with Brownie's arm around his neck, was pointing to a star.

'Fifty million times big as sun, Brownie. Think of it, Brownie. Where's our little planet in this sys'm, eh, Brownie?'

'Migord, Mis'r Mass'on. I wisht I knowed where my feet were to. I tried to get upwards, but be dang if I can, midear.'

'Doesn't the thought terr'rize you, Brownie? What are we? Coming and going like a spark—just bits of life—coming and going, Brownie—and yet—Brownie—we aren't faithful among ourselves.'

'Corbooger, Captain, I do love 'ee, and will stick to 'ee, for you'm a proper gennulmun. Now I do fear when my missus do zee me. She can speak politically fierce. That be her Welsh blood, gordam.'

'Brownie, you fool!' interrupted a voice from the gloom. Get up, now at once, immediately. There's drunk you must be, and brought home by a gennulman who should have knowed better than to get intoxicated.'

'Now, doan't 'ee fret 'eeself, my maid,' came the sepulchral tones of Brownie. 'The Captain ban't innoculated—he'm urrible tired and resting. So I guar-an-teed this gennul-nan a bit o' zupper——'

'Supper? Supper? At this time o' night? Supper? You've got some hopes, you have.'

'Aw, us'v got hopes, midear, even if us hasn't got no bliddy zupper.'

The dogs were licking Maddison's face, Billjohn settled to
sleep upon his chest. He could see an indistinct white blur tha
was apparently the apron of Brownie's wife. He wished tha
she would go away, so that he might lie peacefully with
Brownie. But already Brownie had commenced to get on hi
feet. Maddison pushed Billjohn away, and stood up; the white
blur of Mrs. Brown's apron slid up the sky, and he was lying on
the roadway with Brownie, endeavouring to speak, but unsuc
cessfully.

Mrs. Brown went away. She came back with a pail of water
and threw it over the men and the dogs, then went in and
slammed the door. Brownie crept into the hedge on his hand
and knees, and soon began to snore. Once in the night Maddi
son awoke, remembering where he was, and feeling a quietud
under the stars that made remote all human joy and sorrow
In the water-meadow behind the cottage a corncrake raspe
an unvaried song as it stalked away through sedge and marsh
grass. Up the valley came the roar of waves beating on the
sands of the Bay.

A mouse pursuing its lowly quest among the ferns and dea
leaves ventured across the road, and took sanctuary under hi
boots as Tatters whined in sleep. Then it passed on, climbe
the rough wall, and entered the cottage, to search with the
cockroaches for scraps. He was awake instantly afterwards, i
seemed, and gazing at the round black eyes and spread whit
wings of an owl hovering enquiringly just above his head.

Maddison held out his arms to it; it hesitated, fluttering;
settled on his fist. Slowly he drew down the perching bird
immaculate, cloud-white, gold with the aerial sun. The
large soft eyes stared at him. Tears streamed down h
cheeks.

'A symbol—my White Bird flying in the starry night,' h
whispered. 'My sweet, where have you been?'

He sat up and stroked the soft yellow-grey feathers of its head
Its white downy breast-feathers waved with his breath.

144

' "Turn away no more.
        Why wilt thou turn away?
    The starry floor, the watery shore
        Are given thee till break of day."

'O God, I have betrayed——'

When the white owl had flown away, Maddison got up, feeling stiff and cold and very thirsty, and pushed through the hedge. Among the dewy grasses his feet swished, until he had reached the top of the hill, and was nearer the aspiring larksong. He stood at the edge of a wheatfield, looking at the dawn that was like the brow of his beloved, radiant and flushed with personal sunrise, the brow of godhead, on which shone the morning star, silver witness to the visions of men.

Chapter 13

WHEN at last he came back to the roadway a little fat boy, with eyes merry and black as currants, was poking Brownie with a stick, and chuckling as he did so. He was dressed in a pair of girlish knickers, with frills, supported by buttons to a flannel shirt. His bare feet and legs were brown as a sparrow's.

'Go on, ye old dawbake!' he urged, jabbing with the stick. 'Wake up, ye mazidawk'; and when he saw Maddison he laughed merrily, rolled his black round head as he said: 'This be my feyther, Mis'r Mas'n.'

'Hullo, Tikey,' said Maddison. 'Now, don't hurt Father Get me a glass of water, will you, please?'

'No,' replied the child, as he grinned, rolled his head about and struck his parent with the stick. Brownie opened his eye and stared at his youngest son. Seeing Maddison he sat up passed his hand over his head and said that he were turrible cold.

'Ye've been droonk again, ye ould devil,' gloated Tikey. 'Ye just wait till me mother gets hold of ye.'

A girl slightly larger than Tikey came round the cottage wall followed by others at varying intervals. Eventually the fathe had nearly a dozen young children playing around him. Tikey stole his bowler and put it on his own head. Brownie got up and went round to the cottage entrance. There he saw hi stout wife. She was a Welsh woman from Cardiff, and had me her husband on a steamer trip in the Severn Sea; he had been very sick; her maternal kindness had urged her to hold his head and ever since she had held Brownie.

'Ach-y-fy! You're a fine one, and no mistake. Drunk again

146

Well, well. And with a gentleman who should have knowed much better, do you hear? And what about me and all my small children? And Tikey wanting new boots to his feet, poor bach. But what does their dad care, I wonder. Not very much, I should say. A good-for-nothing——'

'Doan't 'ee talk zo, my maid, doan't 'ee——'

'Indeed, don't you dare to tell me off. I'm a proper wife and mother, and you—why, you're just a bag of good-for-nothing bones and skin, look you. If I should think to stick a pin in you, beer and water would run out till nothing but a greasepot was left whatever. Sunday morning, too. Nice thing for you to go to——'

'Now, go easy, midear.'

'Do you think I might have a glass of water, please?' asked Maddison.

'Indeed! Don't you dare to tell me what to do.' Mrs. Brown's voice as it rose in pitch resembled the crow of a cock. 'There's a nice thing for you to go to ring the bells in God's house after a drunken night. And you a Methodist, look you.'

'Wull, I ban't narrow-minded, midear, and I do love to ring the tenor bell in church though I be chapel through and through.'

'Don't you talk to me.'

'You be doing all the talking, midear.'

'Well, well, Duw Anwyl!' gasped Mrs. Brown, turning to Maddison. 'What do you say to that?'

'I'd like a glass——'

'I be dalled if I like to hear too much political speaking,' muttered Brownie, a forlorn penitent on his legs, and passing a weary hand across his brow.

Mrs. Brown began to cry, and went into the cottage and knelt down by the hearth. From one half of a barrel sawn in two she pulled out a swaddled baby and rocked it violently on her bosom. Brownie invited Maddison to breakfast, and they walked subduedly into the one living-room. Brownie sat down beside his wife on the settle, making attempts to take the infant from her, but she held it away. Brownie put his arm round her neck, and with a swift movement she thrust the baby towards him, dropped it into his lap, and rushed upstairs. Tikey and other children clustered round their father, laughing at the baby, who smiled at them. They clung to Brownie's legs, called him dear daddy, and wrestled with each other for his caresses.

'Poor feyther's been out all night.'

'Ha, Granfer Mas'n, ye can't catch I!'

'Now, then, young Tikey, doan't 'ee bite feyther's ear like that, naughty boy.'

'Mis'r Mass'n, ave 'ee any pennies in 'ees pocket?'

'Tikey, don't pull thaccy dog's tail, or ye'll be bit!'

'Yar, gitout, no dog woan't bite Tikey, cause Tikey will bite dog.'

They yelled with laughter when Maddison seized Tikey and pretended to pull off his shirt. Tikey squirmed and kicked, wriggled and laughed. One of his brothers brought a collection of birds' eggs to show him, another brought a book prize from Sunday school, another showed him a bag of marbles and two chipped blood-alleys, saying that each blood-alley was worth twenty ordinary marbles. Two girls aged seven and nine years sat on the floor and stared at him, until meeting his glance they had to giggle, finally becoming laid out with mirth. Megan, their tall sister of fifteen, with dark eyes and adolescent figure, reproved them, blushing with shame for their behaviour. She held a brimming glass of water on a tray.

'I'm sorry it took so long, sir, but the well be ten minutes walk away, there and back.'

'My dear, I'm so sorry. I had no idea you had to walk so far, or I'd have gone myself. Thank you very much! Lovely water!'

After breakfast he told them that he was going away on the morrow, by the first train.

'Oh, but you mustn't go to-morrow, sir!' exclaimed Megan,

eagerly, 'because us be going to have dancing and singing, and a great faggot fire at night. And there will be fires on all the Exmoor hills, and on the Dartiemoor hills, so parson said last Zunday.'

'Why?'

'It be Peace Day to-morrow,' said Megan.

He remembered. Twelve months ago he had been waiting to lead his dismounted squadron against the German salient at Rheims, the commencement of Foch's offensive, when the armies of France and Britain were so weary and battle-shocked, and the Americans were waiting to make their first big drive against the St. Mihiel salient. Twelve months! Already the war was remote as the raids of the Danes sailing up the estuary, a thousand years ago.

During breakfast he spoke seldom. Afterwards he walked with Brownie, who was shaved and dressed in his best clothes, to the church. In the ringers' room he waited while the six ringers pulled at the ropes; then walked to Rat's Castle, packed a bag, put a volume of Blake in one pocket and a volume of Jefferies in the other, locked the door, hid the key under the threshold, and commenced the return.

At the top of the coombe he rested, looking down at the sea widening to blue-green immensity from the cove. Herring gulls wheeled above the deserted cottage, and among the bushes the roof of the machinery shed formed a brown patch on which jackdaws were perched. He took a final look at the white beach where so often he and Eve had dried in the sun after a swim, and, turning resolutely, walked back to Brownie's for dinner.

Megan had made a squab pie, a dish of meat baked with vegetables and dumplings, and sweetened with sugar. She desired so much to please him; he knew this, and forced himself to eat what he did not want. In the afternoon the children played under an elm in the meadow while Maddison, now feeling tired, lay on the grass and slept with the sun on his face.

After evensong at the church he bade good-bye to them.

Mrs. Brown said that she hoped he would come back soon. The children clung round her skirts and shouted at one another. Brownie leaned against the doorpost, smoking his short cutty while Tikey rolled his head, and laughed between his father's legs.

'Us wull zee 'ee agen someday, zur,' said Brownie. 'Us do like 'ee zo that 'ee must come back and be th' squire, midear.'

This earnest of affection moved his heart so that he could not reply, but only nod to them.

'Us will allus have a knife and a plate for 'ee, Mis'r Mass'on,' Brownie promised him.

'I'll make 'ee eat wums an' snails, ye girt old silly man,' yelled Tikey from the arch of father's legs.

The last sight of the happy Brown family was taken at a turn in the lane, standing in a group and waving to him.

With the spaniels he walked down the lane towards the Bay, to say farewell to the happy sands. His train did not leave until five in the morning; the night sky and the darkling earth were his. Halfway to the Bay he turned into a lane leading through a farmyard, and onwards upon a steep and rugged track, which he called Sky Lane, that led upwards to the planet Mars shining redly in the southern sky. At the top of the hill he saw far below him the dusky flat waste of the Santon Burrows, bounded on the west by a sea shallow in endless foam. The dim roar of the Atlantic lured him to rest awhile; then he went down the sunken lane, picking a way through brambles and leaning umbelliferous plants, and so to the road between the Bay and the village of Branton.

It was quiet as he walked along the deserted streets an hour later, and down the turnpike road to Barum. He quitted the road for the estuary shore, where the incoming tide was gurgling and racing up the channel of the Taw. Curlews were calling under the brightening stars, which shone in the moving waters as he rested on the bank.

For two hours he followed the course of the river; and finding a haystack in a field outside the town, he threw up the spaniels, climbed upon the hay, and tried to sleep. Nightlong came the cries of river birds, while he recalled the past in a tangle of desire and pain. He slept between two and three o'clock, rising before dawn and continuing his journey. He had breakfast with a baker's moulder in one of the narrow, old-town streets near the station. His host—who was about to go to the bakery and had offered him the meal when he had enquired for an hotel that would be open so early—refused to accept payment, so Maddison gave him the spaniel Tatters. This delighted the moulder, and just before five o'clock his guest left with Billjohn for the railway station, where he purchased a ticket to Folke-stone. As the train left the platform Maddison saw Tatters struggling in the moulder's arms, and yelping in agony as he watched master going away from him, he knew, for all time.

THE SCARLET THREAD

Chapter 14

For hours he had been looking through the open window at the countryside brown in the heat. Swishtailing cattle in the shade of trees everywhere sought relief from the flies that buzzed and stung in the sun-glare. The wheels of the carriage seemed to be tearing up the burnished rails as the train rounded a curve—both permanent way and rolling stock were worn after the long burden of men and material borne here, every day and every night of the past five years. This had been the beginning of the main English Via Dolorosa, although few had felt grief as the khaki millions were taken to and from the ports of Folkestone and Dover. Going overseas, many had been gay with drink, shouting with excitement for the unknown; later, returning after wounds, they were self-held in secret fortitude, casual in manner on the verge of unutterable darkness. The train stopped, shook, clanked, jerked on again. The engine was puffing harsh and invisible steam in the shimmering sky.

At last the first outlying houses of the town came into view, and the spaniel must be stuffed into his pack. Billjohn whined and looked anxiously at him as he was thrust into the khaki bag and the flap closed over his head. The train stopped in the station with a jerk that flung Maddison against the seat. He opened the door and jumped out, his bag in his hand. Having not sufficient money to buy a dog ticket, he must get past the ticket collector before the dog was observed. The thought of delay was anguish, for it would postpone reunion with Evelyn; for hours his mind had been urging on the engine, turning the wheels faster, heaving the carriages through space. From far away came the blare of a brass band.

155

Few people were on the train. Two porters stood by the open gate. Billjohn was struggling in his pack. He held out the ticket, looking straight ahead.

'Haven't you a dog ticket?' asked the porter, for unknown to Maddison, the head of Billjohn was looking out of the pack on his back.

'I'm not a dog,' replied Maddison. 'Good morning'; and pushing away the porter's arm, he hurried forward, flung his bag through the window of one of the taxicabs waiting in a row, opened the door, and jumped in.

'Go on, anywhere, drive on, drive on, fast as hell, anywhere.'

'Sure,' said the driver. 'Faster'n 'at even. Oh, yes. Sure. 'S Peace Day.'

The engine roared and shook the cab; the clutch was let in with a jerk; Maddison lay back and shut his eyes, but only for a few moments. The station road sloped downwards, and it appeared to him as he lay back on the shiny cushions that the cab must crash into the houses at the bottom, for the station road joined the main road at right angles. But with rear wheels locked the cab swerved round, almost hitting the pavement, and missing an omnibus by a few inches. They passed under the railway bridge, and entered an avenue, across which strings of flags were hanging. The speed increased so much that Maddison in alarm leaned out of the window, and shouted at the driver to stop; but as this only made the driver twist the wheel so that the cab lurched in zigzags from side to side of the road, he sat down again, bracing himself for the inevitable crash. They rushed over a crossroad, bumping and swaying, almost running over a child with a hoop playing at the corner. In front was the High Street, crowded with motionless people. The driver jammed on the brakes, the cab swung left, swung right, then slid completely round, with its offside wheels in the gutter and the engine stopped.

'You blackguard!' shouted an angry voice. 'You blackguard! You road hog! You nearly killed that child! I saw you!

I'll have you sent to penal servitude! You shall pay for this, sir!'

A crowd was gathering round the cab. In its midst stood an elderly short gentleman, with red face and white moustache, shaking his fist at the driver, who, seated at the wheel, his peaked cap cocked over one eye, was regarding the crowd with sleepy superciliousness.

'You shall pay for this, sir!' fumed the old gentleman, who was dressed in a baggy brown suit, a large brown stock-tie, and brown bowler. 'Do you know who I am, sir? What? My name is Dodder, sir—Mr. Archibald Dodder, O.B.E.'

Several people began to laugh, and Maddison, leaning out of the window, said he was sorry.

'Sorry, sir? Sorry? You say you are sorry? Is that all you have to say? You are sorry, sorry! By heaven, sir'; he turned to an immature soldier in khaki, obviously a new recruit, who was standing beside him, a cigarette hanging on his lower lip. 'What have we been fighting for? For this sort of thing to occur while the colours are passing? Disgraceful state of affairs! As for you, you drunken hog, I shall tell my friend Sir George Bogside, the Mayor, to take away your licence!' he bellowed at the taxi driver, who with glazing eyes was now hanging to one of the mudguards and trying to swing the starting handle.

The old gentleman held a dog on a leash: a decrepit poodle with shaven parts to its body, standing as though tired to death on the pavement.

'Your 'ound won't bite, will 'ee, guv'nor?' enquired the taxi driver, hoarsely.

'Don't be impertinent, sir!' cried the old gentleman. 'Wait until I call a policeman!'

'Wait until you call a policeman,' repeated the man, slowly. 'You'll call a policeman. Well, call a policeman,' he said in dull thick blobs of speech. 'Call a barber to your sloppy dog, too. Wants a 'air-cut, guv'nor.'

He continued his efforts to swing the starting handle, while

Billjohn stood on the seat and barked at the shivering poodle, who ignored him and wearily held his yellow teeth and grey snout to the pavement. A policeman came up. The taxi driver lurched sideways and the old gentleman fussily went up to him.

'I am Mr. Archibald Dodder, O.B.E., sir. Member of the Conservative Club. I give this fellow in charge. I am a personal friend of Sir George Bogside. Now take them to the station.'

'Come on, ol' fella, and have a drink.'

'I want to see your licence.'

The driver seemed to be masticating other blobs of speech.

'That dog wants 'air-cut,' he repeated. 'Bogside. Bogside, ha-ha. See 'r joke? Bogside. Ha-ha. Bogside.'

The crowd had grown considerably, but as nothing seemed to really happen, it slowly loosened, and returned to line the roadway.

'What happened?' said the policeman to Maddison.

Maddison told him that they had skidded, but had done no harm beyond frightening Mr. Archibald Dodder, O.B.E., member of Conservative Club, friend of mayoralty, etc. His irony was lost on both policeman and Mr. Dodder, but the taxi driver laughed hollowly to himself and ejaculated: 'That's right.' The policeman told the taxi driver to 'get on with it', saying that there was no entry into High Street until after the march past of the troops of the Shorncliffe and Folkestone Command. After which he pushed through the crowd, followed by the others, for many murmurs and the tramp of feet told of the nearness of the head of the marching column.

Maddison found himself standing next to Mr. Dodder as the General and his staff rode by on their chargers. How alert and clear-cut were the staff officers, with their red-banded caps whose peaks were gold-encrusted with oak leaves, their red tabs, their shining belts and boots and spurs and double rows of ribbons. The beribbon'd staff! A great longing for the old days of war came over him: for the old friendships, parades, suppressed excitement of standing by for 'gaps' in the big infantry attacks, the horses, the men, the width of life so near to death. Ah, here was the cavalry! What regiments? Badge of Prince of Wales's feathers—the tenth: would Farrell be there? And Tony Slade? They passed, two troops, probably on detachment duty. He scanned the faces in vain. Skull and crossbones, the seventeenth lancers—his heart beat violently—the old seventeenth! Did they remember when they had been sent to attack Bullecourt in broad daylight, on May 12th (or was it 21st?), 1917, because the blasted Staff had believed the Germans in the Hindenburg Line would be asleep after their mid-day meal? The survivors had returned about 3 p.m., looking as though their faces had been soaked in brine, their eyes smarting and fixed beyond seeing.

They passed; and he was solitary again, more solitary than before. Why were no bands playing? Then came a brigade of field guns, with wheels and hubs and guns gleaming dull olive-green with oil polish, chains and buckles burnished, leather traces shining with saddle-soap. If they had only brought a few eighteen-pounders from Ypres or the Somme! This was not what had happened. These watching people knew nothing.

Cyclists; an infantry battalion, with colours. Strange to see regimental colours, things seen only in pictures before the war, tattered with shell-fire, dying men hoarsely shouting around the colours. Battle artists—wasn't there a Lady Someone who painted what were called graphic and heroic battle pictures? So that the onlooker was inspired to feel everything except the truth?

People who could read Julian Grenfell's *Into Battle*, and who were otherwise than silent and quiet afterwards, did not know. *Into Battle* was mystically quiet, a man saying farewell to the sweet fulness of life, a man strong with personal sunshine, as yet undimmed by the still small voice of sadness. But what would Grenfell and Brooke have written had they lived through the

Somme and Third Ypres with the P.B.I.—the poor bloody infantry. Different songs! Sassoon's poems were the true voice of a soldier, a man who was true because he was true to himself, a poet writhen in agony in the toils of the boa-constrictor of mass-human un-understanding. No, these people would never understand, never, never, never——

Someone gave him a jab behind the ribs, someone muttered angrily: 'Take your hat off, sir! How dare you stand covered when the colours of the county regiment are passing?' He gasped with pain, for the thumb of Mr. Archibald Dodder had jabbed by his kidneys.

'I'm sorry,' he muttered, and instantly took off his hat, realizing that all other men were either hatless or, if in uniform, at the salute.

'That was my son's regiment, sir!' said Mr. Archibald Dodder, in a voice of fierce pride, when the colours had passed. 'Were you in the army?'

'Yes, sir,' said Maddison.

'Were you in France?'

'Yes, sir,' said Maddison.

'Were you wounded?'

'No, sir,' said Maddison.

'Well, you weren't a shirker, anyway, that's something.'

With a blank face Maddison moved away.

A detachment of W.A.A.C.'s in their khaki wideawake hats and tunics and skirts, passed, followed by a detachment of W.R.E.N.'s, in blue uniforms. The women were ironically cheered by a few old soldiers standing in the crowd. By their voices they were Cockneys.

'Meet me to-night in dreamland, kiddo!'

'See you round the bonfire, ma'mselle from Armentières!'

'Now we know who won the war! Get the cradles ready, girls!' amidst hoarse laughter.

They understood, thought Maddison: they were not reverent with ignorance.

Meanwhile the drunken driver had been making slow but determined attempts to swing the starting handle. Suddenly the engine roared. Dense fumes of burnt oil poured out of the exhaust. Maddison pushed back the throttle lever so that the engine turned slowly.

'I want to go to Number 9a, The Paragon,' he shouted in the driver's ear. 'Only for God's sake go as slow as you can. Where's my dog? Have you seen my dog?'

The pack was lying empty on the floor of the cab. He searched among the crowd, whistling. Billjohn had gone.

'Oh, well, let him go,' muttered Maddison, irritably, while in his mind he made replies to Mr. Dodder's questions, ranging in tone from angry contempt to chill irony. He felt suddenly weary.

'Number 9a, The Paragon. And drive slowly.'

'Sure. Slow?' hiccoughed the driver.

'As slow as possible.'

'Slow as possible,' repeated the driver. 'Slow—as—poss-ible. Not slow. No, not slow. Slow-as-possible.'

'That's right.'

'Slow—as—possible.'

With a final vain glance around for his dog, Maddison got into the cab. The driver put in the gear, and the car moved forward. Maddison held the catch of the door, ready to jump out; but the car moved along slowly in bottom gear, then it jerked forward, and slowed again, jerked forward and slowed, as the driver trod on and released the accelerator pedal. The car moved along at this rate for about a minute, finally stopping by the last corner house before the crossroads, where the little girl was still playing.

'Why are you stopping?' shouted Maddison. 'Get on, you bloody fool!'

The driver slowly alighted, and with a wide sweep of his arm, he said: 'We—are—here.' He added: 'As—slow—as—possible.' He saluted.

'Of course we're here,' said Maddison sharply. 'You've had too much to drink!'

'Oh, no,' replied the driver, shaking his head many times. 'Oh, no. 'S Peace Day. Celebrate Victory to-day! Can't have —too—much—to drink.'

'Where's 9a The Paragon, please?'

'9a The Paragon? Mrs. d'Arcy Fairfax?' enquired the driver, in a mock-haughty voice. 'We're here, sir!' And waving his arm towards the corner house: 'I've had the honour of 'aving one—having one—with his lordship this morning.'

'I don't understand. Who's his lordship?'

'Naps,' pronounced the driver. 'Naps. A proper toff, is 'is lordship.'

'Do you mean Lord Spreycombe?'

'That's right, milord. No offence meant, milord.'

Maddison looked at the number on the door. It was 9. The little girl was watching him. She had auburn curls, and Evelyn's eyes.

'Are you Jonquil?'

The child nodded.

He hesitated.

'Is your mother in, do you know?' he asked presently.

'Mummie's out with Daddy.' She stared at him. 'But Martha's in.'

'Who's Martha?'

'Martha is the maid. Only don't tell Martha you saw me. She thinks I'm asleep in the nursery, but I'm not, because I runned away.'

'I won't tell her. May I go up?'

'Erhum,' she nodded.

'Will you come with me?'

'No, thank you. It's Peace Day, you see, and I don't want to waste any of it lying down.'

'How's your influenza? Didn't you have influenza a little while ago?'

THE SCARLET THREAD

The child looked gravely at him; she pouted, and frowning at him, turned away. 'Silly,' he heard her say, 'he doesn't know what he's talking about.'

Telling the driver to wait, Maddison climbed the worn stone steps leading up to the front door. The bow windows on either side of the door held paper notices that a desirable flat was to be let.

With relief he saw that it was the basement apartment. There were three above, because there were three bell-pushes. Beside the top bell an old visiting card was pasted.

BRIGADIER-GENERAL AND MRS. L. M. F. D'ARCY FAIRFAX.

And pasted below it a piece of paper inscribed in Evelyn's handwriting:

Ring, and Walk Up.

He waited for his heart to cease thudding in his ears, then walked through the doorway and up the stairs, passing the second flat. Up two more flights, and he came to a white door, which was ajar. He rapped on the door, and waited. The place seemed very silent.

'Hullo, is Mrs. Fairfax there?' he heard his weak voice calling.

When no reply came, he pushed open the door, and stepped across a black carpet.

There seemed to be no one about. An open door showed what was apparently the drawing-room, and he went inside, going at once to the fireplace, because several photographs of Evelyn were silver-framed on the shelf above it. In silence he stared at them.

One was obviously an enlargement from a snapshot. She was standing before a tree, her face upheld, with loosened hair: the same look of spirituality upon it that he remembered in the moonlight when first they had kissed. Another, a portrait study of head and shoulders, seemed to contain in the laughing lips and eyes the spirit of earth-joy. A third showed her, serious and calm in riding habit, and mounted on a tall hunter, hounds grouped below, a house in the background.

A fourth was taken in natural colours with her husband in the uniform of a brigadier-general; how proud she looked, standing beside the soldier with red and white brassard of corps headquarters-staff, double row of ribbons, and four wound stripes. The grave small head of Jonquil, in an oval silver frame, was beside it; and Jonquil as a fat naked baby on her smiling mother's knee. This photograph was soiled, and worn at the edge, as though by long carrying in tunic pocket— probably one carried in the war, he imagined.

On a wall hung an oil painting of a small child in a briar-torn frock. Somehow it was familiar: where had he seen it? He could find no artist's signature. On the frame was the red asterisk of purchase when it had hung on the line at the Royal Academy, and the catalogue number.

He sighed as he stared at the picture; he clenched his hands, and turned away; he returned, yielding himself before it, as though in supplication. The blue-grey eyes were gently sweet in aspect, wide and unstartled: the face oval, the nose little and childlike; the sanguine lips untogether enough to show a gleam of small teeth, and just drooping as though in shy pensiveness of life. The lovely hair was parted, and brushed away from the brow, falling in two flumes to the ears, whence in ropes it slid over the shoulders, through the little hands, and so to the lap, where the ends were loose like soft auburn feathers.

He stood before the portrait in pain as in his mind the flat surface was breathed upon, and made to rise into life, and to grow, till the child form budded into the first beauty of girlhood—to be stolen while immature by an experienced and mature man. From the painting he returned to contemplate the face of the husband, trying to probe behind the level gaze and to estimate his mind and feelings; but much conjecture only increased the pain.

'You're mine, my darling Evie,' he whispered.

The room contained many curios of Eastern travel and of the Great War. A pair of German saw-bayonets, of the type used by regimental pioneers, was nailed above the mantel, an Iron Cross looped to the standard of one by its black-and-silver ribbon. Polished field-gun cartridge cases were used as vases for flowers on the table; a nosecap for a paperweight; there were pickelhauben, Bavarian shakos, the beaver of a Death's-head huzzar, a Zeiss aircraft range-finder. The room was furnished with old oak furniture of the Jacobean period with two lion skins on the floor, agape in stuffy death. An old writing desk filled one corner, open, with paper, pens and blotter scattered about untidily; on top of it a bunch of roses rested coolly in a silver bowl; used coffee cups stood about the room in disarranged chairs, and ash was on the floor.

'Good-morning, mister,' said a hoarse voice. An old woman stood at the door, looking with dreary solemnity at him. Her face was an irregular knobby red, and she wore spectacles with thick lenses that made a look at her uncomfortable.

'Good-morning.'

'Good-morning, mister.'

'I suppose you wonder who I am?'

'I never wonder at nobody nor nothing, mister; especially if it happens in this household.'

He pondered this remark, spoken so solemnly, but decided that it had no hidden significance.

'Please don't be alarmed: I'm not a burglar. I'm a friend of Mrs. Fairfax.'

'I ain't never alarmed, mister. When I seed you standing there, I imagined you were a friend of the family, and if you will excuse an old woman, mister, anyone could see with the wink of an eye that you are a gentleman, in spite of them rough clothes.'

'I suppose Mrs. Fairfax is out?'

'Yes, mister. With the General—or major as he is now, but

I'm in the habit of calling him the General. "It sounds swankier," as Mrs. Fairfax sometimes says to me. Hir-hir-he,' she ended in wheezy laughter, stretching her big mouth.

'I wonder if you knew my cousin—Phillip Maddison?'

'Yes, mister. I know the Captain well. I always called him the Captain. I liked him. He was always a perfect gentleman to me. He doesn't come here much nowadays, since his fight with that there Warbeck.'

'Oh, did he have a fight?'

'Yes, mister, he ended up by putting him, clothes on and all, in a bath of cold water. Hir-hir-he! Mrs. Fairfax and me laughs over it sometimes even now. Do you know Mr. Warbeck, mister?'

'No, I don't. But I've heard of him.'

'Most folks have heard of Warbeck, mister. He's about with Mr. White nowadays, a-teaching him to adopt loose ways of living, I'm very sorry to say. Do you know Mr. White, mister: 'im what Mrs. Fairfax calls Sandurst? "Sandurst's only a kid," she says to me, "but he's a nice kid, only takes life too serious. There's enough unhappiness in the world already, Marty my dear," she says to me. But Mr. White's always been a perfect gentleman to me. Are you staying to lunch, mister?'

'I don't think I'm invited.'

'Go on, mister, you don't want to wait for no invitation in this house.'

'I left my bag downstairs.'

'You leave it up here, mister. It'll get pinched downstairs, for since the war ended the place is full of thieves. Them Canadians, I'm told, from the camp. They say the Haustralians is worse: God forbid they should come here.'

'You think it would be all right for me to bring up my bag?' asked Maddison, doubtfully.

'Lor' bless you, yes, mister. Why, can't I just see the likeness between the Captain and yourself! Lots of gentlemen stay here. You leave your bag, mister.'

'Right, I will. I suppose you don't know where Mrs. Fairfax is likely to be.'

'They were going to see the march past, mister. Then I expect they'll go for an ice or a meringue at Corvano's. Do you know Corvano's, down High Street? It's near the Queen's Hotel—you'll find that there Warbeck in there, like as not. He's a terror, mister. I sometimes wish Mrs. Fairfax wasn't so friendly; but there, it ain't the business of an old woman like me. Although I must say I'm glad we're going to have some extra help with the house now the General's come 'ome.'

Below in the street the taxicab was waiting, while the driver was holding a difficult conversation with Jonquil. Maddison explained that he would have to cash a cheque before he could pay the fare, and the driver airily waved his arm, saying he was not worrying about his money, that a friend of Mrs. Fairfax was his friend, and any old time would do. Thereafter he drove off for another drink.

Maddison went down the High Street to Corvano's restaurant, entering slowly, with an expressionless face, owing to the chaos of hope and apprehension within. The place was crowded; he scanned the faces, in vain, and went out into the street again. She was not there; every face was a strange face in a strange world; everybody seemed happy with the spirit of carnival; gay bunting and merriment everywhere, laughter and talk—he wandered aimlessly down the High Street, searching the faces that passed him by.

He saw the sign of the Queen's Hotel and entered the lounge as a relief and a refuge. He sat down in an arm-chair, and looked around: perhaps he would see Colyer, or Warbeck—anyone who knew Evelyn, so that the dreadful inner heaviness might be eased. A waiter came with a tray, and he ordered beer. As the waiter moved away he noticed two young men sitting near him. One was heavily built, with reddish-brown hair flung back from a wide forehead; he had a large ruddy face, small brown eyes, a slight reddish-brown moustache, a heavy jaw, a thick neck. He leaned forward and spoke to his companion in a deep voice that held tones of uncaringness and scoffing humour. As he spoke he rubbed together the palms of his hands.

'Well, Sandhurst, well, she's been very kind to me. Yes, I suppose you're right. I *am* a rotter to run the poor old darling down. After all, she is a poor old darling, and, oh, damn it all, not very happy. She's a poor old darling.'

This must be Julian Warbeck. Maddison listened intently. Warbeck emptied his tankard, laid it down to be refilled, wiped his moustache, pursed his lips, frowned and growled:

' "She hath wasted with fire thine high places,
    She hath hidden and marred and made sad
  The fair limbs of the Loves, the fair faces
    Of gods that were goodly and glad.

' "She slays, and her hands are not bloody;
    She moves as a moon in the wane,
  White-robed and thy raiment is ruddy,
    Our Lady of Pain."

'I don't know, Sandhurst, I don't know, but it seems to me the greatest verse ever written. Er?'

'I didn't speak, Warbeck.'

'By God, but Swinburne was a great fellow. He *was*. By God, he was. It's great stuff. It *is*. Don't you think so?'

'I told you before, Warbeck, I don't care for you spouting Swinburne.'

Maddison regarded the speaker. He was a thin youth of about eighteen years of age, with a pale face and slightest of moustaches, dark hair, and large hazel eyes. He wore the cadet uniform of the Royal Military College, and as he lifted up his glass to drink, Maddison noticed the small hand that clutched it, the slender wrist on which was fastened a gold

watch. Apparently he was gulping down whiskey and soda.
After draining the glass he shuddered.

His companion grunted, and stared at the carpet, where a
cigarette end was burning a small hole.

'I don't know, I don't know. He was, I think—yes, of course
he *was*—the greatest poet since Dante and Shakespeare!'

> ' "Ah, beautiful passionate body
> That never has ached with a heart!"

'By God, Sandhurst, Swinburne couldn't half write!'

> ' "More kind than the love we adore is,
> They hurt not the heart or the brain,
> O bitter and tender Dolores,
> Our Lady of Pain."

'By God, Sandhurst, I don't know, I don't know; no, I
don't know, by God, I don't. I'm getting drunk. Well, it's a
poor heart that never rejoices,' he exclaimed, the frown un-
creasing and his face assuming a jovial, half-scoffing expression.
'I'm going to have another. How about you?'

'It's my turn to pay, Warbeck. Here, I'll take your tankard.
I think I've had enough. I'm going to lunch with the Fairfaxes
to-day.'

'Why, you've only had a few, and it's weak muck, too. Good
Lord, you aren't half a chap. I'll have a dog's-nose.'

The cadet carried the glass and tankard to the bar, and asked
in a soft voice for a whiskey-and-spash and a dog's-nose. While
he was waiting, a fierce grunt from Warbeck caused Maddison
to glance at him. Sitting still, he was aware that two men had
entered. When they reached the bar, he looked up carelessly.
Both were tall; one was booted and spurred, and the other wore
the uniform of lieutenant in the Royal Navy. He had fair curly
hair and blue eyes, and was leading a young foxhound, with a
silk stocking tied round its neck.

'What are you having, Naps?' enquired the sailor.

'What have you got in the way of a cocktail that isn't entirely poisonous?' said the booted one to the barmaid.

'Oh, I think you've sampled the lot, Lord Spreycombe,' simpered the girl.

'Give me anything out of a bottle that's wet. No, I'll have a martini. Shake it well, won't you? Hullo, young White! Sorry to see you going to the devil. Whatever is that horrible brown stuff you've got?' He pointed with his riding whip.

'It's dog's-nose, but not for me.'

'Dog's-nose? Are you studying botany?'

'No, sir.'

'Oh, I see: it's a drink, and not a wild flower.'

'It's for my friend Warbeck. Beer and gin. He likes it.'

'Oh, is that the poet?' said Lord Spreycombe, half turning to look at Warbeck. 'I've often wanted to see him,' turning completely so that he leant back against the bar. Cocking his bowler hat over his dark eyes, and pointing with a crooked finger 'I've heard a lot about you and dog's-nose. Inseparables aren't you, what? Thanks, Tubby. Well, here's the best! taking the cocktail and tossing it down his throat without letting it touch his teeth. 'Another one like that, I think. I like 'em with the moss on. And how about you, Swinburnus redivivus? Another dog's-nose? Or two dog's-noses?'

Maddison was unable to decide whether the speaker was sneering at the younger man, or whether an unusual manner hid amusement and satirical good-humour. Everything about the Viscount Spreycombe, M.F.H., known as 'Naps' to his intimate friends and to those who read *The Tatler*, *The Bystander*, and *The Sketch*, seemed long and lean. His face, his teeth slightly projecting, his body, his coat, the narrow point of his waistcoat, his thin legs in black riding boots. Dark crisp hair and moustache, red cheeks and thick red lips, keen dark eyes over which long lashes and deep lids lazily drooped. He wore an old Etonian tie.

Maddison noticed that Warbeck repeatedly glanced at the

ie. His face had flushed, he was nervously biting the nails of
his fingers, and grunting uneasily at each remark. He rose
from the chair, rubbed his hands together, extinguished the
mouldering cigarette end, and said with exaggerated courtesy
as he raised affable eyebrows to the other:

'Thank you, er—Spreycombe I think is your real name?
Well, it's a poor heart that never rejoices! Two dog's-noses, I
think!'

'Splendid! In a jug? The bard can have this jug, can't he?'
exclaimed Spreycombe, seizing one filled with water and
chucking the contents out of the window. 'Two dog's-noses for
Algernon Charles the Second. Make it three! The bard is
thirsty!'

The four stood up by the bar and drank. Maddison listened
to the apparently easy conversation of Spreycombe and Warbeck about horses. The cadet spoke hardly at all, but leaned
against the bar, taking occasional gulps at his glass, each
followed by a wry face and a shudder. The cadet stared at the
carpet, looking distressfully round the room, listening to what
was being said.

'Did you enjoy your swim early this morning?' asked Warbeck, who seemed to be more at his ease. 'I saw you, I think,
with the beautiful Mrs. Fairfax diving in heroic manner from
the breakwater. Her harlequin bathing dress is interesting. I
notice you have one of the lady's stockings for luck around the
hound's neck.'

'Oh, that? Oh, yes, I took that from her as she was dressing.
What's the matter with you, White? If you're feeling bad,
Eddie, it's the first door on the right through the passage.'

'I'm all right, sir,' mumbled the cadet.

Spreycombe turned round and swallowed another cocktail.
Then tilting up his bowler hat: 'Coming, Tubby? Ta-ta,
Algernon Charles. Don't drink too much, or you'll boil and
bust at the bonfire to-night. There's some Swinburnian alliter-
ation for you. See how easy it is! Now, don't look so angry—it

makes you look just like a Hun. Bye-bye, Sandhurst. Hold o:
to your purse!'

The satirical voice ceased as the door closed behind it. T
his astonishment, Maddison saw that Warbeck had puckere
up his face and was crying. He clenched his hands and bit hi
lower lip, his face uncreased itself, and, looking up at th
ceiling, he muttered:

'By God, he is a swine. He's jeering at us both. How does h
know all about me, unless she's told him, that long, lear
lounging, insolent hound? It's intolerable. She's about wit
him every day, and she's no more to him than any othe
woman. He's rolling in money. And I—by God, Sandhurst,
—I would cheerfully give my life to have her smile from acros
the road. By God, it's intolerable, the insolence of that mar
And what does she care?

> ' "Wert thou pure and a maiden, Dolores,
>   When desire took thee first by the throat?"

And yet—and yet she's all right. I oughtn't to talk about her-
it's all wrong. She is a poor old darling, and not very happy

The speaker, at whom other men in the room were amused
looking, bit his nails in agitation and anger. His companio
was clinging to the bar, with half-shut eyes. Maddison kne
the feeling of whiskey fumes swirling away balance. He went t
the youth, seized his arm, and led him to the door. His le;
seemed swinging from his hips, and he stared piteously.

'Warbeck, don't leave me,' he managed to gasp. Warbec
sprang forward and took his other arm. 'I ought to go-
t' lunch.'

'He can't drink,' said Warbeck to Maddison; 'he's alwa'
sick. Oh, God, I oughtn't to have let him drink so mucl
That's all right, Sandhurst, old man—you'll soon be all righ
I'll take him now; don't you bother any more. Oh, here w
are: let's leave him here for a bit. He'll recover. He's been i
here before. Don't worry, Sandhurst, old boy. You're all rigl
now.'

Then to Maddison he said: 'How about another drink?'

'Certainly.'

They went back to the bar.

'God, this is a desolate hole, Folkestone. I say, would you mind—I'm sorry I haven't any money to buy you a drink. Father sends me the doings on Tuesdays.'

'The doings?'

'My weekly remittance.'

'Oh, you don't live down here?'

'No, in town. Have you tried dog's-nose?'

'You prefer that?'

'Thank you,' said Warbeck, gravely and quietly, as he eyed Maddison uneasily.

The drink smelt and tasted like the flower of geranium. Warbeck explained that it was a favourite drink of stokers and Cornish miners. He drained his tankard at a draught, and was invited to have another, which he accepted immediately.

'Do you know the Fairfaxes?' asked Maddison suddenly.

Warbeck stared at him, and said slowly: 'Yes, I have the honour to know a lady of that name. Why?'

They glanced at each other, and looked away.

'I've got a spaniel to give them.'

'Well, I should give it to them.'

Warbeck stared uneasily, frowning, and biting his nails. Then he stroked his chin, lit a cigarette, and said in the scoffing voice that Maddison had first heard on entering the room: 'Have you recently shaved a beard?'

'Yes.'

'You're a cousin of Phillip Maddison. And you've written a book called "The Policy of Reconstruction".'

'Yes, who told you, Mrs. Fairfax?'

'Yes, as a fact she did tell me. She said you were a genius, but a bore when you read to her—which about expresses her paradoxical intelligence. Oh, well, she's a poor old darling, and I—I esteem her.'

Warbeck drank again.

'Have you seen Phillip lately?' asked Maddison quickly dreading lest Warbeck continue to talk so frankly.

'He's gone.'

'Gone?'

'They gave him the push. Why? do you ask? Well, he used to be Adjutant of the Rest Camp on the Leas, and got kicked out for never being there. Extraordinary! Why? do you ask? He was with Mrs. Fairfax all the time. Where is he now? God knows. Certainly I don't, and as I don't go to church I suppose it will never be revealed to me. I want to know, because he owes me five pounds. Lina met you in Devon, didn't she?'

'Yes.'

'She told me about your eremite's existence. Haven't you noticed a resemblance to Romney's Lady Hamilton?'

He pointed to a calendar on the wall, advertising Dodder's Disinfectant, and having in its centre a reproduction of the famous portrait. The turned shoulder, the rounded bosom, the lovely gentle feminine glance all recalled to him a memory of Evelyn sitting on the headland sward, resting on one arm waiting to talk to him when he had finished gazing across the Santon Burrows.

'Sorry I can't pay for a drink,' Warbeck was saying apologetically.

'I'll pay. I want to cash a cheque.'

'Thank you.'

'Dog's-nose?'

'It is a good suggestion. And I say—I hate to ask you—but could you, er—until to-morrow, of course, when the doings will arrive from father—could you lend me a pound?'

'Yes, if I can cash a cheque.'

'You could cash one here. Only,' his voice lowered, 'don't say you are a friend of mine, because I owe them a few bob already. The measly manager will probably do it for you.'

Maddison saw the manager, who agreed to change a cheque

for a pound, but no more. This was immediately borrowed by Warbeck who went off to the billiard room in order to play snooker for penny a point. So Maddison was relieved of his presence as well as of his pound, and went out, returning immediately when he remembered the cadet. He found him in a state of semi-consciousness, leaning against the wall of the lavatory; and calling the manager, helped to carry him to his bedroom. They took off his shoes and tunic, and laid him on the bed; and, looking in a drawer to find a clean handkerchief to wipe the boy's lips, he saw a photograph of Evelyn signed with the words *From Mignon*.

He stared at it for a few moments. Sandhurst's eyes were shut. The manager left the room, After further hesitation Maddison, with hands slightly shaking, hid the photograph under his coat, and went downstairs into the High Street.

Chapter 15

HE could not return to her house for luncheon; and after a
solitary meal at a cheap eating house, which made him feel
sick, he walked along High Street which was crowded with
merry people. Girls four and five abreast and arm-in-arm
walked in the centre of the road; young men in mufti and uniform did the same, surrounding the girls and kissing them.
Tumbled hair and flushed cheeks and wild laughter and gay
dresses seemed to wave and flutter in the merry-making throng
like the red and blue and green and black and yellow pennants
and flags and ribbons waving and fluttering on strings, stretching across the road from shop-sign to shop-sign. Mr. Archibald
Dodder, passing by Corvano's Café Royal, wanted to take him
inside and buy him a drink for several reasons, one being that
his only son had been killed in the war, another that he was
sorry he had been so testy with the young man in the taxicab
that morning. Maddison replied that he did not drink; but he
was led by the arm into the restaurant. He slipped away from
his new friend as soon as was politely possible, since his host's
idea of generosity on this occasion was to give him a drink
called a snowball, which was a mixture of every kind of liqueur
and spirit.

His feelings quickened by the drink, he walked up High
Street, wanting to go to Evelyn's flat, but not daring to go lest
she be not pleased to see him. And the General! He quailed at
the idea of meeting the husband, who was also a general
whose wife he had ravished. Yes, ravished was the word—he
had been like Tarquin in Shakespeare's *Rape of Lucrece*. If only
the ravishment had been greater!

The erotic mood, arising out of indecision and hesitancy, was scattered by the thought that he was misjudging Evelyn. *From Mignon. She's a poor old darling, and not very happy. My husband is the average cold Englishman.* He was probably like Soames in *The Man of Property*, a book which he had read with Evelyn at Cryde Bay. He came to the corner of The Paragon and High Street, whence he could see the southern windows of her flat. He would wait there until she came out.

The gay crowd passed up and down the beflagged High Street. Girls thrust ticklers into his face; boys squirted water at him from leaden tubes; a sucked orange was flung at him; a young woman with untidy hair and laughing lips asked if he wanted a girl, and trying to reply lightly he said what he really wanted was a glass of beer. She attached herself to him, but finding him untalkative, she drifted away with the crowd.

Down the road, marching strictly to attention, came a band of urchins, barefooted and in rags. At the head of the column marched the commander, wearing an officer's tunic that reached between his knees and ankles. Behind this seven-year-old marched the band, producing curious noises from tin whistles, cardboard tubes, a concertina, biscuit boxes for side-drums, a zinc bath for a bass drum, bones, and rattles. With heads erect the dozen ragamuffins marched, in the centre an ensign with blackened face bearing draped colours—a shirt tied round the top of a decomposed umbrella. Their procession was an imitation of the morning's march past. Maddison flung the rest of his money among them. Down went colours, drums, trumpets, fifes, swords; the rabble scrambled and scratched. Others copied the example of the benefactor, and soon dozens of coins were flung. A little bareheaded girl ran forward to secure some, and was immediately pushed away by the commander. She stood in the road and cried, her arm up to her eyes. Maddison knelt by her side, trying to convince her that he was not really hurt.

'Quillie wants to play at soldiers,' complained the child, recognizing him.

'But they're so rough.'

'I want to play soldiers. It's Peace Day.'

The child put a warm arm round his neck, laying her head against his cheek, caressing him with locks soft and brown as the breast-feathers of a linnet. Flesh of her flesh, blood of her blood, spirit of her spirit: from the strange and lovely flower had loosened this petal. If only she were his, how he would guard and cherish her, how her innocence would purify his life, a lamb guarding its shepherd.

'Quillie's runned away from Martha. Quillie doesn't care a damn for anybody.'

'Well, if Martha is looking for Quillie, we must look for Martha. She may be crying.'

'Martha often cries. She's gone to have one.'

'Have one what?'

'Have *one*, silly! Martha said to Quillie: "You wait here lovey, while I have one, 'cause it's Peace Day." Martha went into a booser. Quillie runned away. Let's go to the Leas, and roll on the grass with the dogs, shall us? What's your name?'

'William.'

'Quillie likes Will'um.'

'William likes Quillie.'

The child moved her head so that her lips came to his mouth, giving a kiss.

'Willum's nice to kiss. Nicer'n Naps or Sandhurst or Daddy,' she said. Her moist hand was wriggled into his, and she led him up the High Street, making two steps to his stride. Soon they turned up a quiet passage leading to the promenade; but the sight of a man in front made her cry: 'There's Jay Double-u Quillie hates Jay Double-u. Take Quillie away, Will'um.'

She pointed at Julian Warbeck, and clutched his coat. Maddison noticed that Warbeck's eyes, as he approached seemed more deeply sunk in a face more roughly flushed than

178

before. When he stopped before them he frowned as though in an effort of concentration; he thrust forward his head, and said in a thick voice:

'You haven't been very long in re-establishing yourself.'

'You've had too much dog's-nose, my dear chap.'

'What do you mean?' said Warbeck, putting a hand on Maddison's shoulder.

'You're drunk. Please get out of my way.'

'What?' glared Warbeck. 'How dare you tell me that I'm drunk. I'm *not* drunk! By God, it's intolerable, the insults and insolences that I have to listen to from people of tenth-rate intelligence. By God, Maddison, I'm *not* drunk.'

'Well, don't distress yourself, Warbeck. I merely suggested that you had taken too much dog's-nose.'

'I *haven't*, I tell you,' insisted Warbeck, in piteous rageful distress, 'I *haven't* had too much. I'm *not*—hicco—drunk. And even if I *am* drunk, that is no reason why I should have to tolerate your intolerable and insolent remarks. Where are you going with Quillie, ur?'

Maddison feared that at any moment he would leap forward and attack him. Warbeck's big face was full of rage: with nervous agitation he was flinging back the tawny hair from his brow.

'We're going for a walk. If I were you, old chap, I'd have a rest for a bit. Have you had any lunch?'

'Why do you ask me that? No, I haven't had any lunch. And if I prefer not to have lunch, is that the concern of anyone but myself? I—I—oh, it's—I—hicco——'

The child wailed to be taken away, saying that she was afraid of Jay Double-u. Hearing what she said, Warbeck frowned; then his face unpuckered and with a gesture of despair he turned away his face. Maddison saw that tears were running down his cheeks, and heard his sob: 'She's afraid of me—that child of sunrise.'

'Don't worry, I say, Warbeck.'

179

'How can I help it?' groaned the other, 'in a world of miserable beasts, caring nothing for beauty, all doing their best to drive poets to madness! Barbarians, to whom beauty is nothing! I won't let you have Jonquil. She's run away from Martha again. I'm going to take her back to Lina. By God, don't you try and harm her! She's the only lovely thing in England. Give her to me, you long insolent fool.'

He rushed with whirling arms and lowered head at Maddison, who feared that he had to deal with a man much stronger than himself. Jonquil shrieked, and Maddison pulled her aside with him, while Warbeck struck the air and fell sprawling. Maddison felt that Warbeck had not meant to hit him; he was striking at his invisible torture.

'Run, W-Will'um, run,' urged the child. 'Run to the Leas.'

Maddison helped Warbeck to his feet, then ran after Jonquil; and reaching the top of the street, he glanced round and saw that Warbeck had got up and was leaning against the railings of a house, pressing his head with his hand.

Before them were the Leas, and below and beyond, the English Channel. Residential houses and private hotels faced the Leas, with small gardens before them, a pavement and roadway, then a number of grassy lawns bordered by low connected chains stretching from post to post, on which people were sitting, or endeavouring to sit, in spite of the efforts of children further down to jerk them off. Jonquil led Maddison over a chain, and on the grass.

'Let's pretend we're gipsies,' she suggested. 'Quillie will be the queen, eating b-bread and honey, and Jay Double-u can be Bluebeard. Now you say: "Sisterann, sisterann, do you see him c-coming?" and I'll say "Shootbangfire" and kill him. Do you like Jay Double-u, Willum?'

'He's very unhappy, my love. He seems to be tormented by something.'

'Quillie thinks he's a damn swine.'

'Hush, Quillie! No one's a damn swine, really. You mustn't speak like that.'

'Is it naughty?'

'Yes.'

'Then Quillie will say it again. D-damn swine.'

'Does Martha speak like that?'

'No, but Mummie says Jay Double-u's a damn swine, so he is, mustn't he?'

'And what does Father say?'

'Jay Double-u doesn't come any more now Father's come home from ther East. Father plays tennis.'

'Without Mother?'

'Erhum,' she nodded, 'sometimes.'

'Do you like Father?'

'Not so m-much as Martha or Mummie. Or you,' she added, rubbing herself against him.

A band began to play in the bandstand a quarter of a mile along the promenade. Thousands of people were passing and repassing on the asphalt walk of the Leas. Continually his glance searched the faces.

'Don't you want to play gipsies, Will'um?' asked Jonquil.

'Of course I do. If you promise not to say damn any more? Lord, I'm like a conventional parent.'

'All right. Then you be chief, and sit here before the fire. Now order me to go and get wood for a fire. Speak r-rough to Quillie. You see, I were stolen by you, and you beat me, and swear and are always drunk, and you married me. Tell me to go and get w-wood, and I cry.'

She stood up, pretending to cry.

'Go and get firewood,' he ordered gruffly, 'and be quick about it. And snare a rabbit for my supper. And get mush-rooms and wild apples. And if you dawdle, I shall tie you to the caravan wheel, flog you——'

'To a inch of l-life?'

'Exactly. Flog you to a inch of l-life, rub salt into the

181

wounds, leave you to the wolves, and a mouse will come and bring you berries to eat. Now go, and be quick!'

With a delighted laugh Jonquil skipped away, and commenced her pleasant hardship. She returned shortly.

'Quillie's caught a nice bunny,' she said, laying a discarded cotton glove beside him. 'And got some m-mussrooms.' Fragments of an apple core and shreds of a banana skin were laid beside the rabbit. 'Now the firewood,' which consisted of bits of paper, a bootlace, and spent matches.

'W-W-Will'um?'

'Yes?'

'Don't let's play any more. Tell Quillie the story of a poor little stolen girl who was whipped and rubbed with salt and was brought berries by a mousie. Quillie loves W-Will'um better'n Martha or *anyone*.'

'Will'um wishes that Quillie were his.'

'Then steal Quillie!' she tempted.

'For this afternoon?'

'For always.'

'But what about Martha and Mummie?'

'Quillie hates Mummie.'

'But she said she loved Mummie.'

'Only sometimes, when Mummie doesn't whip her, and rub salt into her wounds.'

He thought with delight, you little liar! and kissed her impulsively, and stroked her hair.

'Tell Quillie about the little girl.'

'Her name was Swallow Brow.'

'The little girl's?'

'One day she was playing on the sands with her dog——'

'What was his name?'

'His name was Tintack. He chased a bunny, and lost Swallow Brow, who was stolen by gipsies, one of the band of the Bloody Hand!'

Jonquil shivered with enjoyed terror.

'It was near a large lake. The little girl, Swallow Brow, was rowed in a boat to their secret island.'

'What was that c-called?'

'Heron's Island.'

'How lovely!'

'On Heron's Island the gipsies of the Bloody Hand made her build them a hut, which she did, making her very tired. She lay down to sleep, and in her sleep a swallow, also tired, perched on her head.'

'Why was he tired?'

'He had flown thousands of miles from Africa.'

'Why?'

'Nobody knows.'

'Not even W-Will'um?'

'Not even m-me.'

'Erhum.'

'The gipsy saw them asleep. He kicked Swallow Brow and made her cry. He caught the little swallow——'

'Oh, W-Will'um!'

'And he put it in a cage——'

'It will excape, won't it?' she pleaded.

'If it doesn't pine away and die.'

'Quillie will open the cage,' she insisted, jumping up and down with joy.

'Well, the little girl was beaten and kicked again. She was sent to get a bunny for supper, and sticks. She brought them. In the cage the swallow was beating its wings, and crying. Why, Quillie, what's the matter?'

'Not really crying,' she said.

'Because you know the swallow won't really die?'

'Erhum,' she nodded.

'The little girl made the supper. Then she went to sleep again. In her sleep another little girl called Quillie came to her having floated there on the back of an owl.'

'Me?'

'Yes, you were on the back of an owl.'

'I did ride there once, when I were l-little, I 'member.'

He would tell her no more, although she begged and coaxed; so she went away, returning some moments later, and, finding him still unresponsive

'W-what's the matter, Will'um?'

'I wish I were dead,' he muttered.

'Quillie often feels like that. So do Martha. She says: "Lovey, I'm damnwell fed up with being messed about. If it weren't for you I'd clear off!" '

The mimicry was done with such quaint gravity that he laughed, and his mood passed.

'W-W-Will'um!'

' 'Ess, midear?'

'Why do you speak like that?'

'Oh, I'm copying someone I knew when I was your size. But what do you want?'

'Quillie would like to chuck stones into the sea.'

'Do you know the way down?'

'Erhum.'

'Come on, then.'

They joined the crowd on the Leas, walking towards the bandstand. Jonquil led the way down a zigzagging cliff path, passing wild mallow plants and campion in bloom, and along a dark path through tall pines and firs that stayed all light except broken restless fragments of gold on the brown needles and cones. Lying in the shade were many couples, some sitting apart and talking, some reclining side by side in silence, some bound together by each other's arms, motionless and quiet. A solitary terrier covered with dust was digging a hole in the earth, yapping excitedly to itself, and pausing to sniff the rabbit of its imagination.

The white margin of the sea was freckled with human beings. Upon the brown pebbles the waves of high tide broke and swirled, rushing forward and drawing back for a fresh leap with a crashing rattle of rolled stones. Along a track of matting laid from a pavilion, male and female figures were passing, thin ones shivering as they crept along it in dripping bathing dresses, the fat ones smiling and satisfied. Men with straw hats on the backs of their heads, and dark coats open, lolled on the shingle, idly throwing stones, or watching the most pleasant bathing girls. Several rowing boats packed with human beings were being lazily rowed on the swell by boatmen for five shillings an hour; others were going a short way out to sea in motor-boats, some to beseech the pilot to put back to dry land as soon as possible. Rival boat-loads of long-haired youths in striped shirts were having races, sometimes converging and bumping. Children with oiled-silk and mackintosh coverings on their lower garments were mechanically filling tin pails with pebbles and dried seaweed in order to empty them, making as much noise as possible. Smaller children ran into the back-washes of waves, imploring parents to witness their extra-ordinarily daring and adventurous deeds.

Jonquil and Maddison sat near a man asleep in the sun with a handkerchief spread over his face. Jonquil giggled at the thought of tickling his head with a feather, and he whispered to her that she must not be naughty. But Jonquil was deter-mined to tickle the head of the sleeper, and crept on hands and knees towards him, holding the feather in her teeth as though it were a dagger. Maddison leaned sideways and grabbed a foot; he squealed and tried to kick away the restraining hand. Firmly he pulled her back to him, saying that he was a giant. This delighted her more than the idea of tickling a man's head, and she asked to be told a story.

'About Swallow Brow,' she insisted.

He began a variation of the fable told on the Leas, but Jon-quil insisted on hearing again the same story. So he told it to her, lowering his voice as two girls returning from the sea tip-toed past them. As he was concluding the fantasy by telling her that a dream swallow would live in her heart for so long as she was kind to other little children, he turned without any motive or desire, and looked over his shoulder. The two girls were sitting on the pebbles a few yards away. Both were about twenty years old; a fair girl holding a towel round her, and a girl wringing sea water from black hair that lay thickly on sunbrown shoulders and scarlet bathing dress.

They had not seen him. Jonquil, with a gentle smile on her lips, was still thinking of her swallow. He did not want to be seen by the girls, and yet even as he contemplated going away a desire for companionship upbrimmed within him. He sat still, looking seawards, ready to hear what they might say. Almost at once the clear voice of Elsie Norman said:

'You are an awful ass not to wear a cap, Mary. Your hair will split at the ends. It's your great asset, you know. Besides, it gets so coarse.'

And the reply of the other:

'Oh, it's a nuisance. I shall have it cut, I think.'

'My dear, you would be silly.'

The dark girl did not answer. Jonquil jumped up from his side, and Maddison heard the chafe of her feet on the pebbles.

'Why, it's Quillie!' said the girl in the red bathing dress.

'Who's that with her?' the voice of Elsie enquired. He knew that they were looking at him, and presently Elsie was speaking to the child, asking her where her mother was, and had she run away from Martha again.

'Martha went to have one, so Quillie went and found Will'um. And Will'um says a swallow's in Quillie's heart. And Quillie's been riding on an owl's wings. Hasn't I, Will'um?'

He ignored them, pretending not to have heard.

'Whatever does the child mean?' demanded Elsie, with bewilderment.

'Why, look!' said the dark girl.

'Who do you mean, Mary? That man?'

'Can't you see?'

'Don't speak so loudly, my dear. He may be listening.'

186

Now all three were staring at his back.

'Can you hear, Mr. Willie Maddison?' she called softly.

He turned round.

'Hullo, Mary,' he said.

'Whatever are you doing here, of all places?' exclaimed Elsie.

'Oh, I came here.'

'But your father said you were living on the coast, learning to farm or something. You look just the same!'

'So do you.'

'You remember Mary Ogilvie, don't you, Willie? Do you think she's changed?'

He looked down at the girl in the wet scarlet bathing dress, crouching by his feet. With her hand she brushed the long wet black hair from throat and shoulders, looking up at him, and tossing it behind her neck. Her mouth was slightly opened, and she smiled, so that he saw the tip of a red tongue and the white teeth. She blushed, and her glance fell.

'Hullo, Mary. I met a friend of yours two or three days ago. And I've just remembered that I accepted an invitation for yesterday, and didn't turn up. A girl called Diana Shelley.'

'Diana! Where?'

'At Cryde Bay. You live near, don't you?'

'Yes.'

She smiled up at him, and began to wring her hair. Some drops of sea water fell on Jonquil, who cried out:

'Hi, damn you, Mary!'

'O, Quillie!' said Mary.

'Quillie doesn't care a——'

'O, Quillie!' said Mary, putting her arms around her. You've said that to me before. Look at the butterfly!' laying her cheek against the child's.

Jonquil clapped her hands, and pointed to the white butterfly that was drifting about the heads of the holiday crowd. Tell Quillie a story of a butterfly,' she pleaded.

'You must ask Willie.'

'His name's Will'um, silly! W-Will'um, tell Quillie a story.'

'Later on.'

'No, now.'

'I don't know it yet.'

'Why not?'

'I don't want to.'

Jonquil pouted, and kicked him.

'Temper!' said Elsie.

Jonquil opened her mouth and cried, struggling and kicking when Mary tried to comfort her. She struck her on the cheek but Mary, wincing only a little, continued to whisper that she must not be naughty.

'Quillie will! Quillie will! Damn you! Quillie hates Mary and W-Will'um, and Martha—whip Quillie. She's naughty— whip Quillie!'

'What an awful temper,' said Elsie. 'Spiteful little thing. wouldn't pander to her if I were you. You're too soft-hearted The child wants discipline. No wonder, with such a mother!'

Jonquil lay on the pebbles, quiet now, abandoned to shaking sobs. Mary's face was pensive.

'What do you mean "with such a mother"?' asked Maddison

Jonquil had ceased her sobbing and was playing with two pebbles, and waving her feet in the air. She began to sing t them as though they were dolls.

'Poor stones, nice stones, always by the waves, talking to th sea, so dry and hot. Poor stones, dear stones, Quillie puts yo in her hand.'

Elsie said slowly: 'Her mother has recently returned from North Devon. Did you meet her there?'

He nodded, looking at Jonquil.

Mary said: 'Come on, Elsie, let's get our things on.'

They picked their way nimbly over the pebbles, and h squatted by Jonquil. She ignored him and went on singing t the stones. Mary Ogilvie was dressed first, and ran to the

olding shoes, stockings, and towel in her hand. She sat down
with the child between them. He dreaded lest she speak of
Eve: he longed for her to speak of Eve.

'Have you bathed to-day?'

'Not yet, Mary.'

'Isn't it nice to see all these people so happy?'

She began to dry a foot, bending her leg, so that her brown
knee with the scar he remembered was exposed. A man passed
them with a tray of bananas, oranges, sweets, chocolates and
heap magazines. 'Would you like anything?' he asked Mary,
who shook her head, smiling.

'That's good, for I haven't any money.'

'I want an orange,' said Jonquil.

Mary bought her an orange.

'Many years since I saw you last.'

'It seems unreal, that last day, even now.'

'Up by the Roman encampment?'

'Yes.'

'There's a Roman encampment here, but it's the centre of
icnicking parties. Not solitary like that lovely hill above
Lookhurst.'

Her feet were dry, and she began to pull on a stocking. He
ooked across the water, seeing small yachts and boats with
rown lug-sails. A seaplane droned above, and from the head
f the pier half a mile eastwards floated a brazen curl of music.

'Don't you think Diana Shelley beautiful?' Mary said, pull-
ng the brown stocking over her knee, and swiftly fastening it
nder her skirt.

'Yes. But she seemed strange.'

'Everyone says that. She is very shy. She only lives for
usic. What did she say?'

'Oh, not very much. She asked me to lunch yesterday, I
orget where——'

'Monks' Orchard. It's quite near our place.'

'Yes, that was the name. I forgot to go.'

'She will be disappointed.'

'I don't think so. She only asked me because I admitted I knew you.'

His tone of voice made her unhappy. She stole glances at him, comparing him with the boy who had sat with her in the long grass of the hill above Rookhurst, a week before the war began. She had not seen him in the years between. In silence she finished pulling on the other stocking. Then she asked, after a small hesitation, if he was stopping in Folkestone for long.

'I don't know.'

The seaplane passed with a roar just over the crowd, and hundreds of faces caused the beach to shift its freckled and variegated colour. They looked up at the same moment.

'I just thought I would come to Folkestone.'

He rose to meet Elsie, who looked very fresh and pretty in a linen dress, blue as her frank friendly eyes. The sunlight burnished her hair, fairer now than when the thick plait had conserved its gold. She wore an engagement ring, he noticed. I must smile and talk lightly, he thought, or she will think that I and Eve—— He clenched his hands against his despair.

'Sorry to have kept you so long, my dears. How about some tea? Jonquil, are you going to be a nice little girl, and come home with us to have some cakes?'

Jonquil, having buried the orange, was interested in a cork.

'She'll come,' said Mary.

Maddison and Elsie moved off, to be followed by Mary and an obedient child. They walked across the lower road, and up the path through the pines.

'What do you think of Mrs. Fairfax, Willie?'

'I thought her quite nice. A bit unconventional, perhaps.'

'Yes, many people think that. Daddy used to paint her as a child, you know.'

'So that's where I've seen the picture in her sitting-room before!'

'Her portrait was hung in one year's Academy, and bought by Major Fairfax's father. Funny coincidence, wasn't it? For afterwards the son married the original. She was only sixteen, and he was more than double her age. They married almost immediately—just before the outbreak of war. He had spent years in the Sudan. It's too young, really, to be married at sixteen, for a girl cannot possibly know her own mind at that age. What do you think?'

'I agree.'

'Of course she cannot. It's too young to expect a girl to settle down. Then came the war, and he went to fight, and she was left alone down here with her relatives. But I suppose you know old grandfather Fairfax and the two aunts, don't you?'

'No.'

'Well, I expect you will before long.'

They walked up the path in silence. Elsie said presently:

'I say, you don't look as fit as you should, my dear, living in Devon. You're too thin, and you're dark under the eyes. Perhaps it's the sun. You ought to wear a hat, you know. You had sunstroke once when you were a boy, didn't you?'

'No, that was Jack.'

'Of course. Poor Jack! You and he were friends, weren't you? Don't you miss him?'

'Occasionally.'

'Only occasionally? Why, I should miss my friend much more than occasionally if he'd been killed. How is your father?'

'I don't know. I haven't seen him or heard from him since I left Rookhurst at the beginning of the year.'

'What a pity you aren't more to each other. But you never did get on very well, did you? Neither of you has had a proper chance. But he's very proud of you, Willie. You should have heard him talking to Daddy about you during the war.'

'But I did nothing particular during the war.'

'But you did. You won the Military Cross and the Croix de Guerre.'

'Valueless. Ask the dead.'

'Morbid still! At any rate we are all proud of you at Rookhurst. Your name is hanging in the church porch, on an illuminated scroll. Now, don't go and do anything to spoil that decent record, will you? Take the advice of an old friend, Willie, and keep clear of any entanglement!'

'Why should I be in any entanglement?'

'No reason at all. I merely said mind you don't. Daddy was saying that he was sure you had the brain and the personality to do considerable things, if only you could find your feet. He said that just after you had left, when you and he had that long argument all one afternoon and evening. "When Willie throws off the effects of the war he will go straight ahead." That's what Daddy said, and, you may be sure, he knows what he's talking about! He said you hadn't yet got the world quite in perspective. That's why I thought I'd give you a friendly piece of advice, and warn you not to think too much about people who aren't of any particular importance.'

'Thank you.'

They reached the top of the Leas, which was less crowded owing to a general desire for tea and ices. Elsie and Maddison were joined by Mary and Jonquil, who was now laughing happily. They turned down a side street leading to the High Street, and were about to cross the roadway when a long low yellow car shot past, the driver cutting out the exhaust so that it seemed to be emitting roaring coughs.

'Mummie!' shrieked Jonquil, but the car went past without Evelyn seeing them.

She was sitting beside the driver, who was the dark-eyed red-lipped man he had seen in the lounge bar that morning. Behind sat the sailor called Tubby, and a small fair girl holding a bulldog by its collar.

'I want Mummie, I want Mummie!' cried Jonquil. 'I'm sorry I runned away. I'll never run away any more. Mummie, Mummie!'

'Don't cry,' said Mary, picking up the child. 'We'll go and find Mummie at once. Why, look, the car has stopped!'

The car had stopped before a corner shop. The driver got out, followed by Evelyn, who was dressed in white. The driver bent over the car, lifting out several articles looking like small pails. The sailor climbed out also, and the two men bent over the cans. Then they carried them towards the corner shop, the windows of which were covered by lattice shutters. The place was without flag or decoration of any kind. Over the shutters were the gilt letters:

Wine and   GEO. BOGSIDE   *Spirit Merchant*

They put down the cans before the shop. The taller, darker man lifted one up and flung the contents over the shop front. This was repeated with the other cans. Great splashes of red, white and blue colours began to run down the shutters and the plaster front. Indifferent to the crowd of about a dozen spectators, Lord Spreycombe slung the empty tins of paint upward to a small roof, on which were several shrubs in tubs, above the shop, where an elderly man was sitting with two ladies, apparently having tea. The elderly man happened to lean over just as the third can sailed upwards, so that it nearly struck him.

'What do this mean, my lord?' he called in a high angry voice. 'What do this mean? Outrageous behaviour for the son and heir of a peer o' the realm. I shall have the law on you, my lord.'

'What's that you say, Mr. Mayor? My dear chap, we're helping to decorate the ancient and horrible town of Folkestone. We are responding nobly to your appeal to make the best display on this suspicious occasion; and, noticing that your worship omitted to decorate his own establishment, we considered it our duty, after cracking several bottles, to do it for your washout. And all responsibility must be put upon the magnificent patriotism of your appeal. No, don't wave your arm like that, or you will fall over. Your shop looks very nice indeed.'

The paints were slowly making their shapeless slides down the drab shop front, while attenuated driblets in advance of the main sploshes gave the appearance of string blinds hanging awry. When Maddison was only a few paces from the yellow car Jonquil ran forward and threw her arms round her mother's skirts. Evelyn with an exclamation of delight seized her under the arms and lifted her up, kissing repeatedly the small face.

'Quillie, darling, mother has missed her baby girl——' Maddison heard her say, and then they were looking at each other. Immediately Evelyn set down the child, and with a radiant delight she rushed up to him.

'Bill . . . ! Billy . . . ! You in Folkestone! My dear, but how perfectly priceless! Where are you staying? You must come home to tea and see Lionel. I've told him all about you, and we were thinking of motoring over to pay you a visit. How nice to see your old face again! Let me look at you, my dear. . . . But how long have you been here? And why haven't you been round to see me?

She turned to the two friends, and with extreme cordiality she greeted them.

'What an extraordinary day of surprises and adventures! Do all you people know one another? Why, Bill, I had no idea that my friends were your friends! Elsie, have you known Willie Maddison for long?'

'About twenty years.'

'Good heavings! Mary, dear——'

'Will'um's been telling Quillie lovely fairy stories, Mummie!'

'I'm sure he has, darling, because he's half a fairy himself. How rude: I am forgetting all about my other friends.'

She turned to the tall man, who was leaning on his elbow in an attitude of assumed tiredness against the windscreen. 'Naps. you know Miss Norman and Miss Ogilvie, don't you?'

Lord Spreycombe became upright, and, taking off his hat, he swung one lank leg across the other and made a low sweeping bow.

They all murmured: 'How do you do?'

'This is Captain Maddison.'

'O, h'r'y'u?' he enquired, apparently through his back teeth, raising his black semi-circular eyebrows, and holding out a limp hand. Evelyn slapped it, telling him not to be sloppy. 'He hasn't grown up, yet,' she said. 'Miss Pamment'—speaking to the fair slim girl in the car—'you know Miss Norman, don't you? Of course! And Captain Maddison, otherwise Bill? Tubby, bow to the ladies—Lieutenant Sir John Lorayne. The bulldog's name is 'Oldfast, because he never has yet. Now you all know each other!'

'Don't forget Lord George Bogside, and the Swamp sisters!' whispered Lord Spreycombe, pointing to the group on the roof of the shop, who had resumed their tea in attitudes of stiff oblivion of the outrage.

'Naps, you mustn't be so naughty!' said Evelyn, as she gave Maddison a sweet smile. 'I must leave you before the police arrive. Good-bye, Miss Pamment! I shall see you at the hop to-night, shan't I? Cheerio, Tubby; don't forget to ask me for a dance, will you?'

'Mummie, can Quillie come to the dance, too?'

'No, my darling, little Quillie must go to bed, or she will lose the roses in her cheeks.'

'Then can Will'um take Quillie to the bonfire?'

'For a little while, perhaps, if Quillie is good and will sleep after tea.'

'Thanks awfully,' said Jonquil.

'Isn't she perfectly sweet, Billy?'

He looked into her eyes, which surely shone with love for him: so he gave her a wounded glance. 'Very sweet, Evelyn.'

'Mummie, quick!' whispered the child.

Evelyn looked round. 'Strewth, here comes someone I don't

THE DREAM OF FAIR WOMEN

want to see. Hide me, dear people. Stand in front of me, Naps. Too late!'

Julian Warbeck approached. He strode quickly, in a straight line, his hands in the pockets of his jacket. His broad shoulders were hunched as though he were sunk in some thought. When he saw the shop he stopped abruptly, scowled at the sight of the paints, and growled: 'It is—hicco—raining at last, I perceive. Hiccoo—damn—how fine a rainbow!' With a gesture of lonely humour he raised his hat solemnly to the door-handle, and walked on.

'He's drunk,' whispered Elsie Norman.

Warbeck heard her. He thrust his head forward, frowned so that his eyes were nearly hidden, thrust out his underlip, muttered a contemptuous 'Oh, well', rammed his hat on his head, and strode along his straight line, endeavouring to demonstrate, it appeared, his ability to walk perfectly upright. He marched unswervingly across the road, halted, turned to the right in the middle, and looking fixedly ahead, disappeared in the direction of the Leas.

'The Hun following his dog's-nose,' murmured Spreycombe, but no other remark was made.

When the yellow car was gone, Evelyn said: 'Billy, how nice to see you again. You must come home and have tea with me, and meet Lionel; and go with us to the Victory Ball to-night.'

Looking at his feet, he said: 'I've already said I'd go with Elsie and Mary, thanks very much.'

'Oh, very well,' she replied calmly. 'What are you going as? A slasher of thistles?'

Jonquil said that she also had promised to go to tea with them; but Evelyn said that she must be tired, and must say good-bye, and go home with her mother. So they parted: Jonquil in tears; Maddison in silence, withdrawn into himself.

196

Chapter 16

Mr. AND Mrs. NORMAN said that it was a delightful surprise to
see him, and during tea asked him many questions. Charlie
Cerr-Nore was there; he and Elsie were engaged to be married.
'Old Pigface', the nickname given Charlie at school, seemed
less inclined to like Maddison than when they were boys, but
Mrs. Norman did most of the talking. The name of Evelyn was
not mentioned after Elsie had told them of the meeting with
Jonquil on the beach, and later of the wine-shop episode.

'Your cousin Hugh Spreycombe is a bad young man!' said
Mrs. Norman, fondly, to Charlie. 'He'll be getting into serious
trouble one day!'

After tea Maddison was left with Mary, sitting on a seat
under a mulberry tree at one corner of the tennis lawn. Upon
impulse he asked her to go for a walk with him on the Leas, and
seek his lost spaniel. The crowd was increasing, the cheeks of
the girls were red and shining with exertion and laughter, their
hair untidy, ticklers and paper whisks in their hand ready to be
thrust into any and every young male face. The elder men
strolled with relaxed expressions, carelessly happy, hands in
pockets, caps pulled over ears, smoking. Children bumped
into them, scrambled round them, heedless of anything except
the games they were playing.

By his side stepped Mary, speaking only when he spoke to
her, wearing a panama hat and simple gown of tile-brown
Arabian silk with white collar. They walked past the bandstand, the middle of a vast pool of humanity, from which
uncountable concentric circles of deck-chairs seemed to ripple
with every kind of male and female face, dress, and gesture.

Many couples were dancing. The leader of the orchestra, a mixed one in Hungarian dragoon jackets and obsolete French infantry pantaloons, was ostensibly unsteady upon his legs. Maddison and Mary stood and listened for a time, then continued their walk to the less frequented part of the Leas. Before them spread a wide and smooth expanse of grass, extending on the right till it reached a fence of red corrugated iron about eight feet high enclosing for some hundreds of yards many blocks of residential buildings, on the chimney pots of which rooks were perching. The houses had a drab and dreary appearance.

The buildings within the enclosure had been commandeered by the military authorities during the war, as a Rest Camp for soldiers returning to France from leave. The Rest Camp was empty, the buildings evacuated, but not yet handed over to the owners. Here his cousin Phillip Maddison had been adjutant for the first few months following the Armistice.

He walked on in silence while the din made by the band faded away behind them. The sun which all day long had seemed to be ripping a fierce silver furrow in the sky was now spent in a gold fog which threw long shadows behind them. When they had passed the Rest Camp they came to an empty bandstand round which a few old people were quietly sitting. He noticed an ancient man in a bath-chair with a sheepskin wrapped round his knees. At his feet was curled a fat cat with an enormous head. Near the old gentleman were sitting two elderly ladies, both of them knitting, and one of them talking to a man wearing white flannels and idly spinning two tennis racquets as he sat on a reversed chair. Maddison observed the large brown hands and the ease with which the strong fingers twirled the racquets. The man in flannels glanced at the approaching pair with blue eyes of an unusual lightness which was the more pronounced by the projection of the high cheekbones in a face sunburned and lean. He wore no hat; the fair hair was short and upright, with bald patches receding on each

THE SCARLET THREAD

side of the temple. His nose was thick at the bridge, as though
it had been broken, and had reset irregularly. Mary whispered
swiftly that he was Major Fairfax. 'The others are her husband's grandfather and her two aunts-in-law.'

Major Fairfax, recognizing her, jumped to his feet.

'Hullo, Mary! What have you been doing with yourself all
day? Seen Lina?'

'We met her just before tea, Major. How d'you do, Mrs.
Beayne—Miss Fairfax. Is your cold better, Mr. Fairfax?'

She spoke to the old man, after bowing to the elderly ladies.

'Worse, worse,' grumbled Mr. Fairfax. 'This sea breeze is
very damp. You'll catch a cold in that thin dress. Do I know
you, young man?'

He pointed at Maddison with a bony finger, and peered at
him under eyebrows tangled and ragged and white. A black
clerical hat with floppy brim was pulled down over his ears; a
woollen muffler, after being wound several times round his
neck, crossed the chest of his greatcoat and was tucked under
his arms.

'What's your name, young man?' he enquired in a throaty
voice. 'Here, Tommy, Tommy, Tommy; don't go away,
Tommy, Tommy, Tommy. Milly, why don't you catch
Tommy? Mind that dog over there—they'll fight, I know
they'll fight!'

The old gentleman's querulous concern had been caused by
the cat getting up, arching its back, yawning and jumping from
the bath-chair.

'That isn't a dog, my poor parent,' said one of the women,
smiling at Maddison. 'That's a piece of newspaper.'

'But you can't be too careful, my girl. A dog may be asleep
under the paper. Here, Tommy, Tommy, Tommy; don't run
away, Tommy, Tommy, Tommy.'

He patted his knee under the sheepskin, but the cat ignored
him, and squatting on one hind leg commenced to scratch.

'Exercise is good for Tommy,' he mumbled.

His other daughter was smiling at Maddison, and Major Fairfax was looking amused. Mary said, blushing:

'Mrs. Beayne, Mrs. Fairfax—this is Willie—I mean Captain Maddison.'

Miss Fairfax made a conventional murmur, and Mrs. Beayne, a tall woman wearing tortoiseshell spectacles, addressed him in a deep broken, musical voice.

'How do you do? Now, tell me, are you any relation to that poor little man, Phillip Maddison?'

'Oh, yes; are you?' asked her unmarried sister.

'He is my cousin.'

'Fancy that!' exclaimed Miss Fairfax, rising to her feet impulsively. 'Now, really, I do see some resemblance. Now, tell us, Captain Maddison, where is Phillip? Do you know, he was a constant visitor to the house, and he never came to say goodbye! We are so hurt, aren't we, Margery?' appealing to her sister.

'Oh, very hurt. Your poor heart was quite broken, Milly. As for dear Evelyn, she was inconsolable.'

During the pause Maddison hesitatingly held out his hand to Major Fairfax, and the two men shook hands.

'My wife has told me about you, Maddison, and about your tame birds and animals. I suppose you've been to the house and seen her?'

'No, sir, but we saw Mrs. Fairfax in the town with Jonquil. Mary and I have just had tea with the Normans—my old friends. I only arrived this morning.' Was he betraying his agitation?

'Please don't call me "sir",' said Major Fairfax. 'It makes me feel superannuated.'

'But what about all your birds and animals? Did they arrive this morning?' asked Mrs. Beayne.

'No, they've all gone away and left me. I brought one spaniel with me, but I lost him.'

'Oh, the poo-oor little man!' said Mrs. Beayne. 'How wery,

wer-ry sad!' Her voice assumed a nasal, moaning tone that was produced from the back of the nose, with an effect of long-drawn compassion. 'What a werry sad holiday for the poo-oor bow-wow! Where was the little man lost, and does he know master's address?'

'His name is Billjohn, and I lost him in the High Street.'

'But you must go to the police station.'

'I daren't.'

'Ho, ho,' said Mrs. Beayne. 'It's as bad as that, is it? Bashing constables?'

He recounted his drive in the cab, and they all laughed except the old gentleman, who was too intent on watching the cat. Major Fairfax did not refer again to his wife, and he felt less apprehensive. Constantly he looked at the face of Major Fairfax; he was entirely different from the mind's picture he had formed.

'He was a brigadier-general under Allenby in Palestine,' Mary told him when they had left them. 'I like him.'

'So do I!' declared Maddison. 'I bet he was a popular brigadier!'

They walked towards the gold-dewy sunfall which was pouring the mists over the sea. He walked with downward glance, caring nothing for the beauty that gave such joy to Mary. Past the big red-brick Grand Hotel with its shining glass conservatory they walked, past the Majestic Hotel, now atrophied since it was still commandeered by the War Office, although it had been empty of members of the Women's Auxiliary Army Corps for several months. They came to open fields, where a great mass of timber was piled for the bonfire that night. They turned southwards to the sea, and sat on the edge of the cliff, ragged with coarse grasses, poppies, and blue scabious.

Tussocks of thyme grew down the sandstone slope, murmurous with wild bees singing on the purple flowerlets. A kestrel hawk was hovering above. Mary looked eagerly towards the

golden luminousness of the horizon, as though wishful of
absorbing the life of the light, of drinking the wind. Once she
looked at her companion in wonderment at his heedless attitude, at his dejection. To her came the same helpless feeling
she had felt as a very small child when at a tea-party she had
heard him talk about the nightingale, and which in after years
she had felt when sitting with him beside the tumulus on the
downs above Rookhurst. Always he was so sad. If only the
sunlight could enter into him as it did into her, and make him
happy.

'Mary.'

'Yes, Willie.

'Do you know if it is to be a fancy dress at the Grand Hotel
to-night?'

'It's optional, I think.'

'Would you like to come?'

'I'm going with my aunt, thank you.'

He turned away as he spoke, and she wondered if she had
been rude in answering him so baldly. Do come, she longed to
say; but she could not speak. While she was waiting anxiously
and a little unhappily, she noticed a mouse climbing the rough
stem of a wild mallow growing just below them on the slope.
It sat on a flower. The creature faced them, unafraid, because
they made no movement. On seeing it Maddison lost his
apathy.

'Look at that mouse,' he whispered.

'I've seen it.'

'Don't move.'

The mouse squatted among the veined purple flowers of the
mallow, nibbling the hearts of the blossoms. With small paws
it pulled off the petals, working with quiet earnestness. A
bumble bee burred to the plant, and it leapt up and snapped at
it, and having missed with its sharp teeth, continued to tear
away the petals. The labours ceased abruptly, and the mouse
froze all movement. Looking slowly upward, they saw that the

kestrel had espied it, and was resting on the breeze about ten yards above the edge of the cliff, its barred tail and wings spread, and head pointing downwards. The filaments of wing and tail feathers were nearly transparent, and red as though pulsing with blood; the glow around the sun seemed to have fired the bird, and every featherlet ruffled by the wind was like a flicker of flame.

The mouse never moved; one paw was upraised. Down slid the kestrel, beating wings and depressing the fan of its tail until it was balanced once more on the moving air, leaning forward on the wind and resisting its uptrend in the shifting and slipping movements of its wings.

He felt Mary's hand clutch his knee. She was in an agony for the mouse's danger. The black eyes of the blossom-spoiler were fixed in unwinking terror. If it made the slightest movement, the hawk would descend. Flinging up his arms, he shouted. Mary's cheek was struck violently; the hawk swerved and swooped away; the mouse leapt from its leafy platform and was lost in the grassy runs below.

'Mary, I'm so sorry. What a brute I am! Do forgive me!'

He had hurt her, for there was the mark of his blow slowly raising a stain on her cheek, yet she made no sign that she was hurt. She would not look at him, so remorsefully he put his hand on her shoulder. She stiffened, but relaxed, and smilingly turned to him.

'I am glad it escaped,' she said.

Gently the dying wind tossed the ragged grasses, shaking the poppies, and waving the heads of the scabious. She sat very still; the hand was removed from her shoulders. He spoke no more; the humming of the bees at the thyme came to them.

As the sun fell lower the golden fume became thicker, and the sea-breeze wavered. Mary wanted to talk about birds, but his apathy seemed to have returned, and with it the curious distress within herself.

The dance was not mentioned again, even when they passed

by the Grand Hotel on their return and he stopped to read the notice-boards advertising the Victory Ball, placed outside the gates. On the pavement as they walked past the Leas house the heels of Mary went *clippety clop*, *clippety clop*, and realizing that he was noticing it, a hot colour flushed her cheeks, and she quickly explained that the noise was due to the iron tips on her heels.

'They last longer that way,' she said.

When they returned to the Normans' house Elsie noticed the red mark on Mary's left cheek and asked her how it had happened. He told her, with additions by Mary, of the mouse and the hawk, and Elsie seemed to be amused by the excitement of Mary as she described the saving of it.

'You and your old mouse,' she said with good-natured tolerance. 'You're just like Willie. I believe you'll be a child all your life'; and seeing the sweet luminousness in Mary's face she impulsively kissed her.

'I must flee,' said Mary, 'or I'll be late for dinner.'

'I'll come with you,' suggested Maddison, anxious to leave

'See you at the dance?' said Elsie. 'Cheer up, Willie! You'll soon be dead!'

Chapter 17

THRICE he walked down The Paragon; thrice passed the house, and went on round the corner, and down to the Queen's Hotel. He had a desire for light and faces, to appease the twilight heaviness that was now hardly to be borne. From the Queen's Hotel he went to other pubs; but the bars were crowded by shouting soldiers, sailors and civilians; and after seeing a fight between a half-drunken Canadian sergeant— boasting that the Canuks had never lost a trench, while every British brigade, one time or another, had run like hell backwards—and a half-drunken civilian wearing the silver badge of disablement, which ended in the Canadian being scragged by half a dozen half-drunken British soldiers, he went into the High Street. Arc-lamps above the heads of the people were spluttering and shooting out their stark and coppery rays. He meandered down several streets, coming eventually to the railway bridge, and passing onwards, he reached a wide Roman roadway that led through a plain to where were grouped acres of empty Canadian hutments. The way led to the downs, now dimly dark against the northern summer sky. Sometimes he stopped, harkening to the faint roar that rose with the glow of Folkestone's rejoicing, and was passing, ghostlike, across the lightless huts.

Onward again, with Capella glimmering just above the hill line, as though it were a lantern held for his guidance by some wandering shepherd. Over a fence at the foot of Cæsar's Camp, a blundering through brambles and over flint-strewn watercourses made ages since, a laboured climb up the steep sides, until Capella was hidden behind the ramparts, leaving him with the Lion and the Bear, the Dragon and the Swan. Rests in the long grasses, then upwards until the summit was reached.

He stood on the grassy ramparts, seeing the promenade of lamps below like a snake glittering every scale. Beyond, suspended in blackness, a battle-cruiser suddenly became studded with yellow as all her lights were switched on at every porthole. A white searchlight beam stretched out from among them, illumining the pier, trailing over the houses, and swelling to a dazzling whiteness as it moved up Cæsar's Camp, causing a drove of feeding cattle to stampede in terror. The light-swelling burst in blinding rays upon him, and he put his hands to his face; the dazzle swung away again, a beam of light feeling the sky.

Some minutes afterwards the red-whiteness cleared from his sight, and he walked in darkness round the fosse. Unceasing in the long dry grasses the wind made its myriad lispings, rising and falling like the sighs of the lost generation come from the battlefields of Europe. The starlight made it possible to walk swiftly on the chalky downs. Larks roosting in the tufts sprang up with frightened chirrups at his passing, and fluttered away in the dark to seek other crouching places. He remained with the field crickets and the stars while the rockets streaked upwards from the Leas, breaking at the pause of their curves into red and green showers. Very lights, no longer needed by the detrenched army, soared with them, descending in wavy pool of radiance and drooping like faded water lilies. Then a different points great serpent tongues of flame darted at the sky: the beacons were kindled.

He walked on, feeling the strength of solitude coming upon him. Horned owls screaked in the night wind as they hunted the voles and mice on these hills of the dead, where under the grassy mounds the bones of pagan men were buried, owls that made now, as then, the same cries as they dropped to clutch and crush the furred bodies. In reverie he fancied that some skin-clad man had sat and dreamed here, long ages before the

Romans threw up their earthworks; even now some hill-flower might be drawing colour and life from his calcined bones. Perhaps a Roman had mused here under the stars, pining for the olive groves and fireflies of the south, while the watch-fires winked on the shore, and the galleys rode at anchor in the bay; helmet—breastplate—short sword—the trieme he may have borne—his bones; all, all were dust. And here may have climbed some Canadian lad, uncomforted in the night, sick for the wheat plains of his western home, for the lakes and the mountains, and the orchards on the slopes above the Pacific— far from this northern sea, so cruel to those that served it, its waves shot-over and splinter-lashed, mournful with crying gull; guarding on its bed cracked submarine and rended battle-ship, skulls weed-grown in the mouths of guns rusting in the deep green water. Ancient Briton and alien Roman, Saxon and Norman, Colonial and Englishman, all had breathed the salt wind of the hills, and pondered the star-meaning at night; were they of Something that strayed, and lingered awhile, and found Itself again?

The solitary human on the hill sat with reverie, watching the flames below licking the night. A broken pale circle surrounded the fires—these were the faces of the people who were rejoicing at war's end. His restless spirit urged him to descend the hill and to seek one face in the thousand, but he remained, for here the night was quiet and kind—like the patient and faithful death that found after earthly linger the weariest travelling morsel. He pressed his face into the grass, the tears falling slowly from his eyes. He would not go to the dance: he would sit in some four-ale bar, and finish *The Policy of Reconstruction*. He leapt up, shouting with sudden joy.

Later, pacing tranquilly the ambit, he found a dump of stakes and hurdles, left by a company of military engineers. Till he was fatigued by the carrying he bore many backloads to the earthwork, dropping them near a flagpost which marked the highest point. He sought some dried furze, and set light to

the beacon. At once the wind carried the golden flame-rush
from spike to spike, with hissing crackle and floating spark
The pinewood stakes soon fired up; he brought more hurdles
heaving them on, and then sat down and dreamed with the
flames.

He sat by the fire, celebrating Peace Night on the hills of the
dead, alone with the field crickets that sang to the heat, a straying moth, and the timid steers snuffling and peering at the edge
of the fire-glow. Embers were blown bright by the wind and
then wasted. On the Leas the bonfires were brightly burning
at intervals up and down the coast dull white blotches spread
in the sky. These were the naval flares, each a million candle
power, which once had burned the night long on the Calais
Dover submarine boom. Wherever he looked inland the dark
earth in a hundred places was specked with fire. The nearest
beacon was three miles away, but he could see the curl and
twist of the wild flames breaking skywards. Northwards, eastwards, westwards, whithersoever he looked, the beacons were
burning—tokens of joy at England's ended darkness. He
pitched the unburnt ends on his own fire, which flamed
immediately, and sudden emotion choked his throat and sight
he felt that the spirits of dead soldiers were with him. Sheep
and cattle shuffled in the darkness beyond the fire, and from
the grass came a million signs that stirred the flames, and
passed into darkness again.

Chapter 18

ABOUT eleven o'clock he arrived at the big bonfire in the field adjoining the grounds of the Grand Hotel. A vast crowd surrounded the fire. Some of the spectators were lying on the grass in attitudes of abandonment. Only a few small boys braved the heat of the ruddy mass and dared to venture within a fifty foot radius. Several young civilians and soldiers, overcome by heat and drink, were sprawled on the ground.

He saw the big face of Julian Warbeck in the crowd, and going near, discovered that he was talking to a lank individual of about fifty years of age, wearing a monocle, and a very small cap that looked like a schoolboy's. Warbeck's face was welcome in that lonely crowd, and he stood behind them, waiting for an opportunity to speak. Warbeck was saying in his rough voice:

'Well, Mr. Everard Dodder, well, I care nothing for what you say. I think—yes, I think—that for you, without erudition or intuition, to pronounce an opinion on Swinburne—on *any* poet'—he spoke with anger—'I think, by god, yes, I think that it is an insolence that is intolerable.'

'I merely remarked that Swinburne, in youth, never seemed to have innocently enjoyed himself. Furthermore, my young friend, I was reading the poet before you were born.'

'And you don't think he *is* with Shakespeare?'

'I do *not*.'

'Oh, well I don't care for your opinion.'

'Now, don't let us quarrel. Won't you just come to my house—it's only a step away—and have a friendly little cup of coffee?'

209

'Have you no barley-water?' enquired Warbeck sarcastically. 'I am afraid coffee would fly to my head, and then I should be so brilliant that I would put the fire out!'

'Well, perhaps as it is Peace Night, I might find a glass of oporto.'

'An excellent disinfectant against melancholy, sir!'

The elder man laughed, or rather from his lips stretched back from his yellow teeth came a series of sounds like 'tee-hee'.

'That, my young friend, is the wittiest thing I've heard you say to-night.'

'It was a third-rate remark,' said Warbeck contemptuously.

They moved away, and Maddison watched their departure. Mr. Everard Dodder, a younger brother of Mr. Archibald Dodder, was a cadaverous man dressed in a black Norfolk coat, with schoolboyish knickers, stockings and white spats. He carried a little swagger cane as though he were a lady and the stick were a hair found in a plate of soup, and as he walked he lifted high his feet.

They passed round a segment of the fiery circle, and Warbeck left his companion, to stride rapidly towards a group of people who had just moved into view. The leader was a girl whose face shone whitely in the ruddy light which plied its rays upon the ermine coat she had wrapped about herself. Recognizing her, Maddison's heartbeats made him feel faint. Two men strolled immediately behind her, one in a dinner jacket, hatless, and hands in pockets; the other a figure that brought from the onlookers a startled murmur of admiration. The figure of a tall, lank man, sooty black, his face obscured by a mask, in trunk hose, doublet and cape, carrying on his shoulder an executioner's axe with crimson haft and polished head that gleamed bloody with the play of firelight. To the girl Warbeck raised his hat, bowing low, and began to speak. She seemed amused by what he said, for she slightly struck him with the fan she carried. After hesitation and anguish Maddison went towards her, behind Mr. Everard Dodder, who now with a slight

toop, round shoulders, and hands behind his back, appeared
o be searching the ground for his lost confidence.

'Ha, ha,' Maddison heard him say. 'I'm so glad you're so
innocently enjoying yourselves, what?'

'Rather, Mr. Dodder!' And Evelyn slipped and whispered to
Maddison, while giving his wrist a quick squeeze. 'Darling,
where have you been? My heart's been aching for you.'

The soft voice, and the agony of caress in it, made him in-
capable of speech.

'Billy, come into the dance. I'll get rid of Naps and Lionel.
Lionel's the one in a dinner jacket. He likes you. Now, come,
darling boy.' Aloud she said: 'Rot. Of course you can come.
Fancy mooning about all alone! Lionel, this infant's lost. He's
coming in to dance.'

'Hello, Maddison,' said Major Fairfax. 'Alone? My dear
chap! Where are your pals?'

'I haven't any, sir.'

'What about us, m'dear old chap? Come into the dance.
Everything merry and bright.'

'But I can't come in these things,' he exclaimed, looking at
his clothes.

'You can come as an oddmedodd, my dear William—you're
absolutely the part!' said Evelyn.

'Come and crack a bottle of bubbly, Maddison. The place is
absolutely flowing with it.'

'That seems to indicate that the Old Country is all right at
last, sir,' said Warbeck, rubbing his hands together.

'I'm so glad they're so innocently enjoying themselves, what,
Lord Spreycombe?' said Mr. Everard Dodder, looking at the
crowd through his monocle.

'I'm so glad you're so glad,' retorted Lord Spreycombe,
swinging his executioner's axe. 'Coming in, Major? The plebs
begins to gape. Mrs. Fairfax?' He offered his arm, and they
walked away through the people who quickly made way
for them. Major Fairfax and Maddison followed. Mr. Everard

Dodder reassumed, on his lordship's departure, his upright and confident posture.

By the entrance of the hotel Evelyn twirled round snapped her fingers, cried '*Voilà!*', gave her husband a ravishing smile and said to Maddison: 'Bill, I quite forgot! I've found—what do you think?'

'A grocer that doesn't sell bad bacon?'

'Be serious. I found what you've lost.'

'Not Billjohn?'

'Yes.'

'Where is he?'

'At home. My dear, he came up to me soon after I left you this afternoon, wagging his little tail, and awful glad to see me. Aunt Margie—you've met her, haven't you?—has lost her heart to him. Now ban't I a praper maid tew vind un, midear?'

Lord Spreycombe sauntered in through the door. Major Fairfax looked at her with an admiring pleasure, as she bent forward from the step above them, holding her cloak round her knees with her left hand, her bright glance passing from Maddison to her husband and back again.

'I'm awfully glad about Billjohn,' said Maddison. 'Would you like him?'

'Rather!'

'You can have him.'

'But you must want him for yourself. I'll tell you! You walk him out for me; remember, you may want to give him away to someone else shortly! Your friend Mary's here.'

'Oh, good,' he said with assumed enthusiasm.

They entered the lounge of the hotel, on the sofas of which men and women were sitting, all talking, most of them smoking cigarettes, many of them laughing without restraint. A few men in evening clothes, some with hair dishevelled, and other in fancy dress, stood in groups, holding glasses in their hand and talking loudly to girls and women, also holding glasses or eating ices. A dance had just finished. Major Fairfax said to

Maddison that he must be thirsty, and led the way to the bar.

'Help yourself, Maddison,' he said, handing him a plate of sandwiches and a glass of champagne. 'Have some wine. Beaded bubbles winking at the brim, eh? By jove, it's a blessed change from everlasting whiskey. Ever been out East?'

'Only during the war, sir. Gallipoli, and afterwards France.'

'Wonderful show, Gallipoli! Read Masefield's book? Unforgettable, like the landing at Suvla. Lost most of my pals there—stout fellows, b'god. Have some more wine! Merry crowd here, aren't they? War forgotten. Wish I could forget. Yet I don't think I want to. Which way did Naps Spreycombe go? Oh, here he is, with Lina. Shall I pour you another glass n'dear?' he asked her, in a friendly and courteous voice.

'I am still within that capacity you warned me to observe, darling.'

'How about you, Naps? Back teeth submerged yet?'

'Lud, no,' drawled the executioner, raising his mask, and showing the slanting eyes. 'Thanks v'y much. D'luck!' drinking to Evelyn.

Maddison felt an almost overwhelming happiness. He dared not look at her. He noticed that women standing or sitting near appeared to be appraising her; and the glances of some were reservedly critical. He knew as they spoke to their companions that they were discussing her. She seemed to be unaware of other women's notice as she stood so naturally and easily with the clear wineglass in her hand, her small brown shoes close together.

'Well, Billy, what do you think of my costume? You don't appear to have noticed it.'

'It's ripping,' he said, munching an egg-and-cress sandwich. 'No, I don't mean it literally; it is very fine indeed. A grand advertisement for Dodder's Disinfectant!'

'My dear, isn't Everard Dodder a scream? And Archibald, too!' She came close.

'I drink to you, Eve!' he whispered.

'Darling,' she murmured, looking him straight in the eyes.

The crown of her head was adorned with vine leaves o
autumnal tone, and her auburn hair was unbound and falling
down her back and over her right shoulder. She wore a sleeve-
less garment of Rose du Barri, which was torn from the supporting left shoulder-strap, so that the front fell diagonally
across her bosom and the white bodice was seen. Her wais
was girdled by a narrow brown sash after the original of her
attire, which was one of Romney's portraits of Emma Hamilto
as a Bacchante.

'Billy, take your eyes off me. Haven't you seen my neck and
shoulders before?' she whispered by his side, as she offered him
a plate of anchovy paste sandwiches. 'Go on, eat all you can
Put three in your mouth at once. That's right. It's lovely to
see you so happy. Do you like my fancy dress? But wait till you
see Mary Ogilvie in her highland kilt and bonnet!'

'I don't want to see anyone but you.'

'You mustn't talk like that! Have some more wine. Don'
you think Naps looks perfectly bloody with his skinny legs? I'm
a bit tight, Billy. I want to kiss you! I do! Billy, his sister is
here, but she won't know me, but I'm not worrying. Her lady-
ship's rigged out as Queen Elizabeth. Billy, I feel absolutely
tight. Do I look it? Ask me for a dance, won't you?'

'All of them!'

'Good evening, Mrs. Fairfax,' said a quiet voice near them
It was the fair girl who had been sitting in Lord Spreycombe's
car that afternoon. Sir John Lorayne was with her, in the uniform of an admiral of the Royal Navy a hundred years ago, a
patch over one eye, a telescope under an arm.

'My dear Horatio!' exclaimed Evelyn. 'From what shades
have you come to meet your old love?'

'Oh, I've been having a quick one round at the American
cocktail bar, Emma,' replied Lord Nelson.

'He insists on dancing with you, Mrs. Fairfax,' said Miss
Pamment. 'So I brought him along.'

'May I have the honour? I've lost my dance programme.'

'You may. I've lost mine, too—my programme, I mean, not my honour. I've still got that, Horatio. I can give you the next, if you like. Don't you think Bill is absolutely topping as an oddmedodd?'

Lorayne and the fair-haired girl exchanged glances. Something gave a wild yell in the distance: it was the leader of the band giving a warning that the interval was at an end. Another musician banged the big drum, a third blew a blast on the trombone. Maddison swallowed the wine in his glass, and asked Miss Pamment if she would dance with him, receiving an unenthusiastic reply that she would love to.

'I'm going to dance, Major.'

'Good man! You'll find me here afterwards.'

He moved with the crowd through an archway, and came to the ballroom, ablaze with electric light, Allied flags, coloured balloons, and festoons of paper chains. With a crash of tinpots and other instruments the band started. He saw that the orchestra consisted of negroes.

'Why, what's the matter?' asked Miss Pamment, golden-haired and slim in a gown of bronze and gold taffetas. She paused with his arm round her waist, and looked with innocent surprise into his face.

'What extraordinary music, Miss Pamment! It's much harsher than ragtime!'

'It's called jazz, I believe.'

'What's that?'

'It has just come over from America. Don't you think it rather thrilling?'

'I think it's fine. Let's dance!'

'Rather!'

He was light on his feet. The beat of the music provided a rhythm that led him away airily as one of the balloons swaying over their heads. He was wildly happy. All the orchestra grinned at the dancers. One negro playing the piano yelled to him as he passed, and his white teeth flashed. Another banged a bass drum, rattled bones, clashed cymbals, and thumped a row of tinpots; three were playing banjos, and a dusky boy was playing a wind instrument that sent the most heartbroken wails above the din and clatter. They were continually bumped into by other couples; when this happened he usually apologized and received a spontaneous apology from the man, but often a stare from the women. He was not looking where he was going, owing to a desire to see Evelyn. When after the dance and the encore demanded by hand-clapping he was sitting with Miss Pamment in an alcove, she explained the reason.

'You see, Captain Maddison, it hurts to be bumped if you are a woman; and besides, we have a dread of appearing untidy in public. A girl would rather be starving than slovenly. Men are not so fastidious, are they?'

She smiled, and he wondered if she were referring to his worn shoes, flannel trousers, old tweed coat and the faded school tie of red, black and yellow bars; certainly she did not appear to have noticed the oddmedodd's attire.

'John seems to be happy, doesn't he?'

He looked across the empty floor, and saw that Lorayne was standing above Evelyn, who was seated, and laughing at something she said. The woman on his right, an angular Pierrette, was discussing them with her partner, and he heard her say: 'No one seems to know who she was before her marriage. She is curiously reticent about that point. But I should say she was hardly out of the top drawer! Who's she got hold of this time? Drunky Redhair and the Cadet both seem to have been disposed of.'

Miss Pamment heard as well, for she smiled at him and whispered. 'The voice of envy, Captain Maddison.'

He nodded; but he felt the icicle of fear in his heart.

'Have you known Mrs. Fairfax long, Miss Pamment?'

216

THE SCARLET THREAD

'No, I've only just met her. But Lionel Fairfax we've known for ages.'

'And has Sir John known her long?'

'A week, I think.'

'I imagined that Mrs. Fairfax and he were old friends, since he came as Lord Nelson.'

'An absolute coincidence,' she replied immediately, and went on in her demure voice: 'Mrs. Fairfax has a genius for making friends quickly. The conventions that enslave us ordinary folk have no chance to bind her. She has a great number of friends, and not a few enemies, I fear! Have you known her long, Captain Maddison?'

'Oh, yes. Are you great friends with Spreycombe?'

'Not awfully much. He lives near my grandfather's place, and I've met him there, with his old father, Lord Slepe. John's younger brother, who was killed in the war, was Lord Sprey-combe's fag at Eton. Are you an O.E.?'

'No, I went to a small school in the Westcountry—Colham School.'

'Oh, yes, I know it. Isn't that where Rupert Bryers, the poet who was killed at Gallipoli, went?'

'He was a great friend of mine, Miss Pamment, and once we planned to run away to America together.'

He told her about the adventure; and when the band com-menced, Sir John Lorayne bowed to Evelyn, and slid across the floor to Miss Pamment.

'Have you been enjoying yourself, John,' she asked.

'Very diverting, old thing,' he answered. 'Bit choppy though, so I thought I'd put back into harbour.' He nodded and grinned at Maddison, who bowed to him, then to Miss Pamment, and walked across the floor to Evelyn, around whom two young men were hovering. He went to her to claim the next dance.

'This is ours, I think, Lady Hamilton?'

'I think it must be, Oddmedodd.'

217

'But Mrs. Fairfax, you promised,' exclaimed one of the young men, with straw-coloured hair and china-blue eyes, who was dressed as an Indian rajah. 'The one before the supper dance, surely! I haven't got my programme—beastly bad form to have programmes.'

'A rajah and an oddmedodd claimants for a dance with Emma Hamilton! What an embarrassment for her!'

The Indian rajah stubbornly stood before her, and looked disdainfully at Maddison. Giving him a swift and expression-less glance, Maddison said: 'I'll see you later'; and bowing, he went away to the bar and drank another glass of wine with Major Fairfax.

'I see Mary over there, Maddison,' said Major Fairfax. 'An awfully pretty girl, don't you think? She hasn't been dancing much.'

'Perhaps she won't like to be seen with me in these clothes, sir.'

'Rot, m'dear fellow. Don't you ever let trivial details upset you—although, of course, I quite understand that in this case it's out of consideration for a lady. Good lord, you fought and suffered for England, and this is the night of rejoicing. You go to it, m'boy.

'But I don't know the lady with her.'

'Come along with me, m'dear chap. I'll soon put you right.'

Chapter 19

MAJOR FAIRFAX took Maddison to the two women sitting out in an alcove, and introduced him to Mrs. Pamment, the mother of the girl with whom he had just danced, and the aunt of Mary Ogilvie. The band was playing a brassy tune which most of the five hundred dancers were humming as they moved round the polished floor. He asked Mary if she would dance with him. She nodded and got up. She wore a tartan kilt and stockings, with red heels to her black buckled shoes, and a short slashed waistcoat of black velvet over a shirt-blouse with flowing white cravat. There was lace at throat and wrist. On her dark head she wore a bonnet with blackcocks' feathers, and the plaid over her left shoulder was fastened with a large brooch enclosing a cairngorm stone in a silver clasp wrought in the shape of a thistle. She stood slender and straight in her maidenly composure.

They merged with the moving throng.

'Enjoying yourself, Mary?'

'Yes, Willie. Isn't Mrs. Fairfax beautiful?'

'Yes.' He added after a while: 'You look ripping, too.'

They bumped and were bumped.

'I've been on the downs making a fire on Cæsar's Camp.'

'How lovely.' She wanted to say: I wish I'd been there, too.

'It was strange up there, seeing the flares and hearing no guns. I was homesick for the guns; awful thing to say, isn't it?'

'I think I understand,' she said. 'I don't see how anyone who went through the war could ever forget.'

In his mind was lighted by memory a sombre picture of flame and smoke and shards upbursting from broken earth like the

THE DREAM OF FAIR WOMEN

blown coal-dust fire round an iron wheel-hoop in a blacksmith's forge; and moving slowly in corpse-rotten mud were men with faces toadstool-pale under their helmets, men with dislustred eyes, hollow-minded and beyond fear. They were men who had bidden farewell to wife, mother, child—who had loved the green fields, the evening talk in some town tavern. They were entirely human, of no class or creed, of no race or nation; and they were dead.

He moved with the hectic throng, with the mass shuffling clockwise to the bombilation of negroid music. Pierrots and Irish colleens, gladiators and chanticleers, jesters and Quaker girls, Chevaliers and newsboys, Charlie Chaplins and milk-maids, Bohemians from the Quartier Latin, butterflies, fairies, and nymphs. Pale cheeks and sunbrown cheeks, painted cheeks and pencilled eyebrows, lamp-blacked lashes and blue-rubbed eyelids. Eyes that were sweet and young and gentle, eyes that were old and hard and false-bright with liquor. Pupils shining with love and happiness; liquified by belladonna and diminished by morphine sulphate. Natural lips and car-mined lips, lustrous hair and dyed hair, hair in waist-long tresses and in plaits, hair false in coil and pad and gummed whisker-curl. Young and old, they sought personal happiness, he thought, one among pom-poms aswing and scarves floating above the sussurration of skirts and the sibilation of shoes. They clasped aloofly, firmly, tenderly, amiably, delightedly, abandonedly, round waists and shoulders and necks. The brilliant lights shone on the Peace Night revellers.

Afterwards Maddison and Mary sat out in the palm court beside a fountain. Laughter and talk filtered from the lounge over the tiles and round the ferns. Through the glass frame-work the night sky glowed with the reflection of fire on the dews ascending.

'I suppose I'm the most disreputable person present,' he said suddenly. 'A real oddmedodd!'

'What is an oddmedodd?'

220

'One of those creatures whom the winds roughen, on whom the rains fall. A scarecrow—whom men fix on a cross as a warning, but which even the thieving crows despise.'

'In Devon we call them mommets. I think they are lovely things—like owls and stars. When I used to see them in the Great Field, as a child, I used to feel so sad for them.'

'So did I—in the Big Wheatfield at my home.'

She looked at him, her eyes wide and tender. He would not look at her. Once again she realized that she was thrusting the unwanted affection of friendship upon him. The pride in her heart that would have raised a barrier before any other man was overlaid and crushed by the desire to comfort him. She spoke to him no more as he sat with averted head, and when the beating of the big drum announced the supper dance, and he did not move, she arose, hesitated, said 'I think another dance is beginning', and waited unhappily. 'God, the Somme battlefields at night!' he muttered. In the candlelight she saw his face, and his eyes were contemplative and filled with pity for something infinitely beyond his personal compassion. He looked at her and smiled; and she was unable to say anything.

They walked over the carpet of the lounge, strewn with cigarette ends, coming to the hall through which other couples from nooks and crannies were passing to the supper room.

Evelyn waved to him.

'Thanks, Mary,' he said, and hastened to Evelyn.

'Sit next to me,' said Evelyn. 'That is, unless you'd prefer to sit with Mary Ogilvie.'

'Wouldn't you prefer the Indian rajah?'

'Jerry Tollemache? Billy, why did you desert me? I begin to think you don't care a hoot for poor little Eve.'

'I'm—Eve—do you love me?'

'Darling, only you. Men seem insipid since I met you. Sounds like a song, doesn't it? "Men seem insipid since I met you." Darling, I'm awfully drunk.'

'I'm not—yet! But, by God, I'm going to be! Christ, I love

you! I say, oughtn't I to take Mary to supper, as I've danced the supper dance with her? Look, she's standing all alone over there. Just a minute, I'll fetch her.'

When he returned to the table Eve was sitting between Major Fairfax and another man. There was no room for them. Maddison and Mary sat down at the next table, which Sir John Lorayne had managed to secure. While a crowd of men bore plates and jugs and glasses to their ladies waiting patiently in ballroom, lounge, dining-room, and even on the stairs, they sat down in comfort. A manservant who, with tattooed wrists and torn ear, looked exactly what he was—a disguised A.B.— was most anxious lest they might miss any dish, and brought them during the meal and in rapid succession plates of sandwiches of lobster, crab, salmon, cucumber, ham, tongue, chicken, gentlemen's relish, and egg-and-cress; and then fancy cakes, chocolate biscuits, shortbreads, dundee, madeira, and cherry cake. He fetched for their approval dishes of banana-custard, trifle, fruit salad, jellies and blancmanges, caramels, junkets. In his horny hands he held tall jugs of cut-glass with cider cup and claret cup, moselle cup, all with ice floating in the amber and ruby liquids. Afterwards came *pêche melba* and strawberry or vanilla ice cream and cold Mocha coffee. And Turkish cigarettes brought from Constantinople by Tubby himself.

'Well done, Harnett,' said Tubby, nodding pleasantly at him. 'Now go ashore and enjoy yourself.'

'Very good, Sir John,' replied Able-Bodied Seaman Harnett, coming smartly to attention and instantly disappearing in the direction of the bar where, before leaving, he was observed to swallow several drinks rapidly.

'I say, do look at that horror over there,' said Miss Pamment in her demure voice, laying on Maddison's sleeve the fingertips of a slender brown hand. 'Isn't she a scream?'

The scream and horror was an elderly woman sitting by herself in a corner. Her large fat face was patched in red where moisture had run through the powder. A tortoiseshell comb in the pile of her yellow frizzy hair flashed with diamonds, as did the corsage of her purple gown and every joint, it seemed, of her fingers. She seemed to have no neck, and the folds of her quadruple chin rested forlorn and vast on her chest. She wore gold stockings and shoes.

'I've been watching her,' continued Miss Pamment. 'She hasn't had anything to eat. I suppose no man is brave enough to approach her.'

'Ho, you forgets yer little Tubbers, darling!' said Tubby, mimicking the cockney voice of A.B. Harnett. 'Ever since me carver George told me th meaning of *no-blessy o-blyge* I've always been the perfect little gent. Now's me chance, what?'

'Tubby, don't be an ass!' begged Miss Pamment with a smiling look of admiration on her fair face. 'I say, you'll only get snubbed by her if you do.'

Tubby had seized a plate of sandwiches in one hand and a plate of cakes in the other, and balancing them in imitation of a waiter, he went with long strides to the lonely woman. With an amused look Mrs. Pamment watched him, until he came back with a grin, and whispered as he sat down.

'I've got me reward. She said "Ta, much, dearie." I thought, as a matter of fact, of asking her to join our merry little party over here, but me nerve failed when I saw the sparklers so prolific-like, for I didn't want me ma-in-law to be jealous.'

'I wonder if she'd like something to drink,' said Maddison. 'Shall I ask her?' He went over to the woman.

'Thank you awfully,' she replied. 'Now, I call that reely kind, I do.'

'Champagne?'

'Ta much, dearie.'

After waiting some minutes he got a bottle, wondering how he was going to pay for it, and a clean glass, and went back to her. She made room for him to sit down, somewhat to his consternation, and began to talk like one who had been repressing some anxiety. Covertly he watched Evelyn, laughing and talking at the next table.

'I suppose that nice boy who brought me some food is your brother? No? Well, the Scotch girl is surely your sister, isn't she? I mean to say, I could have sworn you was brother and sister. I had a boy somewhat like you once. He was killed only last year.'

'In the war, I suppose, madam?'

'Yes, shot down, the poor little darling, and only eighteen, too; but the lad would go, and neither me nor his father wanted to stand in his way. A flying observer, in the R.F.C. he was.'

'Yes,' said Maddison, realizing the futility of words.

'Well, cherry-oh, as my poor little dead Herbie used to say Cheery-oh, Mr. What-do-you-call-it! My best respects!'

The restraint of her grief, and the melancholy tone of her voice, somehow made him feel serene.

'Are you alone?' he asked.

'Yes, dearie,' she sighed. 'Me and Father came down to Folkestone to see our other boy, who's got some swell friend down here. I suppose you don't happen to know anyone of the name of Warbeck—Lieutenant Warbeck of the Flying Corps. Or a Mrs. d'Arcy Fairfax?'

'Are you Mrs. Warbeck?'

'Oh, no, I'm Mrs. White. Only my boy, Peter, is always mentioning those names in his letters, so the lad's father and me thought we'd come down and see him here when he wouldn't come home for Peace Day. I suppose he's a bit ashamed of his old parents. I mean to say, anyone could see with half an eye that I'm not quite a lady, couldn't they?'

She looked anxiously at him, and he replied truthfully but evasively that he had not thought about it.

'Don't you find I jar on you a little?'

'No, of course you don't!'

'Well, my Peter told me my manners jarred on him. That' my mistake for trying to make the lad a gentleman. We sen him to the best school we could get him into—perhaps you know Harrow, do you? And then he went to Sandhurst—it's reely the Royal Military College, but they all calls it Sandhurst. It makes Peter nearly cry when I call it "College".'

'I think I met him this morning.'

Mrs. White was very anxious to hear all about her son, and he told her that when he had left him he was resting in order to be fresh for the evening, which was the literal truth.

'Dad went to bed tired. I mean to say, he isn't used to drinking very much, and he worked very hard in the war. We had a little place in Brum before the war, making magnetos, but you should see it now, Mr. What's-your-name! Peter hates it; he won't go near it.'

'I suppose he knows you've come?'

'Oh, yes. We wanted to get into the place where he stays, the Victoria, but he wrote and said it was full up, so Father and me come here instead. It's the leading hotel, isn't it? Do I drop any aitches?'

'No. Do I?'

She laughed.

'I'm waiting up in case Peter comes. If you see him, you might tell him I'm here, will you? I mean to say, I shall be here till I go up to our suite on the first floor. Now, that's reely kind of you. No, I won't have any more wine, thank you, dearie, or I shall be snoozing off, and I want to see the little lad when he comes.'

When she had mentioned the name of her son, Maddison had felt the heaviness coming again in his breast. Nor did the sight of Eve laughing in another man's face ease the weight of depression. She and Lionel were sitting at a table with Lord Spreycombe and his elder sister, and another couple—a man dressed as an Arab sheik whom Maddison recognized as a staff-major on the headquarters of the Cavalry Corps in France, and a girl dressed as a Turkish woman. Lady Rachel Cerr-Nore, as Queen Elizabeth, sat upright and stiff, partly on account of

Evelyn's presence, partly because she did not feel at home in the very mixed and overcrowded assembly, partly because her ginger wig was intensely hot, her ruff made her chin sore, and the whalebone corset was oppressive. She had the slanting dark eyes of her brother, but her lips were not so red or thick. She was not enjoying herself; but she answered with friendly graciousness the frequent remarks of Evelyn, whose brilliant colouring of face and eyes was drawing the attention of all at the surrounding tables. Her own table, with the exception of the unbending Lady Rachel, was kept in continuous laughter by her drolleries and conceits

Then occurred a scene which might have taken place on the stage; indeed, for the old gentleman concerned, the world was his stage. Sir Rudolph Cardew, the veteran actor-manager, beautifully mellow after a pint of Perrier Jouet and a bottle of '64 port, sauntering in a detachment of reverie through the assembly with his monocle twirling on its black riband, his patriarchal white hair so glossy and his dress clothes so pluper-fect, stopped before her as though she were the only woman in the room, and in a hush he bowed to her companions, and fixing the monocle in an eye, his cadent voice was heard to say:

'Ah, Mrs. d'Arcy Fairfax, had I been dead a cycle of centuries, and you passed by me grave, me bones would rise joyfully, ah, joyfully, at the sound of your voice, and dance in me tomb.'

Maddison, sitting beside Mary, heard the words, and saw the animation fade from her face, leaving it grave and slightly startled. 'Isn't she lovely,' whispered Mary in his ear. And taking the tips of her fingers the old actor bowed low over them and touched them with his lips, bowed to Lady Rachel and to Major Fairfax, allowed his monocle to fall, passed his fore-finger and thumb down the broad riband, and sauntered to-wards the further door as though he were in an empty room twirling his glass. The bibble-babble of conversation rose loudly again.

Shortly afterwards the drum was banged, and many young men cheered. The strings of balloons were pulled down by waiters, and everyone scrambled to obtain one. A dinner-vagon laden with toys was pushed across the floor, and ticklers, scrammel pipes, whistles, swallow-burrs, flags of the Allies, fools' caps and bladders, rubber imp faces with tongues that stuck out on squeezing, and a score of other delights were picked up and laughingly inspected.

'Billy, why so solemn?' asked Evelyn, as they stood together waiting for the band to begin after supper. 'What frets the child of nature now?'

'Perhaps you'd rather dance with someone else?' was all he could reply.

'Well, if you feel like that——'

'Don't misunderstand, for God's sake!' he pleaded, and she whispered:

'Hush, people are looking. Come, dance!'

The jazz band had begun. It was like dancing with air, she was so light on her feet. They were bumped: he held her close.

'You're trembling, Billy.'

'You'd never tremble, would you?'

'I wouldn't show it if I did. I believe you're jealous. Ah, that's it! Well, you needn't be. But I can't keep on saying forever that I love you, and you not believing me, can I?'

'Eve, Eve——'

'Hush, not now. Be patient. Ah, you're dancing better now. That's how I like to see you—smiling, with the brightest eyes I know, when you like. Billy, you're irresistible when you laugh. Now you're withdrawing into yourself again. Enjoy, enjoy, ENJOY, while you can.'

Suddenly she gripped him so that he winced and gasped.

'I'd like to bite through your lips, you fool! I saw you talking to Mary Ogilvie, making spells with words, then you go off, free as air. But you can't play that game with me, even if you do think you're Jesus Christ.'

227

THE DREAM OF FAIR WOMEN

The lights were growing dim; red, blue, yellow beams flickered on the mass of dancers.

'Billy, I'm drunk, don't listen to me. Billy, you do love me, don't you? Darling Billy, be your own sweet self. Billy, this is the loveliest dance I ever danced.'

The beams flickered madly. They ceased. Bright lights were switched on.

'O, blast those bloody lights!' he said loudly, blinking.

Hundreds of coloured paper ropes and chains and tape were thrown in curl and festoon and whizzing lunules over the multiloquent heads. The revellers wove and interwove in their abandon to natural joy, speaking to anyone and everybody, blowing whistles in the ears of strangers and allowing themselves to be enwound with brittle web and chain. Above the din could be heard the rattle of the hunting horn blown by Lord Spreycombe, and his strident yells of 'Tear'm, tear'm, tear'm, li'l bitches, l'il bitches, tear'm, tear'm.' Pushed hither and thither, clasping Eve to his chest, Maddison experienced a surge of happiness so strong that he felt if only his voice could equal it his shouts would roll round the earth: that the spirit of the moment's fraternity must never be lost, never be allowed to subside, but must gather impetus and be grasped, so that human enmity and strife should perish for ever! He would achieve it through *The Policy of Reconstruction*. And with shining eyes he looked around him, his head above most men.

Chapter 20

At the end of the dance Maddison saw strolling into the ball-room a soldier he had not noticed before. The newcomer was tall and with a small dark moustache, in a blue patrol jacket with high collar, and his trousers with red piping down the seams were fastened under his Wellington boots. On his shoulder straps he wore the three gilt stars of a captain's rank and a row of medal ribands on his left breast. The slim and elegant figure had an air of aloofness, and as he came nearer, occasionally glancing at the faces of men and women seated round the walls, he recognized his cousin Phillip. He got up and went towards him, noticing with pride that the first ribbons of the row were the Distinguished Service Order and the Mons Star with silver rosette. Phillip's face was still thin, but not so pale or haggard as when he had last seen him; he wore his black hair short and his deep blue eyes had the same speculative look that had been so pronounced in him as a boy.

Phillip stared, and said, as he came forward to shake him gladly by the hand:

'Willie! My God, I'm glad to see you!'

'But where did you come from? I had no idea——'

'But what are *you* doing here? I thought you were at Rookhurst!'

'I've been living in North Devon. Where we spent that leave together, after the Somme. Remember?'

'Yes. If only I'd known you were there! I'm wandering about spare at present. I've chucked the service.' His eyes were moving restlessly about the room. William saw him stop his breath, and knew, before he glanced round to confirm it, what was the cause.

Phillip offered him a cigarette with a hand that shook as it held out the case. 'I say, Willie, how about a spot to drink? Let's get out of this crowd.'

They went to the bar, and over whiskey and soda Phillip told his cousin that he had been at his home for two days, and that the peace celebrations in the London suburb where he lived had so depressed him that he had been 'unable to stick the lousy place any further.'

'I got my new Falcon motor-bike and came down here— two hours blind over bumpy roads—I've left it in a garage. I used to be in the Rest Camp on the Leas.'

'I know.'

'Who told you?'

'Lina.'

Phillip's eyes were tragic. He took a gulp from his tumbler. William's heart was beating in his throat and ears. They did not look at each other.

'She's here to-night.'

'Yes, I thought she might be. I say, have a gasper?'

'No, thanks; I've still got this one.'

Three wassailing old men were standing near, and one of them kept repeating with drunken enthusiasm:

'I tell you—she's a ravishing girl. But our day's gone. Day f' youth. We'r hashbeens. All pretty women, g'bless'm, after th' boys. Day f' youth. Drink up, g'en'men.'

'I say,' whispered Phillip, 'let's go away. That chap is Colonel Tarr, my late Commandant, who got me kicked out.'

'The man they called the Flapper King?'

'Yes.'

They moved away to another bar.

'Phillip.'

'What.'

230

'Were you kicked out because of Lina—indirectly, of course, I mean?'

'Yes, I think I must have been.'

They gulped their whiskey.

'I've been drinking champagne; I'll spew if I drink any more whiskey,' said Maddison.

'Willie, I'm awfully glad to see you. It's so terrible lonely now the war's over.'

'I know.'

They drank again.

'Phillip, do you know Major Fairfax?'

'Is—is he here, Willie?'

'Yes. An awfully nice chap.'

The colour was coming back to Phillip's cheeks.

'Tell me, Willie, how did you meet her?'

'In the Nightcrow Inn. I got your message, thanks.'

'What message?'

William did not reply.

It so happened that as they stood in the hall by the lift about half an hour later they encountered her as she was returning alone from the cloakroom. She stopped as she saw Phillip. Her eyes became large and she did not smile. Phillip looked at her steadily.

'Well, Phil?' she said, as though with an effort to put a smile on her lips. 'Why do you stare at me like that?'

His voice was low and unsteady.

'Only because I have not seen you for so long a time.'

'Why didn't you tell me you were coming down? It is rather a—a shock, meeting you so suddenly like this.'

'Let's get some refreshments, and we can talk,' stammered Phillip, trying to smile.

'Refreshments? My dear boy, you're not at a suburban hop. We've had supper.'

'I—I—beg your pardon,' stammered Phillip.

She said decidedly: 'I must go back to the ballroom.

231

My husband is waiting. Would you like to meet him?'
'Can't I speak to you a moment, Lina?'
'You are speaking to me.'
'I—I mean in private. I won't keep you a moment.'
'Phillip, my dear, I'd rather not. I—I—you make me say things I hate saying. Do be sensible. I can't say any more than I've said already.'

'I understand. But I must—just—tell you something before I go. I have just come on my bike—seventy-five miles—to see you. Well, I've seen you. I came to keep a promise. Remember? No, doesn't matter. Don't think anything more about it. I understand. Hark, it's twelve o'clock!'

He held out his hand, while she looked at him with inscrutable eyes.

'I'm just in time to shake you by the hand on the day of days —what did we plan for Victory Night long ago? It doesn't matter. You have forgotten. Well, I'm not worth remembering. Good-bye, Mignon. It is over now. Yes, it is over,' he murmured, without reproach, without disesteem, only sadness.

Turning to his cousin he shook hands with him, said 'Good-bye, old man, and all the best!' and taking his uniform cap from a peg, walked out of the hotel for ever.

She shivered, and said wistfully to Maddison: 'Coming?' But when he made no reply she went on alone. He walked unsteadily into the lounge, a shadowy place of soft carpets, couches, and deep arm-chairs holding still couples from whom came a low laugh, a whisper, an unheeded protest. It seemed to him that he walked in a dream, that he would awake and find himself in his room at home, and that the strange wartime and the stranger peacetime would fade as phantasms of a night's unrest, that it would be time to get up and prepare for school. This feeling passed, giving way to an obscurity of inescapable thought, wherein it seemed that life was an illusion, that natural reality was the calm and untroublous after-sleeping known as death. The after-sleeping was real, and life a little wayward sojourn from it, like moisture in clouds that inevitably, predestinately, went back to the ocean.

He sat down in a dark corner. In the distance was audible the thrumming of the band. He had been reclining only a short time when he saw the figure of Eve enter the door, and hesitate, turning one way then another, searching. The exhausting emotions of the last forty-eight hours, the lack of sleep, the tension of expectancy, these were beginning to produce uncaringness; he sat still, imagining that he cared nothing for her. When with a low exclamation she found him and swiftly moved to him he rose to his feet, swaying a little, and offered a chair. She sat down, making place for him beside her. In the dim room, lit by candelabra on the far side, she faced him; but not with the faltering glance of a minute past. Those eyes now were very gentle, the lips near his own; mouth came to mouth, bosom to bosom, and girdling arms; and having sought and found, eyes closed upon reality, drawing over themselves the cloak of rapture, wilder than any known, since it bore away all fret, all doubt, all wasting pain.

The candles on the far mantelpiece burned on in small flickering gold points, yet radiant to him like the branched buttercups of May meadows. In the mirrors they shook and quivered as though respondent to his own felicity.

'Eve, I can't live without you,' he murmured against her breast.

'Darling,' she whispered, 'I've been whirling life around me ever since we parted, in order to forget.'

'You *wanted* to forget me? O God, I can't believe it, Eve.'

She pointed to an eastern window, filled by the moon rising over the black chimney stacks of the Leas houses. He stared at it, thinking it was like the powdered face of a broken-hearted clown. Her fingers caressed his neck, and he returned to enfold her, burying his head in her lap.

'Eve, Eve, why do all these men love you? Do you love them first?'

'Still asking questions? Well, I'll answer. I don't know why they love me; I wish they wouldn't. The second question I won't deign to answer.'

'For God's sake, tell me. Do you love them?'

'No, you damned fool. Do you think I give myself to anyone?'

He could not answer.

'Do you?'

'I don't know,' he said, miserably, pressing his brow in the soft hollow between neck and shoulder.

'Pah, all you men are alike. I'm going!'

He held her. She relaxed.

'Forgive me! I do believe you. Please, please forgive me.'

She made no reply. He looked up and saw she was crying. He took her closer; the tears wetted his cheek. The slow falling music of a waltz came to them, the moon filled dark corners of the room with a pale cold night.

'Why are you crying?'

'Because everything I do seems to bring pain to someone else, and b-because one part of me is w-wastrel of love, and w-wicked——'

'But you love me, don't you? Kiss me, kiss me. I care only for you.'

'Not for yourself, your visions?'

'I hate them.'

'That is not the faithful visionary speaking—the strong spirit I loved in you.'

'Do you still love me?'

She did not speak.

'Eve, for God's sake——'

'Hush, my darling. They're playing the Eton Boating Song. It makes me sad—all the boys I knew—who are dead. My heart is filled with dead men.' She wept. 'Billy, you do love me, don't you? If only I could trust myself to you. Really I am very weak. Ah, no. I am stronger than you—poor lost child—whose hands beat at my heart—when I think of going home after this, to *his* home—and after the wine——'

'Lionel?'

'Yes, my lawful husband,' she laughed bitterly.

The Boating Song ended and there was a silence following, in contrast to the usual bruit after the jazz. Then shadowy couples strolled into the lounge, rested, and drifted out again when the implacable rhythms started. Others came in, searching for dark places, murmuring: 'How about over there?' or 'Is there anyone on that couch?' and perhaps 'So sorry! Couldn't see you!'—a laugh, a moving away, and then stillness.

The moon rose higher. They could see the tearstains on the powdered clown face. A clock chimed the half hour.

There was no rest. They sat together, yet apart.

'Billy, who was that woman alone in the corner you were talking to at supper?'

'She said she was Mrs. White.'

'What did she want?'

'She said she was waiting for her son, Peter White.'

'Oh, yes, Sandy. I know him slightly. He is rather a nice little boy. He was supposed to come to luncheon to-day, but didn't turn up. He likes playing with Jonquil on the floor. Oh, Billy, Phil did frighten me.'

'Another one!'

'I swear he isn't, Billy. I can't help it if men get silly over me. I think I shall go and burn my hair and face in the bonfire, and then no one will care about me.'

'Eve, I'm sorry I am so suspicious—my weak nature.'

She was the Eve he had known in Devon. He kissed her, whispering:

'Eve, come under the pines down the Leas.'

'Yes.'

'We can slip out through the conservatory.'

'Yes, wait here. I'll get my cloak.'

'I'll go and get a drink.'

235

'All right. Wait for me in the lounge.'

He went to the bar, and rapidly poured several glasses of wine from an opened champagne bottle, gulped them down, then hastened to the lounge. This was the life! Together they went out into the night.

The crowd was thick round the bonfire, which had just crashed; out of its glowing pile arose flames lambent in the moonlight. Some soldiers were hopping to the tune of mouth-organs and a concertina played by A.B. Harnett, caps on the backs of heads, bottles sticking out of jacket pockets. They stopped to watch them.

'Dear fellows,' he said, thinking of the men of his old squadron. 'Ten million like them dead——'

'Hush, my darling. The dead want you to be happy, remember.'

She pressed to her heart the hand she held so tightly, and then to her lips. Together they went down the cliff path, and so to the dark pines. The tongue of the wind drew itself over the black tops, stirring to sound every needle. Gently he un-cloaked her, spreading the thing of white furs on the forest floor where was no moonlight, and drew her down into the darkness and hid his face in her hair.

Sunken to a glowing mass was the bonfire when they passed it on their way back. The soldiers were gone. Stray couples stood gazing at the pale wavering flames. Lonely figures were asleep near it. Through the conservatory they slipped into the lounge, in darkness now the candles were guttered. It would be three o'clock soon, but still the dance revolved unwearied the banjos strummed tautly, the negroes shouted their wide-mouthed pleasantries. Major Fairfax told them that 'one of her pals named Warbeck had just been slung out, after knocking all the hats off their pegs, stamping on them, and fighting five waiters'. He himself had been engrossed in a game of poker, and hoped that he hadn't been too selfish of been away too long. She replied that they had been outside in the moonlight, whereupon he suggested a dance, and they joined the throng.

Maddison watched her till they were absorbed in the heterogeneous stir and movement, then he went on the Leas, feeling a great contentment. It had been a marvellous night! What a fool he had been to waste himself by doubt and thought! To-morrow he would begin a new life: he must send to a publisher *The Policy of Reconstruction*, dedicated to *Evie*, *Eva*, *Eve*, *Eveline*, *E-v-e-l-y-n*. The darling! She had invited him to stay in the spare room of the flat. Never again would he be unhappy! The dawn would come soon. The dawn, silvery and gold and radiant like Eve herself!

The Leas were deserted, the lamps extinguished, the bonfire a heap of embers from which rose and played lilac and blue flames that swayed one way or another like a cloud of gnats. A great heat was thrown out. He lay down on his side, head pillowed on left arm. Almost at once he must have slept, for he awoke in the steely pallor of dawn, to crawl nearer the fire, followed by a mongrel dog that had been curled against his back.

Chapter 21

Thrushes were singing when he awoke again, with the mongrel licking his face. The fire was a rough flat circle of white ash around which a few dishevelled figures were lying. Dozens of bottles, black, green, and transparent, whole and broken, labelled and plain, were scattered with paper, orange peel, stoppers, Mr. Archibald Dodder's brown bowler, boots and shoes, a set of false teeth, a woman's torn skirt, walking sticks, flattened hats, fragments of food, and a dead swallow winged by the heat. At one edge of the fire stood a discoloured iron seat, evidently uprooted from the promenade and cast on the bonfire during the frolics. Across the embers the Grand Hotel quivered and faded in the hot air arising, seeming insubstantial and remote as the happenings of the night before.

He arose and stretched, then went down to the deserted beach, and bathed in the sea. He returned fresh and clear-minded to the Leas, resting gratefully in the beams of the high-rising sun. On the blue and silver water fishing boats were waiting slack-sailed for a breeze. Strolling to the town, he bought a newspaper, glanced at the uninteresting headlines about the Versailles Treaty, and dropped it in the gutter. To the lower quarter down a steep cobbled road he went, going into an eating house and ordering some breakfast. A tousled girl with undarned stockings and dragging slippers brought him some kind of fried fish called aussie, margarine, marmalade and a pint of strong tea which he drank from a thick mug. He discovered that aussie was a euphemism for dogfish, and gave half of it to the mongrel, with all the margarine. Afterwards he went to look at the Bogside shop, finding that the paint had not been removed, and that several miserable flies were stuck to it. While he gazed the cur dog was sick, and deserted him.

At eight o'clock he decided that he might call at 9a The Paragon. He walked there through a square of Georgian houses with stucco fronts and bell-pulls, small front gardens filled with laurel and privet bushes, and railed off from flagged pavements by rusty rails and stone pillars. A number of cats were sitting in the roadway and on the pavements before the houses, while male and female servants were sweeping and shaking rugs and mats. The square of houses looked on to a railed garden bordered by trees and shrubs, on the lawn of which thrushes and blackbirds were hopping with sparrows and eagerly running starlings. He saw a big cat crouching under a shrub, its yellow eyes fixed on a wren stittering above it. He recognized the monster as belonging to Major Fairfax's grandfather, and threw a piece of earth at it.

'I'm glad you've 'it 'im,' spoke someone behind. 'Great fat ugly birdketching fleabitten eunuch.' He looked over the bushes and the railings, and saw a female servant standing there, leaning on a broom.

'Do you mean Tommy?'

'Yes, that's Tommy Three, the great fat ugly creature. All through the war he had to have his meat, though we was starving. I wish some dog would ketch him and wring his neck, but lorblessme, sir, Tommy Three can fight any dog. And the old gent would die on the spot if his cat was in peril. Tisn't right, I think, to keep cats in luxury while working people starves. And him that was a parson, too!'

'Mr. Fairfax was a parson?'

'Yes, and more godly in his young days than now, with all his talk of British Israel. Nice thing, I don't think, to say that the English are really shonks and 'Ebrews, the lost tribe of Israel. Well, talking won't shake no mats, even if it does put us above the monkeys, as some say, which I doubt, as talk means scandal, leastways in this house. If you see Tommy Three, just

239

chuck more dirt at 'im, the great fat ugly birdketching eunuch!

'I will. I like birds.'

'So do I. Me kettle's boiling over. Good-morning, sir.'

She waved the broom, and bobbed down the stone steps into the basement. Maddison walked to the corner house of The Paragon, and went upstairs. Martha met him.

'I suppose no one's up yet?'

'Only me, mister, and my little ducky prancing about upstairs, pretending she's a sparrow, hatching a nest of eggs in the basin, hir-hir-he!'

She wheezed with laughter, stretching a big mouth.

'You'se Will'um, aren't you, mister? I beg your pardon, that's the name my little ducky calls you by.'

'Yes, I'm Will'um. I hope there wasn't trouble over Quillie's running away with me.'

'No trouble, mister, only a few more grey hairs for me, but I'm old, I don't count.'

At that moment the voice of Jonquil called outside:

'Martha, one of the eggs is aggled. But Quillie's hatched three—such lovely little swallow babies. May Quillie come down, Martha?'

Martha moved outside, and hoarse whisperings came to Maddison. A gurgle of delight, bare feet pattering, and Jonquil in a yellow sleeping suit had leapt up to him, wrapping arms round his neck, and legs round his waist.

'W-W-Will'um! Quillie's so happy you've come. Martha, Martha, just you listen to Will'um telling all about Swallow Brow and the fairies.

'Hir-hir-he,' chuckled Martha. 'You are a caution, lovey. My, you'll be one for the gentlemen when you're older. Hir-hir-he! Ain't she a dear little love, mister? Have you seen her mother when she was a little 'un?'

She pointed to the portrait in oils, and he nodded.

'Your dog's here, mister.'

'Yes, yes, Will'um, your dog's here. Where is her, Martha?

'etch Will'um's dog to Quillie, at once, Martha. W-W-Will'um!'

'What?'

'Your dog barked suthing awful last night. Didn't he, Martha?'

'Yes, lovey, he did. We tied him up in the box-room, but he houted the roof off almost, and so I had him with me in the itchen, and he whined there. And when I went to bed, well, e 'ollered fit to fetch out the lifeboat.'

'Where is he now?'

'Gone, mister. Done a bunk as soon as I opened the door to ake in the milk just now.'

She looked very much like a sad frog, with the deep upper p, the wide mouth, and her convex glasses. Jonquil dismounted from him as impetuously as she had leapt up, and Martha urged her to go upstairs and get into bed again, until he came up to dress her.

'Quillie wants Will'um to dress her.'

'But that ain't proper, lovey.'

'Why not?'

'Hir-hir-he,' gurgled Martha, screwing up her eyes, ' 'tisn't ght for a gentleman to dress a lady.'

'But Will'um isn't a gentleman. Course not. Why, look, you usy old fool Martha, his shoes aren't polished and his hair's ll rough. You're not a gentleman, are you, W-W-Will'um?'

'No, Quillie.'

'Course not. So you can dress me, can't you?'

'I'll do my best. But I haven't had a lot of practice.'

'Doesn't matter. Come on upstairs, Will'um, and I'll show ou my nest of swallows.'

'Do you think it will matter, Martha?'

'No, certainly not, mister. Why, she's only a baby. Criky, ere's the master!'

The sound of a door being opened and closed in the hall, of a ot-thud on the carpet, had made Martha say this.

'Morning, Maddison. I wondered whose voice it was. Why,

Quillie, you look very fresh, m'dear. Been swimming
Maddison?'

'Some hours ago, Major. Afraid I must look rather untidy
as I haven't been to bed yet, and my bag—is—is—it's where
left it.'

'Where's that?'

'Oh, here, I'm afraid.'

'My dear fellow, don't apologize. You must stay a day or s
until you get settled. Let me put your bag into the bathroor
meanwhile—I expect you'd like a tub.'

Major Fairfax was in a dressing-gown and slippers, an
obviously on the way to the bathroom himself, so Maddiso
thanked him, and declined.

'M'dear chap, don't stand on any sort of ceremony with u
We're very simple folk here, y'know. You go and bath, an
I'll write some letters. They've got to be written, and it's im
material whether before or after my bath. Lina's still sleepin
—she's fagged out with the excitement. Martha, get Captai
Maddison a towel, will you? And some tea—I expect you'\
a thirst after last night, eh?'

'But, Father, Will'um mustn't have a bath now, becau:
Quillie wants him to dress her. Don't you, Will'um?'

He felt that he had betrayed Jonquil in the stormy time th:
followed. Told with firm gentleness that she must go upstair
Jonquil rushed behind him and refused to go. Her father to)
her not to be a foolish child, and ordered her to proceed, whi
Martha stood by and muttered to herself. Major Fairfax caug]
hold of her arm, leading her to Martha, and saying that sl
must be taken up immediately. Jonquil protested and kick(
him with her bare toes, hurting herself, so that she cried ar
fought him the more. The father held her quite still, at arm
length, and said in a severe voice:

'Jonquil, you're making a fool of yourself. I tell you that yc
must go upstairs with Martha, and immediately! Are yc
going to do it?'

'No, no, no, no, no, no! Quillie wants Will'um! Quillie ates you. Let go of Quillie's arms. You hurt Quillie. Let go, ou damn swine!'

Whereupon she was spanked, and screamed the more. Iartha seized her, and bore her struggling upstairs. Major airfax said:

'Childish temper! Mustn't give way to a child or a horse, Iaddison, if you care for them. Here you are. You go in and et on with it, and I'll sling you in a towel. You'll find every-ning in there. Don't hurry!'

He opened the door, and Maddison entered at once, realiz-ig that his host wished him out of the way. Hardly had he ken off his coat when he heard the voice of Evelyn asking hy Jonquil was crying: the indistinct reply of Lionel, and the und of her leaping upstairs, doubtless to comfort the child, hose naughtiness had been caused by the calamity, to her, of n intense delight suddenly becoming an acute pang.

A long howl, and a scratching at the door, told him that Bill-hn was on his scent. He opened the door, and the spaniel dled in, talking to his master in faint whines and gurgles, not ing near him, but gazing with lolled tongue.

'You don't seem awfully happy, Billjohn.'

'Owwow-yeelo.'

'But I threw you out of the taxicab to save you from being ttled to bits, Billjohn.'

'Himhimhim-yeelo.'

'I'm very clever, but I can't control destiny, my dog. Or ther chance, because they are the same things. You think m omnipotent, don't you?'

'Imimimimimimimimimimi,' whined Billjohn, settling on e coat, trousers, and shirt, which master had flung on the or; and, sighing deeply, he swallowed all the moisture in his outh, and curled to happy sleep.

Evelyn, clad in a dove-grey kimono, went into the bathroom he was about to go out, and gave him a swift kiss as she passed him. Major Fairfax was able to devote extra time to the writing of letters, which consisted so far as Maddison could see in smoking Egyptian cigarettes and reading *The Times* and *The Daily Mail*. These he dropped beside him, with tobacco ash, when Maddison entered, and offered a cigarette. Martha brought tea, two cups of which he drank, owing to his host preferring whiskey and soda.

'Lord! It is good to be back in England after the desert Maddison, and to take a drink cold instead of lukewarm. The whiskey is vile, though. Bad stuff since the war.'

He swallowed a tall tumbler of it.

'How long do you think you'll stay in Folkestone, Maddison?'

'I don't quite know, yet, Major.'

Major Fairfax hesitated, then lit another cigarette from the stump of its predecessor, and Maddison felt uncomfortable thinking that the other would interpret his remark to be a hint.

'I've put Bill in the spare room,' said Evelyn, at breakfast.

'Good,' replied Major Fairfax.

After two days, when Maddison said he must be going Lionel said:

'My dear Bill, Lina and I are only too pleased to have you And bring your Mary in whenever you want to,' with a kindly knowing smile. Later, when he was alone with Evelyn, Maddison asked her why Lionel had spoken about Mary Ogilvie.

'Billy, dear, you are most dense. Naturally I had to make up something—to tell a damned lie, in other words—to account for your presence here in Folkestone. A woman has to act all her life, and if she doesn't she is usually downtrodden.'

'But who would tread you down?'

'Every man I ever met. Such as Julian Warbeck. My dear I was terrified when he called this morning. He had a black eye! He never gets drunk like other men, or rather he never behaves like other men when he is drunk. His face gets flushed and he talks with sonorous bombast. And the pity of it is that

e is really a nice boy, and a clever one, too, but absolutely
wasting himself. He won a scholarship to Balliol in 1915, but
since the war he has never troubled about it. I suppose you
wonder at our being, or rather having been, friends. My dear,
Julian used to be with a reserve regiment of cavalry stationed
near here—at Shorncliffe—and they gave a dinner and dance
one night. I saw him again, once, afterwards; he read Swinburne to me, with the inevitable result! Woe's me.'

They were sitting by the Leas bandstand while the afternoon
holiday crowd sauntered by, and tired-looking elderly men
pulled at bath-chairs containing wrapped invalids.

'You see, Billy, I can't help men being attracted by me.
Julian came along at all hours of the day to see me, and I
couldn't very well close the door in his face—and he wouldn't
take any hints. I didn't mind him, and Aunt Margy—the one
that is so fond of Billjohn—was amused by him, and before
Lionel came home I used to spend most of my time at their
house. Neither Aunt Margy nor Aunt Milly minded that, as
the men used to come there.'

Conversation was made awkward by the town band rendering, with a solo by a precise cornet player, the most popular air
from *The Gondoliers*. The concircling chair-loungers clapped
the performance so enthusiastically that an encore was given.
Afterwards he returned to the subject, which Evelyn seemed
most willing to discuss.

'Julian began to send me poems, which I thought awfully
long, but good, and told him so. Later, I discovered that they
were by Swinburne—"Faustine"—and bits from "The
Triumph of Time". Then came a shower of sonnets and a
translation of Catullus which he insisted on reading to poor
little me. People began to talk, and as he made himself
notorious by drinking, I had to write and ask him to keep away,
with the result that you see now. It's very hard for a woman
like myself to live, you know, Billy. There are so many pitfalls.
God alone knows what the populace thinks of me, and

certainly I don't care. But I care for the respect of my friends

'Eve.'

'Yes, my darling?'

'Do you think Lionel knows that I—that we love eac
other?'

'No, my dear. What makes you ask?'

'He looks at me sometimes with a funny look. I can't quit
make him out. I felt terrified when first I met them on th
Leas, because they were your people.'

'I shouldn't worry. I understand Lionel perfectly. My dea
of course he does not suspect anything.'

'You know, Eve, I feel a vile person, enjoying his hospitality
and pretending to be his friend, when we——'

'But aren't you his friend? You told me this morning tha
you liked him very much.'

'I do like him.'

'Then why are you making all this pother?'

'But don't you understand?'

'I think you think too much.'

'I see.'

'Now, Billy, don't be silly. Do you think I'm a fool, wh
can't understand what you mean? Do you think I am quit
easy in my mind, all the time? But what can we do? I canno
bear the idea of hurting anyone, and there is only one way t
avoid doing that.'

'What is that?'

'By not hurting them.'

'Yes, I suppose you are right. But, Eve, I can't bear you pre
ferring me to Lionel, when he's there—he feels it——'

'Ha, ha! And yet when I do show my wifely affection, yo
close up, and go away, and God knows when you're likely t
return!'

'Billy, sit forward, there's a youth over there I don't want t
see. Don't turn round.' And when he had gone she said: 'Yo
remember my telling you about "Sandhurst"? He is anothe

hat strains the web of friendship. A dear boy, but weak and foolish.'

'How about William Maddison? Also weak and foolish?'

'He is my heart's own.'

Was she mocking him? She saw his eyes, and made the action of kissing with her lips.

'Eve, I wish we were back in Shelley Cove, or on the headland.'

'So do I.'

'I would be there for ever with you. That is real life, in the wind and the sun. Listen, this is what I wrote yesterday:

'The music they are playing now is only the pale ghost of primitive happiness, that has long ceased to be in our civilized state, but lain dormant in the inherited part of the mind, to merge one day as music. These people dream when they hear music: they would be bored to hear the source of it, which is the wind in those dry thistles and elderberries and gorse of the headland, on the hills loved of ancient men, over which burned the stars by night, and the sun by day.'

His voice was rapturous, she stared with delight at his face.

'You make me long to rush away to Devon again. But that is impossible—yet awhile.'

'Let's go on the downs this evening.'

'My dear, haven't we promised to have a musical evening with the Aunts? Musical thistles and elderberries and goose? We'll go to-morrow. Come and bathe now, and then we must go home to tea.'

After dinner all three went to the house of the grandfather in Radnor Park Gardens. The odd short maid recognizing Maddison gave him a bright smile, but the sight of Billjohn took this off her face.

'There'll be ructions,' she prophesied.

Mrs. Beayne, the elder of Mr. Fairfax's two daughters, met them in the hall. Her deep voice, rough yet musical, greeted them as she came forward.

'It's so nice to see you all. And you, too, my poor bow-wow' —the voice was now comically nasal—'runnin' away from master. Naughty baow—waow! P'raps it was a lady baow-waow.' Billjohn, with wagging tail, was standing with his fore-feet in her lap, and licking her hand. 'And how's Billjohn's master? Recovered from the shock of meeting Eve's relatives on the Leas?'

'He's qute recovered, Aunt Margy. Why, only this morning he was saying how nervous he was when he saw you, and how he wanted to grow his beard again!'

'My poo-oor boy, how bad you must feel!'

Inside the drawing-room lit by a ragged gas mantle old Mr Fairfax was sitting in an arm-chair, a skull-cap on his head. Opposite him across the fireplace was another armchair, and sprawling on a red bandanna handkerchief was the cat Tommy. As they entered the room the domesticate stretched itself luxuriously, opening wide its maw, and turned on its back. But made aware of the spaniel's presence it sat up, glowered, arched its back, and uttered a growling menace. Billjohn, tail wagging, went up to it, was spat upon several times, his ears were clawed, and he hid under the table.

'Who let that dog in? Drive it out into the street. Don't let it touch the cat. Here, Tommy, Tommy, Tommy, don't be worried. There now, Tommy is quite upset. I know he'll get indigestion. Milly, go and get some milk and soda-mint. Who's this young man?' he enquired, turning to look at Maddison.

'My poo-oor parent,' said Mrs. Beayne, with mock com-passion. 'My poo-oor parent, calm yourself.'

'How do you do?' beamed Miss Millicent Fairfax. 'I am so glad you could come. And do you sing? You must sing. I am so sorry about your dog.' Her voice lowered. 'Don't take any notice of father. He is so old, Captain Maddison. We must be tolerant of grown-ups.'

He wondered what age she was herself. Miss Fairfax was

248

considerably smaller than her married sister, and she might have been any age between twenty-five and forty-five, because of a girlish manner entirely unassumed, and a gown of peacock blue velvet trimmed with white rabbit fur. Frequently she clapped her hands, made whooping noises of hilarity, and leaned back to laugh unrestrainedly. Describing her to Maddison, Evelyn had said: 'Her hair is of a shade between the colours of mahogany and chestnut, her lips are red as red ink, and her wrinkles are filled with powder, and, therefore, approximately level with its general surface.' The face of her sister, Margery Beayne, lacked any aid: the big eyes held a look of sadness which gave her, with the abundant white hair and smooth cheeks, a melancholy dignity.

'She has been divorced twice,' Evelyn had explained.

'Lionel, tell me at once who this young man is?' ordered the old gentleman.

'Bill Maddison, Grandfather. You've met him.'

'What's he doing in Folkestone?'

'He's staying with us at present. How's your gout, sir?'

'Worse. Is he paying anything?'

'I'm sorry to hear that. But the weather ought to do it good.'

'But it doesn't. Come on Tommy, Tommy, Tommy, up, up, dear old Tommy, Tommy, Tommy, up on poppa's knee!' he coaxed, but the cat, eyeing him to see if he had anything to give, and finding nothing, ignored the invitation.

'Now Bill Maddison,' began Mrs. Beayne, sitting near him, and lighting a meerschaum pipe. 'Now, my boy, I want to hear about your wonderful family of animals. The beautiful Eve, on her return from the Garden, naughty gel, told us a little about them, and a lot about you. Werry embarrassing, for a hermit wasn't it? Oh, werry, werry embarrassing, wasn't it, Billjohn, my handsome baow-waow? Milly, this naughty baow-waow has been using henna on his head. Oh, Billjohn, you sly little man. Trying to cut out the town doggies? Don't be too loving, my dear, don't be too loving, or you'll come to a bad end, like me, won't he, Evelyn Fairfax?'

'Don't mind Aunt Margy, Billy,' was the laughing reply. 'She can't be serious for a moment. But talk to her about foxhounds, beagles, bassets, and anything that barks and wags a tail, and she will be your pal for life.'

The stars are now shining in the pool above the boulders of Shelley Cove, he thought. Jefferies, my Jefferies!

Mrs. Beayne looked pleased, and continued: 'Now, don't put him off me like that, Evelyn. Now, Bill Maddison, who is looking after your animals in the cottage, and why did you leave them?'

'Well, they're all gone, Mrs. Beayne.'

'How werry sad!'

'I knew I shouldn't keep them long when I took them young.'

'That's just our general experience, alas! But won't you miss them?'

'No.'

'How callous you sound. Well, one grows callous in this hot-bed of gaiety.'

He imagined that Major Fairfax was regarding him intently, and was alarmed by the questions to which he endeavoured to give some sort of flippant answers. He felt a relief when the old gentleman was taken to bed on the arm of his daughter Milly, helped upstairs by Major Fairfax, and accompanied by the cat.

Miss Fairfax played the piano on her return, and sang two songs, while Aunt Margy sat in her father's chair and sewed. Evelyn sang Tosti's *Who?* Maddison was moved by its beauty, and glanced at the husband's face during the song, wondering what he was thinking as he gazed at the singer.

'That's a werry nice song,' said Aunt Margy, looking up at its conclusion, over the rims of her tortoiseshell spectacles. 'A werry touching song. Isn't it, Billjohn, my handsome baow-waow? No, Billjohn, you mustn't lick Auntie's face. Don't be too loving, me darlint, or you won't be happy.'

A dog tail was thumped on the carpet; the quiet sewing resumed. When Maddison was commanded to sing something, he at once refused; but they were insistent. A long search through a heap of old music scores revealed only one song that he knew, so he sang *On Richmond Hill There Lives a Lass*, gaining confidence towards the end.

'Werry charming, werry charming,' said Mrs. Beayne. 'Wasn't it, Billjohn? Now who was Master thinking of when he was singing?'

After selections from the *Moonlight Sonata* and *The Yeoman of the Guard*, Aunt Milly, clapping her hands, suggested a card game called 'Rummy'.

'Those dear Tommies used to like it so,' she said musingly. 'Lina, have you heard from Pat lately? He was such a nice boy, wasn't he? It is so nice in these rough times to find a young man of good family who has nice manners.'

'It's hard to find a man anywhere,' chuckled Mrs. Beayne. 'Even burglars no longer hide under beds.'

'Margy, you are disgraceful!' reproved her sister. 'Now don't light that disgusting pipe again!'

'The world has made me what I am,' sighed Mrs. Beayne. 'I was driven to smoking a pipe by my life in the tropics with Arthur.'

'She's terribly cynical,' said Aunt Milly. 'She calls Mayfair and Cheltenham the tropics! Don't heed her, Captain Maddison.'

'Cynical comes from a Greek word meaning "dog",' ventured Maddison, and Evelyn said: ' 'Ear, 'ear; Poet Bill on the classics is hot stuff. Sugar in your coffee, Poet Bill?'

Miss Fairfax returned, after coffee, to the subject of young men, and in particular of the nice young flying 'ace' who used to come and visit them.

'Lionel, you should have heard Pat Colyer recite "The

Green Eye of the Little Yellow God". It was wonderful, wasn't it, Lina? He was such a nice boy, and so brave. Lina, has he written to you lately?'

'I had a postcard the other day, from Brighton or some such place. He's a very negligent correspondent. Simply said "cheerio" on it. Oh, I'm sick of rummy. Let's play poker.'

Poker palled, as everyone betted extravagantly—with matches. The ragged mantle swung to the snore of the gas. Maddison longed to be away from house life, and after the game went to sit by the open window. Across the quiet square came the tinkle of a piano, and a street lamp was blinking through the trees. He leaned out on the window sill, among flower pots, to be joined by Miss Fairfax, who began a conversation in a romantic voice.

'Don't you love the night, Captain Maddison? I do. Look at that lamp over there. And the rustling trees. I love lamplight. If only I were a poet, what things I would write. Do you know Ernest Dowson's "Cynara"? I used to recite that when I was in the Glad-Eye Concert Party for Entertaining Soldiers. Of course, I had to leave out lines here and there! I always think of poor Dowson when I see a street lamp; why, I don't know, but I always do. You know it of course:

' "When the feast is finished, and the lamps expire
Then falls thy shadow, Cynara! The night is thine;
And I am desolate and sick of an old passion,
Yea, hungry for the lips of my desire."

'I always think, when I hear that poem, of a poor young boy who is going to the dogs. It is so very sad. I won't mention any names, in case you know him, but he is in love with someone out of reach, because she is married already. Perhaps you can guess who I mean, but it wouldn't be fair to give names away. She is very beautiful, and inclined to be foolish, but a very good gel, and very straight. She confides in me, you see; so I know all her little troubles. We are like two gels together—two sisters. Well, the poor boy—he isn't twenty yet—he is such a sweet boy, too—oh, awfully sweet and so unspoilt—yes, dear Sandy, I wish I could be of more help to him—he thinks I don't know, too, you know—well, the boy is in bad hands. He associates with low companions. He sometimes drinks too much, and he is such a child, and not used to intoxicating liquor. This beastly war is to blame—oh, if they would hang that wicked old Kaiser, the cause of it all! It's very sad, isn't it, Captain Maddison, to see a young man going to waste, and the spectator unable to help him at all?'

'Yes, it must be disturbing, Miss Fairfax.'

'It is. You know, so many men lose their heads over Lina. It worries her, poor gel. Don't you think that Mary Ogilvie is perfectly lovely, with her small head and raven-black hair, and large brown eyes?'

'I knew her as a child, Miss Fairfax. She was always gentle and quiet.'

'I know. Lina told me all about it. She is such a kind gel, and although she is usually quiet, she understands! Ah, how I wish I were her age once more! Hark at someone playing the Missouri waltz. It haunts me, it brings back memories of the long, long, long ago. Doesn't it to you?'

'Yes.'

'Oh, what a beautiful night! Look at that tiny little twinkling star up there in the sky. It's like the eye of a baby—Jonquil's eyes twinkled like that when she was in long clothes. Such a darling baby—oh, I did like nursing her. Lina is such a fortunate gel—but I do wish——'

The sentence was not finished owing to a crash in the area below.

'Oh, dear, there goes one of father's geranium pots. How very unfortunate!'

'I am a careless chap,' he apologized. 'I was trying to see if I could find Spica the Virgin.'

253

'My poor unknowing boy,' said Mrs. Beayne, removing her tortoiseshell spectacles, and giving him a look of mournful compassion. 'My poo-oor unknowing boy, you will search in vain for anyone of that description in Folkestone.'

'Really, Marjorie, your cynicism is positively banal! You make me blush for you!'

'Present company excepted, my poo-oor sister. I was giving our young and unsophisticated friend a piece of werry, werry good fact. And don't blush for me, dearie. Save them up for your Ideal.'

He said, smilingly: 'Spica is a star, Mrs. Beayne.'

'And so it should be to one of your years, my child. I realized that you were a poetical star-gazer. My poor sister, I fear, is werry, werry ignorant, and her mind is not so white as her cheek. Well, dear people, I'm going to bed now.'

Shortly afterwards the guests left, and Milly whispered at the door that she had so enjoyed their little talk.

'You must come again,' she breathed in his ear. 'I will get Mary to come, too. Don't worry over Margy's words. Life has been rough with my beautiful sister, and she has lost all her ideals. What a lovely night! Oh, the bright stars! Au revoir, dear people, I have so enjoyed your coming.'

She blew many kisses to them on her hands, and twirling round, disappeared into the gloomy house.

Chapter 22

MADDISON found himself a room in the lower part of the town, paying seventeen shillings a week for it, including breakfast. Lionel was so cordial in assurances that he was welcome to the flat, that Maddison's feelings of being a sponger were allayed. After breakfast, as he turned the corner of The Paragon, he met Major Fairfax coming down the steps.

'Can't stop, Bill. Got to catch the London train. But go up! Back to-morrow.'

He hastened down the road, a brown bag in his hand. A window above was flung open, and Evelyn looked out, whistling. Her husband turned round, and she continued to wave until the lime-trees hid him. Then looking down, she invited Billy to come up.

Jonquil was playing on the floor of the drawing-room with a few pails, a mop, some brooms, and a basin. Evelyn was writing at the desk, her back turned.

'W-W-Will'um—look, here's heaven. I've got swallow angels on these trees, and that's a big pond. Can you hear something?'

A peculiar noise was coming from the kitchen, as Martha sung to herself as she washed up cups and plates at the sink.

'Yes. It's Martha in the kitchen.'

'Silly! That's not Martha. That's Satan in hell growling as he burns up the souls of drunkids an' boozers.'

He laughed and kissed her, and lay down on the floor beside her, stroking her hair.

'Good-morning, Billy. It is so nice that you like my daughter.

255

Youth clings to youth, what? I wondered if you were going to notice me.'

'I saw your back. Shall I come across heaven to you?'

'I am still on the earth. Quillie, darling.'

'Yes, Mummie.'

'Go and build up a little hell for yourself in the kitchen, with Martha, will you?'

'But Quillie wants to stay here with W-Will'um.'

'But Mummie wants to talk with W-Will'um alone.'

'You go to hell instead.'

'Quillie!'

'Oh, all right.'

She gathered up the basin and one of the brooms, and dragged them through the doorway without a word. When they were alone he stood behind her chair and put his hand on her wrist.

'Stop writing. I want to speak to you.'

'Just a minute. I must finish this note.'

'To whom are you writing?'

'To a friend of mine.'

'Oh!'

'Don't be huffy.'

'I'm not. I should not have asked.'

'I'm writing to Pat Colyer.'

' "The well-bred young gentleman who recites so beautifully." "My wit, like your temperament, is essentially adaptable." Blime, what I missed by not going to Eton!'

'I say, aren't those relatives of Lionel's a scream? My dear, Aunt Margy alarms me. She hasn't the slightest use for convention herself, and lets everyone know it, too. You remember her remark about the stocking? Well, just for a rag, I wore a harlequin bathing dress on Peace Day. I gave a stocking to Naps for bravado when he asked for it, and he tied it round the neck of a puppy he's walking. Aunt Margy saw it afterwards, and gave me such a look. One has to be very careful with Aunt

Margy—she knows things by intuition. When she looks at me sometimes, I do, indeed, feel a lady of uneasy virtue! Often when I see her I think—"There goes Evelyn Fairfax forty years on."'

'Oh, no, Eve.'

'Oh, yes, Billy. You will be white-haired, too, very tall, and distinguished—probably a famous playwright; but I hope you will not vaporize yourself too much—and I shall make short witty remarks from the gallery to you in the stage box. Won't I, Billjohn? Damn there's the bell. I wonder who that is?'

Martha knocked at the door. 'If you please, Miss, Mr. Warbeck wants to see you.'

'Ask him in, Marty.'

'May I come in?' enquired a suave voice. 'Good-morning, Evelyn. A note in the remembered calligraphy appended on the postern invited me to walk in.'

'Hullo, Jay Double-u. How's the black eye? How very smart you look. Do you know Captain Maddison?'

'Yes, oh, yes, we know each other. Evelyn, may I smoke?'

'Gippies and Virgins on that table. Help yourself.'

'Thank you,' replied Warbeck. 'A Virgin, I think.'

He was dressed in a bright brown suit, very tightly fitting, bright brown boots, with a high collar, a yellow bow tie, and stiff white shirt-cuffs. His reddish hair was oiled and brushed back from the high rounded forehead. Between the thick lips, in one corner of the mouth, he inserted a cigarette, struck a match on his heel, lit it, and spun the lighted match through the open window.

'It whined like a spent bullet!' cried Maddison.

'Yes,' replied Warbeck. 'That's why I did it. Evelyn, may I sit down?'

'You may.'

'Thank you.'

'You won't mind my finishing my letter, will you?'

'Can you write while I smoke?'

'Don't be an ass, Jay Double-u.'

'Thank you.'

The visitor lay back on the sofa, and looked quickly a[t] Maddison and away again. Evelyn went on writing with [a] quill pen, which scratched audibly. Warbeck cleared hi[s] throat, sat up, and addressed the other man.

'Well, how do you like Folkestone, Maddison? Or have you not considered whether you like it?'

'I find it rather an amusing place, Warbeck.'

'Oh, yes, it is an amusing place. Didn't I meet you on Peace Day? I'm very vague about it all.'

'Yes.'

'Did I borrow a pound from you?'

'I believe you did.'

'Here it is. I am most grateful. Thank you.'

'Thanks very much.'

He passed over a treasury note.

'Er—Mrs. Fairfax will probably shriek with derision when [I] ask the question—but have you read Swinburne?'

Evelyn laughed, and Warbeck wrinkled his forehead.

'No, I haven't, Warbeck.'

'Oh!'

He began to gnaw his nails.

'I've read some of Bernard Shaw.'

'I prefer that lesser writer, Shakespeare,' replied Warbeck satirically.

'And one book by Wells—*Tono Bungay*.'

'Yes, it's a good book. Yes. Wells has a great and earnes[t] mind. A trifle vulgar, perhaps, in his uninspired moments— but I hear friends manage to tear up most of the backslangin[g] letters he writes to critics in the press. One day we shall mee[t] and be friends.'

Evelyn laughed mockingly again.

'As for his fraternal friend Bennett, whose *Pretty Lady* Mrs Fairfax so adores, well, I should like to meet him, too—an[d] borrow one of his motor-cars. I have a fur coat already.'

'Don't swank,' called out Evelyn.

'Oh, well,' sighed Warbeck, and returned to his nails.

She appeared to be writing a long letter. Maddison got up and went into the kitchen. Jonquil was throwing pots and pans about the room, which Martha grumblingly picked up.

'Why, what are you doing, Quillie?' he asked.

'She's a terror, mister. Said that the place was hell, so she's smashing of it up.'

Martha broke into wheezy laughter. 'Dearie me, mister, that kid is the funniest thing I ever did see. And if it wasn't for her, I wouldn't stop here, only I promised the master when he first went away that I would. I could earn more money outside, if I'd a mind to. But I don't like leaving the baby, mister.'

'Don't you get on very well with Mrs. Fairfax, then?'

' 'Tisn't that, mister. Her and me gets on all right, mostly. But I long for the old life.'

'What, acting?'

'You are a comic, mister,' she wheezed. 'Acting! Hir-hir-he! No, I used to be in a laundry. Many a gentleman's shirt I've ironed. And washed, too. Not a few spotted with wine, either! Too true, they were! Like that there Warbeck. He's a funny fellow, mister.'

'I know he is. I've seen him before.'

'Used to come in here a lot. Very witty fellow, and has always been a perfect gentleman to me, though I am only an ugly old servant. But when he's in booze, mister, he's terrible. Dearie me, you ought to hear Miss Milly talking about him. She hates him. "A nasty fat 'Un," she called him once, and ordered him out of the house—not her house, but this house, what belongs to my lady.'

'Do you know Mr. White well, Martha?'

'Yes, mister, and he's one I feel very sorry for. He's only been in here once since she came back from Devon, and he came to me with tears in his eyes and said good-bye. But she never did like him very much. Too soppy, she said. But he was always a perfect gentleman to me.'

'Is that Sandhurst you're talking about, Martha?' asked Quillie, who during the conversation had been quietly occupied in building a heaven, with swallows, out of the ruins of hell.

'You get on with your own business, lovey, and don't poke your nose into what doesn't concern you.'

'Don't be so rude and silly, Martha. I know it was Sandhurst you meant. Quillie likes Sandhurst—he used to play with her.'

'Ain't she cute, mister? Calling 'erself Quillie. Come here, lovey, and let Marty kiss you. She's Marty's baby, mister. Ain't you, lovely?'

'Er-hum. And Will'um's, too.'

As Will'um went across the carpet to the drawing-room, he heard Warbeck say in tones of submission: 'It will be everything to me, and so little for you to give, old thing. Won't you?'

Warbeck glared at him as he entered, sighed loudly, and turned away.

'I'll let you know, but I can't promise, Jay Double-u.'

'Thank you. Will you write to me?'

'Yes.'

'Thank you. Well, I'll go now. Have you finished my volume of *Atalanta in Calydon*? Shall I take it now or leave it?' He pointed to a book lying on the table.

'I've read it, thanks.'

'What do you think of it? Or don't you think of it at all?'

'I read it with interest.'

'H'm. Oh, well! Don't you think the chorus beginning "When the hounds of spring are on winter's traces" great?'

'Yes. I mean no. Have you written any more lately?'

'Er—what? Oh, no. I'm just a scribbler at present. I shan't mature for some years. But, take a tip, and buy my first editions when they come out. Yes, I've written a sonnet or two since I saw you—er—would you care to see them? Oh, damn, I haven't got them with me.'

'In that case I'd like to see them. But, first, will you throw that yellow tie away.'

'Certainly, Mrs. Fairfax,' he said, ripping it off and throwing it out of the window. 'Good-morning.' And shaking hands with Maddison, he went out.

'Did you notice the old-world courtesy, Billy? Poor old Julian—always full of beer and Swinburne, neither of which I care very much for—but, then, I've got no taste. He has asked me to dine with him one evening next week at Corvano's restaurant. It's his twenty-first birthday.'

'Will you go?'

Down in the street Warbeck was chasing a puppy running with the yellow tie in its mouth.

'No, I don't think I shall. Quick, look! How funny! Poor Julian. He's got something fine in him, but it is covered by silly traits that time, I suppose, will work out of his nature. But that applies to all of us. I wish he'd go and do some work.'

Her husband had spoken to her almost the identical words about Lord Spreycombe, who had a wife and two small children, that morning; but Maddison did not know that. He regarded her with bright eyes and happy face.

'You know, Lina, I think you're jolly fine with men.'

'My dear, what makes you say that?'

'You're so generous. You see the good in human character. You never emphasize the weaker side in people you could afford to despise, I suppose, if you wanted to.'

'Silly Billy,' she said, coming to sit by him. 'Silly Billy, you don't know me at all. You're in love with a dream-woman, an Eve in moonlight—and that's why, in a way, I'm sorry you came here. For your very own sake, child. O, yes. Darling, come here on the sofa beside me.'

They were interrupted by: 'Mummie, can Quillie go out on the Leas?'

'Not alone, darling girl. Quillie might get stolen.'

'Quillie would like that.'

'Why?'

'So's Will'um could rescue her.'

'Precocious huzzy!' cried Evelyn, snatching her. 'Hug Mummie close. Quillie is Mummie's very own daughter. Kiss Mummie, my silkenhair. How Mummie wishes her own hair was soft like Quillie's and not coarse and thick.'

'Mummie.'

'Yes, darling!'

'Is Jay Double-u coming again?'

'I hope not, darling.'

Silence, while Quillie caressed her mother. Then a murmur of 'Mummie'.

'What, sweetheart?'

'Can W-W-Will'um live with us always when Daddy goes back to ther East?'

'My dear, what a question! I wish he could.'

'So do I, Mummie.'

'Why do you wish he could, Quillie?'

Silence again, and gentle breathing; child head snuggling closer, bare arms twining tighter, and the soft confession ' 'Cause Quillie loves W-W-Will'um.'

'W-W-Will'um,' mocked Evelyn. 'You are the spit of your naughty mother.'

The letter was posted, and the three went for a walk along the promenade. Jonquil walked between them, holding their hands, her pale blue silk pinafore blown by the cool sea breezes. The sun-hot asphalt burned through the thin leather of their shoes. People sitting on the seats were interested in them, and sometimes smiling remarks were made about the child. They walked to the bandstand, and sat down in the front row of the deck-chairs. Jonquil espied a friend, and darted away to play with him—an urchin with a fat collie pup. Billjohn rushed after her. The band was playing a soothing air. Maddison lay back in the chair and with closed eyes yielded to the golden happiness given by the sun on his face. He suggested that Evelyn should do the same, but she preferred, he was told, the protection of a wide hat.

'You liked the sun in Devon.'

'This is Folkestone, where it isn't done to take off one's hat.'

'I thought you were so unconventional.'

'Dear Will'um, you talk too much.'

Jonquil returned with the squirming pup in her arms, at which the spaniel was playfully leaping, declaring that she wanted five shillings, in order to pay a little boy.

'You can't have that mongrel. Tell him to take it back.'

'Here, take your mongrel back,' Jonquil ordered the grinning urchin, who called the pup and swaggered away.

Their position was such that everyone passing could see them. The first friend to come up was the stripling form of a cadet; he passed twice before deciding to go to them.

'Hullo, Sandhurst,' smiled Evelyn.

He saluted stiffly, and gave Maddison a timid look.

'Do you know Captain Maddison?'

'Yes, I've met him before. How do you do, sir?'

Maddison rose and shook hands, saying:

'Don't call me "sir" again, whatever you do. Lord, I'm only twenty-two! Come and sit down.'

'Thanks awfully.'

He hesitated for a moment whether to sit beside Evelyn or Maddison, and sat beside Maddison.

'Sandy, dear, the wind's so cold on my left side.'

'Oh, I beg your pardon, Mrs. Fairfax!' said Peter White, jumping up and sitting beside Evelyn.

'What have you been doing with yourself, Sandy? I haven't seen very much of you, have I?'

'I only had forty-eight hours' leave last time, and I meant to write and apologize for not turning up to lunch. The fact is—'

'You were blotto, I suppose?'

'Yes.

'Silly child! You know it isn't good for you.'

'I suppose I am an awful fool.'

'Not so bad as that, my dear   How long are you here for? When did you arrive?'

'I arrived last night. I've got six days.'

'Sick leave?'

'Yes,' he grinned shamedly.

'Swinging the lead again?'

He confessed that he had not been so ill as he had insisted to the medical officer.

After an hour with him, Maddison realized from his manner that he was desperately in love with Evelyn. He felt no jealousy, only pity, since Evelyn did not love him. He liked him; the boy had a radiant mind. White's head was boyish and well shaped, with a little chin, mobile wide mouth, and snub nose. The alert, hazel eyes showed a temperament too sensitive and emotional; it was obvious as they talked that he was trying to be friends. So might he himself have been in 1914, when desperately in love with Elsie Norman. The terrible darkness of adolescent love! Yes, he must befriend the boy.

At tea that afternoon he discovered that Sandy was passionately fond of wild birds, and of the writing of W. H. Hudson.

'I've got most of his books, Captain Maddison. I'll lend them to you. *Far Away and Long Ago* you will love. Miss Ogilvie—you know her, don't you—has got it at present. It's a most beautiful book. Mrs. Fairfax read it, didn't you, Mrs. Fairfax?'

Evelyn, sitting on a low stool and talking to Tubby Lorayne and Miss Pamment, looked up. 'Who's that taking the honourable name of Fairfax in vain? Sandy White. My dear Sandy, only tradespeople are allowed to call me "Missis Fairfax". To the others I am Lina.'

She looked steadily at him, and he blushed.

'Now, tell me what you want.'

He stammered it was only about a book.

'I was telling Captain Maddison——'

'You mean Bill?'

'Yes. I was telling him you had read a book called *Far Away and Long Ago*. It's wonderful, isn't it?'

'Perfectly splendid, my dear. How about some more tea? Will you run and get a jug of hot water? Thanks so much.'

Eagerly he went out with the jug, and while he was out of the room, she said: 'Poor Sandy, excitable as a child. Frankly, I didn't read the book, and I didn't have the heart to tell him so. Don't ever say I told you that, for heaven's sake.'

They laughed. Maddison felt an icicle forming in his breast. When Sandy came back he tried to talk to him; but the boy seemed to have lost all heart, as though he had heard what she had said. Soon afterwards he left the flat.

The return of Major Fairfax from London was to be made just before dinner, according to a telegram which came at noon on the following day. Maddison was sitting on a lionskin at her feet, awaiting in silence the dread arrival, when a chance remark recalled the incident of her careless acquiescence to Sandy's enthusiasm. Although he persuaded himself that she had said it in order not to hurt his feelings, yet a persistent pain of doubt remained. He thought, too, of the incident of the time-table and the Scarlet Crane's-bill, but dared not mention it. Her hand straying through his hair made sharper the pain, so that suddenly he knelt at her knees and hid his face in her lap.

'Once you said that love was the only justification of life. I thought that dream was. I was wrong, Eve, my beautiful one, I should die if I lost you.'

'Would you, Billy?'

'I am tortured when I think of your many many friends. Damn those men who treat you with familiarity!'

'Dearest Billy, why this thusness?'

'I can't help it. I must tell you, or die. Why should they flaunt your beauty as though you were someone other than Evelyn Fairfax. Why should you write for nearly an hour to a bloody little bas—a beastly little nincompoop like that fellow Colyer!'

'Lorlumme, the lad nearly swore! Poor Pat!'

'Blast him! Poseur! "My wit, like your temperament"—Good God!'

'Jealous little thing.'

'I'm not jealous.'

'You are.'

'Not in the way you mean. I am not jealous of you, but jealous for you, for your beauty, for your spirit. I would be content to be allowed to guard you. You are very precious, Eve; to me you are, O, as glorious as the sun.'

'So you are content to guard me, are you?'

'You don't understand,' he muttered, apprehensive at her tone of voice.

'Of course not. I'm just a fool. How like a child you are. Almost persuadest me thou art a man!'

He sprang away, but she pulled him back.

'If you hurt me, I shall hurt you. But I hate this idea of guardianship. You talk like Lionel. I am Eve. You are Billy. We are necessary for each other's harmony. Why think further?'

'But, Eve, you are too fine to be spoiled by unworthy——'

'Gosh, help yourself to flowers. In other words, you want me for yourself.'

'Yes, I do want you, but openly, what is called honourably, for your sake.'

'Silly fool, why wrap it up in all that involved talk! Still, it's part of your dream to do that, isn't it?'

'O Eve!'

'O Billy!' she mocked, looking at him with brooding sweetness in her eyes. He was humble before her, and she tilted his chin. 'No woman could resist you at times. Not even proud

266

little Mary Ogilvie. But you haven't wanted to kiss me when I've wanted to kiss you, so you shan't start now.'

'Don't talk like that, Eve.'

'All right. Let me finish. At other times you are a bore, and no woman—even Aunt Milly—could stick you!'

He edged away from her, and said in an altered voice: 'I don't understand you sometimes.'

'How like a man!'

'Eve, I——'

'You're a clumsy old thing. Oddmedodd Bill—the scarecrow of love! I've been waiting for the scarecrow to come alive, for the vivacious and eager youth to step out of the straw and rags of mournful brooding, to say one thing—I've been waiting to kiss you, and you've been using as many words as possible, all mighty fine, no doubt, but a waste of time. Billy, don't you love me?'

'You know I do.'

'Then why not say so?'

'I love you.'

'You're a clumsy old fool, little wild boy with the brown eyes, but—I—adore—you—for—it,' she said, kissing him between each word. He cursed violently, as below in the road a boy with evening papers shouted his wares.

'Lionel will be here soon. The London train is in. Damn!'

'Your fault, Billy! Your words, words, words, my darling!'

On hearing his whistle below, she sprang up, tidied her hair in the glass, and went outside, pulling-to the door. It did not close, and Maddison heard him say:

'Well, old girl, it's been successful. But I may have to go off very soon.'

'Oh, L-Linky, dear, I hope not,' she said softly and tenderly.

Through the crack in the door Maddison saw her arms around his neck, and the kisses that impulsively she gave him. He had a glacial desire to walk out of the house, but controlled

himself; and almost immediately Major Fairfax was in the
room and greeting him cordially.

'Well, Bill, it's fine to be back.'

He pulled a new pipe out of his pocket.

'Awful hot in town. Serious water shortage. I got this pipe
for you. Noticed your own was a bit battered. Straight grain.
Got one for myself.'

'Haven't you got a present for little me?' asked Evelyn.

'I haven't forgotten you. Come into the other room, and I'll
show you. Jove, I'm hungry. Is dinner ready? Stopping, Bill
aren't you?'

'Thank you, Lionel.'

'Good man.'

He was left alone, with a straight-grain briar pipe in his
hand. Then, noticing some rug-hair and dust on his knees he
hurriedly brushed them. In one of his socks was a hole.

Chapter 23

MAJOR FAIRFAX observed this after dinner, and Evelyn at once ordered Bill to bring to the flat everything of his that needed repairing. The two pairs of socks that he brought a few days later were not worth mending, she declared, and, over-come with compassion for the state of his feet, she took him shopping. First she called at the bank, in order to cash a cheque. The manager asked her if she was entering for the tennis tournament.

'We confidently expect General Fairfax to pull off the men's singles, you know, Mrs. Fairfax.'

'Yes, he's quite good, isn't he?'

'I was watching him the other night, playing with Miss Pamment. A really brilliant couple. For such a little lady the smashes and volleys of Miss Pamment's are really remarkable, don't you think?'

'Do you know, I'm afraid I haven't seen her playing?'

'Oh, yes. Awfully hot weather, isn't it?'

'I love it, Mr. Walpole.'

'We poor slaves, you know, Mrs. Fairfax.'

The manager moved away, and Evelyn pushed the cheque over to the cashier.

'Let me see my account, will you, please?'

The notes were flipped and counted, recounted, and pushed under the grill. A clerk brought the ledger, and she inspected it. The next call was made at a wool shop. Major Fairfax, as before, preferred to wait outside. Maddison and Evelyn went in together. 'What colour would you like, Billy?'

'Auburn, for your hair.'

269

'My poo-oor boy, as Aunt Margy would say. Carroty socks!'

'Then yellow—the colour of my favourite flowers.'

'Daffodils?'

'No: hawkbit—a kind of dandelion.'

'What funny taste! They're weeds,' she said, teasing him.

'Have you looked at the disc of one? Lovely things—small suns.'

She smiled at the girl who was humbly waiting behind the counter.

'Let me see some heather mixture, please.'

She went to get some skeins, and Evelyn said to him: 'I, too, love dandelions. But not yellow socks, besides, Jay Double-u sometimes wears yellow socks with black and red lines. Beastly things. That reminds me, why did you pay that tenner into my bank?'

'What tenner?'

'You know perfectly well. I think that a mean way to treat a gift.'

'But I was awfully grateful for the loan.'

'Silly fool! Still, have it your own way.'

'I'm very grateful.'

'You look it. That's what Naps says: "I'm very grateful".'

'When's he coming back?'

'Naps? The lord only knows. Joke, ha ha. He's gone north to the moors. My dear, we shall be eating grouse soon. I can tell you, it's very convenient having such aristocratic pals.'

'It must be. Sorry I'm just a nobody.'

'You're not. You're a very big somebody—to me.'

Eventually she bought needles, and nine two-ounce skeins of three different shaded wools, and with the parcel under his arm they went into the brilliant light of the street.

'The infant wanted yellow, Lionel. Awful taste!'

'No, we mustn't let him become a Bohemian, must we?'

They had ice creams in ginger beer and meringues at Corvano's restaurant, meeting there the aunts Millicent and

Marjorie. Evelyn asked them if they would like to go with them on the next Monday to the theatre.

'My dears, it's such fun. I managed to get a perfectly good box for nothing! You must come with Lionel and Bill and me.'

'That's news to me, darling,' said Lionel. 'How did you manage it?'

'Ah ha, that's a secret!'

'But, Lina, how perfectly priceless!' exclaimed Milly Fairfax, clapping her hands. 'What a gel you are, to be sure! On Monday night? I shall have to put poor father to bed early.'

'Don't forget Tommy,' said Maddison.

'Oh, yes, and Tommy! Don't you laugh at my father! But Lina, darling, do tell me how you managed a free box! It's the new revue, *What Next, Dearie?* they're trying out for London, isn't it? Oh, what joy!'

'No. *What Next, Dearie?*'

'Oo-oh!' said Lionel.

Maddison said: 'I say, won't you all dine with me here, first?'

Millie clapped her hands. 'What will Father say about all this gaiety? Do you think I dare ask him, Lina? He might disapprove. He is so early Victorian about me; poor Father!'

It was decided that they would dine there on the Monday evening; and Maddison reserved a table.

At lunch that day Evelyn told her husband that Julian Warbeck had invited her to dine at Corvano's on his birthday. She said that she had not accepted, as she meant to speak to him first. She winked at Maddison, unseen by Lionel, as she spoke.

'I would rather you didn't, Lina, old girl. I don't want you to be talked about, m'dear. Besides, I don't think you ought to have anything to do with him whatever. He doesn't live down here, does he?'

'In London somewhere, I think.'

'He ought to get back there, and do some work.'

'He's supposed to be a poet.'

'That's an awfully convenient thing to be. Personally, I

consider that most so-called poets are indolent by nature, and
are simply time-wasters.'

'You're an old materialist, my dear.'

'Possibly I am, but then, I've seen more of life than you have.'

'I wonder!'

'I don't.'

'Oh, you're so terribly old and wise, aren't you, Lionel?
Billy and I are young ignoramuses.'

'Yes, I suppose I do seem terribly old.'

'My dear, I was only ragging you.' Her hand sought his
under the table. Lionel went on:

'But it's a good thing, I sometimes think, that I am old.'

'You're not, you silly,' laughed Evelyn, and he smiled at her.

'But do you really think, Lionel,' asked Maddison, 'that
poetry is the child of indolence?'

'Certainly not, Bill. I have no theories about poetry. I'm
simply stating facts. There are, I know, exceptions—men of
clear vision, who live blameless lives, and whose achievements
are magnificent because they themselves are magnificent. All
a question of curbing, in youth, the desire to let things slide.
But that's true of every one of us. All character that's worth
anything is built up bit by bit. That's the sort of man I care
about.'

'Yes.'

'Nobody's faultless. We all make mistakes. Some make the
same mistake several times. But they needn't worry. The time
comes when they realize it was a mistake, and they don't do it
again. Result—head held a little higher, moral fibre toughened
a bit. But it's all a question of realizing it for oneself. But you
don't want to hear my platitudes. Have another cutlet?'

'No, thank you.'

'Won't you, really? You haven't eaten half a meal, m'dear
fellow. Lina, shovel it on to his plate. Go on, Bill, get it down
you—you want to fatten up a bit. Have another glass of beer?'

'Thanks.'

As soon as they were alone Evelyn said:

'At lunch Lionel was referring to me. He ought to have been a parson.'

'I thought he meant me. It was not a pleasant thought. Eve, I think I am one of those indolent wasters he spoke about.'

'Silly boy! Of course it doesn't apply to you. Anyone can tell from your face what you are.'

He said: 'Then the blacker hypocrite I must be.'

'Don't worry, Mis'r Masson. It would never enable you to get anyone's fortune.'

'Eve, tell me how you managed to get the free box for *What Next, Dearie?*'

'The author's a friend.'

'How long have you known him?'

'Aren't you inquisitive!'

'Tell me!'

' "Should a woman tell?" '

'Please!'

'Why should I? Where are you going?'

'For a walk.'

'Hope it keeps fine for you!' she called out as he opened the hall door.

His dinner jacket, for which he had written to his home at Rookhurst, arrived two days before he would need it for the theatre. It was accompanied by a letter from his father.

'FAWLEY HOUSE,
ROOKHURST,
11th August, 1919.

MY DEAR WILLIE,

Your letter was delayed owing to my temporary absence from home, and on my return I was most pleased to hear from you. I send the suit as requested, together with a pair of pumps and some black socks, which (I imagine) will be too small for you. The whole suit (which reeks of lavender and mothball, but that is Biddy's business; blame her, not me), I expect, will be too small: it was made, you will remember, just before the war. Clothes are so very expensive nowadays, and may I suggest that the coat and trousers could be made bigger if you get a tailor to open the seams; I am at present wearing a suit that has been turned (my old Harris tweed), and Biddy assures me that it looks 'proper'. Biddy, by the way, is as well as ever, and just the same. I have told her how happy and well you are, and she is delighted, and begs me to send you her love.

'The Normans (so I am told, but cannot be sure) are in Folkestone for the summer. But you may have met them. We suffer a good deal from lack of rain, but it is a general drought according to the papers. I am expecting your uncle Richard to stay the night here shortly, for a few days. Recently I saw him in town, he looks fagged out, poor chap; he had a very arduous time during the war in the Special Constabulary, and was blown up by a Zeppelin bomb. Your cousin Phillip, it appears, is giving him cause for much anxiety, owing to the resigning of his commission, which, as you know, was in a regular battalion, and for no reason whatsoever, apparently. These are unsettling times.

'Everything is much the same, and I live on, not quite knowing why. The garden suffers from want of rain. We had the Otter Hounds here last week, but they did not kill, you will be glad to hear. The rooks have not come back to us; the rifle and machine gun range drove them away. They have not yet begun to plant out new trees to replace the beeches felled during the war. Colonel Tetley asked for you the other day. Peggy Temperley is going to be married soon, to whom I don't know. Mr. Temperley has bought a Ford car.

'The Americans seem to be behaving in a peculiar manner, don't you think? I mean in regard to France and the Peace Treaty. A great pity, after the splendid way they came over last year. As a nation they are magnanimous only by impulse, splendidly magnanimous, like some of the actions of youth.

they cancel their magnanimity because they are not mature in that quality. Wilson is a great man, but his type should never be a statesman, for his realm is higher and his work is to inspire the minds of others when they are tranquil, and not concerned with material things like government.

'Let me hear, when you have a spare half hour or so, how you are getting on. I have not any idea as to whether or no you have got a job in Folkestone, or how long you have been there. I am glad you have got such nice friends, and trust you will retain their friendship. That, in my experience, is one of the hardest things in the world.

'This must go to the post now, so I will conclude. Accept my best wishes, my dear Willie, from

Your affec. Father,

JOHN MADDISON.

'I forward herewith a circular from your old school. Apparently they want particulars of your service, for the Roll of Honour. It has been here since June, but I did not know your address.

J.M.'

Maddison promptly tore up the circular from Colham School. 'My standard of honour still needs to be raised,' he muttered, as he opened the window and threw the handful into the air. 'No Rolls of Honour for my sort.'

Major Fairfax offered to lend him a suit when, with laughter, he tried on the dinner jacket. And in these borrowed clothes he took his friends to dine, at half past seven on the Monday night, to Corvano's restaurant in the High Street.

They entered through wide swing-doors, which were held open by a big flat-footed commissionaire in a chocolate and yellow uniform, with gargantuan moustache and hands. His local name was The Beetle-Squasher. In the lounge dozens of copper-topped tables stood, with people sitting at them, drinking beer, wine, spirits and coffee. Beyond was the dining-room. People looked up as they entered, including Julian Warbeck, who, dressed in a tail coat, was standing at the bar, a glass of whiskey before him.

'How do you do,' he said gravely, and bowed.

'Good evening,' replied Major Fairfax, as they passed.

'O my God,' said Evelyn, 'I forgot to write to him!'

When they were seated at their table in the restaurant, a place of mirrors that reflected infinite roomsful of waiters, diners, and red and gilt upholstery, Julian Warbeck, with flushed face, went and sat at a table laid for two, near them. Of the soup he took a single sip, flinging the spoon into the plate and pushing it away. He put a cigarette into his mouth, felt for matches, frowned, and rising, went to their table, bowing gravely and asking for the loan of a match.

'Have you such a thing? Thank you. I am compelled to smoke in order to ward off the pangs of hunger. That human carrion-crow brought me soup that had hairs in it. Unlike those on the heads of human beings, they were numberless. Your matches, sir. Thank you.'

He bowed, gave a cold look at Evelyn, and returned.

'He's drunk,' said Mrs. Beayne. 'But the poor child makes an effort to hold his liquor werry werry well. And his wit pleases me.'

His waiter, who certainly bore some resemblance to a crow owing to flapping coat tails, black eyes, coracoid nose, apparently no mouth, and absolutely no chin, brought a bottle of champagne and took away the soup. Julian, after an ostentatious inspection of the fish, groaned audibly that it was anæmic cod again, and gave it to a cat that was rubbing against his legs. Another bottle of wine was brought with the chicken, and at the end of the dinner a bottle of brandy. After drinking five glasses of this as quickly as possible, he called the waiter and said something to him. The waiter hopped over to their table, and said that the gentleman would be honoured if they would drink his health.

Maddison looked at Major Fairfax, who asked: 'What do you think, Bill?'

Maddison referred to Evelyn, who in turn asked Mrs. Beayne, receiving in reply: 'Why ever not?'

So five liqueur glasses were brought, four and a quarter of them being filled. After hesitation, Julian Warbeck came over to their table and said solemnly:

'I would rather you did *not* drink my health. I have changed my mind. I have just recollected, with a recrudescence of pain and embarrassment, that Miss Fairfax, the last time I saw her, ordered me out of her father's house with words of a screaming voice about policemen and—p-oo-um—excuse me—p-prison! I care nothing for any of you. I heard the sneering remark of you, sir!' glaring at Maddison; 'and were you not so obviously an outsider like your lank cousin, I would—by God—Oh, why should I tolerate such insolence?'

He gnawed his lips, puckered up his face, clenched his right hand and gave an agonized look toward the ceiling.

'Forgive me, Lina.'

'I should go home to bed, if I were you, Jay Double-u.'

'You want to get rid of me. You think I'm drunk, don't you?'—facing Major Fairfax—'but I'm *not* drunk. I've known Mrs. Fairfax for six months, nearly—I could tell you the very day I met her—and I asked her to dine with me this night— my coming of age. But that's nothing to do with anyone—no one cares about me. But wait! One day the world will listen to me—when I am dead! Oh, forgive me. I have no friends— not even a Watts-Dunton, to whom I can crawl.'

His voice changed, and looking straight at Evelyn, he said:

'You, Mrs. Fairfax, for whom I have the deepest regard and respect, you promised to write to me about dining with me to-night. I have received no such letter. I hoped that you would come at the last moment. You came all right—yes, you came. Oh, it's intolerable, intolerable!'

Diners at the other tables began to turn and watch him. The

human carrion-crow hovered near, moving about silently.

'I owe you an apology, Jay Double-u—and truthfully, I forgot all about it until I saw you here. Please accept my apology.'

'Thank you. Will you drink with me?'

'Fetch a chair and sit down for a bit, won't you?' invited Major Fairfax. 'Have a cigar. We've got to go shortly—to the theatre.'

The chair was brought, and he sat down while they drank his health. Just as Maddison was about to sip, Julian protested.

'I would rather you did not drink my health, you—oo, um—excuse me, ladies—you sneering beast!'

'My dear Warbeck, I assure you I wasn't sneering!'

'You were! By God, I won't tolerate it. You shall *not* drink my health!'

'Would you like me to pour it back into the bottle?'

'What,' roared Warbeck. 'You long, lounging, insolent hound! By God, you are all against me. With the saliva of your pale tongues you would quench my mind-fire! You would drive me back to the gallipots. By God, Maddison, you dark devil, don't you look at me any more!'

'Look here,' said Major Fairfax, rising. 'Leave this table, or I shall call a constable and have you confined. Your brain must be deranged.'

'Deranged? How dare you, sir?' The voice sank. 'Yes, you're right. I'm nearly burnt out. Yes, you're right. O well! I—no—I——' Tears stopped the words.

They rose from the table and left him. Miss Fairfax was trembling with fear and indignation, and Evelyn's face was inscrutable. They waited while the commissionaire beckoned their cab, and Maddison heard Lionel say to her: 'You see, I was right, m'dear.'

'Oh, yes, you told me so,' drawled Evelyn. 'But, then, you always tell me so, don't you?'

They went through the lounge in strained silence.

Behind were voices in argument.

'Put it down to my account.'

'We keep no books 'ere, sar.'

'I cannot pay now. To-morrow.'

'Perhaps you care to leaf a guarantee, sar.'

'Don't touch me, you greasy fungus!'

'I call plizman!'

'Intolerable insolence! I tell you I will pay to-morrow.'

'What is your name and address?'

'I will not speak to you. Leave me. I will pay to-morrow.'

Taking his opera hat, a cloak lined with blue silk, and a silver-mounted ebony stick, Julian Warbeck strode towards the swing door. The restraining hand of the proprietor was pushed away. But way to the street was barred by The Beetle-Squasher.

'Just a moment,' said Maddison, going back to the restaurant.

'Forgive me, Warbeck, but had I known that it was your birthday, and that you were expecting—I mean, that you were going to be alone, I would have asked you to join our table. I know how rotten and miserable it feels to be alone.'

'I don't care what you say!'

'Very well. Good-bye.'

Warbeck gripped his arm. 'Don't go.'

'I must.'

'Have a drink with me. For God's sake, don't desert me!'

'Sorry, I must go.'

'Very well, go! I can do without your friendship.'

Maddison went back to the cab. Nothing was said about Julian, but as they were going to their box, Eve whispered that he was a dear.

Chapter 24

THEY occupied the lowest box on the right-hand side of the theatre; a very superior lady attendant showed them into their seats. Miss Fairfax sat nearest the stage; by turning round in her seat she could see almost the whole house. Maddison sat next to her, a big box of chocolates on the lap of his intensely-creased trousers. Evelyn, who found interest in the people who sat in the stalls, was between Mrs. Beayne and her husband, politely attentive to the remarks that he made.

Mr. 'Jimmy' Skinner, lessee and part-owner of the 'Entente Cordiale Theatre', regarded the house through a monocle from the further entrance to the stalls. A silk hat was thrust far back on his great rugged head. He pulled at a long black cigar, and as he sent wreaths of smoke over the stalls he inspected methodically all the women. He bowed deeply towards Evelyn's box. Evelyn waved her hand. Lionel looked at her; glanced away.

Someone knocked at the door of the box. The door was half opened. A young man with a clean-shaven browny-red face looked in. His even white teeth showed in a smile. His dark hair shone; his stiff shirt gleamed very white.

'May I come in?'

'Hullo!' cried Evelyn. 'Come in and meet my Aunts. This is Mr. de la Hay, the author of *What Next, Dearie?* Major Fairfax, my husband. And Captain Maddison!'

'I say, don't give me away like that,' laughed the man, in a clear baritone voice. His eye-sockets and lids were blue with greasepaint. His languid glance was equally given to all in the box. 'Wait till you see if it gets across.' He laughed again. 'I'm awfully nervous.'

'Mr. de la Hay sings and dances, as well as having written the book and the lyrics,' said Evelyn. 'Isn't that the right term—"write the book"?'

'I must tell you a story,' replied the actor. 'My last show flopped so badly that the last two houses were practically "paper"—complimentary tickets to friends, etc. We sold one stall, however, and when the chap asked at the box office "What time does the show start to-night?" the b.o. manager replied: "Any time you like, sir." Ha ha ha! Isn't it good? I thought of giving it a line in my next play. I say, I must run away now. Forgive me. I say, Mrs. Fairfax, Consuelo wants to see you sometime—you met her at rehearsal, if you remember. She asked me to tell you she was "at home" in her dressing room if you'd like to go and see her.'

'Rather!' said Evelyn. 'I talked to Consuelo Fitzroy,' she explained to Lionel, 'about going on the stage. She's perfectly sweet. You'll see her in the show—she sings and dances with Aubrey.' To de la Hay: 'Is there time to see her now?'

De la Hay gracefully lifted her hand, and glanced at her wristlet watch. 'Yes, but we must rush. We open in about four minutes. Good-bye, and I hope you enjoy the show!'

He held the door open for Evelyn, who went out with him. The door closed.

'Goodness gracious me!' exclaimed Miss Fairfax. 'How does Lina make so many charming friends? She never told me that she knew any of these people! What a lucky gel she is! Did you know, Lionel?'

'She mentioned she had met some actress or other,' replied Lionel, and he turned to watch the members of the orchestra entering through the door under the middle of the stage.

'There's Miss Pamment with her mother,' exclaimed Miss Fairfax, 'just coming in. How absolutely ripping they look. Oh, to have money to buy nice things! How do you do?' She

281

inclined her head: 'And Sir John. How graceful he is. How do you do? Just a typical sailor, isn't he? So breezy!'

No one seemed to have heard her comments.

'And there's Sir Rudolph Cardew, the veteran actor, who is eighty this year. How do you do, Sir Rudolph? Isn't he sweet, Billy—but I shouldn't have called you that, should I? And yet—Captain Maddison is so formal. May I call you Billy?'

'I wish you would, Miss Fairfax.'

'Don't call me Miss Fairfax, please, Billy! Everyone calls me Milly. Won't you?'

'I would love to—Milly.'

'That sounds so much nicer.'

'And may Aunt Margy call you Billy?' asked Mrs. Beayne in her deep voice. 'Don't worry, I shan't ask you to kiss me next.'

'I shall do that without asking, Aunt Margy.'

'Here, you two!' laughed Miss Fairfax. 'I feel quite gay. Drinking that man's health has affected me.'

'I must keep an eye on you, my poor girl,' said her sister.

Milly leaned forward eagerly. The orchestra was tuning up; the conductor, who also played the piano in the middle of the space alluded to as the trenches by many successive comedians, was vamping softly to himself; the 'celloists were reproducing deep grumbles from their instruments; the violinists sending little plaintive sighs into the murmuring audience.

'There's Mr. Norman, with his daughter and her fiancé. Oh, to be able to paint, Billy! And there's Mary Ogilvie—isn't she sweet? So young and innocent—oh, if I were twenty again!'

'You are twenty in spirit,' replied Maddison.

'Dear Billy, how sweet of you,' murmured Milly, sighing. 'Ah, the lights are going out! I wonder where Lina is? Enjoying herself, I expect.'

The overture commenced, and the audience sat back and settled down in their seats. Once the overture was really going, the conductor abandoned the piano and waved his arms with an easy familiar movement that seemed to entrance Miss Fairfax. A red light shone for an instant beside the conductor, a buzzer sounded its note of warning, and at the click of his baton on the illumined music frame before him the music suddenly subsided. An anxious pause, while he gazed round with uplifted arms; another tap, the lights in the theatre sank; with a sigh of indrawn breath Milly settled further into her seat as the haunting refrain of the theme song of the revue, *Your eyes tell me a story, dearie*, throbbed rhythmically to the roof.

The curtain swayed upwards, revealing a company of actors and actresses, and nearly synchronizing with a burst of song, the words of which were unintelligible to the listeners.

Maddison looked for the actor—what was his name?—but could not see him. In the middle of the chorus—when the girls on the stage, clad in summer gowns and wide hats with ribbons, turned to the men in evening dress standing by the scenery—he leaned forward, scanning the faces. Each man raised a hat made shiny with glycerine, each man offered an arm to a girl, each pair wandered off, talking inaudibly. As the last pair left the stage a small man dressed in oversize clothes entered, with a grin at the audience, for 'a spot of old man giggle-water', meaning whiskey. Obviously not Eve's friend. This entrance into the hotel was only effected after difficulty, for he appeared to be unacquainted with the revolving door, ran round and round, faster and faster, evoking roars of laughter from the audience which became applause as he was flung in, after several somersaults. Meeting the manager, the comedian asked for a job, saying that he was a retired general, whose experiences in the army had developed initiative, resource, personality, although otherwise he had no qualifications.

'What were you before you joined the Army?'

'Happy'; and those in the cheaper seats cheered. He sang a song about war babies, and went off.

'Vulgar beast,' remarked Milly, looking scornfully at the stage. 'When is that nice Mr. de la Hay coming on?'

'The author, you mean?' asked Maddison, ironically.

'Yes, but he's acting as well, I think, isn't he?' replied Milly

'Over her head,' murmured Lionel to Maddison. Immediately Maddison wondered how much Lionel understood. And where was Eve, and why did she not return?

The orchestra increased to a crescendo. Ah, there he was Clapping of hands. 'Bravo,' cried Milly, in a voice that she wanted to be bold and loud, but was actually like a dove cooing

Maddison felt more depressed as he watched the confidently-dressed de la Hay, heard the rich clear voice, the laugh, the easy gestures, the way he raised his silk hat and carried his cane. He was a neat and precise and supple dancer.

'That's Consuelo Fitzroy,' whispered Milly, excited, after putting on spectacles to study the programme. 'That's Lina's friend. Oh, isn't she lovely. How graceful! Surely they must be in love with each other to be able to sing and dance like that together! Isn't her smile too, too lovely? Oh, I hope she asks me round behind the scenes, too. I would so love to meet Miss Fitzroy. The stage always thrills me—Oh, dear, it was such fun during the war when I was with the Glad-Eye Concert Party. We used to go miles away to sing to the Tommies, free car rides, nice food to eat, nice people to talk to—oh, dear, I am almost sorry the war's over. That sounds awful, doesn't it?'

'I know the feeling, Milly. I often have it myself. They were the days!'

'They were! You're perfectly right, Billy.'

The chorus returned, entering from everywhere at once, and in curious steps, trooping on the stage and pointing playful but accusing fingers at the lovers. The chorus finished, they went away with similar dancing steps, and an old gentleman with long side-whiskers made a tempestuous entrance in search of his daughter, who began to sob on a sofa while her lover lit a cigarette and tossed the match among the orchestra. He leaned negligently on his stick, a smile on his face, waiting for the millionaire's rage to abate. Maddison saw that he was, behind his stage smile, inspecting Lionel and himself. The father, peaking in a harsh Americanese voice—'Isn't he just like the Americans,' observed Milly, who had met none—gave her a week to decide whether she would marry the Honourable Willy Rinkle-Wyse-Whystle, or refusing to wed him be turned adrift with no prospect of inheriting the hundred million dollars made out of pork and beans during the war. His daughter scorned the money made out of pork and beans during the war, and threw herself into the arms of the penniless lover, a thing which drew forth congratulations from the not-to-be-deceived onlookers.

After a series of comic interludes, songs, and dances, in which it was revealed to the audience that the poor suitor was a real peer and a detective as well, and that the Honourable Willy Rinkle-Wyse-Whystle was in reality the leader of a notorious band of blackmailers journeying round the world to various hotels, followed too late by the detective, the curtain descended on the first act, accompanied by much noise from the orchestra, and those in the cheaper seats of the theatre made a rush to get beer before the refreshment bar closed. Sir Rudolph Cardew, the veteran actor, was observed to make a distinguished exit from the stalls, taking his famous hat with him. He returned no more.

'It's jolly good fun,' exclaimed Milly. 'I wonder where Lina is?'

'Well, Billy, enjoying yourself?' asked Mrs. Beayne.

He nodded.

Evelyn returned and sat down. Several faces were turned to the box, watching the brilliance and animation of her face. They went outside, to smoke in the lounge; and on returning missed Maddison.

'Where's Billy?'

'Look, he's sitting beside Mary Ogilvie,' whispered Milly. There was a vacant seat, I noticed. I always thought they liked each other—a perfect little pair, aren't they? Oh, the orchestra is about to begin. Hush!'

THE DREAM OF FAIR WOMEN

The scene was a market square in China. The music was
conventionally oriental. The play commenced with all the
players grouped together on the stage; Chinese ladies in a
semi-circle, the principals in front—including the millionaire
of pork and beans, who had apparently forgiven his daughter
at least during the chorus—and the same sunburned gentlemen
behind in evening dress and shiny hats, and all singing in manly
voices the words of a song that was destined to become most
popular.

> *I want to tease my little pixie,*
> *That I've left down in Dixie,*
> *I want to kiss her bright blue eyes,*
> *And win for her my prize!*
> > *She's*
> > *The cutest,*
> > *The neatest,*
> > *The sweetest,*
> > *The most dinky*
> > *Peach I've known*
> *So when my wild oats are sown*
> *I think I'll toddle home.*
> > *And*
> > *Tease my*
> > *Very homely,*
> > *Very lonely,*
> > *Very comely*
> > *One-and-only*
> > *Pixie.*

The audience roared their applause when this lyric had been
sung for the third encore; but someone, possibly a drunken
soldier in the gallery, threw some halfpennies on the stage,
which the ex-major-general, now a Chinese waiter with long
flapping boots, a pigtail with a telephone receiver tied to it,
and the imprint of a white handmark on the seat of his pants,

picked up and asked 'Who's given me another gratuity?' which occasioned much clapping from the ex-soldiers in the seats near the ceiling, one being so carried away that he shouted out: 'Write to *John Bull* about it', which suggestion was cheered by those on the uncomfortable wooden forms beside him.

Next came the song of the evening—the song to whose tune half London and New York were to dance the following winter —*Your Eyes Tell me a Story, Dearie*—sung in unison by the detective-peer, whose identity was as yet unknown by any except the audience and the daughter of the millionaire.

'It is very beautiful,' whispered Miss Fairfax, 'very beautiful and haunting. What a beautiful voice that man has! Hullo, Billy. Had a good time with Mary? Hush! I mustn't talk.'

> *For your eyes tell me a story, Dearie,*
> *A story as old as the waves of the sea:*
> *The words are as wise*
> *As the light of the skies,*
> *Which your eyes have made bluer for me.*

She looked at Lina, who was leaning slightly forward. How sweet was her profile, and how the reflected light from the foot-lights made mystery of her dark eyes and eager lips. How proud she was to think such a lovely creature was her niece!

No one coughed or moved in the theatre during the song. The audience was rapt, entirely quiet. Maddison leaned back in his chair, swaying, his left hand on the back of Eve's chair, steadying himself. Miss Fairfax, made emotional by the music, wondered why his face, which could be so alight with joy, was now so sad. But, she remembered, all poets were sad. She was speculating upon the cause of his sadness when she noticed that the face of Mary Ogilvie was turned in their direction; the girl was sitting only a few yards away. She was dressed in a gown of pale pink, and Miss Fairfax realized that the oblique gaze of the beautiful eyes, so liquid and dark, was solely for the young man who was staring as though bewitched at her niece.

287

On the stage the last words of the last verse were floating in a golden cadence down to the listeners:

> Toil and Sorrow
> Will not borrow
> Love and laughter
> Ever after
> From my life.
> If I have you, dear,
> To bill and coo, dear,
> You'll never rue, dear
> When you're my wife.

Her own heart beating faster, since the sentiment had been for herself, Miss Fairfax took her eyes off Mr. Aubrey de la Hay the singer, and started. For she distinctly saw her niece with a swift turn of her head kissing over her shoulder the hand of Billy as it rested on the back of her chair. Immediately afterwards Evelyn caught her glance, and smiled.

'I was so carried away by the song that I couldn't help it,' she leaned across and softly said. 'If it had been old Archer Dodder I would have done it. Milly, what a lovely song——'

Again the chorus, a repeated duet, and then a storm of clapping ended the scene, and the lights went up. She glanced quickly at Billy, puzzled, for he seemed indifferent to the kiss on his hand. Lina had shocked him, she thought. Temperamental boy! He was now in his most charming mood, bubbling over with wit and laughter.

The next scene was laid in a desert oasis, with palm-trees, camels, sand, at evening. Apparently the band of blackmailers had just left. The detective-earl and his love in Arab dress sat by a fire, eating dates. Far away in the background sounded the muezzin call to prayer, a faint voice crying: *Allah is great, Allah is God, there is no God but Allah.* 'And he lives down in our alley!' sang a voice from the gallery. Cries of 'Hush! S-s-sh!' An evening star appeared simultaneously with a crescent moon

A dancer fluttered on, fluttered round the stage, like a moon-moth. Maddison stared at her: she was Eve, the moon-silvery wavelets of Shelley Cove, the Comorant rock, the dark mouth and eyes. Too soon the dancer fluttered away; the sun rose on the sleeping lovers.

Towards the end of the act Evelyn's hand touched his, clasped, lifted, and slightly pointed. Julian Warbeck had entered the box opposite, and was standing behind the huge form of Mr. 'Jimmy' Skinner, who, with the mayor and two ladies, was sitting there. Miss Fairfax made an exclamation of astonishment, since during the first act she had prophesied that by then he was lying in the gutter. The audience was left in apprehension for the lovers just before the curtain dropped, as with wild yells a band of Arabs rushed forward and captured them.

Apparently some sort of release was effected while the stage hands were rolling properties about behind the curtain, for the next scene was at Monte Carlo. The hero was seen to be gambling heavily, and heard to be muttering several times 'Curse muh luck', as the croupier raked in shovelfuls of notes and gold. At last, ruined and reeling, he was left alone, while Willy Whystle laughed saturninely in the background. The blackmailer having departed, a veiled figure entered. Immediately after a cry of 'Darling!' and several kisses he sang a song entitled *Blue Bird or Blue Blood, which will you choose, dear?* the effect of which was marred by the noise of voices in argument; and Julian Warbeck was seen violently to leave the box opposite.

A comic interlude before the curtain, and then the audience was treated to Paris by night, with a student's rag at Montmartre, accompanied by airs that seemed always trying to be like *La Bohème*. Afterwards Miss Fairfax said:

'Oh, how I would love to go to Paris, to that jolly Bohemian quarter. Lina, can't we go together on a Cook's tour when i—oh!'

She put her hand to her mouth, and confided later to Bill
that she really oughtn't to have suggested it when Lionel had
been home only a short time. She was garrulous until the play
began again, when its reel and rush in exotic setting and
gorgeous display absorbed her enthralled attention.

The final scene showed the Earl of Chewingom married to
the millionaire's daughter. With aristocratic fervour he
announced that the ancestral pile need not be sold after all
Pork-and-beans was quite happy; he married his first sweet
heart, a widow dragged on the stage for the finale. The ex
general married the cook, who likewise sprang from nowhere
All the bronzed young men in evening dress managed to find
each one of them a lady of his heart in the fashionable throng
upon the stage. Everyone sang, everyone was happy. The
principals took many calls, alone, and holding hands. Maddi
son noticed that the hero smiled twice, with a flash of white
teeth, at Eve.

'Author! Author! Author!'

'There! He'll be famous,' cried Milly.

Evelyn laughed. 'Aubrey told me they paid twelve men to
clap and shout "Author". He's a most amazing person
Whither away, O Will'um?'

'I wanted to arrange with Mary about a walk,' he called
back over his shoulder.

'Ah ha!' said Milly. 'Hush!'

Mr. de la Hay strolled on to the stage, before the curtain.

'Oh, he's charming!' whispered Milly. 'Order, order!'

Crushing his opera hat against his chest and releasing it
again, and flicking it under an arm, the author waited, smiling
for the applause to subside. He held up his hand, after rapidly
pinching his nostrils.

'Thank you. Thank you. Ladies and gentlemen, I am glad
you like my little effort. I have tried to give a little clean
pleasure. The future of the drama, I believe, lies in a different
direction to the old. We've been too dreary and serious hither

o. Why should the highest form of art be tragedy? Why not give joy a chance? I don't believe in plays like Ibsen's *Dolls House*, or Shaw's unpleasant plagiarized verbosities. The function of the theatre is to amuse, not to bore the weary by adapting the dith-y-rambic twaddle of mouldy philosophers. We've had enough of sombreness during the war—and now we're going to be merry and bright. Ladies and gentlemen of Folkestone, thank you for your kind appreciation.'

He was cheered and clapped, and lit a cigarette to show his self-possession.

'He'll be famous,' declared Miss Fairfax. 'Oh, what a blow he struck at that ass Bernard Shaw! Hullo, Billy, you've been quick. And he's quite right, too! It's the new spiritual awakening of youth we've read so much about. We *have* suffered enough in the war, and we want happy things now. Don't we, Billy?'

He nodded.

'Come, my dear boy, cheer up! Laugh, and the world laughs with you.'

'Think, and you think alone,' said Maddison. 'My God, I never heard such damned impertinence as that speech.' He got up again and went out of the door.

'Milly, dear, where's your intuition?' asked Evelyn.

'Oh! You mean Mary? But surely she——?'

'You wait and see!'

'Really, anyhow, he was positively rude!' cried Miss Fairfax.

When she saw him outside, and looked at his face, Milly's quick romantic sympathy was aroused; he waited to hold open the swing door, and as she passed through she squeezed his arm. 'There, Billy, we'll always be friends, won't we?'

Outside the theatre, underneath an arc-lamp that showed the stark whiteness of his shirt-front, stood Julian Warbeck, his cloak thrown over his left shoulder. Seeing them, he took a long pull at the cigar he had recently lighted, and dropped it on the pavement, respiring solemnly in its direction a length

291

of smoke. Then he swept off his hat, and took three strides towards them.

'Forgive my intrusion, but I want to apologize. Major Fairfax, sir, have I your permission to speak a moment with Mrs. Fairfax?'

'What do you want, Jay Double-u?' demanded Evelyn, in tones of quiet finality.

'I am going away to-morrow by the early train.'

As he made this announcement he looked unflinchingly at her eyes, and drew in through his nose an audible breath. She said:

'I am very glad to hear it. W-what are you going to do?'

Her voice, with its deep-throat stammer, with its subtle inflexion of an impersonal caress, seemed to agitate him inwardly, for a frown as of pain creased his wide forehead. He looked on the ground, made with his shoulders a slight gesture of despair, and in a voice of controlled roughness he said:

'I realized many things to-night. I realized that I had been a fool. I am still a fool, but nevertheless I am going away.'

'I wish you luck.'

'Thank you. I am going up to Oxford.'

He looked as though he expected her to show surprise. In a calm voice she said:

'Write to me and tell me how you get on. Remember, I believe in you, Jay Double-u.'

'You are very good.' He stopped, bit his lip, then went on: 'Yes, you are good. I shall not easily forget your kindness to a friendless man.' He paused, as though trying to remember a speech he had been preparing: 'Oh, yes. You, Maddison, I can see, are one of those men whose faces grow grey with their own pitiful breath. The world of men and women will conquer you, Maddison, and too late you will realize that the Garden of Proserpine is closed against you. But I shall remember you——'

'Come, Lina,' murmured Lionel. 'Warbeck, we must go now. Good luck!'

'Thank you.'

'Good-bye, Jay Double-u, and good l-luck! Mind you're not sent down!'

'All men of vision are sent down from Oxford.'

He gave a piteous look at Evelyn as she turned away. Maddison saw his eyes wet with tears, and went forward to shake him by the hand. Warbeck turned, and strode into the darkness beyond the artificial light.

At the corner of The Paragon they bade good-night to the aunts; Maddison said he would see them safely to their house, although they protested that it was not necessary. Evelyn whispered to him: 'Come back after; I'll leave the door unlocked.' And he moved off with the aunts. After bidding them good-night, he returned to The Paragon with slow steps, hesitating outside. He went away, but came back rapidly, leaping up the steps to turn the handle and bump his head against the door which, unexpectedly, did not open. It was locked. He waited a minute, two minutes, then went away in the direction of the Leas.

It was after two o'clock when he let himself into his lodging down in the lower part of the town, watched by a policeman whose tread was silent. He found Billjohn couched on his pyjamas, beating his tail furiously.

Chapter 25

I<small>T</small> was cool in her high drawing-room after the long self
enforced walk on the heated asphalt of the Leas, cool and
restful with the open windows and pale lemon curtains moving
with the sea breeze, but . . .

'Eve, can't you understand——?'

'Listen, Billy. When you are with us, I feel an affection for
Lionel that is a genuine fondness; but when he and I are by
ourselves, I feel that I cannot tolerate him. If I am sitting
quietly meditating, he will ask me if anything is the matter,
and when I say that I was just thinking, he wonders what it is.
You see, the male spirit always tracking me to my most secret
and remote retreats, where is only room for myself! Even the
happiest lovers have solitary tracks of the spirit to walk alone.
But he doesn't understand that.'

'He loves you, Eve. I know he does. I've watched him.'

'In his own way, I suppose he does. I wish he didn't.' She
went on knitting the heather-mixture sock.

'I suppose you wish that about me?'

'Now what makes you ask such a silly and unnecessary
question? I shall have this sock made by to-morrow, if I keep
at it.'

'Eve, I think I ought to go away.' He waited.

'Very well, as you think, Billy.'

He went out of the room, going upstairs to Jonquil's nursery
in the attic, climbing into blinding sunlight through the win
dow on to the leaded roof that scorched where hands and body
touched.

Lionel, returning from his tailor's a few minutes later, said to

her as he took a cigarette from the silver box he had won at
polo, tapping it on his broad thumbnail:

'Bill's an extraordinary fellow, but an awful good one—the
best type, a little too sensitive perhaps, for the hurly-burly of
this life of ordinary mortals. He has a curious air of being un-
affected by experience which for a fellow who has been through
nearly five years of war is remarkable. At eighteen he was
fighting on Gallipoli—a boy still—too young to stand the shock.
He was telling me the other day about his boyhood, and his
friendship for a fellow who was killed, and, d'you know,
m'dear, I was profoundly moved by seeing the wistful joy on
his face at those memories. He might have been sixteen, and
relating the exploits to his guv'nor—how they built a hut on an
island, noosed pike in the lake, made fires in a spinney, and got
rooks' eggs in half a gale. It must be fine to have sons and
watch them growing up. If only Jonquil's coming had been
different. . . I daren't ever risk losing you with another—er—
infant——'

Seeing her steady gaze upon him, and the cessation of her
knitting-needles, his eyes became impersonal, and he said,
rising:

'How about going on the hills this afternoon? The breeze
will be great up there. Let's ask young Mary and Bill. By jove,
yes, of course. We ought to have had her round here more
often. Why didn't we think of it before?'

'Well, she's such pals with the Normans, isn't she, and you
know how that woman hates me, just because I was——'

'I know, m'dear, but you mustn't worry about people who
don't understand and who don't matter in the slightest. Those
middle-class people are always the most terrible snobs.'

'You are a dear,' she murmured, kissing him impulsively.
'I'll ask Mary for this afternoon. We'll picnic, shall we?'

Jonquil went with them. The broad Roman road curving at
the base of the encampment, that had been beaten by the feet
and chariots of the cohorts which had made it and outlasted

the artillery tractors, the lorries, and the troops twenty
centuries afterwards, was slippery with dead sun-dried grasses
Maddison, as they walked slowly along it, thought of the grass
that had been growing in humbleness throughout those centuries, while men had wrought and made their bitter wars, and
perished. Mary walked silently at his side.

'I wish there was another war.'

'Why?' she said.

'I wouldn't come back then.'

Evelyn and Lionel were walking behind them, and a long
way in front Jonquil was hopping about with Billjohn
prancing around her.

Mary looked as though she were going to say something, but
the thought wavered in hesitation, and was not expressed
With almost a birdlike stillness she walked on the brown grass
by his side, her tread quiet and even, except when the iron-
tipped heels struck a flint. A touch on his arm, and he was to
look at Jonquil, who was rolling in her white silk frock with the
dog upon the grass. Mary said:

'She is a darling child.'

'Yes.'

'Jonquil, stop rolling on the grass, you dirty child,' sharply
called Evelyn behind them. Colour came into Mary's cheeks.

'Oh, all right,' said Jonquil, getting up and running on till
she and Billjohn were as small as a white butterfly and its cast
brown chrysallis.

They went up by the same track he had climbed on Peace
Night. Halfway to the top they sat down, yielding themselves
gratefully to the slope. The sun high in the south-western sky
was like a blistering splash of quicksilver aroll in a crucible of
blue porcelain. With her fingers Mary moved aside the grasses,
peering for shells and flowers. She touched the gold disk of a
hawkbit.

'Billy's favourite flower,' said Evelyn. 'Put it in his buttonhole, my dear.'

Mary did not pick it, but continued to touch its toothed petals with her forefinger, hiding her face by pretending to examine the flower.

'It's so happy,' she said at last, glancing at Evelyn.

'Here you are, then, Billy,' said Evelyn, picking one and tossing it across to him. 'Here's one that isn't so happy.'

'Thanks very much,' said Maddison. He sprang up and ran to Jonquil, who was picking all the flowers she could find.

'W-W-Will'um!'

'Er-hum?' he mimicked.

'Quillie trodded on a bumble bee and killed it. Look!'

'Oh, Quillie, what will the poor bee-babies do?'

'Well, you see, Will'um, it bit Quillie.'

'But bees don't bite, Quillie. They sting.'

'Erhum. But this one is lousy, Will'um: it bit Quillie, and nearly stang her, too, making Quillie damn well fed up with it. Let's climb to the top and you be an English soldier, and I'll be a bore.'

'You'll never be that, my dear.'

'Only in pretending, I mean. I'll shoot you.'

'Oh, I see. You mean a Boer. It's too hot.'

'Yes, it is, isn't it, Will'um?'

'Yes, my darling.'

They sat down on the strawlike grass. Jonquil snuggled close to him. Because she was a miniature Evelyn, because she was lovely and feminine and faery-frail, he put his arm round her, while love surged in his heart, not like a turbid stream, but like the wind which bore the glistening thistle-seeds in the shining air.

'W-W-Will'um!'

'Yes, my sweet?'

'Will you marry Quillie when she grows up?'

'If you like.'

'You do love Quillie, don't you?'

'Very much.'

297

THE DREAM OF FAIR WOMEN

'Better'n Mary?'

'Er-hum.'

'Honest to God?'

'Hush, Quillie! Yes, really.'

'Then will you give Billyjohn to Quillie?'

'But he's already given to Mummie.'

'Erhum. I know. But Mummie said to Father that she—that she didn't want Billyjohn, not *really*, only she said she did so's not to hurt you.'

'Look at that lovely butterfly over there, Quillie.'

'Yes. Don't let's kill it, shall us?'

'Oh, no.'

The clouded blue settled on a scabious head, opening and closing its azure wings. It was cool on the hillside where the wind stroked the harsh bents and drove up into scarlet flight the soldier-flies which dwelled in the grassy wilderness. Below them brown cattle were grazing as they moved along their chalky paths. A swift shadow glided over the grass; looking up they saw a hawk veering across the windy uptrend. Mary saw it, too, for she pointed. It was almost like old times, with Jack. And Jefferies had loved the shadow of the hawk on the grass. Jack and Mary——. He climbed up towards Mary.

On the Roman earthworks the wind came like the spirit of water, cool and boisterous, rushing by unseen, pouring over Cæsar's Camp. Mary trod on the swarded ramparts, leaning against the air-tide which moulded the light garments against her slim body. Maddison leapt up beside her, drawing a deep draught into his lungs, and breathing out slowly with an exquisite content. Afar the glittering sea stretched into summer mist that hid the French coastline. Tiny dark specks smouldered in the mist. They saw the cross-Channel boat nearing shore, with its grey wake left scarcely perceptible on the sea, even as the reality of war was scarcely perceptible by any who had not been near it. Folkestone sprawled along the sea's edge, a heap of soiled and crushed bricks that in places flickered

298

silvery flashes where from skylights and windows the sunlight glanced.

'Isn't it lovely, Mary? Like the downs above Rookhurst.'

'It's lovelier there, Willie.'

She saw his eyes fill with tears before he turned away his head.

'I often come here,' she said, 'and listen to the wind music. Everything makes a different noise—the broad grassbents and the tussocks, the thistles, the carlines, and even the short rootlets on the turf. And I'm certain I've heard a harebell ringing.'

'Quillie has too.'

Jonquil lay on her tummy in the fosse, swinging her legs and biting at grass. Mary realized that he was not listening to what she said. Lionel and Evelyn were climbing to the summit a hundred yards away; he was staring at them. The wind lifted his hair; the colours of the school tie he wore were dull and drab. The spaniel lay panting in the shade behind them. A hawk-shadow cut across them; a rising lark stopped singing, and dashed to the ground. Turning suddenly to her, he said with bitterness in his voice:

'You see, nothing is allowed to remain happy for long.'

She looked at him, hesitated several times, lost a little colour in her cheeks, then said quickly, while her brown eyes seemed to grow larger and to take to themselves a soft auburn glow, 'Don't be unhappy.'

He looked away from her.

Jonquil began to hum and sing, and they listened to her song about a bee that was killed by a cruel little devil.

'Aren't I, Will'um?'

'What?'

'A cruel little devil.'

'I'll whip ee, my maid!'

'Quillie wouldn't cry. But sorry I sweared,' she said gravely.

'You dear thing.'

'But Quillie killed a bee dead.'

'Well, it's gone to heaven now.' Aside to Mary he said: 'The conventional remark.'

'I hope it won't sting God,' said Jonquil.

Mary, who had been sitting still, touching the grass, suddenly laughed. 'I know it's very wrong, but I can't help laughing.'

'But why should it be wrong, Mary? Do you believe in God?'

She nodded. The colour had returned to her face.

'I don't. Shall I tell you why?'

'Yes, if you like.'

'I thought no more of God after I had fought in France. Listen, I'll tell you something. Once I bayonetted a German in a trench raid. A poor little undersized Saxon, about eighteen I suppose. I wanted to be able to think I had killed a German, you see, so I killed one unarmed, and very small. He was in a dug-out, reading. I took the book back as a souvenir. Poems of Keats—translated into German. I got the Military Cross for that raid, which was, owing to the feeble troops against us, particularly successful. And every night Grandpa Fairfax on his bony knees says, "I Thank thee, O Lord, for giving us Victory." '

She looked into his eyes, unsure of herself, yet her glance was maintained, although the dreaded colour was in her cheeks.

'You're just the same Willie I've always known,' she said, as though speaking to herself. 'Funny little thing you are, really.'

Even in the vivid sunlight a soft fire seemed to illumine her face and throat. Her black hair, her dark eyes, the rise and fall of her breathing, gave him a curious feeling of satisfaction, and he must turn sideways, as though ignoring her, and touch with his fingertips the empty shell of a banded hill-snail.

'Mary, are you staying in Folkestone much longer?'

'I'm going back to Devon next week.'

She watched him playing vacantly with the snail-shell. He ceased as Evelyn's laughter was heard.

'Poor bee, quite dead, never see his babies, poor bee. Quillie killed you, la la, yes she did,' sang the child, far away and happy in her sun-dreams, waving thin legs in the air.

'Mary, will you come for a walk one day before you go?'

She nodded.

'To-morrow?'

'Yes.'

'In the afternoon?'

So it was arranged.

'Can Quillie come, too, Will'um?'

Mary heard him sigh. He lay down in the grass with closed eyes, the sun on his face, listening to the grasshoppers which chirruped while waiting for love and the evening dewdrops.

'Can I, Will'um?'

He rolled over, taking her in his arms, kissing her several times. She lay inert, with pouting lips and eyes growing angry, then struck him in the face, struggled free, and ran away up the hill.

After a few moments he got up, and followed her slowly to where she was sitting, her mother's arm around her shoulders. He climbed to the summit and stood beside the flagpost, looking down at the fields in which the corn was being cut. Toy horses were drawing the reaping machines, toy men propping the sheaves into stooks; there was the faint rattle of the machines and sometimes the pop of a gun, and the coursing of dogs. Evelyn sat below with Lionel and Jonquil, apparently a family content in the sun. The black patch of the bonfire he had made on the night of July the nineteenth had been disturbed only by wind, which had winnowed the ash and left charcoal and charred ends on the baked earth. A scattered flock of rooks and jackdaws passed over the hill, cawing and roistering. Eastward the line of downs dipped into a valley grown with oaks, and a mile beyond on the slope a chalk quarry had been carved. Patches of gorse grew on the downs, sheep were straying, there was a scent of thyme in the air, and always the burring of bees.

He walked round the fosse, thinking of the Roman earthworks above Rookhurst, of Jefferies, and the friends of his boy-hood. Mary knew those downs; Mary had known them before their spirit had perished. Climbing to the summit again, he saw the Fairfax family walking towards the farther skyline. Mary was lying in the grass where he had left her.

'Hi! Coming?'

She got up and climbed to him, sometimes slipping, but scrambling to her feet again. He went down to meet her, taking her hand and pulling her to the summit. Together they ran down the reverse slope into the fosse, seeing the others standing by some gipsies on the road behind the encampment.

A bay horse unclipped and ungroomed was hobbled near, cropping the grass. Lurcher dogs approached in silence, pointing at Billjohn, who pranced about and told master of dangerous objects. Three brown barefooted children ran for-ward and begged for pennies. A fire smoked under the hedge, a cooking-pot by it, and fresh skins of rabbits were drying in the sun. A baby wrapped in a sack slept beside the wheel of an old unpainted caravan. Two young men sat under the hedge, straws in their mouths, and a white-haired crone squatted in shade on the caravan steps, smoking a black clay pipe. They took no notice of the newcomers, and the lurchers did not growl, but sniffed with casual intentness at the excited Billjohn.

Jonquil stood by her father, listening to a brown young gipsy woman telling her mother's fortune. Smilingly Evelyn sat on the ground, her hand in the gipsy's rough lap.

'Yes, my good lady,' she was saying, 'you will be very happy, but sorrow will come, and like a thunderstorm in summer. But your heart will carry you through, my pretty one. Do not give it too quickly to strangers, my lady. You will see many stars, but one will not fail; but keep a brave heart, my pretty lady. Won't you let me cross your palm with more silver, my lady, for the good fortune that a true Chal has told you. Very hard to live, my good lady, and we can make no baskets of green grasses, my good lady, because they are withered early. Bless you, my good lady, for your heart is kind.'

'I did hope you would say something about a dark, sardonic lord, and danger,' said Evelyn. 'Didn't you, Lionel, what? Hullo, Billy. Wherever have you been? Let her tell yours.'

'Won't you have yours done first, Mary?'

She shook her head quickly. 'No, you have yours told.'

'Only half a crown, my lady. I can see you have a good fortune, my lady. I can see it in your face, my good lady. But let me tell you of that nice gentleman you think of. Only half a crown, my lady. Two shillings. I am a true Chal, old and wise as the earth. The stars speak to me at night. Come, my lady, only two shillings.'

Mary looked appealingly at Maddison, and her lips framed the whisper: 'Let her tell yours, Willie.'

He gave the gipsy half a crown, and she took his hand upon her weatherstained lap.

'You have much before you, my gentleman. You must never lose hope, my gentleman. Beware of sweet laughter, my gentleman. You have a journey, my gentleman, but your feet will not falter. You draw life from the stars, my gentleman. Many secrets will be told you, and you will cross water, but you must not turn back, for water to you is as treacherous as a snake in a bird's nest, my gentleman. There is a lady who loves you, my gentleman. Bless you, my gentleman, for you have a kind heart. Now, my lady, let me tell your fortune.'

But Mary shook her head.

'Quillie, let the lady tell yours,' suggested Evelyn.

'No. Quillie don't like her,' declared Jonquil, getting behind Mary.

The baby in the sack woke and began to cry. Jonquil went and stared at it.

'What an ugly baby.'

The baby's mother, the fortune-teller, picked it up and retired to the shade of the caravan, on the steps of which she sat, unfastening her bodice and putting the wailing infant to her breast. Jonquil looked at her with intense eagerness, but said nothing, and walked seriously behind them to a hollow where they decided to have tea.

While Maddison prepared a fireplace of flints, and Evelyn spread the cloth, the others went off to get wood. She did not speak, and after a minute he asked her what was the matter.

'Nothing, Billy. Why should there always be something the matter?'

'You don't speak to me.'

'I didn't like to interrupt your thoughts. Once—once you used to share them with me, but now you never tell me anything. But, my dear, I do not want you to do anything against your wishes. I want you to be happy. That butter will run to grease in the sun, I'm afraid.'

China mugs were laid in a row, and the vacuum flask containing milk taken out of the basket. A pot of guava jelly followed, with cakes and a paper spill of the china tea.

'Eve, I can't—I can't—I mean, Lionel——'

'I hope no one takes sugar, for Martha hasn't put any in the basket.'

'Eve, this can't go on. I——'

'Mary is getting sticks, why not go and help her? Dear me, no teapot. But we can make tea in the kettle, as we did on Vention Sands. Remember? No, you've forgotten.'

'I hardly remember anything else. Because of that, Eve, I feel we ought to tell Lionel.'

'But tell Lionel—what? I thought our love was over and done with. You behave as though it is, anyhow.' Her voice altered. 'You say you want to tell him. Just what do you want to tell him?'

'Don't be alarmed,' he replied, forcing a playful note into his voice. 'I wouldn't be so treacherous!'

'Then what do you mean?'

'Eve, I love you, I think about you all day and all night. Eve, let us tell Lionel, so that you can leave him. I know he'll

understand. People either love or they don't love. I don't
believe you ever loved me,' he said, desperately.

'You are unkind,' she lamented, 'and you know well how
you w-wound those who are fond of you. William, dear, if I
went away with you, I should only be a drag. You are as wild
as one of those swifts above us. They are swifts, aren't they?
And, Billy, you will hate me for saying it, but if we did take the
final step, how could we live? You told me you had only your
army gratuity. And that won't last for ever, will it, Will'um?'

'No.'

'Whereas at present you should try to think of others a little.
Don't be hurt, old boy—it's bad friendship that doesn't help by
telling the truth about things like that. God knows, I'm selfish
enough myself.'

'You are most generous.'

'There's Mary with some sticks. Isn't she a topping girl? The
only woman in Folkestone that I would really trust. Perhaps
Milly—but Milly, poor old dear, wouldn't understand.'

'You aren't going to tell Mary about Devon, surely?'

She looked at him through narrowed eyelids. 'I wouldn't
be so treacherous!'

'Eve, quick, tell me. Do you love me, really?'

'I think of you most of the time, really.'

'Not all the time?'

'Not all, Billy. I think of Jonquil occasionally, and ordering
dinner, and—those secret tracts I told you of. You meet me
there, sometimes. Darling W-Will'um.'

'Eve!'

'Yes, Billy.

'Does Quillie imitate you when she stammers, or do you
imitate her?'

'I imitate her.'

'I thought so.'

'I even imitate you, W-Will'um!'

'I know you do!'

'Aren't you flattered?'

'I'm too miserable to be flattered.'

'Miserable? For why, my dear?' she asked softly.

He did not reply. Mary was there, and Lionel and Quillie

He stuck four short sticks into the ground and built up within a flint keep a small hut of the thinnest twigs. Inside he put a spring of dry furze. Around and over the hut were placed sticks, like a wigwam. Everything was done most carefully, and the process watched excitedly by Jonquil, amusedly by her father, eagerly by Mary. Evelyn sat apart and said: 'Hurry up with that there prize fire, Will, my lad.'

'I must arrange the stones exactly right, or most of the calorific energy will be lost,' said Maddison from the ground, looking up at Evelyn.

'Damn your calorific energy. I want some tea to quench my calorific thirst. Blast the smoke!'

'Lina, remember the child,' reproved Major Fairfax.

'My dear, your grasp of scientific words is comic. Bill, blast the smoke, please—a miniature blast furnace—blow on it. That's right: the flame eats the smoke, as my common old grannie used to say. Blast the smoke!'

'I know worse than that,' his daughter informed him.

'Don't let me hear you, or I will have to punish you Quillie.'

'No, all right, Father dear.'

Secretly laughing, Maddison put more sticks on the fire Immediately the furze crackled, smoke made him cough, and the flames lit the sticks. The kettle was put on. When it began to sing, Jonquil claimed that she knew what it was saying.

'Tell me,' said Lionel, kneeling beside her.

'There's a droppo water inside that—that's lost itself, and is running round hollering for its ma.'

'Its what?'

'Hollering for its ma. It's lost, silly. Martha and Quillie once found a lost little boy, and I gave him a sweet, and

Martha said: "He's hollering for his ma, lovey." See, don't you?'

Evelyn looked at Maddison and winked.

'That's hardly the way for a lady to speak, Quillie.'

'Martha isn't a lady—she's a old woman instead. And she says "Thank gord for it!" She does really, Father—you needn't look so unbelieving at Quillie. Don't she, Mummie?' appealed an unhappy Jonquil.

'Yes, my darling, of course she does. Mummie will have to speak to Martha about it, but Quillie isn't naughty at all for saying it. It's perfectly natural. She's mother's very own darling. No one shall hurt Quillie—she shall grow up as free as a wild swift in the lovely air of heaven. Mother will not let her white childlike soul be warped by restraint into what is called a woman of the world like herself. Isn't that the *Policy of Reconstruction*, Billy? What else is the kettle saying, Quillie.'

'Quillie can't hear any more,' she said, almost tearfully.

'I can hear a dog growling inside,' Mary told her.

The child forgot her misery, and put her head near the kettle, so that the auburn locks fell away from the ears fragile as burnet roses.

'Quillie can, too. And a l-l-little swallow. And a starling. And—and a old man selling ba-nanas and choklicks on the beach. And—and a noise like M-M-Martha singing a song as she brushes Quillie's hair and saying " 'Old still, lovey. Good-bye, Dolly, I must leave you, though it breaks my 'art to go." Like the soldiers of the Queen singed when they went to catch that wicked old Kruger, who ate babies!'

Major Fairfax lay back and shouted with laughter, a thing Maddison had not seen him do before. No man with a subtle mind *shouts* with laughter, he thought. Poor Eve.

'Quillie, your father is amazed by you. I never thought you had it in you.'

'Father's been away all the time, hasn't he, Quillie?' said Evelyn. 'Mind, darling, or you'll be scalded!'

The kettle tunes lost themselves in a soft rumble, and Maddison emptied the spill of tea into the water. They sat round the spread cloth, feeding a stern-swinging Billjohn with tit-bits. Afterwards they explored the encampment, Lionel and Maddison together, the others at a distance.

'I've chucked smoking till after the tournament,' said Lionel, as Maddison filled his old pipe from an oilskin pouch. 'You'll come and watch us, won't you?'

'Rather. I like watching your partner play. She's so full of life, and it's a joy to watch anyone like that.'

'I know what you mean. Here, light your pipe inside my coat, out of the wind. Bill, I notice you stick to your old love very faithfully.'

The matchbox was dropped. Maddison knelt down to recover it, and struck another match kneeling down.

'I don't know what you mean, Lionel,' his voice said from the ground.

'I haven't seen you smoke that pipe I gave you yet.'

They went down the hill to the three girls. The kestrel soaring above them uttered its wild cry; in the tussocks the free grasshoppers sang to the sun.

Chapter 26

EVELYN, in a black evening gown, heard his slow footfalls mounting the stairs. She left her writing desk, and sat on the sofa. He came into the room.

'Hullo, Billy. Had a good walk?'

'Yes, thanks.'

'You don't seem very enthusiastic.'

'Mary is a most intelligent girl.'

'Of course she is. What did you talk about?'

'Nothing.'

'Extremely intelligent! Why not sit down and tell me all about it? You look tired.'

He sat down at the other end of the sofa.

'Where's Lionel?'

'Dressing.'

'I must dress.'

He looked at her. He moved across to her, and hid his face in her lap. She stroked his hair.

'Little boy's hair you have. Little boy's eyes, too. Poor little boy. Trying to free all the birds in the world's trap! Poor little boy.'

'Eve, do you mind if I don't dine here?'

'But why, my boy? Mary's coming—she'll be disappointed.'

'Well, I feel that—I'm—not wanted.'

'Silly, of course you're wanted. Lionel wants you. I want you. Mary wants you. Quillie wants you, so does Milly and Margy.' She kissed him on the nape of his neck. 'Now run up and change—they'll be here in twenty minutes.'

He ran upstairs into the attic room, and changed into the

THE DREAM OF FAIR WOMEN

borrowed suit. Evelyn was giving a small dinner party, to which the Pamments with Tubby Lorayne, de la Hay, Mary Ogilvie, and a subaltern named Tollemache were invited.

The dinner was a success, owing to Eve being charming to everyone at the same time, but most charming to Lionel. De la Hay said he must run off as soon as the meal was finished, since the show began at eight o'clock; he would, of course, return afterwards. Everyone liked him, as he was so friendly and consistently cheerful. To Lionel and Maddison he was particularly friendly.

Afterwards the aunts came over from Radnor Park Gardens for coffee and liqueurs. The room was filled with a soft light from the shaded lamps, the evening air was cool, the modulated murmur of voices rose with the smoke of Egyptian cigarettes. Above the stack of the house across the way a large star was shining, sometimes dulled by invisible smoke from a chimney pot. Mary was asked to play the piano, the *Missouri Waltz* being requested by Milly. She played it, and then some of the airs of *What Next, Dearie?* Tubby Lorayne began to dance with Evelyn. Maddison watched the star, identifying his life with it. When the music stopped he walked to the piano to talk to Mary.

'Will you play some Debussy?' he asked.

'Yes,' she said, turning round nervously. 'Would you like Debussy?'

'Do, please,' came a polite chorus of assent.

She played the *Sunken Cathedral*, then an Hungarian dance; after which they said: 'Don't stop, please', Major Fairfax saying: 'If only I could play like that! Mary, you're a genius, m'dear.'

'What shall I play?' she said quickly.

'Oh, any old thing,' said Evelyn.

'Remember this, Willie?' Mary began to play. He went nearer the window, so that he might see more of the sky. The melody was broken in the middle, and the preludian trills of *Hymn to the Sun* sent his mind wandering far from the life of

310

streets and houses, to the seashore at night, the cries of curlews, the lighthouses flashing on Lundy.

'It's like the Taw estuary at night,' said Maddison, kneeling down beside the piano stool. 'When there is a frost, you can hear the feeding flocks of curlew and golden plover calling in the darkness. It's like a thousand golden bubbles rising out of the water.'

'Golden plover are simply toppin' on toast,' remarked Mr. Tollemache, trying to make a joke. 'Do please play some more rags, I say, Miss Ogilvie. Play "Your Eyes Tell me a Story, Dearie". Marvellous, the way you remember them.'

Mary played. Friendliness brooded in the warm shaded light of the room. Mrs. Pamment was talking to Mrs. Beayne and to Major Fairfax about her eldest son, his captain's 'doggy' in a battleship in the Bosphorus. Tubby Lorayne and the Pamment girl were sitting side by side in a deep couch talking in intimate and subdued tones. Milly was preparing herself to make a recitation; Tollemache, the tall youth with china-blue eyes and blonde shiny hair who had been dressed as a rajah at the Victory Ball, was talking to Evelyn about some runs he had recently with the Devon and Somerset Staghounds.

'You ought to come down to Exford, Mrs. F., you ought really. You'd get some simply toppin' runs. We killed a twelve-pointer the other day out of Horner Wood. Only you need two 'osses for each run.'

'I'll bring fifty!' said Evelyn.

Maddison looked out of the window at Spica Virginis, which now seemed to be resting on the rim of the chimney pot. Miss Fairfax recited, gave an encore, sat down again looking hot. People passed in the street below, their laughter and voices audible in the air of the summer night. Upon the pot edge quivered the point of light, until it dipped and was lost.

The handle of the door was turned, and they heard Martha's voice saying: 'You come out of there, lovey.'

The door opened, and Jonquil's head peeped round.

'W-W-Will'um!'

'Quillie, you naughty girl, go back to bed this instant!' said her mother, in tones of surprised pleasure.

'Quillie wants Will'um a minute. Come on, Will'um.'

She came into the room, in her flannel sleeping suit, bare-footed. All the women petted her, especially Aunt Margy, while Martha grinned happily at the door, and said: 'She would come, miss.'

He went upstairs with her, led by the hand. She sat on a chair. 'Will'um, can you hear anything?'

He listened.

'Only the sea.'

'Yes, but what else?'

'Your feet on the rung of the chair.'

'Silly! Look over there! Can't you hear it crying?'

She pointed to a piece of sacking lying by the grate.

'Why, of course. It's a baby. Where did you get it?'

'It's Quillie's. Quillie had it after supper. The doctor brought it to Quillie in a black bag. It's now crying something awful. Isn't it, Will'um?'

'No.'

'It is.'

'It isn't.'

'Oh, Will'um, do pretend!'

'I can hear it now. You must get into bed and keep it warm, or it will die. Good-night.'

'W-W-Will'um, don't go, or if you do I shan't let you be its father any more. But if you stay, I will let you be the father of all my other dolls, and my Teddy, which was borned before I met you, but I will say you are their daddy.'

'Right-ho, my faithful spouse. Now I must go down, and you must go to sleep with your baby, or it will die.'

'Yes, Will'um.'

She took a sort of rabbit from the sacking, and leapt into bed, holding it to her heart.

'It's stopped crying, hasn't it, Will'um? I say, do you think that baby the gipsy had was stolen?'

'It might have been.'

'It looked a gentleman's baby, didn't it?'

She tugged him down, giving him several kisses.

' 'Night, Quillie.'

' 'Night, Will'um.'

He went downstairs. Mary was sitting on a hassock near the window, looking out at the night. Her small chin was resting on her hands. Tollemache was seated beside Evelyn at the piano, performing with her a musical exercise known as chopsticks.

'I say, Mrs. F.,' he said, 'you've got a simply toppin' idea of rhythm, really you have.'

Maddison was spoken to by Mrs. Pamment and Lionel; Mrs. Pamment made room for him beside her, asking him to tell her about his cottage. She was a Devonian, she said, having been born a Chychester—'the family of blue eyes and long noses'. She was kind, and her manner sympathetic. He told her about the otter cub and the seagull, forcing himself to talk lightly. But all the time he listened to Eve's voice, and heard what it was saying so vivaciously to Tollemache. He spoke ramblingly, lightened his mind, faltered, felt ill. In an embarrassing silence the voice of Tollemache was heard saying: 'Well, if I can get the motor-boat you'll come? It will be simply toppin', Lina.'

He had called her by this name a moment previously.

'Rather, Jerry, I'll come.'

'I must go now,' said Maddison, a minute later. 'If you'll forgive me running off. I've got some work to do.'

'See you at the tournament to-morrow, Bill? Come and lend Miss Pamment and me your moral support.'

'Rather.'

He stood, hesitating, in the middle of the room, looking on the floor.

'My sister Constance has a place near you in Devon,' said
Mrs. Pamment. 'You must go and see her when you return to
your romantic castle. It's on the Santon Burrows, most
appropriately called "Wildernesse".'

'Yes, do come,' said Mary.

'Yes, I will, thank you,' he replied, while on a stool Mary was
watching his face, hands under her chin, her eyes dark and
patient, as if suffering.

Chapter 27

On returning from the tennis tournament, from which he and
his partner were knocked out in the semi-finals, Lionel was
met at the door by Martha with a telegram.

'I didn't bring it to the ground, mister, as I knew you'd be
busy playing. It come soon after you'd gone.'

He tore open the orange envelope and spread the flimsy
sheet, then handed it in silence to his wife, and looked at
Maddison with a composed smile.

'My dear,' said Evelyn in a low voice, pressing his arm, 'how
utterly miserable!'

'Don't worry, old girl. I expected it, you know. I've been
lucky to have had so long. Marching orders, Bill!'

'When for, Lionel?'

'Says forthwith, but that means twenty-four hours' grace.
I shall have to go on Monday morning. Damn!'

'I'm coming with you,' declared Evelyn, 'that is, if you'd
take me as your groom or batman. Now if I were to dress up
in uniform and cut off my hair, no one would know the
difference.'

'Wouldn't they? You'll hear from me, darling, if you cut off
your lovely hair!'

It was the first time Maddison had heard him use the word
darling.

'Nevertheless, I shall come,' she averred.

When Lionel was in his bath, Evelyn and Maddison were in
the drawing-room. He stood by the window, looking down the
street towards the sea, and she sat on the couch, turning idly
the pages of *The Tatler*, which contained a photograph of Lord

and Lady Spreycombe and their guests having luncheon on a
Perthshire moor.

'Shall I go, Eve?'

'You can stop here if you want to, Billy. But don't let me
prevent your going if you prefer to be with other people.'

'You know I don't.'

'I don't know it. I can go only by your behaviour, which is
rather extraordinary. Why can't you be happy and contented,
like Tubby Lorayne or any other man? He said to me when
you cleared off during the tournament that your behaviour was
peculiar. His term was "wet", and although I found it hard to
follow all his curious sailor's talk, yet the meaning was
obvious.'

'Eve, I'm sorry I am so dull, but——'

'Oh, you exasperating man! No wonder Elsie Norman
wouldn't have anything to do with you, if you behaved to her
as you behaved to me. Couldn't you see that the whole of
Folkestone, all the wooden women, there this afternoon, were
talking about me? I wonder how many engaged girls other
than Muriel Pamment would have remained quiet while I sat
with Tubby? None. Muriel is a decent girl herself, and a
decent girl is as rare as a smile on your face.'

'What would you expect any girl to do? Bash you on the
head with a racket, or aim balls at you?' he said, trying to
smile.

'Billy, she wasn't jealous, was she?'

'I think she must have been. She kept looking at you.'

'Are you sure. Wasn't she looking at Tubby?'

'Anyhow, you seemed to like talking to Tubby rather than to
me,' he said dully. 'I felt you were snubbing me.'

'Snubbing you? Because I speak to Tubby? I spoke mostly
to Tubby because you were in one of your introspective moods,
and I didn't want to interfere with the four hundred and
seventieth chapter of *The Policy of Internal Combustion*. I
addressed most of my remarks to the Matelot because, one,

he is bright; two, he is cheerful; three, he is about the only man I know who doesn't introduce the personal note into the conversation; also, your gloomy face makes people talk. Why can't you laugh and be happy? You can be very attractive, if you want to be. I try to make you happy, but I fail, apparently.'

'I care for you so much,' he said, going to the window. 'So much, that I can think of nothing else. Certainly not honour.'

'Honour! Well, one day you'll hate me; and when that time comes, remember that I was, according to my own standards, trying to be decent.'

'I know you are,' he said.

'Come and sit by me, quietly. Just hold my hand; hold my hand, Mis'r Ma'sson, and do not be unkind. Be just your dear natural self again. You make me fret, you know.'

She lay back with closed eyes, breathing quietly. He sat upright, staring at the sky through the window. The minutes went by. He began to think that she cared for Lionel more than she liked to admit. He suffered. Martha in the kitchen could be heard laying plate and cutlery on the silver tray. The splashing in the bathroom ceased, and a man's voice was heard humming intermittently. She lay still. The bathroom door clicked, and his hand was squeezed and held. He was alarmed; his hand was gripped tighter; he submitted. Was she going to tell Lionel this way? He fortified himself. On the thick carpet a foot made a dull thud, and Lionel looked round the door.

'Shall I turn the water on, Lina? Hello, aren't you feeling very fit m'dear?'

The eyes opened, freeing tears that rolled down her cheeks. She leapt up and went without a word swiftly past him and into her room.

Lionel sat where she had been sitting, and with deliberate movements selected a cigarette, tapped it on his thumbnail, and lit it. He drew deeply at it, inhaled the smoke, and released it through mouth and nose.

'Bill.'

'Yes, Lionel.'

'I want to tell you something.'

Maddison waited. Now it was coming. Lionel inhaled, and exhaled slowly. Maddison breathed slowly, to ease his heart.

'Bill, I want to speak about Lina—why she isn't coming with me out East. Lina's a mixture of all sorts of things, wild as a Dartmoor pony, impulsive and generous, sometimes foolish and sometimes inconsiderate, but that's only because she's young. But you probably have observed that already. People talk about her, of course; they do about anybody who is out of the ordinary run. They talk about her and that fellow Sprey-come, a man I don't like and don't want her to know; he's a waster who has badly let down his class. Do you like him?'

'I hardly know him, Lionel.'

'She's promised me she'll drop the fellow, and I'm awfully glad. She's so intensely alive that she sees no harm in doing things that another woman, less vivid, would think twice about doing. But I shan't be here to help her—I—well, I won't go into the question of why she isn't coming out East with me. She will later, when she's settled down a bit and found that the hat she's looking for is on her head already. You understand?'

Major Fairfax exhaled a tremendous amount of smoke suddenly.

'Bill, don't be offended, but to-morrow—you understand— my last day—Lina and I will probably take a luncheon-basket and the two-seater and spend the day out somewhere, perhaps at Dymchurch or Rye. But come to breakker as usual, and Martha will give you lunch and tea, and you can take Jonquil out, if you wouldn't mind being nursemaid for once, or Martha can look after her if she's too troublesome. And I hate to ask you to keep away, it seems so beastly selfish, but you under-stand, old man, don't you . . .'

318

The next afternoon, while Lionel and Evelyn were away, Maddison went down to the beach and bathed with Mary and Jonquil. The child hopped about in three inches of water, splashing and giving little squeals when a wave came. She danced and sang, not at all shy of the crowd by the wet coconut matting that led from the bathing building to the water. She said she didn't care for the waves, and stretched herself in the sun on the wet silver-nailed pebbles, but when a big ninth wave rolled and crashed she leapt up and threw stones at it, and shouted: 'Nasty wet old waves, Quillie thinks you silly. Take that, old waves.'

They went for tea to Mary's aunt, Mrs. Pamment, afterwards returning to the flat. It was deserted and quiet, except for the snores of Martha asleep on a hard kitchen chair, with head fallen forward on folded arms.

'W-W-Will'um, don't wake her,' hissed Jonquil; 'she's a bit fed up to-day.'

'With Sunday dinner, I suppose.'

'No, Will'um. With life. Let's come to Grandfather's.'

They went round to Radnor Park Gardens, and found the two aunts and old Mr. Fairfax in the garden, with the cat Tommy on his knee. Seeing Billjohn, it leapt off and flew at him, spitting and making a savage noise. Billjohn fled, and Mr. Fairfax shouted irritably:

'Tommy, Tommy, Tommy, goo' boy, don't be frightened. Call your dog off, Mr. Maggleton.'

Billjohn yelled and fled round flowerpots and over flower beds, with the furry fury after him smacking with clawed paws and spitting. The noise made several dogs bark in other gardens, and Maddison threw a stone at Tommy.

'How dare you do that?' fumed Mr. Fairfax. 'How dare you! Leave the house at once. No one asked you in. Go away, Mr. Maggleston, go away this instant.'

'Hush, Father, hush,' begged Millicent. 'Think of the neighbours. They can all hear.'

At last Billjohn fled through the gate leading to an ivied lane at the bottom of the garden, and Tommy jumped on to the wall behind his master. Billjohn stood and whined in the lane.

'I beg your pardon, sir.'

'No use doing that now. The damage is done. Who let you in?'

'We walked in, sir.'

'How dare you? Why didn't you ring?'

'I pulled the bell, sir, but unfortunately it came away in my hand. The early Victorian wire was rusted through.'

'What?' cried Mr. Fairfax. 'You've broken my bell! And then you walk in?'

'I thought that better than running away. If you will let me send a tinker to-morrow, sir——'

'You must pay for it. Milly, see that he pays for it. And that window broken by an old boot on Peace Day. No doubt he flung it.'

'Father, don't be silly. You'll make yourself ill. Billy, don't take any notice. Poor dear Father is tried by the heat.'

No wonder, thought Maddison, since he was muffled up in a great coaching overcoat and a woollen scarf. The old gentleman suddenly became less irascible, and asked him if he was a British Israelite.

'No, sir.'

'Would you care to read some of the literature on the subject?'

'No, thank you, sir.'

'What did you say?'

'Poor Father is deaf,' explained Milly.

'I said I was rather busy at the moment, thanks very much,' cried Maddison. 'Besides, to be frank, I am not enthusiastic about being a member of Israel's lost tribes.'

'Ah, all godless, you young men. You like Shelley, don't you? That mad atheist, whose books my father burned!'

'First editions? What luxury, sir!'

'I can't hear very well, I'm sorry, Mr. Magglestone, but I'll ask Milly to fetch some literature.'

'Thanks, sir. I'll lend you my "Policy of Reconstruction" to read, if you like. The chapter on "Religion in Wartime" will interest you.'

'The war was made by Satan. It was prophesied in the Old Testament, Mr. Magglestone.'

'Maddison, my poor parent,' shouted Mrs. Beayne, who had come into the room, and was smiling at Maddison.

'Maddison, hum, yes. Not one of the Wiltshire Maddisons, surely?'

'My forefathers lived there, I believe, sir.'

'Then you must read about British Israel, because you come of a good stock, young man. Milly, fetch my books after supper. Mr. Maddison, you must stop to supper. Now, hearken to me. You read your Bible, of course.'

'No, sir. I prefer reading Shelley.'

'Hush, Billy!' reproved Milly. 'Father may hear you!'

'This war would have been saved if the world had realized that the old prophets had foretold Armageddon. It was for the English to realize that they are the lost tribes of Israel, the chosen race of God. Here, Tommy, Tommy, Tommy, come on my knee, then, Tommy, Tommy, Tommy.'

'The war would have been saved if people hadn't been so religious,' declared Maddison.

'Hush, poor Father *will* hear you,' said Milly. 'You mustn't joke like that,'

'You don't tell him to hush when he tells me about the Lost Tribes.'

'Now you're becoming rude, Billy.'

'Oh, yes, of course. I must never say what I think. Only a decayed intellect must dominate the world!'

'There's a difference in your age, and Father's age, remember. Besides, it's perfectly true that the English *are* the Lost Tribes of Israel. If only you weren't so conceited, if you were more idealistic, you'd take the trouble to read about it, and then, I'm sure, you'd jolly well find out you were wrong!'

Milly's voice was quite angry.

'People understand nothing,' said Maddison, in a bleak voice. 'They still think the Kaiser caused the war—they don't see how all of them helped to make it—all of them, by being what they were. Poor old Kaiser, when he was a little boy he had to study twelve hours a day under a rigid Prussian tutor. Poor little boy.'

'How dare you talk like that in this house!' cried Milly, in a voice thrilling with anger. 'How dare you! Have you no patriotism, that you talk like that to one who has lost dear friends because of those *brutes*. Those awful *beasts*, who cut off the hands of little children! Really, Billy, you make my blood boil! You're joking, surely.'

'I must go,' replied Maddison. 'Good-bye, thank you for everything. Good-day, sir. Billjohn! Heel!'

He left the house of Mr. Fairfax, who, Eve had told him, gave away half of his small income to the cause of proving that the English were the Lost Tribes, while he and his daughter Millicent, who had remained single in order to look after him, lived on the barest necessities of life.

'Religion is a filthy bird-lime; it snared the White Bird of Jesus Christ!' he muttered. 'It ruined His feathers—the white lime of sepulchral minds, the whitewash of honour hiding dead thoughts! The lost tribes! My dear Mr. Fairfax, may I be so bold as to remark that I hope no one will ever find your lost and lousy tribes?'

Composing such remarks from his agitation, with which he devastated Milly and her father, the headmaster of his old school, and many others, who directly or indirectly had caused him to writhe in the past, Maddison walked up and down the Leas, a pain at the base of his skull; and when Evelyn appeared with Milly and Lionel, calling out 'Billy!' in her charming voice, he longed to be alone with her, so that with his head surrendered to her compassionate breast he might find sanctuary from the thoughts that, like hounds, pursued him.

'Milly, I beg your pardon for being so rude.'

'It wasn't the rudeness so much, Billy, as what you said, that distressed me!' cried Milly, hotly. 'But still, we'll forget it, shall we?'

They departed, taking Jonquil; and he had to remain and answer as brightly as possible the bright remarks of Milly. She insisted on taking him home to supper, where Mr. Fairfax spoke seldom to him. At half past nine he complained of a headache, and said that he thought he would go to bed. He had acute indigestion. Mrs. Beayne said to him at the door as she let him out:

'Good-night, my dear boy. Go home and have a good rest. If it's any help, remember Aunt Margy sympathizes, if only because you like dogs. Good-night, Billyjohn, my handsome bow-wow. Bring your nice young master to see us again.'

He went on the Leas, remaining there till the promenade was almost deserted, and every other lamp had been extinguished, a sign that it was nearly eleven o'clock. Then he walked down The Paragon, on the other side of the road, and in the shadow of the garden hedge opposite the flat he watched the lighted window at the top of the house.

A man on a bicycle with a long stick came and put out the big light at the crossroads. Two church clocks chimed the hour within a few seconds of each other. He walked up and down. The light in Evelyn's bedroom was switched on, so that both sides of the top flat were illuminated. At a quarter past eleven the drawing-room became dark, but he did not move away. He leaned against the garden railings, his hand on his forehead, and trembling slightly. The hall-door opened, but he did not hear; and Lionel had come down the steps, softly on the rubber soles of his shoes, and spoken, before he looked up, wondering wildly if he should run away.

'What are you doing there?' enquired Lionel, curtly, as he crossed the road.

'I just happened to be passing,' he heard his own voice saying.

'It's Bill! My dear old man, I'm sorry I spoke like that. I saw someone hanging about, and constantly looking up—one can see quite clearly from up there—and I came to see. Hope I didn't scare you, Bill.'

'No, Lionel, no.'

'You sound a bit shaky, old man. By jove, you're trembling. Come for a quick walk to warm your blood. Nerves a bit groggy, still, I expect, after that blasted war. Don't heed what Grandfather or Milly says—they don't realize anything that happens. Cigarette?'

'Thanks awfully.'

The darkness on the Leas was comforting, and they walked past the deserted Rest Camp, coming to the cliff path.

'Shall we go down to the sea?' asked Lionel. On the wooden seat under the trees they sat down, smoking their cigarettes, a muffled blackness around and above them.

The silence was oppressive. Lionel did not speak. Maddison felt that he wanted to speak, and was waiting for himself to say something. A wind stirred the tops of the pines, making an aerial soughing remote and high above them; the waves rushed on the unseen shingle, paused, sucking back and waiting, rushing forward again. Then he was aware of little noises all about them, squeaks so shrill and sharp that the ear nearly missed them. A leaf rustled as a mouse ran swiftly to its hole under the root of a tree.

'Bill, old man, I shouldn't stay up half the night if I were you. I know the restlessness of youth, but if you strain yourself now you will regret it so much later on. You haven't been looking quite so fit lately. Is there any trouble—I don't want to be inquisitive—but sort of elder brotherly, if you understand. You regard me as a pal, don't you?'

'Oh, thank you, Lionel. I—I don't really deserve to have a pal.'

'Rot, utter rot. Look here, I'm rather concerned about you, and I'm going to take the risk of offending you. Now, I'm going to ask a dashed personal question.'

'Yes.'

'Are you worrying over any girl—I mean, of course, little Mary Ogilvie?'

He made no reply.

'I rather thought so. Well, Bill, take my advice, and leave her alone for a bit. Go away, and get some job, and work hard. Then things will come out all right. You see, if a decent girl like Mary is fond of a man, and knows, as she will, that he is fond of her, she wants to believe that he will go through any-thing to win her. A girl wants to be won, Bill, just as much as she wants to be loved. Now, forgive the next impertinence, and remember that I'm keen as mustard to help you, because I—well, I damn well like you.'

'You're too decent, Lionel.'

'Bill, have you got any private income?'

'Nothing. I've got about seventy pounds left of my gratuity; after that I'm broke.'

'Well, Bill have a little rest first, and then see about a job. Carry on with your writing afterwards. I haven't seen any of your things, but I think you've got the qualities in you, not quite matured yet, that will make you all right. You've got sensibility—anyone can see that—and love of beauty and the true things of life. Meanwhile, get a job.'

'Yes, I think I must. I feel convinced that sooner or later I shall succeed in my work.'

'I'm sure you will. But it's usually a case of later, y'know.'

'Lionel.'

'Yes?'

'I only like Mary as a friend.'

'Oh.'

Nothing was said while Lionel lit a cigarette from the stump of the old one.

'Is it anyone else I know, Bill? Don't be afraid to tell me. Is it Lina?'

He did not answer.

'You silly old ass,' said Lionel, patting his shoulder, 'you're a bit afraid of me, I do believe! Well, I will tell you a secret—there's no confidence betrayed in the circumstances. You remember when I looked round the door yesterday? For a moment I admit I was surprised when I saw you holding Lina's hand. Then I knew by her eyes and the abrupt manner of her departing that she was upset by my going away. Thereby hangs another confidence, Bill. However, Lina told me afterwards how pally you had been to her, and how you had kissed her when you saw her distress. Why, Bill, that's the very reason why I like you so much—that spontaneity, saying and doing the thing you feel. Lina herself was surprised, and, as she told me, felt a warm affection for you.'

After a pause he went on:

'I think your affection for Lina is a great compliment to her, and to me as well. Dare I confess it: I feel you're my younger brother? I'm dashed fond of you, really, Bill, old man. But I mustn't get sentimental. About Lina. She is a woman who attracts men—she has grace and beauty and that elusive quality that only the most feminine of women possess. I, as her husband, realize that I am in a sense the guardian of that beauty. You see, old chap, I am telling you this because I know you are a decent fellow——'

'I'm a waster, Lionel.'

'Nonsense, Bill! Of course you think so—what decent man doesn't? Again, even the best of men think things that they are ashamed of, and the very fact of their being ashamed shows that they have the right stuff in them. Now, the advice I am going to give you is this. Do not waste yourself on anything that is not worthy of your true self—if you do you will have to

326

repay in bitterness and pain, one way or the other. I'm not referring to you personally: I'm giving you a sort of impersonal irrelevant advice, if you understand what I mean by that.'

He paused.

'I do try to be myself,' said Maddison, desperately.

'We all do, Bill. Now, Bill, you are the sort of man who can do extraordinarily fine things—once you are sure of yourself. So I can say to you, with every sincerity, that I value your friendship and affection for Lina. When you go away, I hope you will be able to run down now and then and see her; and, above all, don't take any notice of what people say—there are always a lot of mean men and women—with little, petty souls— who are only too ready to talk. You must know the sort of thing I mean, Bill, but don't worry.'

A long silence.

'And, Bill, don't idealize women. Suffering lies that way. Face reality and crush down the vision of what you desire— don't idealize anyone too much—you will suffer, if you do——'

The listener made no reply. Through the dark a curlew whistled its sweet and husky journey-notes.

'Bill, my heart went out to you when I saw you standing by that lamp-post. I realized suddenly that you must be very lonely without a mother, or sister, or brothers, and a father you've lost touch with. I wish you were coming with me.'

'So do I.'

'Yet your way lies in another direction. A man must work out his own destiny, Bill. Go to London and get a job. Live carefully—follow your ambition, your writing, I mean, in your spare time, and then one day you will meet someone whom you will want to marry. I know, Bill: for I have felt as you are feeling now.'

A minute's silence, and he said: 'Well, Bill, what are you thinking of?'

'Nothing, Lionel,' he said, feeling that at the slightest further kindness he would lay down his head on the seat, and weep. In his mind he was seeing Eve as she knelt before the fire in his cottage, looking at him, and yet past him, with wet eyes, a woman weak and helpless and passionate, for she was in love with a man, and that man was himself. If only he had left the cottage and gone to sleep on the hillside, if only he had not set himself on fire by thrusting the torch of that auburn hair against his throat. He ought to have confessed about Devon—he was deceitful, treacherous, faithless. Yet he loved Eve, and now he was speaking to Lionel, whom he almost loved as much as one could love another man.

'Good-night, Bill.'

They shook hands and Maddison walked swiftly in the direction of the Leas; in silence he despaired, till his spirit seemed to break from actuality and stream with Shelley's wind down the golden trackways of the stars.

Chapter 28

AFTER an early breakfast at an eating house next morning, Maddison hurried round to The Paragon. Outside a one-armed man with a scarred face, standing by a barrow, clicked his heels and saluted. He returned the salute, and said good-morning, while noting the four brass wound-stripes on the man's left sleeve; and the silver badge of disablement in his buttonhole.

'Beg pardon, sir, but would you tell the General that the outside porter is present, and, he hopes, correct?'

'I will; but how do you know I am the General's friend?'

'Beg pardon, sir, but I thought you must be, as I've seen you about with the General so often.'

'Right. I'll give your message.'

'Very good, sir.'

The ex-soldier came to attention.

He stepped into the hall, seeing that the ground-floor rooms were still in a state of incomplete decoration, owing to a strike of the workmen. Up two flights of stairs he came to the second floor, occupied, in Evelyn's description, by a 'disagreeable little red-nosed uneducated elderly man retired from a grocery business', who was at that moment, as at most of his moments, quarrelling behind closed doors with a bewigged woman, whom he claimed as his niece. Up the third and fourth flights, and he came to the door of the Fairfax flat.

He knocked, and waited. He knocked again, and after a further wait Martha came and opened it. The hall was piled with uniform cases and trunks.

'Why didn't you walk in as usual, mister? It wasn't locked.'

'Oh, I see. Are they here?'

'In there, mister.' She pointed to the bedroom door. 'The missus isn't very well, mister. She's got one of her headaches, what she sometimes has when she isn't very well. She's very upset because the General's going away, mister.'

'Yes, I suppose she is.'

He sat down in the drawing-room and waited. He glanced at the papers, only to throw them down again. About five minutes went by, and a door was pulled open and Lionel strode into the room. Maddison did not look at his face.

'Just coming, Bill,' he said quietly, walking round the table twice, taking a cigarette, and patting his pockets for matches. He seemed very hot, and wiped his brow with a handkerchief. He avoided Maddison's eyes. Maddison looked on the floor. 'Matches?'

'Doesn't matter—don't want to smoke, Bill.'

The cigarette was thrown out of the window.

'The porter is outside, Lionel.'

'Oh, good. We haven't much time. Lord, I hope I haven't forgotten anything.'

'Shall I call him up?'

'If you wouldn't mind. Martha, where's the decanter?'

'Here you are, mister,' gasped the maid, rushing in with a jingling tray bearing decanter, siphon, and tumblers. ' 'Ave a good stiff peg, mister.'

'Thank you. A little present, Martha.'

He handed her a five pound banknote.

'Thank you, mister, but I don't want that.'

'Go on, take it; don't be silly. And look after Jonquil and Mrs. Fairfax, won't you?'

'Yes, mister, of course I will. Don't you fret, mister. Here, drink a good stiff peg, mister.'

There were tears in Martha's old eyes, and she looked at Lionel with a grieved expression.

The porter, who had been beckoned from the window by Maddison, rang the bell, and Martha went out.

'I drink to our friendship, Bill!'

They clinked glasses, and drank, looking at each other. 'One more, Bill.'

Major Fairfax raised his second tumbler of almost neat whiskey, and looked straight at him.

'Here's good fortune to you, Bill.'

'Thank you. And to you—I—oh, good fortune, Lionel!'

They clinked glasses again and drank, or rather gulped.

'Hat, stick, gloves, waterproof. But it won't rain. Money. Notecase—matches—damn, I want some matches.'

'Take mine.'

'Thanks. Is that luggage gone?'

'All correct, sir. Is Lina going to the station?'

'No, we say good-bye here. You see—train—I hate scenes—'

'Yes. Shall I go on?'

'Will you? Right-ho. I'll catch you up.'

'I'll take your riding coat, sir.'

'Will you? Thanks. See you there.'

'Aren't you going to say good-bye to the aunts?'

'Done that already.'

'Well, I'll go now.'

'Right-ho, old man.'

Maddison felt like a galloper to the General. God, if only the war was still on, and he were Lionel's aide! God, he loved Lionel—too late, too late for any friendship now. With the heavy hunting waterproof coat on his arm, he left the flat, just as Evelyn in dove-grey kimono, fastened by a silk rope and pompons, slipperless and loose mane of hair flying out behind, leapt up the stairs to fetch Jonquil. She looked at him in passing, without recognition or greeting. He went downstairs, pretending not to see the little man in the flat below peeping through one door, and his niece through the other.

He loitered till Lionel joined him, and quickly they walked

to the station, finding that they had ten minutes before the train left. They strolled slowly up and down the platform while the boxes were labelled for London. Major Fairfax talked about a number of irrelevant things, and hearing the whistle of the approaching engine he took hold of Maddison's left arm just above the elbow, and said:

'She's beginning to realize that the hat she's looking for is on her head already. Bill, go and see her as before. She wants a real pal. And, when you go away, run down sometimes, won't you?'

'Yes, I will, Lionel.'

'Twelve months. Well, it's worth it, Bill, I'll take my coat. Thanks. Smoker, please!' to the porter.

The trunks and boxes were dragged into the guard's van, people walked past seeking empty carriages, hatless heads looked out of open windows. Passengers found seats. The guard stood by with his green flag. Lionel jumped in and leaned his elbows on the window frame.

'Good-bye, Bill.'

'Good-bye, Lionel.'

'Write to me.'

'Yes.'

The guard waved his flag, the whistle shrieked, the train moved.

'Look after Lina for me,' came the last words, almost in lip movement, and Maddison whispered 'Yes'. Until the train rounded a curve and so hid him from sight, he stood unmoving, except for a hand sometimes waved. Then he walked very slowly back to 9a, The Paragon.

THE BROKEN WEB

Chapter 29

When Maddison walked into the room, fortified to say good-bye, trying to prevent the tears from coming into his eyes, Evelyn was listlessly sitting on the couch, in the grey kimono, her hair loosely coiled. She greeted him quietly, turning her glance to rest upon him for a moment, before staring out of the window again.

He waited, standing by the fireplace. It was still early, before nine o'clock, and the sea breeze was scarcely stirring. He looked round the walls, at the Zulu knobkerries and shields and assegais, a rhinoceros-hide Kaffir-whip, and other souvenirs of African travel; at the water-colours, and photographs of Rodin's sculptures; at the picture of the darling child who was Evie, whose blue-grey eyes looked, even as Eve's were looking now, beyond the beholder. He moved sideways, wondering if Eve were seeing him; and she was, but with what a strange look.

'Bill.'

'Yes?'

'Are you my friend?'

He nodded.

'Can I tell you something very secret.'

'Yes, of course.'

She drew her legs up on the couch, and the swan's-down slippers dangled from her toes.

'Bill, Lionel made me go down on my knees and pray with him.'

He nodded, looking on the floor, thinking that such behaviour went with loud laughter.

335

'Billy, I really did pray.'

He nodded, not looking at her.

'I wanted to love him. O, why——'

He waited.

'Yes, I prayed to love him. Then he—he kissed me. I felt s
good, somehow. Then he—O, I can't tell you.' She hid he
face in her hands. 'O, I could have jumped out of the window

Martha knocked, and came slowly in.

'Would you like a cup of tea, ma'am? And some nice ho
toast and butter?'

'Thank you, Marty darling. And bring some for Captai
Maddison, too.'

'Of course, ma'am.'

Martha went out slowly and quietly, thus conveying her sym
pathy for the missus.

Evelyn leaned back and shook free her hair, dividing it int
two tresses, which she pulled over her shoulders and com
menced to plait. He went and sat by her. His knee presse
against the pink feet. She looked at him over her right shoulde
head thrown back obliquely, while slowly plaiting the left tres

'You look sad, Eve. Tell me.'

She shook her head sadly.

After a while he took the right tress in his hands, and bega
to divide it into three, for plaiting; but gently she detached hi
hands.

'No, Billy.'

'Shall I ask Martha to help you?' he exclaimed, rising.

'No, thank you. Martha has her own work to do. Billy
want you to be serious a moment.'

'Yes.'

'It must end, Billy.'

'What must end?'

'You know very well what I mean. You mustn't make lov
to me any more.'

He said as calmly as he could:

336

'I had no intention of doing so.'

But he winced at her immediate reply of: 'I am glad I see things differently now. I feel a swine.'

'I'll go to-day.'

'Where will you go?'

He shrugged his shoulders. 'Anywhere.'

'Don't be hurt,' she begged him, taking his hand, which lay limply in hers.

'Listen, my dear. I've given Lionel my word of honour that I'll write and tell him immediately if ever I feel I love anyone more than him. We went down on our knees and he asked me to pray to God so that I shall grow to love him. Oh, Bill, I felt that my heart would break! I shall never love him. I wish I could!'

He said nothing.

'You understand, don't you?'

'Perfectly.'

'Billy, don't be unkind.'

'Am I unkind? I'm sorry. I do understand.'

'But you say it in such funny tones as though you didn't care. And I did so want you to understand that I am trying to play the game—a bit late in the day, perhaps, but I am.'

'I understand.'

'You understand nothing at all!' she cried, striking him in the chest with her fist. 'God, you men are awful!'

He waited, expectation deep within him; but to his surprise she began to cry. She clutched a cushion with her fingers, while hiding her face in her other arm.

'Dear Eve,' he said, taking her wrist. Her hand unclutched the cushion, and held two of his fingers.

'Tell me, Eve, why you are so unhappy. Don't be afraid. I like Lionel, too, you know. Don't cry, my sweet. There, lie still in my arms; I'll always be with you if you want me.'

How strangely small she seemed, hiding her face on his chest, while he protected her head with his arms, and stroked her hair, passing his hand over her head and down to the hollow at the nape of the neck. Her hair was adorable. He pressed his lips on her hair. He felt tender and strong.

'He will come home soon,' he whispered.

'Blast him!' she sobbed.

How could one ever understand a woman?

'I'll tell you,' she said, sitting up. 'I wanted to love him. I held him in my arms. Then—then he—O God—then he asked me "to excuse him", while he "got something".' She hid her face in her hands, shuddering.

'Billy, I just withered. O, I hate him!'

He stared out of the window, wide-eyed, serious.

'I expect—wasn't there—I mean didn't you nearly die when Quillie——'

'God, you men! You know nothing!' she cried, running out of the room.

She came back five minutes later, followed by Martha with a tray of tea and buttered toast.

'Sorry for being such a fool,' she said. 'I feel better now. Have some toast. It's beautifully done, Marty dear. No, the tea isn't too strong—just right. Now go and get your own breakfast, you poor dear.'

'I say, Bill, you should have seen our daughter saying good-bye. Kissing him demurely and holding out a polite paw. "Good-bye, father, and hope you have a nice voyage. Quilly must go now, as Swally is crying!" Complete staggeration of paterfamilias! Exit, right, to nursery.'

'Poor Lionel!'

'Oh, I don't suppose he worries. He isn't very fond of children.'

'All his capital is sunk in one big company.'

'Whatever does that extraordinary expression mean?'

'You're his wife.'

'He's awfully keen on his job.'

'I speak metaphorically of his emotions.'

THE BROKEN WEB

'Then I'm going. Call a spade a spade by all means, even call it a bloody shovel, but don't call it an implemental stratum disturber. See you in five minutes. Come shopping?'

'Yes, I'll hang about outside shops with a basket, if you like.'

He saw her in twenty minutes as she looked round the door in the dressing gown after her bath, but it was fifty minutes before she was dressed, and then she called him into the bedroom to fasten the back hooks of her white frock. They went round to her grandfather's, where she told them that she was 'bearing up as best she could'. Aunt Milly cried 'Of course you are, dear old gel.'

They went into Corvano's for ice creams. Mr. de la Hay sat there. He rose, bowed, and smiled.

'Hullo, Aubrey, sorry I'm late. How's the show.'

'Oh, going well. We're going to Manchester next week. 'Morning, Maddison.'

'Good morning.'

'Sit down, Aubrey. Lionel went off this morning.'

'Did he? It's hot in the train, I expect.'

After a few minutes Maddison closed his volume of Shelley, of which he had read nothing, and got up. 'I've just remembered an engagement. Will you excuse me if I rush off?'

'Of course, Billy. Will you be back to lunch?'

'Well, it is an engagement for lunch, and tea as well, I expect. Tennis, you know.'

'Then I shall see you at dinner?'

'I'm dining out, too.'

'Really. Well, good-bye—hope you have a good game.'

They both smiled at him, and he went down to the beach with Billjohn trotting at his heels too hot to explore the myriad smells that came to it. He tried to read. With dreadful slowness the time passed. He went to see Mary; went away; went back again to the restaurant, to see with anguish the empty chair where she had sat. All the afternoon he waited on the Leas, but she did not come. He had eaten nothing since the morning.

At nine o'clock he went round to The Paragon.

There was no light in the drawing-room. In the kitchen he could hear the soft steaming of a kettle. Martha sat within, with folded arms, staring at the gas stove. She looked up wearily as he walked in.

'She's gone out, mister.'

'Where to?'

'I don't know, mister. She expected you to lunch and tea, and a cover was laid for you at dinner, but you didn't come. She's been solitary all day, mister. I think she misses the master very much.'

'Yes, I expect she does. Wasn't Mr. de la Hay here, then?'

'No, mister. Would you like a cup of coffee?'

'No, thank you, Martha. I suppose you don't know where she's gone?'

'No, mister. She said she couldn't wait here any more, and went out.'

'I'll go and find her, then.'

'Yes, mister.'

He went on the Leas, walking quickly and scanning in the light of the lamps the faces of the people he passed on foot and on the seats. He could not see her. The time came when every other lamp was switched out, and he was a mile past the bandstand. Thinking she might be on one of the lower walks he left the promenade and went along a parallel path a few yards below the top of the Leas. Seeing a dim figure coming slowly towards him he sat down on a seat and hid his face in his coat collar. It was a woman, and she went past slowly, but whether or no she looked at him he did not see. A man was following her. Stealthily he passed the seat, overtaking her some distance away. He listened. He heard the footsteps stop, and a man's voice saying: 'Good-evening. What are you doing all by yourself, little girl, and so late at night?'

The man continued, in a slightly altered voice: 'Surely I met you on the beach this morning?'—and Eve's reply: 'If so, I've quite forgotten.' There was a pause. 'Well, perhaps I made a mistake,' said the man. 'Don't let it worry you,' said Evelyn, amiably. 'Good-night. Is that you, Billy?'

'Yes,' he said, jumping up. The man slipped away.

'Where have you been, Billy?'

'I've been looking for you. Who's that bounder?'

'Some lonely soul or other, trying to find happiness, I suppose. Is that the definition of "bounder"?'

They stared at each other.

'I've been looking for you everywhere, Eve.'

'Did Martha tell you I was out?'

'Yes, I came to find you.'

'That's very kind of you. I didn't know I had such a friend.'

'I went away this morning because I felt unwanted.'

'That's rather a habit of yours, isn't it, my dear? It has its cause in jealousy, weakness, and conceit.'

They went up to the promenade, and strolled in the direction of home, speaking seldom. Outside the flat he said good-night, but did not go away; and she said quietly:

'Well, good-bye Billy. Write to me sometimes, won't you?'

He could not speak.

'Just think, Lionel's far out to sea, now. Looking over the rail towards the last English lighthouse. I wish I could send the dear old boy a wireless.'

'Yes,' he stared at his feet. 'O, Eve, it's all so sad!'

Some singing soldiers passed, arm-in-arm, walking back to Shorncliffe Camp. When they had gone she said casually:

'I had a wire from Sandy White to-day, and I rather wanted to ask your advice about him. But if you would rather not——'

'You know I'd do anything in the world to help you, Eve.'

'You have a funny way of showing your devotion. But you're of such fine tissue, I suppose, that my coarse nature upsets you.

341

You ought to have been a woman, Billy, and I ought to have been a man. You would be a nun.'

'Don't, Eve. You're not coarse—I believe you are too fine for ordinary men.'

'And you are too fine for ordinary women. There, don't we esteem each other!' she said bitterly.

'It often seems to me that you delight in hurting people.'

'Only those I love.'

'And your love is like the chafing sea.' He added: 'But I love you just the same.'

'You mustn't say that any more, Billy.'

'No. I'd better go,' he said quietly. He waited.

'Won't you come in a moment for a cigarette?'

'Are you sure I shan't be in the way?'

'Don't talk in that unnatural manner. Be your own dear self, Billy.'

Martha gave them coffee, and Eve said: 'You poor dear, have you been waiting up for me? Go to bed, Marty.'

They sipped the coffee, and smoked cigarettes. Motor-cars passed outside, and then the big lamp at the cross-streets was extinguished by a man with a long stick. Only one shaded reading lamp illumined the room.

'I'll show you the telegram,' she said, rising to get it. When he had read it, and re-read it, Maddison asked her who was meant by Mignon.

'That is supposed to be me.'

'A term of affection?'

'I suppose so. Surely you know it is a French word, meaning darling? Where were you brought up?'

'Not in France. He is in love with you, Eve.'

'In his boyish way, I suppose he is. I can't help it.'

He gave her back the telegram, and she said:

'I suppose he'll be hanging about for six days. I don't want to see him. I don't want to receive his wild letters, or his poems, or to read the books he sends me—and I don't want to be unkind. What can a woman do? Tell me, Billy.'

'It seems to be rather a question of what—men—should not do.'

'You've said it exactly. You're very wise sometimes, my friend. In fact, almost a prig. No, I didn't mean that.'

'It's true, anyway,' he said bitterly. 'And a conceited egoist, weak, and without charity.'

The coffee finished, and three cigarettes, he rose to go.

'Don't make any noise going down, will you?'

'I'm going back to Devon in three days.'

'Why?' she asked, and he saw what he imagined to be a look of fear in her eyes.

He did not reply to her question, but walked to the window and stared at the dimmed street below. She said:

'Have you been with Mary to-day?'

'Yes.'

'I see.'

She looked at him sideways.

'Very well, go back to Devon with her.'

He said that he would go back to Rat's Castle, and never see anyone again.

'Never, never, never ' he declared, the tears coming in his eyes.

'Then go, with my blessing. Good-bye, my dearest one.'

She stretched her arms above her head, bending backwards, rising to her toes with an exquisite flexion. The arms came down slowly on his shoulders, and she rested her head on his coat, as though she were weary. He stood still, thinking of Lionel. With arms wound round him she confessed that she did not realize before how terribly jealous she could be, and how miserable he could make her.

'Billy, I can't live without you, really I can't. I knew it to-day. Don't distrust me, Billy. You are more than my life to me. You don't care about Mary, do you? I could have killed you when I saw you talking on the beach this afternoon, with your head so close to hers. Hold me, Billy. You wild bird, you have caged your mistress. Billy, speak to me.'

He held her head against his heart, smoothing the childlike brow, and smiling as he laid his cheek on the adorable hair.

'Poor poppy,' he whispered. 'Did someone pluck it, so that its petals withered, and the seeds it had dreamed of in the sun were lost. Poor poppy, token of hope in the parched and over-burdened earth. You see, I remember all you say. And I slashed the poor thistles.'

'Ah, but then I told you to go to the devil!' she murmured, snuggling into his arms, as though she were Jonquil.

'Well, that's calling the bloody shovel a spade!'

'You're laughing at me,' said the muffled voice.

'Funny, how bony a woman's head feels,' he said, clasping her head. 'I mean the lovely shape it feels. I mean, your head is so innocent in its shape, so trustful. I can't express myself. Now I must go.'

'Don't go. I feel afraid without you. Sometimes the world terrifies me.'

'It terrifies us all at times.'

'You don't often feel afraid, do you, though?'

'Nearly all the time.'

'What?' She lifted her face, and looked at him. 'You're just pretending. Why, you're the strongest man I know!'

'Don't mock me.'

'I swear I'm not!'

'But Lionel's much stronger than I am.'

'Lionel's a weak man. Weak, weak! A-ah!' She clenched her teeth. ' "Hail to thee, blithe spirit, bird thou never wert!" '

'That's Shelley! I didn't know you read Shelley!'

'Ah, you don't know anything about me, my dear! There's Jonquil crying! Just a moment!'

'I'm going now.'

She leapt up the stairs.

'No, I'll be back in a minute!'

THE BROKEN WEB

He felt himself to be strong.

'See you to-morrow.'

He opened the door, softly closing it behind him and going downstairs. The stars shone serenely above The Paragon. Till one o'clock he paced the lower road by the sea, alone with the spaniel and the cool night wind that flowed tirelessly from the waves. Then he went to his lodging, and taking *The Policy of Reconstruction* from his suitcase, wrote until sunrise.

Chapter 30

IT was a happy breakfast, he and Eve and Quillie.

'You are so sweet to me, Eve.'

'But it is you who are so sweet to me, Billy!'

After swimming, and luncheon, they took the two-seater from the garage, and motored out of Folkestone, down the hill into Sandgate, and along the level road to Hythe; through the narrow streets of Hythe, left-handed round the sharp corner where Phillip, coming from the London road, had once crashed on his motor-cycle, she told him. The London road went to the right; they took the left fork, along by flat marshy fields behind the shingle-ridge and the sea, past the School of Musketry, and the deserted hutments and concrete hangars of an aerodrome stretching far into the distance.

Hiring a skiff, he sculled her up the military canal. She sat in the stern, holding the rudder-lines. A party of blue-suited soldiers from hospital sitting on the towpath whistled and passed remarks to them as they glided by.

'You're all right, mate!'

'She's a pretty little girl from nowhere, nowhere at all,' chanted one.

Another sang with lung-gassy wheeziness: 'All day long he —call-all-ed her snooky-ookums.'

'That's a boatload fit for a hero,' remarked a wag with half his face shot away.

'Company, eyes front!' ordered another, presenting arms with a crutch.

She was called *Lizzie*, *Lil*, *Mademoiselle from Armentières*, *My beautiful ba-byee doll*, and other names.

346

'I love them all,' she said as he pulled through the weed-beds, for the water was low owing to the drought. 'I wish I could be everything to all men. Does that sound silly?'

'It sounds just like my charitable, my beautiful Eva!'

He sculled on in the hot sunshine. When far away and by themselves, he let the sculls slide on the water. Slowly the skiff drifted into the bank. He held a willow while she stepped out. They sat in the shade of the willow, while with a withy wand, a thread of cotton, and a bent pin baited with a bread-pill he tried to catch the red-finned roach which passed slowly in shoals among the submerged weed-forests. He watched his lovely Eve, softly radiant as in the early summer sun of Vention sands, taking off shoes and stockings, and with cotton skirt tucked up, dabble her toes in the coolth of the water. The ripples threw a soft light on her face shaded by a large hat, making more lovely the glances she gave him.

A pair of royal swans with three dun cygnets in their wake bore down upon them, and hove up, gravely accepting the pieces of bread she tossed to them. Then with bare feet they walked down the towpath, taking the kettle and the tea basket, and explored the desolate aerodrome. They visited the officers' quarters, now empty and littered with paper, wondering how fared the vanished inhabitants: the pilot who had drawn these charcoal sketches of girls' heads on the asbestos sheets of the walls, how fared he—in whatever world he moved or slept? And where the hand that had pasted up the coloured drawings and photogravures of actresses and society beauties from *The Sketch*, *The Tatler*, and *The Bystander*.

Contemplation of these dusty relics of a lost and scattered generation made them silent as they wandered from hollow grey cubicle to hollow grey cubicle, and down the empty corridors, where hung scarlet fire-buckets; and cobwebs. On the hot asphalt of the paths from one hut to another they ran on their toes because of the heat, making a tour of these quiet places. They had tea in one of the lofty mechanics' sheds, once filled by the sickly mist of castor oil, and the haar and roar of tested rotary engines. Now it was a place of mice and moths and dried oil-patches, with green sorrel growing unsunned amid rotted paper by the concrete walls.

As they went back to the skiff she saw a bird rustling through the grass between two sheds. She caught it. It struggled, its heart throbbed, its beak gaped. It was a lark with a trailing wing, broken by the claw-stroke of a hawk. Tears rolled down her cheeks; it was so frail and thin and weak and helpless.

'O, look, look, my little hurt one!' she cried in a small voice.

His heart spilled over, and he embraced her, smoothing her cheek, stirred to the core of his being by her woman's tenderness. He took the bird from the nest of her hands. The shoulder joint of the wing was festered. He lifted the wing, and it came apart from the bird. The lark fluttered one ragged wing.

'Good-bye, bird,' he said, and putting it on the ground, trod out its life.

'Billy!'

'Nothing is lost in earth or air.'

'O, Billy, how could you?'

'Never will I forget your pity, dear, dear, gentle Eva.'

'Was that a lark?' she said, as he sculled slowly towards Hythe.

'Yes.'

'Once you said I was like a lark. Remember?'

He nodded.

She smiled pensively, trailing her fingers in the water.

'Billy, thank you for a lovely day.'

'Thank you, Eve.' He added: 'And thank you, also, Lionel.'

'Don't be cynical!'

'Sorry. I merely felt he should be included in the general acknowledgments.'

'And you call yourself a thinker! An apostle of freedom!'

She drove home silently. He sat beside her, the spaniel with paws on the side of the car, ears and hair of head blown back, nose ever flairing the wind for the smells that made its eyes dreamy.

'Eve, sorry I was unkind.'

'Darling, you are sweet. I realize now how brave you were to put that poor lark out of its pain. I've been thinking, too, how decent you've been to Warbeck, to Sandy White's mother, to Lionel.'

'And to Grandpa Fairfax!'

'He's just a bloody old fool, darling. No one takes any notice of him! Come in and talk to me. We've got lovely sea trout for dinner; I told Marty to serve it luke-warm, with mayonnaise and the thinnest cucumber slices. And Lionel's wine merchant delivered some champagne this morning, with a note from Lionel, asking me and you to drink his health.'

'Poor old Lionel.'

'Don't waste your sympathy. He's all right. He loves being alone, really.'

'Do you honestly think so?'

'Yes. Do you know, on our honeymoon, just before the war, he made up a foursome at golf the third morning. While I looked on.'

'Quite right, too. He wasn't your property!'

'And isn't. Everyone belongs to themselves.'

Upstairs, he said suddenly:

'But in rare cases they immingle. Do you know, I believe the retort of Jesus, when the Pharisees were trying to trap him, meant this: Whom God hath joined—that is, who are wedded in impersonal love, as well as human love—let any man try and part them, if he can! He meant it wasn't possible. You try and part two swans! Likewise, or contrariwise, those who weren't wedded in impersonal love—such as Shelley and Harriet Westbrook—God parts them asunder. They weren't "meant for each other"! Whereas old Grampa Fairfax interprets that witty, profound, ironic, *truthful* retort—better epigram than any made by any Lord Chancellor—as: Whom the Church service hath joined, are tied for life whether they like it or not.'

Observing the strained look coming on his face, she knelt beside him on the couch, and smoothed his hair with her hands.

'But how terribly clever W-W-Will'um's becoming! Very soon the Rev. Elliot will be packing up from the Parish Church and donning a captain's uniform of the Salvation Army!'

'No, but seriously, Eve——'

'Darling, I am terribly serious. Of course you are right!'

'Dinner is served, ma'am.'

'Thank you, Marty. Now Bill, remember you mustn't pop the bubbly cork into the ceiling until we've had the soup—best American tinned!'

350

Chapter 31

AFTER supper they sat by the open window as twilight stole up the street and dissolved the harsh fronts of the houses. They held hands, but did not speak. The street lamps winked brighter, and shadows were thrown by the big light over the crossroads. Martha had finished washing up, and sat with arms folded in the kitchen on a wooden chair. Jonquil was in bed and sleeping.

Evelyn gently withdrew her hand from his clasp, and stood up, saying that she was going for a walk down by the sea. He stood up and walked to the door, opening it for her. She passed with a murmur of thanks and went into her room to get a fur coat, for the early autumn evening was chilly. He waited outside in the hall, leaning against the wall and immediately falling into a reverie of Jesus and himself. When he heard her voice calling his name, he started up and said:

'Hullo?'

'Come here a minute, Billy.'

He pushed the door open and walked inside. The room was in darkness, except for the wafted lights of street lamps on the ceiling. She was standing still by the wardrobe.

'Come here, Billy.'

The seductive tone of her command made his heart beat quicker. He went to her, where she stood with her fur coat thrown open.

'What a Conradian atmosphere in this room,' he said. 'Listen: "The fragrance of an eastern scent, mysterious and ancient, seemed to steal upon him like the whispered breath of desire." How's that for a pasty-faced imitation of Conrad?'

He touched her cheek with the back of his fingers, an
smoothed her eyebrows; he stroked her hair and made the tip
of fingers and thumbs meet round her neck, but the contact wa
light.

'Well, Eve, what do you want me for?' he said through hi
teeth.

'Be the darling Billy you were in Devon,' she murmured.

He bent his trembling knees so that their faces almos
touched, and his eyes were level with hers. In the dimness he
features were immobile and marble-chaste—the brow mad
whiter by the dark hair above it, the large eyes with their dar
lashes, the lips that she moistened as he held her face in hi
hands and tilted her head.

'Are you going to marry me?' he asked. 'If you say yes, I wil
kiss your sanguine lips as they have never been kissed before
And I'll go and tell Father everything, and take you with me
and get the money due to me under my mother's marriag
settlement. Then I'll write to Lionel, and tell him that I lov
you, and that you love me. For you do, don't you?'

She nodded, sighing.

'Your eyes are like the little wild grey wood dove,' he
murmured.

'Darling W-Will'um,' he heard her whisper as though from
her breast. 'Will'um—there, I'm imitating Quillie again!
can never be myself. O God, what, who am I really?'

'And you must write to Lionel, too, because you promised.

'Kiss me,' she murmured.

'Not now, Eve.'

'Have you forgotten how soft my lips are?'

'No, how could I? For you rub them with lipstick so
often!'

'Brute! Kiss me.'

'Will you marry me?'

She did not answer.

'Answer, Eve. Will you marry me?'

352

'Modern version of honour—lover desires to make honest woman of another man's wife in other man's house!'

He turned from her roughly.

'Billy, to be serious. You think too much about ethics. You are fighting against God, or trying to! Conscience, Naps says is only social fear. Oh yes, Naps is quite as clever as you, if you only knew it! He's a deep man!'

'Damn Naps! Eve, can't you see—I am thinking of you, Eve, and also of Lionel.'

'And of your silly little vision.'

'Sorry. I haven't made myself understood. I—I tell the truth, and try to be less weak for your sake, and you reply "silly little vision".'

'You can't care for me very much if you prefer your principles—which, apparently, you make up from any idea which comes into your head—to my love. For that is what you really mean. You have a tremendous desire to reform me, I know, and I suppose it is a very worthy one, but I think that if you would realize that a woman *is a woman*, and not a Francis Thompson's dream or a Swinburne's Dolores, you would be nearer to universal truth. I don't want to hurt your feelings, but so many men have tried to improve my third-rate brain with their first-class minds that my poor head can't hold any more! Except Naps,' she added. 'He is the most natural man I know—he's never needed any policy of reconstruction!'

He made no reply.

'Well, Billy, are you going to sulk?'

He was sitting on the edge of the bed. He rose abruptly and put an arm around her shoulders, pulling her to him. His heart was cold.

'Oh, no, you don't! Do you think you alone have feelings? You can't snub a woman, and make her curl up with shame, and then expect her to melt for you at your first regretful impulse. No, Billy!'

z   353

THE DREAM OF FAIR WOMEN

'I think we are looking at things from different viewpoints' he said.

'A wonderful discovery! I do feel flattered! I've been tellin you the same elemental truth about man and woman ever sinc I met you, and you, with your wayward disregard of all othe opinions except the ones you happen to hold at any particula moment, never listened! Well, my words fall on stony grounc Now I'm going down by the sea to be alone. No, don't yo dare to touch me! Let me pass, please! Thank you.'

She went out of the flat. From the open window he watche her running down the stone steps, and along the lamp-lit stree to the Leas. She faded into the night; and when his strainin eyes could see her no more he sprang up from the floor wher he had been kneeling, and followed.

He went down to the lower promenade, peering at th couples whispering under the trees. He met her almost at onc and, as he had dreaded, she was with a man. He would hav passed, but she said gaily:

'Hullo, Billy.'

'Good-evening, Lina,' he replied, happy in his relief that he companion was an old gentleman.

'Do you know my friend, Captain Maddison, Sir Rudolph? she said to him. 'Billy, this is Sir Rudolph Cardew.'

'I saw you at the Victory Ball, I think, sir?'

With the courtly and reserved manner which for more tha half a century had been part of his nature, the veteran an retired actor-manager swept off the black hat which was one c the classic sights of Folkestone and Piccadilly. Throughout th races and tribes of the world, with their varied and multitudi nous head-dresses (Sir Rudolph was wont to explain), no ha similar in height, breadth and length was like the hat speciall made for and worn by himself. Sir Rudolph's hat was a fourth dimension hat. It was black, and at a casual glance appeare to be a bowler hat; but its crown was the shape of an acorr Sir Rudolph's beautiful white hair was long and thick, an

when both hands were not behind him as he walked with all
the world for stage, one was moving an ebony stick as though
it were a wand, and the other was stroking his beautiful
moustaches. He wore a black cape and a black-framed monocle, and spoke in the rich clear voice of one who on the stage,
before rapt audiences, had known every joy and sorrow, and
with a magnanimous calm was allowing life to pass him until
Death, the Final Curtain, should fall.

'How do you do, Maddison?' the old gentleman said, placing
his hat on his head and confirming an imaginary spell with his
stick.

'The leaves are falling, pushed by the buds of a new generation. No longer are the airs of the night warm. When will
come the rain, an old man wonders.'

Thinking that he was asked a question, Maddison made a
hazard that the rain would come at the full of the moon; but
when he realized that Sir Rudolph expected no reply to his
soliloquy, he broke off in the middle of his answer.

'Mrs. d'Arcy Fairfax, I am forced to admit that what you
were saying just now is, alas, true. Why, my little grand-
daughter has but one idol, and who do you think that idol is?
Why, Miss Mary Pickford. The buds of the new generation!
Well, Mrs. d'Arcy Fairfax, although I have no wish to de-
preciate the kinema, may an old man who knows you be
allowed to say that mildly, ah, mildly, he would deprecate the
loss, for his profession, of a charming voice. What do you
think, Maddison, of the ambition of Mrs. d'Arcy Fairfax to
become an actress for the kinema?'

The old gentleman removed his monocle and swung it on its
black riband; and before Maddison could think of a suitable
reply he said that he must be returning home; and with a
sweep of his original hat Sir Rudolph was gone.

'What a decent old boy. But are you going to be an actress
for the movies?'

'No. I made it up,' she replied shortly.

They walked for a quarter of a mile, silently in starlight, and then he said that he was sorry he had upset her. She took his arm, and was her dear self again.

'Billy, I am a beast to you. And you are so decent to me.'

In her fur coat she was so warm and luring that he swung her round and enfolded her for a kiss, but she put the back of her hand over her mouth and whispered:

'No. No. You mustn't. Not here. Someone may see us. O, Billy, you are naughty.'

'I can see stars shining in your eyes.'

'Billy, why aren't you always like this?'

He thought that nowadays she was seldom like that to him; but the fault obviously lay with himself. In future he would make his dream a thing apart from the world of men and women; and even as in ecstatic happiness after so much repressed misery he resolved to make it so, he knew that such philosophy was false, if Christ were the touchstone. And had he not realized Jesus through himself? Every man was Christ's brother, if only he believed in himself—in spite of all teaching, all else—Christ's equal. The seeds of Christ lay under the asphalt promenade of every man's education and civilization. God, what a discovery! He would make it the climax of *The Policy of Reconstruction*!

'O darling Eve, I am happy because one human being seems at last to understand me.'

'Not because Eve is with you?'

'Because Eve is with me in spirit I am free as the wind to-night.'

'Poof, your mouldy old spirit. Still harping on that string? I'm going home.'

He was left alone. He wandered on the deserted path and sat down on the steps of the sea wall. It was the end. He could bear no more. He would go away. What was there left? The countryside and the dreams it gave. O Spring, come soon!

He leaned against the stone pillar, and the wind bore him

away, so that he was a boy again, speaking to the brook his thin legs had so often leapt. The sun sparkle was there as of old; soon would come the swallows, the darling swallows, to change it into song. Under the current waved the green water grasses. A kingfisher passed over the shining stream. A silver dace rose for a fly. On the hawthorns the buds were opening; chaffinches were singing in every hedge.

The faithful solar spring! Faithful to bring the early speed-well beside the cart-track, faithful to lead the windflower through the dead leaves, and the green woodpecker laughing in the glade. The country was faithful and unchanging; never would it betray the dreams it gave. And Christ was the essence of the world's beauty! God, now he understood Thompson's *Hound of Heaven*. 'Halts by me that footfall.' *The Policy of Reconstruction* led to Christ, discovered out of his own experiences. Truth! Even so, why were his hands clenched, his lip bitten in anguish. *I started life with Evie; then Eva; then it was Eve; then Eveline, and now*—Willie Maddison—Evie what? Willie, Evie—they matched. Eva's lips were full and red, her eyes shy and wondering, sometimes bold. Eve was a wife at sixteen! Eveline, Evelyn—so worldly, so at ease, like a grape solidified in a lime stream. Yet sometimes the bloom of Eva—Devon—he groaned, and ran up the steep path to the Leas.

He met her by the bandstand. She was sitting on a seat, hat-less, her hands in the pockets of her fur coat. He deliberately made his tone gay, and asked her why she had run away from him. She shrugged her shoulders, and said she was cold, and was going home.

He walked beside her, putting his hand in her pocket and holding her fingers. Their fingers interlocked. Outside the flat he was about to stop, but she held on to his hand and said with a firmness that thrilled him:

'No, I shall not let you go this time.'

He felt small, and yielded to her cherishing will. They walked up the stairs, finding the light burning in the kitchen, and old Martha with crossed arms and forward head dozing on the same old hard chair. 'Oh, Marty, you poor dear, go to bed,' said Eve, kissing her; but she insisted on making them coffee and serving it to them in the drawing-room. Wearily she set down the tray, and wearily went upstairs.

'Now, I must go, too,' he said, rising when the coffee was finished. He would go back to Shelley Cove, and live alone again, the greatest thing of his life behind him.

'You needn't,' she murmured, looking away, her head on one side. 'Come and sit by me. There, my dear, don't worry any more. Poor Billy, I have worn you. I realized it to-night, when you were striving to please me. Billy, you touched my heart.'

'Eva!—I shall call you Eva! A little girl in a pink frock, a large-eyed darling with a basket of red cherries, giving them all away with a shy sidelong smile.'

The adorable head was bowed before him, and wistfully she said:

'Just do one thing more to please me, Will'um?'

'Only one thing more, Eva?'

'Only one. I want you to come on the roof with me, under the same stars we saw in Devon.'

'Not the same, Eva. They were June stars. Now it is almost autumn. O sad, that all things must pass away!'

He carried up a lion's skin and some rugs, and they climbed through the window. On the dewy roof she spread it, telling him to lie down. She took off his shoes. She tucked a rug round him.

'You are my little boy to-night, Will'um. I am your mother.'

Yes, he would start walking back to Shelley Cove in the morning. This was the climax: he would leave at the climax. Thinking of Jesus, he felt strong within himself, strangely happy.

She took off her own shoes, and lay next to him, wrapping a rug about herself and throwing a loose one over them both and drawing it up to their chins.

In the west a half moon was sinking into the battlements of he chimney pots, black against the sky. Her hand sought his and held.

'Are you cold, Li'l W-Will'um?'

'Warm, Eva—darling Eva with the basket of cherries.'

'All for you, darling Will'um.'

He stirred unrestfully, and she asked him to have her fur coat for pillow. He said hoarsely:

'No, not that inanimate coat. But I will have your hair for a pillow. For the last time.'

She pulled up the hem of his rug, and snuggled under it. He turned and unbound her hair and smothered his face in its softness. He bound his eyes with it, seeing in a misty net the stars that seemed to be watching him steadfastly. The peculiar fragrance of the tangled tresses gave him a sensation of drawing down star-breath for his mortal breathing. The cold cheeks were near his own that burned as with fever, and he turned to her, hiding his head on her breast. He lay with his brow against her throat, wondering if he could keep back the surrendering words of love that sought to pour themselves from his lips. He felt that his former longing for her was only a shadow of his feeling now. He smothered his face in her hair, turning away from the stars, and put his arms round her, murmuring with hot breath against her chin.

'Care for me for ever and ever. There is no other refuge for me. Christhood is the phosphorescence of old miseries blighting the present sunlight. In you I lose all the broken past—my childhood, the war, all wretched things. You are true—all the while, Eve. You are sunlight. I just stumble trying to find Truth, ancient sunlight. Love me from everlasting to everlasting!'

'I love you from everlasting to everlasting, Will'um.'

'Eva, when you are with other men—I get so afraid. I think all sorts of things. Eva, I can't bear any more. Really I'm very weak, not strong, like you.'

THE DREAM OF FAIR WOMEN

She held him close, as though he were a small child that needed love and sleep in warm arms to soothe away fear-of-loss and night-fret.

'Let me love you, Eve.'

'My love is worthless, Billy dear,' she said gently. 'Just lie quiet, and rest your poor brain.'

He lay in her arms, then struggled free to kiss her throat and mouth, while feebly she strove to hide her face, but she was leashed by her tresses.

'Never more to hear your voice, to feel you near me, to touch your lips—I cannot bear it,' he groaned. He leaned over her, kissing her tears, beseeching her love.

'Billy, I'm not worthy of your love; really I'm not.'

'Kiss me, Eve!'

'I believe that is all you care about me.'

'I love you, Eve.'

'No, Billy, you don't. Sometimes I think love is impersonal.'

'You're mine, darling Eva, you always were mine. Why didn't I meet you years ago, in the spring woods, with your torn frock and long thick hair! Swimming with me, among the lilies of the Longpond!'

'Don't, Billy.'

'You're sweet and pure, my Eva!'

'O, Billy, you mustn't——'

'A-ah, I will!'

'O, Billy, supposing——'

'Christ, I love you.'

She relaxed, she yielded. The gold moon sank behind the battlements of the chimney pots.

When he awoke, the stars were shrinking away from the dawn. Eastward over the housetops the sky was touched with ruddy gold. He smiled at the sky, and slept again.

Chapter 32

SWIFTLY the long golden days perished. Everyone in Folke-stone seemed to be spending money, to be dancing. Young ex-officers, in lounge suits costing double and sometimes treble as much as pre-war suits, lived at the hotels, enjoying the fruits of peace—or rather, the windfalls come to them upon discharge from H.M. Forces—their gratuities, called blood money, ninety-one days pay for each year, or part year, of commis-sioned service during the Great War. Maddison had only about ten pounds left. He insisted on paying Evelyn three guineas a week while he had his meals at the flat. She made no mention of it after a preliminary protest.

The leaves of the trees fell early, uncoloured, withered, nerveless. The hard blue sky pulsed with heat.

They went riding together, Maddison having sent to Rook-hurst for his kit. Evelyn said he looked very distinguished in his field boots and spurs, and fawn cavalry-twill breeches cut in Conduit Street, buttoned high up the inner side of the kneecap.

'Were you ever in a cavalry charge, Billy?'

'Once.'

'What was it like?'

'Well, for days afterwards the infantry transport officers round Arras were "winning" new chargers—the best of them having only broken knees and barbed-wire gashes on their shoulders, running wild about the cratered fields.'

'Don't. We must forget the war—it was too terribly sad, Billy. Let me tie your stock—it isn't quite right. Too small. I ought to have lent you one of Lionel's.'

With deft fingers she rearranged the white ends of cloth, turning them up and over and pinning with a gold fox's-head pin.

He rode a hack hired from the stables, while she rode a black hunter borrowed from Mr. Archibald Dodder. The old gentleman, waving aside both Maddison and the groom, himself adjusted girths and stirrup-leathers, seeing that cheek-straps and throat-lash were not too tight, that curb and snaffle reins were flat and uncrossed; and himself throwing her up into the saddle.

'Now indeed you are Evelyn, with a "y",' he remarked, as they walked their horses along the Roman road under the downs. 'Straight from one of the stately homes of England, what?'

She smiled at him. She wore a dark blue habit, and a veil over the rim of her black bowler hat and tight round her chin, covering her face.

'You wait, Billy—one day I shall be the Countess of Slepe.'

'What fun! For think, you'll be the first peeress of the New Age—formed on the Bertrand Russell principles!'

'That's a cheap remark.'

'I agree entirely, darling. My wit is adapting itself unconsciously, like that of the schoolboy who defined adolescence as "that short period between puberty and adultery".'

'I feel as though I'm a meat safe in this veil,' she said a moment later. 'I think I'll take it off.'

'I wondered why you wore it.'

'To keep the flies off, dear Billy. I say, I must tell you a story. The first time I rode to hounds I was with Lionel, when we stayed with his great-uncle, Sir George Fairfax, in Leicestershire There was an old woman among the field—a perfect scream—kept talking, whenever there was a check, in a loud mannish voice. "Damn these corsets," she said once, and proceeded to rip them off. Just then hounds gave tongue, and we dashed off, and she flung the corsets into a bullfinch—you know what a bullfinch is: a tall thorn hedge? Well, we had a bit of a run, and checked, and then on again; it was a bad fox; and eventually returned to the same bullfinch—and there were the corsets hanging high up, flapping in the wind for all to see!'

They cantered on the downs with only larks for company, cracking hunting whips and hulloa-ing, once startling a lean hare from its daydreams, and pretending to chase it with a pack of harriers, while from their carrion feasts of dead sheep the crows and daws rose goistering at the thuds of hoofs. On being told of the fun, Jonquil said she would go next time, and she rode between them, a sprite in blue velvet cap and brown leather gaiters, upon a Shetland pony.

'Don't go so fast, you pig, Will'um, 'cause Quillie's 'osse's legs is smaller, see Will'um?'

'Isn't she quaint, Billy? 'Oss! She picked it up from Naps.'

'Oh, really.'

'Don't say "oh, really", like that. It's only swank, like my veil.'

'We all spoke like that in the jolly old cavalry, if you understand, don't you know, what? "My wit, like your temperament, is essentially adaptable!" I even wore a monocle for three months during 1915! With a gold rim; for the plain glass ones, which looked much more effective, always pulled down my lower lid.'

'Is that in "The Policy of Self-destruction"?'

'Yes; with your veil and Colyer's O.E. tie.'

'You seem to include everything, Billy. Come on, Nigger, let's leave the wise young man behind! Hoy-ee!'

'Mummie, Mummie, wait, you silly damn fool!' shrieked Quillie. Evelyn held back her curvetting animal.

To-day she was riding astride, in dark brown breeches and waisted coat, and gold-pinned stock so silk-soft under her chin. Purposely he lagged behind to watch the lovely centaurean grace of mother and daughter, which renewed in his heart the pangs of desire and possession. He determined to go and see his father at the end of the week, and find out what money was due to him under his dead mother's marriage settlement.

The next day they went on the downs without Jonquil, riding to an ancient thorn growing out of a big, rounded, grass-grown hump, the burial-place of ancient British warriors. The bark of the hard branches was pared by the teeth of the animals tethered so long, and she told him that misfortune would come to them for bringing this hurt to the tree. It was an old saying in the village where she was born, she said, that thorns must never be injured or even climbed, otherwise they would bring disaster. She embraced its old twisted trunk, laying her cheek against the wood, as though silently beseeching the tree-spirit to stay its wrath. He was so moved by her strange beauty that he put his arms about her and the thorn, pinning her against it, and saying that if he had the power he would shut her up within it, so that he could build himself a stone hut and forever have her nigh him, sharing her only with perching magpies and crows. She complained that he hurt her, and although he would comfort her she seemed not to realize that he was there, and turned her face to the tree. Nor would she tell afterwards what silent words her heart had spoken to it, but seemed vaguely to resent the questions.

They sat by the grassy barrow while he picked up rough flints, wondering whether any wild man had held them in his hand, to throw them down when his mind saw no arrowheads in them. The flints were there, unworn by the elements; the skull of the hunter was calcined dust under the turf; but where was the life that had filled it? Thought was sadness. He glanced at Evelyn; only in the mutual surrender of flesh and spirit to its compliment was to be found harmony, which saw sunrise and sunset with an equal mind.

He did not go to Rookhurst at the end of the week, nor at the end of another week. The strange hot tide of summer lapsed slowly from the songless land. Never had there been such a harvest of corn and stoneless fruit, but the root crops were stringy and ruined. Still no rain clouds came to the sky; the swallows gathered, disappearing suddenly, weeks before their time.

Rare butterflies danced on the Romney marshes—Painted Ladies, Swallow-Tails, Camberwell Beauties. Mr. Everard Dodder, an enthusiastic entomologist, vowed that he had seen a Large Copper. Evelyn asked him what the inspector would say at the police-station if he put it in a killing bottle, but no reply was given. He did not approve of herself, she told Maddison, and hadn't the wit to see any jokes.

'Damn him! He's the Chairman of the Folkestone Watch & Ward Society, and wants all the paths down the Leas doubly lit at night.'

'Eve, can you lend me five pounds? I'm awfully sorry, my money's gone. I must go and see my father.'

'Of course, my dear. But don't go yet. I may let the flat next month, and go to Deauville for the winter. Stay till then; why not? Don't look so surprised, my dear.'

'But, Eve——'

'We can't go on like this forever, can we? Be sensible, Billy.'

'But, Eve——'

'My dear, I thought that discussion had been settled.'

'But, Eve, supposing—I mean——'

'No, no, my dear; there are no complications, fortunately.'

'Fortunately?'

'Be sensible, my dear man. For one thing, I should lose my darling Quillie. Sorry, I must dress now.'

'Are you going out?'

'I'm dining at the Grand to-night. Dancing afterwards.'

'But with whom? You never told me!'

'Martha will give you dinner here. I'm dining with Jerry Tollemache.'

The fair-haired, blue-eyed, pink-cheeked subaltern called for her at 7.15 p.m., wearing only a silk scarf and a felt hat, the brim turned down all round in the correct fashion, with his evening clothes. From the window Maddison watched the red sporting car turning the corner by the Leas. She didn't even look back and wave.

'I shan't be in to dinner, Martha.'

He went round to Radnor Park Gardens about nine o'clock, and silently endured the remarks of Mr. Fairfax about the weakness of the Government in not carrying the sword into Germany, British Israel and the relapsing of the world into the Dark Ages, intermingled with groans about the maid's extravagance with the coal in the kitchen, and complaints against loafing ex-soldiers who wouldn't work but were parasites on the dole, until the old gentleman was rendered ineffectual by the isolation of bedclothes.

'Poor Father, all his hair fell off one day in his bath twenty years ago, and he's never been easy about anything since,' said Milly. 'But we've all got to guard against the ailings of age, haven't we, Billy? Well, old chap, how are you enjoying yourself. Lina's gone out to the Grand with Jerry Tollemache, hasn't she, lucky gel? Well, Billy, how goes the book?'

'I've almost finished it, Milly.'

'Now when am I going to see it?'

'I must get it typed somewhere, and then send it to a publisher.'

'Now I might be able to help you to find a publisher,' suggested Milly, with an air of having much influence. 'A very dear old friend of mine wrote some poems once, and sent them to a publisher in Ludgate Circus, whose advertisement she answered, who pronounced a very favourable opinion, that he was prepared to publish them if she could manage to pay so much—I forget the amount—towards the cost. She was overjoyed; and her poems were published. Unfortunately, like all good work—they say that *Tarzan of the Apes* was turned down by publisher after publisher—it was above the public's head, and didn't sell; but she was able to buy all the other copies up at, I think, what she called remainder price, and so when she does become famous she will have all her first edition. I told Julian Warbeck about it, and do you know, the fat Hun rudely roared with laughter! He used to talk about his own first editions, too, and he hasn't even had one book published.'

'Oh, my book's no good.'

'Cheer up, Billy! Why this thusness?'

'It's rotten.'

'Tut-tut! Come and sing to me. I'm lonely, now that Margy's gone away.'

Soon he left and walked along the Leas in the direction of the Grand Hotel. The windows were lighted up—contrast to the darkness of the war, when any glint might have been seen from the sea. A fine night for a Zeppelin raid. Ah, those days were gone. So was his gratuity. He laughed bitterly; the spaniel jumped up at his hand unheeded.

For several hours he paced in front of the hotel, and stood under the lighted windows, listening to the loud chatter of voices and the beat of banjos. Midnight passed. A policeman stared at him. When the policeman was relieved by another, Maddison saw them both staring at him. At one o'clock the second policeman, repassing, spoke to him.

'Waiting for anything?'

'For a friend, yes. Fine night, isn't it?'

'Very fine, sir.'

'This damned dance will be over soon, I hope, then I'll have a chance of seeing her. Any idea when it ends?'

'About one o'clock usually, sir. Well, I wish you luck. Good-night, sir.'

'Good-night, officer.'

He had nearly poured out his misery to the policeman; but the 'sir' had made him preserve the policeman's fugitive image of himself.

At ten minutes past one o'clock he watched, from behind a hedge, Evelyn coming out on Tollemache's arm; watched them getting into the red car, until it roared away down the Leas.

He hurried as quickly as possible to The Paragon. The car stood outside the corner house. The drawing-room was lighted. Evelyn pulled down the blinds. The light went on in the kitchen. After ten minutes the kitchen light was put out. He imagined them drinking tea. Two o'clock struck. The same policeman passed, silent on rubber soles.

'Night's keeping fine, sir.'

'Yes,' agreed Maddison, trying to keep his teeth from chattering.

'Good-night, sir.'

'Good-night.' He added: 'Officer.'

About half past two the light was switched on in Evelyn's bedroom. A shadow passed over the drawing-room blind, as though the man was walking about. The bedroom light went out half a minute afterwards. The shadow did not reappear on the blind.

Maddison waited in the shadow of the opposite house. Three o'clock struck. The shadow moved on the blind. Two minutes went by, while his heart thumped in his ears. Would the street door open in darkness, as it had when she had let him—Maddison—out, silently, when he——

He heard whispering. He picked up the shivering spaniel, lest Billjohn growl or bark. A figure came down the steps. More whispering, and the soft closing of the door. He saw a match glow against a downheld face. A cigarette glowed as the starting handle was swung in front of the car. The engine ticked over at once. The driver got in and softly closed the door. The car went slowly to the High Street, with dim lights. It turned the corner, the white headlights flicked on, the car roared away down the road toward the Shorncliffe barracks.

Maddison walked down to his lodgings in the poorer quarter of the town.

Chapter 33

ONLY a sheet covered him, yet his body was as fiery as his brain. The bed was a wide one, and jangled as he moved. He shifted from a hot side to a cooler side, only to make it hot, especially where his head lay on the pillows. These he dropped on the floor, laying his head on the dry straw bolster, which gave no relief. Every thought was of Eve in Devon, of her mirthful eyes and sanguine lips, tender for himself. His mind retraced the flagstones to her house, up the steps, passed through the locked door, and drifted wraithlike into her room. Pain dragged it forth from her dark chamber. To other places it went with her, with an Eve now freed and joyous; to meadows with celandines, the flowers of hope, telling that spring was coming, with its sweet birdsong in the very air. Hazel wands and ashpoles, home of the willow wrens, pollen dusting the red nut flowers, doves fluttering above at their raft-like nests, the windflowers below. Green corn asway, and sighing, swallows under the meadow oaks, whitethroats slipping through the nettles; everything come again, brought by the faithful solar spring. All this loveliness shaping itself into one thing, and seeing, he drew up his knees, as though to hug to himself the vision. She who saw the same vision was with him, and in a passionate adoration he clasped her feet, kissing them, wrapping his arms round her knees, till his body was merged into hers, his spirit commingled and absorbed, floating in the blue-stained air, dissolved where was no time, where meadow and tree hung a-dream, where blossom was one with root and leaf, where song and colour and scent became a quivering radiance of whitest light. With a wrenching of the mind he was dragged away from his prostration before the godhead of perfection, of immingled love, to be forced to realize that it would never be. He beat away the bat-wings of imagination, but return they would; he buried his head in the mattress, pressing his eyes, but still they persisted. He clasped the cold bedrails, and kneeling, leaned his bare chest against the top bar, while the spaniel whined and licked his hand.

The house was quiet, with a deadness that bore upon him like onrushing oblivion. He went to the window, standing on cold oilcloth. A flagpost in the squalid backyard was black in the sky; the cord tapping against the wood.

'O Christ, I can't stand it,' he groaned, beating his head with his fist. Becoming calmer, he lit the candle, and stared, as he had stared a hundred times before, at the photograph of Evelyn he had taken from Sandy White's drawer.

He dressed and tiptoed down the stairs. Closing carefully the door, he walked up the silent and deserted street to Radnor Park Gardens. No lights shone in the houses; everywhere was sombrous thickness through which loomed the buildings. He prowled round the square several times, longing to speak to a human creature, and sometimes kneeling down and embracing his dog, and imploring him to understand. Always the same was the spaniel; humbly affectionate and happy, returning immediately at the low whistle that was like the call of a curlew.

He passed the flat, quiet like all others. The darkness was like the ghost of a grey fungus trying to grow upon him. He lit a cigarette; it was tasteless; he threw it against a garden wall, on which it showered red sparks. Down The Paragon he walked, across the High Street, and so to the Leas. Faster and faster, till the path was reached to the sea. Dropping down the lower promenade, he jumped on the shingle, lifting down the dog to him. By the edge of the sea he sat, looking across the Channel waters to the lighthouse of Gris Nez. Farewell, O sun, farewell. Spray from the battering waves wetted his face, and the pebbles abraded in the backwash roared a million watery protests.

In his mind he heard the nightingales singing in the woods of his boyhood. He began to sing in a minor key, feeling all his life in his breast, in his eyes, and smiling to himself as the pure, the sad, the divine notes of a voice that was only partly of himself arose beyond the noise of the waves, arose with the voices of nightingales. Star-breath was in the Voice, he was immortal, and now he might keep tryst with an Eve freed and joyous. He was a nightingale who would return to earth no more; he would sing himself away into the wind, to his mother, who had given him her life, and fled away beyond the sun.

'Farewell, O sun, farewell,' he sang, the tears streaming down his cheeks.

Rising resolutely, he took off his clothes and stepped into the sea, bracing himself to meet a big wave. It swept over him, leaving him upon the pebbles. He dived through the next roller, and swam beyond the crest, where it was calm. On his side he struck out for the open sea, in the direction of the French coast. Half a mile from the land he ceased to swim, and floated on his back, while the waves lifted him gently, and the black bubble-rush murmured past his ears.

He seemed to have no body; he was suspended under the stars, which slid in silver streaks up the passing swell of the black water. He lay effortlessly, fatigued, without thought, abandoned to the sea; then he heard the frenzied barking of the spaniel on shore.

With slow strokes he returned to the distressed dog, often rolled under the surge. Some time later he crawled feebly on the pebbles to lie glimmering in the starlight, beside the spaniel licking his cold face, feeling that death was very near in the darkness, tender and compassionate, and ready to bear him away to the after-sleeping.

Chapter 34

THE next morning, going to The Paragon, Maddison saw a great Mercèdes car, grey with dust, standing outside No. 9. The notice in Evelyn's handwriting seemed to have a new significance; he rang, and walked up. Martha opened the door.

'She's out, mister. There's a gentleman waiting.'

'Captain Colyer?'

'Yes, mister.'

After hesitation he walked into the drawing-room. Captain Colyer was seated in an arm-chair, his feet upon the rungs of a smaller chair, an Egyptian cigarette between his lips and squashed stumps of others in an ash-tray on the floor, beside a tumbler of whiskey and soda.

Captain Colyer asked him casually if he knew where Mrs. Fairfax was.

'I've no idea, Colyer.'

He remained seated. He sipped his drink. Maddison regarded the ribbons on the breast of his azure tunic—the red and blue of the Distinguished Service Order, with two dull silver rosettes; the purple and white of the Military Cross; the purple and white lines of the Distinguished Flying Cross; the red, white and blue of the 1915 Star; the watered rainbow of the Victory Medal; the blue and yellow of the General Service Medal; the red-striped green of the *Croix de Guerre avec palme;* the red of the *Légion d'honneur*, and five or six foreign decorations of which he did not know the name.

'I wish you wouldn't stare at me.'

'I'm awfully sorry—I was admiring your decorations.'

372

'Then I wish you wouldn't—it's like being in a restaurant.'

'I beg your pardon.'

'I don't mind what you do so long as you don't stare at me or expect me to have conversation with you.'

Colyer looked sideways out of the window, finished his drink, and languidly poured himself another. Trying to break the constraint, Maddison said presently:

'Have you been here long, Colyer?'

'Why do you ask?'

'I was wondering if Lina had seen you.'

Colyer yawned and drawled: 'Do you think I'd stroll in and treat her house as an hotel, or a club? Why do you ask? Have you a share in it?'

'Only a cad would say that.'

'You are entirely mistaken, and your mistake arises from an ignorance of the ways of gentlemen. Obviously.'

Immediately Maddison screamed:

'Christ, if you don't shut up, I'll kill you!'

'That remark rather illustrates what I have just said. You know I am practically a cripple.'

'I didn't know. I beg your pardon.'

'You are forgiven, owing to your ignorance. Have you been for a walk?'

'Yes.'

'Have I interrupted it?'

'I don't understand.'

'I mean, are you going on with your walk?'

'Oh, no.'

'Then you don't mind if I go on with my sleep, do you? I am rather fatigued.'

He finished the drink, put the tumbler on the writing desk, and stretched his long legs on the chair, closed his eyes, sighed, and lay still.

Maddison went round to Radnor Park Gardens, and was told by Milly that Evelyn had just left to go to the High Street.

She would take that opportunity, she said, of giving him a friendly talking to.

It appeared that Lina had recently met a widowed lady, a friend of theirs who should be unnamed, who had shocked and surprised Lina by telling her that she ought to remember that as a married woman, and with a husband abroad, she really could not be too careful. Lina was so hurt because she feared that she was being talked about in Folkestone. Of course people always talked, especially in seaside towns! Apparently Lina's innocent gaiety had been mistaken by the harsh mind of this world. Nevertheless, when there was smoke there was fire, and she, Milly, as Lina's pal and *confidante*, felt that it was an obligation to her niece and confiding pal, as well as her duty to her absent nephew, the son of her poor dead brother, to drop a hint to dear old guileless Billy, just as she had dropped a hint to his sweet cousin Phil some months back, to consider Lina's reputation as a married gel and a mother. He must not be offended if she suggested that he went away for a time, and it would increase the respect for him of someone-she-knew-who-should-be-nameless (with a laughing fingershake) if that some-one in Devon heard that he was working hard, determining to make a position! Maddison looked on the ground as though in deep contemplation of her words, thanked her, and went away hurriedly, in the direction of the High Street.

After an hour's search he went back to the flat, walking up slowly owing to the heat, and because he felt a weariness. The rubbers on his shoes made little noise, and he went into the kitchen to ask Martha if she had returned. Hardly had he entered when Evelyn strode across the hall and in a cold voice requested him to go out of the servant's hall, and to speak to her in the dining-room. He held open the door of that room for her, and closed it behind him. She faced him; his glance fell.

'I never thought you could be so contemptible as to spy,' she began. 'I saw you last night! And if Jerry Tollemache hadn't been so tired, I'd have kept him longer still, just to show you.'

374

'Eve, please——'

'Stand back!'

'Eve, but why is Colyer here?'

'That is an impertinent question,' she said. 'And even if it were not, you have not the slightest right to ask it! I am not your property, remember.'

'Eve, why are you so changed?'

'Why did you creep upstairs just now?'

'I came up slowly because I was tired. Eve, please——'

'You have many words, and with them an excuse for everything. And as a guest in my house, what right have you to insult any friends that I choose to invite here?'

'None whatever.'

'Then why did you glare at Pat, and threaten to kill him?'

'I admit I lost my temper. What else could a man do, when he is sneered at as I was? Have you no care for me, that you treat me like this?'

'Very little indeed. I am tired of your following me about like a shadow, questioning my movements. When you're not doing that you're babbling about the resurrection or something of mankind by association in childhood with birds and weeds and wind, and other unintelligible weariness. Jonquil may be charmed by such dreams, my dear Billy, but for one whose mind is mature and healthy they seem pallid and—forgive me saying it—even degenerate.'

He stared at her and said as he turned away his head:

'Had you ever loved me, you would never have said—what you—said just now.'

She replied: 'Do you mind going?'

He did not move. Her words seemed to make the world recede from his feet, leaving him in a void of uttermost darkness.

'Eve, Eve, don't! Don't, for God's sake. Say good-bye—one kind word—O God.' He clenched his hands.

'You are keeping me from my friend.'

375

He seized her hands and pleaded: 'Don't—don't—words are like flint arrowheads.'

She said in a curt expressionless voice:

'I should have thought by the way you continue to remain here that your skin was too thick for my pointed remarks to be taken in. Will you please go?'

He looked at her.

'If I were less desperate, I think I would kill myself, but no.' He stopped, and as she pulled away her hand he said slowly: 'If I were dead, then never, never, never could I make you understand that I—you—my feet tread——'

He faltered.

'What rot you do talk, don't you, Billy?'

He faltered on in distress. 'That is why the Light-bringers come among men—Eve—Eve——'

She turned away and pulled open the door. She waited in the hall, tapping the barometer. He went out of the room and through the hall door, turning to whisper,

'Farewell.'

'Good-bye, Billy,' she said, waiting by the door.

She gave him a sweet glance as he looked up at the turn of the stairs; meeting his own, her eyes became sad. He was frenzied by doubt immediately. The door closed. He went down the stairs and wandered about the Leas, trying to understand what had happened. I know her true nature is pure and steadfast, he told himself a hundred agonizing times. She loves me and yet she—why does she—Colyer, why was—Tollemache kept there because—O God, why, why—perhaps at that moment Colyer——

He groaned, and dared not to think it. He walked the Leas for hours, seeing her after lunch by the bandstand with Jonquil and Colyer, but she was too far away to notice him, and he tried to read his worn copy of *The Story of My Heart*, constantly turning to the engraving of Richard Jefferies opposite the title-page, his only companion. He observed the figure of Sandy

White in the distance, hurrying along, but he avoided him by going down to the sea.

It was afternoon when he went back to the flat. The Mercèdes still stood outside the corner house, a big pool of oil under its bonnet. Jonquil was outside, waiting for Martha to take her for a walk. She was amusing herself by feeding a flock of sparrows with crumbs. He said: 'Hullo, Quillie', but she gave him a glance that was almost a scowl, and continued her talk with the birds.

'Et tu, Quillie,' he muttered, turning away to hide his tears from this miniature Eve.

A man in a bowler hat and a black suit came round the corner from the direction of Radnor Park Gardens as Maddison, overcome by anguish of loss, went up the stone steps. The man looked at him keenly as he went past. Another man in a bowler hat and a black suit came down The Paragon from the direction of the Leas, on the other side of the road. Both carried rolled umbrellas. Both had big waxed moustaches. When nearly opposite No. 9 the second man stopped, and the first man turned back, joined him, and contemplated the car. Wondering aimlessly why they wore such hats and carried umbrellas in the hot weather, Maddison went up to the flat. The men followed. Evelyn met all three in the hall.

'Are you Mrs. Fairfax, ma'am?' said one of the men.

'I am. Who are you?'

'Is there anyone named Captain Colyer with you, please?'

'Yes.'

'May I see him, please?'

'If it is a question of a mistake in giving a cheque, I am prepared to settle that immediately. Captain Colyer told me this morning that he wasn't sure——'

'Just so. Perhaps the gentleman would oblige by giving us a minute?'

'You'd better come in. Wait in there, will you please? Hullo, Billy, how are you? Pat, you're wanted in the next room.'

Captain Colyer lounged against the mantelpiece, a cigarette in his hand. Maddison noticed that his face was very pale.

The men did not go into the dining-room. They waited in the hall. The door was half open. Colyer drew smoke repeatedly from his cigarette. Then he walked languidly to the door, and said:

'Good afternoon.'

'If you wouldn't mind stepping in the next room a minute. We are from the Criminal Investigation Department of Scotland Yard, and want to ask you a few questions.'

'My dear fellow, with pleasure,' replied Colyer. 'Of course I'd be only too pleased to help you——' The dining-room door was shut.

Evelyn went to her desk, and pulled papers about till she found something she had been looking for. It was a cheque-book. As she did not speak, Maddison sat by the open window and watched the sea above the narrow opening of the street leading to the Leas. About half a minute later the dining-room door opened and Captain Colyer's voice, earnestly persuasive, was heard saying:

'My dear fellow, I tell you I have not just come from Harrogate. As for the car, that is probably a coincidence. There are many Mercèdes on the road. My friend Lord Child, the great fly-fisherman, of Hampshire and elsewhere, has one, Sir Charles Ovey has one——'

'You can tell that to the Inspector—and to Captain Colyer!'

'My dear fellow, I am Captain Colyer. Honestly I am. Air-mechanic Tompkins, the fellow you're after, is my servant—or was, until he cleared off with most of my kit. So he's taken to using my name as well, has he?'

'You can explain that at the station. Now, come along before we fetch you.'

'My dear fellow, you're making an awful fool of yourself. And remember, you can't arrest an officer in uniform. It simply isn't done!'

THE BROKEN WEB

Evelyn looked unhappily at Maddison. 'Pat, what does it all mean? Surely there's some mistake.'

'I say, I know this gentleman,' said Maddison, hoping swiftly that the pathetic imposter might escape in his car, or leave for France by the cross-Channel boat. 'Really, I'm sure there's a mistake. If it's a question of a cheque—I mean— nowadays one is sometimes hard up——' Ideas of his manuscript's value passed through his head.

'That's all right, sir. Brown, go and get the Assistant Provost Marshal.'

'Awful sorry, Lina,' said Colyer in his languid tones. 'Most awful bore for you. I'll get Tompkins a court-martial for this. God, what a joke! Fancy arresting one for one's deserter batman!' He laughed at the detective, who smiled grimly.

They waited about ten minutes, and Evelyn, laughing once again, asked Martha to bring in some tea. The detective thanked her but refused to have any.

'It isn't poisoned,' smiled Evelyn.

'Against the regulations, ma'am,' said the detective, stoutly.

They finished tea, while Colyer lounged by the grate, one hand behind him. Then someone was heard to be coming upstairs, and a cultured but rough voice said:

'Where is he? Wait here, Sergeant!'

'Very good, sir.'

A short fat man came into the room. He wore white flannels, with the khaki tunic of a major, with a red brassard marked in black letters APM.

'How d'ye do, Mrs. Fairfax?' he panted. 'Sorry this should have occurred in your house. Been playing a game of tennis. Should have been informed of this.'

'A memorandum was delivered at your office at 10 a.m. this morning, sir,' explained the C.I.D. man.

'Was it, was it? Well, is this the imposter? I put you under arrest,' he puffed, wiping his brow.

'Major Cornwallis, I'm sure there's some mistake,' protested

379

Evelyn. 'I've known Captain Colyer for a long time.'

'He's been a deserter since Armistice Day,' replied the detective grimly. 'And his other names at Bournemouth, Torquay, Brighton, and Eastbourne, are Compton McCudden and Perceval Capel, both with those ribbons. Sometimes, sir, he is a colonel, or wing-commander, whichever uniform he's got on—the old R.F.C. khaki, or the blue Air Force. Before the war, sir, he was a bank clerk, according to the information we have. He was, sir, a second-lieutenant in the Machine Gun Corps until cashiered at Grantham in 1916 for giving a cheque that was dishonoured.'

'I suppose they got him again when conscription came in, the blackguard?' puffed Major Cornwallis.

'Awfully sorry you should be worried, Lina,' drawled Colyer, ignoring the A.P.M.'s remarks. 'I suppose I'd better go. Of course, I'll come back shortly. It's rather fortunate that my father is a director of the Northcliffe Press, because everything can be given proper publicity, even an account of my arrest by an Assistant Provost Marshal in tennis flannels—somewhat dirty ones, too.'

'You impertinent scoundrel,' panted Major Cornwallis. 'Take off those ribbons!'

He went to Colyer and tore off his ribbons.

'Well, I couldn't tear off yours with such a noise, could I?' exclaimed the prisoner, eyeing the lonely ribbon of the Coronation Medal on the A.P.M.'s breast.

'Hold your tongue, sir!' bellowed the A.P.M.

'Oh, very well, sir,' drawled the other. 'Very well. It will not be myself who will be cashiered, sir. Do you mind calling a cab? I'm entitled to one, you know. What? Haven't you read King's Regulations? Au revoir, Lina; and my regrets for this unfortunate exhibition of ill-breeding and unsoldierly conduct on the part of Major Cornwallis.'

'Don't trouble to come to the station, sir,' he said, turning to the A.P.M. with a sudden sneer. 'Why not return to your game of tennis? But mind they don't mistake you for the ball, you fat little bounder! Personally, I should think a Turkish bath would get off those disgusting rolls of fat quicker.'

Evelyn was staring at Colyer with amazement. The suave manner, the tired drawl, the impassive languor, all these were gone. He spoke his sarcasm quickly, in a voice that held a suggestion of cockney accent.

'One moment, sir,' said the plain-clothes man. 'May I see his left hand? There should be a finger missing. Yes, I thought so.'

'Probably done to avoid service!' said Major Cornwallis, who wore, Maddison noticed, no active service chevrons, and no ribbons except the blue and red of the George V Coronation Medal.

'That,' said the prisoner, scornfully, holding up his hand, 'was shot off by the Cavalry-Captain Baron von Richthofen! There's been a war, you know, and some of us have got hurt! And some of us have profiteered, and got fat!' he jeered at the A.P.M.

Long after they were gone, Evelyn stood by the window, looking at the narrow strip of sea beyond the promenade. Quietly Maddison sat down, waiting for her to speak. She stood so still and for so long that he grew restless, and went out to see Martha. The servant did not seem inclined to speak to him after her one remark—'He was always a perfect gentleman to me, mister, and more I can't never say of no one'—so he went back.

'Billy.'

'Yes, Eve.'

'You didn't tell them he was here, did you?'

'No.'

'On your honour?'

'On my honour—such as it is.'

'He need not have lied to me,' she said slowly: 'I often wondered. Once, when Naps Spreycombe was here he asked him something about Eton, and when Pat seemed flustered and avoided the question, I doubted. No, there was no need for him to lie to me. I knew he was hard up. I would have given him all I could spare just the same. Why didn't he trust me? You see,' she added, 'I keep no friends.'

She spoke forlornly, lowering the glance of her eyes, spoke with a gesture of heaviness. Sinking on the couch, she added:

'I begin now to realize the worth and truth of that injured man—my husband. He at least didn't want to stifle me in his pocket all the time. He did let me be myself. He is a gentleman, by heavens, he is!'

At her words he walked up and down the room, while she lay with her face on her arm in an unhappy attitude. For some minutes he paced restlessly, then went into the dining-room, looking at the pictures on the walls, at the photographs, at the water-colour paintings. A giddiness came over him, and he sat down, resting his head on hands supported by his knees. Somewhere a clock chimed six times, but he did not move. The minutes wasted. A step sounded by him, a hand caressed his hair. He remained unmoving.

'Look up, old fellow,' she said; 'I'm sorry I was so beastly to you.'

He stood on his feet, facing her.

'Eve, Eve——' was all he could falter for a minute. The upward look in her eyes was steady and grave. When he could speak steadily again he tried to conceal by a half-playful manner the desolation of his thoughts. 'Why, you dear old silly, you will never find happiness your way—you will break your own heart.'

She said, examining the top round leather button of his coat, and biting it gently with her teeth:

'I shan't break yours, that's a sure thing, for you haven't got one.'

She laid her head sideways against his coat, as though to

hear his heart beating. He pressed it there with his hands, stammering:

'Won't you trust me, Eve? Won't you trust me? I will be faithful forever.'

'But you don't trust me.'

'Yes, yes, I do.'

Her arms found a way under his coat and held him.

'Ah, but you are wild and untamable, and in my longing I hated you, and shot my spiteful arrows at your faithful heart. You have no shield against me, have you, little W-Will'um?'

He shook his head, not daring to tell her how he longed to grovel before her, to surrender himself to her. She became remorseful, and hugged him closer. He dared not yield. He stood there, afraid, weak, confused, in his unshielded heart strange barbs of pain.

'I want to show you something in the attic,' she murmured. He saw a pulse throbbing in her neck. He trembled. She led him from the room. He followed her up the stairs, holding her hand. She could not look at him, but hid her face against his chest, and pulled him down on the couch in a dark corner.

Afterwards, in sweet happiness, she said:

'Billy, do you want to please me?'

'Always, my darling.'

'Come to Canterbury, to the Thanksgiving Service? I'll get the car.'

'Of course I'll go with you, anywhere, my dearest one.'

Chapter 35

He did not telegraph to his father when the next morning he set out by rail to Rookhurst, in order to tell him that the most important thing in his life, the finding of his life's partner, was accomplished. On arrival, he went into the King's Arms for a glass of beer, but stayed drinking and talking until closing time at two o'clock. Then he set out to walk to his home across the fields. Only Biddy, the housekeeper, was in. When her surprise and joy were over, he was able to learn that his father was fishing in the Longpond. This surprised him, and he walked along the right-of-way across the Big Wheatfield, and down to the mere below among the trees.

Once there was a forest there; for more than a thousand recorded years the black cawing of rooks had arisen with the jactitating cries of daws, and the clatter of pigeon wings in the branches of great beeches. The forest was gone, the long three miles of it, except for thin and scattered boles of immature growth. Nowhere could he hear a rook. They were gone, too, and in their place were yellow and cracked chips of wood, and round sawn tree-stumps, everywhere dulled by weather. As he went along a wheel-broken timber track, of yore a path so thickly mossed and a-crackle with autumn beech-mast, he passed a shed of corrugated iron and concrete, with locked doors, and peering in one of the windows he saw the gas engines that had driven the circular saws. Quickly he walked on, closing his memory, forcing himself to believe that he did not care.

Around the lake the timber had not been thrown. Alders and willows, hawthorns and oaks, elderberries and ash-trees, these remained as before. He walked along the shore and on the dry path under ornamental firs and hollies, searching for his father. By the boathouse, still in the identical state of ruin, he found him, sitting against a tree in the shade, reading. A long and warped bamboo rod was fixed on the bank in rests cut from a hazel. Billjohn growled, the angler looked up, put down the book after carefully noting the page and closing it, and stood up. Father and son smiled.

Externally John Maddison had not changed much during the war. He was still tall and lean, wearing a tweed suit that had been turned, the trousers rolled up twice, so that the tops of his heavy shooting boots were seen. He wore a fisherman's tweed hat that had been his father's, yet it seemed no older than the rod or the book. The gold watch-chain still hung in his waistcoat. His eyes were clear and deep below the lined brow, but more grey showed in his beard.

'Well, Willie!'

'Good-morning, Father.'

'This is most unexpected.'

'Yes.'

The conversation paused. The son looked at the float of blue-painted cork and slender heron-quill, among the water-lily leaves ten yards from the bank, immobile in the calm water. With pleasure he recognized it as one made by himself.

'I borrowed your rod and tackle, I hope you don't mind.' He began to speak to Billjohn, and to fondle him.

'Rather not. Have you caught anything?'

'Only a couple of roach. I'm trying for carp.'

'It's very hard to get them. But this is a good place. Isn't the water too bright?'

'I remember my brother Dick caught one here once. Six pounds. I've got on a small boiled potato.'

'A blackberry might be useful at this time of the year.'

'Yes, I thought of that.'

'Have you put down ground bait?'

'Yes, two days ago.'

They watched the float for a minute, while Mr. Maddison filled his pipe. Afterwards he offered his pouch to his son, who thanked him and packed his own charred and chipped briar. Blue skeins of smoke drifted from them, and between the puffs the father asked the son how long he had been in Rookhurst.

'About an hour. I came by a slow train—awful—stopped at every station.'

'I expect you're tired.'

'No.'

'Is that your spaniel? He is a well-bred dog.'

'Yes, that's Billjohn.'

'He's like old Fidelis, somewhat. Your mother's dog. But I suppose you don't remember him.'

'Yes, I do. He died when you—when I—O, years ago.'

'Yes, he's been dead a long time, poor old Fidelis. Let's see, you're twenty-two, aren't you? Heavens, how time passes. Yes, that's a fine dog. Intelligent. Is he broken into field work?'

'A little, a very little. You can have him.'

'But he's yours; you mustn't give away your dog.'

'But I'd like you to have him. He'd be happier here.'

'Aren't you stopping very long?'

'Well, Father, I came really for the day, just to see how you were, you know, and also to have a talk with you about something. That is, if it wouldn't bore you, but I would like your advice, that is, if you would give it.' He spoke nervously, and watched the float, which never moved.

Mr. Maddison said simply:

'I should only be too glad to help you in any way I could.'

'Thank you, Father. The wagtails seem happy, don't they?'

In twos and threes the birds were skipping in flight over the water, dipping their breasts with the faintest splash and making a sunny flicker of riplets. Sometimes one would perch on the broad leaf of the water-lily, to take a gnat or fly. Water-fowl lay in the middle of the broad mere, near Heron's Island;

they were asleep and silent. A pigeon from the opposite shore flew towards them; but suddenly alarmed, it clapped its wings over its head like the snap of seasoned sticks and clattered off.

'Yes, they love the water. I often come here to watch them.'

The water level was low, and greenish-white vegetation hung dry in the lower branches of the waterside trees.

'How is Colonel Tetley, Father?'

'Not very well, poor old chap. He had a stroke in the spring. Old Bob died only last month. You remember him, of course.'

'Poor old Bob.'

'He was found in the rearing field, sitting on his log.'

'Well, we all have to go sometime.'

'Yes. I suppose you've been to Skirr Farm, and heard the glad news?'

'No, I came straight here to find you, Father.'

'They've got a baby boy.'

'Who? Mrs. Temperley. How awfully splendid!'

'I'm his godfather,' confessed Mr. Maddison. 'His name is John William—after their fallen son and yourself. So you see, you will have a great responsibility. Mr. Temperley bought a Ford tractor, for ploughing, on the strength of it. Beastly thing —they've tried it out already—it goes snorting in the fields.'

'I must go and see them. I am so very glad—there will be a Temperley to farm the Big Wheatfield.' He added as an after-thought: 'But he won't climb the Rookery. Father, it seems so strange without our beeches.'

'I've got used to it. They cut them into baulks for the timber tracks in the Ypres Salient.'

'Yes, I remember your telling me. Murdering trees for murdering men!'

'I used to talk to some of the Canadian lumbermen who came over specially to throw timber. They were splendid fellows. A pity, but it had to be; everybody had to give during the war. Well, what's your trouble, old chap?'

'Oh, nothing much, Father. I'll tell you later. It's such an awfully long story, and I hardly know where to begin.'

'Have you known her very long?'

'Who?'

'The girl you are going to tell me about. What is the matter? Does her mother regard you as totally ineligible?'

'I haven't seen her mother yet.'

Mr. Maddison replied by a laconic 'Oh', and played with Billjohn.

'Is she fond of the spaniel?'

'Of Billjohn? Oh, very fond, Father.'

'Is she? Now, I rather suspect that a roach is nibbling that potato. I shall reel-in, I think, and try paste.'

'I expect the carp will be near the surface, Father. It's a good plan to throw a brandling worm, fly-fashion, so that it dangles over a lily leaf. Father, she is the sweetest woman in the world.' He looked on the ground, and nervously kicked over a tin.

'Would you mind kicking this tin of potatoes, instead?' asked Mr. Maddison, meaning to be humorous. 'I haven't yet tried the bread paste. Although I don't suppose it will be much good. They're not going to bite, that's what's the matter. So she is not bad-tempered, you say?'

The son took out an envelope, and impulsively thrust forward a photograph from it, saying casually:

'Well, you can see for yourself.'

'Just a minute; I think I've got a bite.'

He struck with the top of his rod, and pulled out a piece of waterweed hanging to the hook.

'As I thought, those roach have been nibbling. Just a minute. I'll reel-in. I've got deer-fat rubbed on the line to make it float. It keeps it dry, too. Now may I see the goddess?'

Trying not to show his uneasiness at his father's jocularity, he held out another snapshot. The stolen photograph was in his breast pocket; he dared not show it.

'Here's another, Father. Taken on horseback. She is a splendid horsewoman.'

'Yes, she certainly looks very pretty. That's a nice hunter. Good shoulder, plenty of bone. Is it hers?'

'No, it was lent by a friend.'

'I see. Yes, I can see her face better in this other photograph. She certainly is a beauty, but photographs can be so deceptive. Is she coming to Rookhurst?'

'Oh, no, Father. She lives in Folkestone.'

'You met her with your friends there, I suppose. Well, old chap, I don't want to interfere in any way, because you are a man now with your own life before you; yet I feel I ought to say that you should not think of marriage until you are assured of enough money to keep a wife. Unless, of course, your lady is wealthy, and you are prepared to live on her money.'

'I don't think she's got any money of her own, Father.'

'So much the better, my boy. You will be able to feel later on that you have worked for her. By the way, I see in the *Morning Post* that the Government are still sending approved ex-officers, free, to Oxford and Cambridge, with a grant of money. It seems to me a very good opportunity. I'd like you to go to my college, your grandfather's and great-grandfather's too.'

'Yes, Father.'

'I'm glad. Often I have felt that I have been—well, too, too, well—that in my hope for you to do well in life I have been over-anxious. Because I am a failure myself, I suppose.'

Mr. Maddison commenced to knock out from his pipe the tobacco that he had recently lighted; and having tapped it out, he continued to rap the bowl on his heel, so that his voice came from an averted head.

'Old chap, you've done so splendidly during the war, I realized when you were fighting, and I was digging potatoes, that I—well, that you—I mean, that we'd gone a bit too far apart— I don't know.'

THE DREAM OF FAIR WOMEN

'It was my fault, Father, really it was. I never told you anything, because I daren't, being too much of a coward. Aren't
you going to fish any more?'

'Well, you were only being a boy. I'm afraid the water is too
bright, and too low, as you suggested. Well, I'm very pleased
to see you again, Willie. What's it like in Folkestone?'

'Awfully hot.'

'But I suppose you don't notice the weather very much, do
you? Bathe a lot, I suppose?'

'Yes.'

'Well, one is only young once. We'll talk about the future
another time, shall we?'

'Thank you, Father.'

After lunch he tried to make himself tell his father that
Evelyn was already married. During the meal Mr. Maddison
had asked the name of his 'lady-love', and being told that it
was Fairfax he had referred to Evelyn as Miss Fairfax. Thinking of Milly, the son grinned nervously to himself, and seeing
the grin, the father changed the subject. After lunch he
said:

'I think I'll go for a stroll, Father.'

'Right. See you for tea?'

'Yes, Father.'

He walked to 'The Firs'. He found Mrs. Norman alone.
After greeting him, she asked if he were coming home for good.

'No, only for a few days.'

'And then are you going back to Folkestone?'

'Yes, Mrs. Norman.'

'Well, you ought not to. Mrs. Fairfax will do you no good at
all. She is a bad woman!'

Her face set as she spoke, and she avoided looking at him.
He rose from his chair, passed his hand across his head several
times, and when he could master his voice he said quietly:

'Mrs. Norman, she is going to be my wife. Will you listen,
please?'

'Certainly, Willie. But I really don't think that talking will make any difference.'

Briefly he told her about Devon, ceasing when Mrs. Norman laughed sceptically, and feeling rage; his rage passed, leaving a cold dislike.

'Forgive my laughter, Willie, but it is so comical.'

'Really. But surely laughter and scorn have no place in the intimate confidences between friends, Mrs. Norman?'

'Hoity toity! Well, you never had a sense of humour. But I'm sorry if I've hurt your feelings; but, my dear boy, do consider, how can you marry that woman? Is her husband dead?'

'No, Mrs. Norman, but we love each other, and he must divorce her.'

'Apart from the religious aspect of divorce, which I'm very sorry to say I'm afraid you don't realize, I'd like to ask you if Major Fairfax is willing to divorce her?'

He could reply nothing.

'Willie, you will mess up your life, or rather Mrs. Fairfax will do it for you. But it is to be expected of one of peasant blood.'

'What do you mean?'

'Mrs. Fairfax was born in a cottage at Snedlebarum, four miles away, my dear Willie. Her real name is Eve, or Evie, as she was called, and her mother's name is, or was before she died, Caw—one of the Caws of Snedlebarum—an idle, vicious lot. She has no—er—father; at least he was not married to her mother. That, in brief, is the origin of Mrs. d'Arcy Fairfax. But, of course, she has told you already?'

He did not answer.

'Harry will be in shortly, so you can talk to him,' said Mrs. Norman. 'You will probably think him more sympathetic than I am, but he can't desire you to be happy more than I do. And I've told you the plain truth. I say nothing about your relations with the husband, although you assured me on more than one occasion that he was one of your best friends. Willie, Willie, why don't you go straight? It isn't English, you know, to behave as you're behaving!'

And having made this appeal, Mrs. Norman left him alone.

'Christ!' he muttered to himself. 'O Christ!'

He went into the garden, and lay in the hammock, in the shade of the walnut tree.

'Evie Caw—Evie Caw—how odd it sounds. Poor little Evie Caw. Were you born under the beeches, under the rookery, my darling Evie Caw? Anyhow, my darling, I'll never be unkind to you again! Or go off like a bloody little egoist because you speak to any other man! God, what a fool I was! God, what a fool! A suspicious fool. Darling Eva, nothing shall ever part us. Except death,' he muttered to the sky up through the rustling walnut leaves. 'And love is stronger than death.'

When Mr. Norman came briskly to him Maddison met him with a smile.

'I'm glad to see you, Mr. Norman.'

'Good boy! Now tell me all about it, old chap.' The kind grey eyes looked at him.

For nearly twenty minutes, speaking intermittently and in a low voice, and never meeting Mr. Norman's eyes, Maddison talked of the meeting in Devon, of Major Fairfax, of Evelyn. Of other men he said nothing. When he had finished, Mr. Norman leaned forward and spoke in a confidential voice.

'Well, old fellow, so you're in love with my little model, are you? I don't wonder, and I don't doubt—you, I mean. Otherwise, to be quite frank, I do not feel like congratulating you.'

'But, on my honour, I love her with all my heart and soul. And she loves me, too.'

'With her heart, that organ for pumping blood and nourishing the nerves that control the emotions, yes. But not her soul. She has none.'

'But she has. She is a poet! Some of the things she has said to me! And her profound feelings, her sensitiveness to beauty! I can talk to you, because you will not think I'm insane or merely a libertine. You have seen her eyes—can't you see her soul in them?'

'Oh, come now, Willie! You're old enough to know better than that! That soul-in-eye business is all rot! I have known Eve since she ran about in the fields in rags. I have seen her weeping over a swelled frog that some boy had stoned in the stream. Yes, and then watched her cutting it open to see what's inside! I have watched her taking her father's dinner to the mowing meadow, and I have seen the men stare at her, even when she was twelve years old. Now listen. When she was fourteen, she got a job as under-kitchenmaid at d'Essentville Castle—for a short time only.'

'O God. Spreycombe!'

'Exactly. I blame no one, mind. I am just explaining the rise of a very vivid personality. It is said they paid her mother to take her away from young Spreycombe—I tell you in confidence, mind!'

Mr. Norman continued in a reflective voice: 'She is a natural lady. She was a refined child. Mother a drinker, a husband-beating scold. Father a poacher. Where she gets it from, I don't know. It's simply a genius for assimilation.'

'She is a child of sunrise!'

'Well, yes, sunlight is one of the life-forces, and there is more in her than there is in the ordinary mortal. I don't mean that she is over-sexed. But when you spoke just now about her being a poet, I know that you are a poet. She is an absorbent mirror, in which you see your own abstractions. I do not mean she is deliberately insincere. Many people think she poses—my wife thinks so. But I don't. I know she calls up the deepest part of a man's nature, absorbs it, and is himself for a while. That is her terrible attraction, her sincerity; but as each mirror is shattered . . .'

'Mr. Norman——'

'Of course you think you love her. I knew it when I saw you. But you won't always love her, Willie.'

'I will! On my honour, I will. I cannot help myself.'

'My dear boy, in the face of your sincerity, I do assure you I feel an awful prig. But really, you're so very young! Old fellow, you must accept what I say. It's hard, I know.'

'But, Mr. Norman——'

'Listen, dear boy. Tear yourself away! Force yourself to accept the inevitable! Break it off!'

'Never! I'll never desert her! She realizes at last that other men——' He tried to make his voice steady. 'Everything else is gone in my life. What is the countryside to me now? With my love she will be different. I swear to you that I am saying a truth. Believe me, for God's sake, Mr. Norman!'

'Willie, why did you say with your help she would be different? My dear boy, it is worse than I thought. Have you found her already with another lover? Forgive my crudity, but we understand each other.'

'Mr. Norman, you don't understand——'

'Willie, you must not shirk the truth. Don't delude yourself. There will come a time, if it hasn't come already, when you will have to realize that she is behaving to another man, to other men, exactly as she has behaved to you.'

'Mr. Norman——'

'You'll have to face it, Willie!'

'You don't understand, really. I *know*, Mr. Norman, I *know*.'

'Poor old Willie!' said Mr. Norman. 'Afraid I can't help you.'

'There is such a thing as honour,' remarked the quiet voice of Mrs. Norman, who had come in tennis shoes, unheard, across the grass.

'Must you, Deb?' said Mr. Norman.

Mrs. Norman shrugged her shoulders. 'Come and have some tea, Willie, and don't let's say any more about it. Remember, however, I'm thinking only of your good. Come and see the model of the War Memorial Harry has designed.'

'Don't forget Bill Nye, will you?' said Maddison to Mr.

Norman. 'The poor little devil they shot for desertion—but it was simply wildness. Don't forget to put his name on.'

'I'm afraid it's not in my hands,' explained the artist.

'He should be on the Church Roll of Honour. I see they omitted him.' He sprang up. 'His breast, too, was pierced and shattered by the bullets of our common inhumanity, just as Jesus's was!'

'Well, come and have some tea, old chap.'

'Thank you all the same, but I think I'd better go and see Father.'

'How long are you staying?' asked Mrs. Norman.

'I shall go back to Folkestone to-night, Mrs. Norman.'

'Well, then, you ought to be ashamed of yourself, that's all I can say!'

'I'm not a bit ashamed. Forgive my rudeness. What is honour to me? I've never had any honour, as my school reports used to insist.'

Mr. Norman said reflectively: 'The war has upset your normal development. It has upset hundreds of thousands, too—you and Eve among them. Some have got it worse than others. A most difficult period for young people—that poor Warbeck boy, for instance, and Sandy White—and you, Willie. Won't you stay to tea?'

'Thank you, but I—good-bye, Mr. Norman. Thank you very much. I'm afraid I don't feel very well. Good-bye.'

'My dear boy, I wish I could feel that I was of any use. If ever you need a friend——'

'Yes, thank you awfully. Good-night, Mrs. Norman.'

'Good-night.'

Maddison went back into the King's Arms and had a few pints with the landlord in the kitchen, becoming more and more friendly until the landlord's daughter said she wished the war was still on, for the 'place was a bit more lively with them Canadians about the place', when he said suddenly:

'Good-bye, I must go.'

'You'll be all right after a bit of a walk, Mas' Willie. Good luck, my boy,' said the landlord. He walked rapidly home.

'Well, I waited tea until six o'clock,' said his father, in the library. 'Biddy made some of her special teacakes in your honour. I don't know if any have been kept hot.'

'Don't bother, Father. Thanks all the same. I'm not hungry.'

'You had tea, perhaps?'

'No, I mean yes. Honestly, I don't want any. Please.'

He sat down, wondering why he was there.

'I don't believe you've had any. Come, don't be diffident, old chap.'

'Oh, please, Father! I'm not hungry, thank you, Father. O God, why must you—I beg your pardon.'

'Is there anything the matter?'

The son fidgeted on his chair, and mumbled that nothing in particular was the matter.

'Is it about the girl?'

He looked out of the window, unable to meet his father's grave and sympathetic gaze.

'If it's that worrying you, what can I do? Nothing. Absolutely nothing.'

'Father, I find it very hard to tell you.'

'I'm sorry. Don't tell me if you would rather not.'

'It isn't that, Father.'

The father waited.

'She's married, Father.'

'Then she is the wife of your friend?'

'Yes.'

'Well, if I were you, old chap, I shouldn't go back. It may be hard at first, but it will be best for everyone eventually.'

The son did not move.

'Otherwise you will find yourself involved in something beyond your control.'

Father began to walk about the room, as he had years ago

when he was a child, detected in some little crime, and about to be sent upstairs for a thrashing, for the ultimate good of his character. Well, Father couldn't thrash him now!

'Willie,' he said, sitting down again, 'has it gone very far?'

'We love each other, Father.'

'And does Mr. Fairfax know?'

'No, Father. He's Major Fairfax.'

'So you've been living in his house, and——'

Maddison breathed deeply. He sat very still. Suddenly he sprang out of the chair.

'Yes, sir, I was the honoured guest in his house. Mrs. Norman has already emphasized the moral turpitude, the black treachery. Now you know what a blackguard you have for a son. Where's your cane? But you won't get a scream out of me now! The war is between us, you must realize!'

'There is no need to speak like that.'

'I beg your pardon, sir. I have no excuse at all for such a breach of good manners. I forgot I was a guest in your house.'

'I do not forget that I am your father. And you needn't consider yourself a guest—you're the son of the house, sad as it is. You're a bit tired after your journey. Sit down, my boy, don't be so restless. Why not let me ring for some tea?'

'No, thank you, Father. But forgive me mentioning it: is there any money due to me?'

'Any money due to you? From the Army, do you mean? I'm sure I don't know.'

'No, I meant from my mother's marriage settlement.'

'There was a marriage settlement, yes; but that doesn't come to you until I die. Most of it was in Russian stock—and you know what to expect from those blackguards.'

'But didn't Mother leave some when she—when I was born?'

'Your mother left a little money, yes, Willie. But she left it to me. She did not know you.'

'Oh, I beg your pardon—I rather thought, from what I

remember Biddy to have said to me some years ago, that it was left to me. But I see that it was not so.'

'Biddy has curious ideas at times,' said Mr. Maddison, dryly. 'But if I can help you at all, please let me know. Can I be of any assistance to you now?'

'No, thank you, Father. It is very kind of you to offer. I must go very shortly.'

'But you've only just come.'

'I must go back to-night, thank you, Father.'

'I should stay awhile, if I were you,' said Mr. Maddison. He frowned. He felt his tea suddenly heavy in his stomach. Divorce! The young idiot!

'You haven't a damned penny to bless your name with. It's rubbish, a youth like you, just starting life! You ought to get a job, you know, instead of loafing around. You'll develop into a waster—as I always feared.'

'It's very hard to get a job nowadays.'

'Have you tried, I wonder.'

'No.'

'Humph. Well, I was afraid it would come to something like this when you were a schoolboy! You always were idle, and deceitful. It's a thoroughly bad business!'

'You wait!' screamed Maddison, leaping out of the chair. 'You wait! The whole bloody world is against me, but I shall be stronger than all your damnations! You wait! One day you will see if I am idle and deceitful! You know nothing, nothing!' He sat down, hiding his face in his hands.

Father and son were trembling.

'Biddy has made your bed up,' Mr. Maddison managed to say; 'you ought to go to bed.'

'I should only be climbing out of the window again in the night. I did that once before, if you remember. If only I had fallen and broken my neck! O Christ!'

'I don't know why you are talking like this.'

'I've told you why, Father!' he shouted, springing up again

and walking up and down the book-lined room. 'You say I was indolent as a boy, you wise grown-ups, with your canes and your religions and your blockades of food for children—and your wars and all the lousy hellishness arising out of the negations of the little boy's dreams. Christ, I won't stay here another moment! O, you good people! You grind away the natural, the godlike part of the mind, and have your wars, your burnings at the stake, your crucifixions, your—O Christ, I can't bear it!'

'I don't know why you're talking like this,' said Mr. Maddison wearily. 'Unless it's because you've been drinking again. You said you'd chucked it when last you were here. I'm sorry you've gone back to loose ways.'

'None of you—you're all—Mrs. Norman hasn't the least glimmer of what Christ means—I'm not condemning her, but —she is a good woman in herself—but when I think of her— and the human race generally—absolutely helpless because people follow false ideals—I—we——'

'My dear boy, you are overwrought. Why not go to bed and rest?'

Mr. Maddison was seriously alarmed, for the agitation in his son's features as he flung himself about the room.

'Honour! *Dulce et decorum est!* Ten million didn't go home again, but I did—Willie Maddison the unwanted, the waster! God, it's quite true! I've never done anything worth a damn in my life—d'you hear?—except to be a target for our naval shells on Chunuk Bair—and later to help to destroy some poor miserable little German boys of eighteen—now I live in my friend's house after I've made love to his wife! And I'm not a bit ashamed, really! That's an awful thing to say, Father, but it's absolutely true! I'm a degenerate—creepy crawly—as you once called me as a boy. Why don't you order me out of your house? I'm no more use to England—why don't you kick me out?'

'I don't know why you're bullying me like this,' said Mr. Maddison, in a thin voice.

399

The tone of Father's voice, the worn look on his face, made the son remorseful for his words. He realized that he was stronger than Father. Father looked grey and tired, and his hands were trembling. He flung himself on the sofa, sobbing.

'There, now, Willie, there now!' said Mr. Maddison, hovering near. 'There now, old chap.'

'Father,' he said, in a choked voice, while tears ran down his cheeks. 'Sir, forgive me speaking to you like that. I'm a cad and a—a rotter. But Father, everyone seems to be against—against me. I walk all night sometimes, to—to tire myself so that I may sleep—but it's no use—and the—nights are long—longer than the frosty nights on Gallipoli—after the deluge, when half of us were frozen—dead in the ice of the trenches. Father—the silence of the night hurts more than frozen eyeballs and the—the ice between the brain and the—the skull, and the—concussion of big naval shells. So forgive me—I am —always—really—really despair, and yet, yet——'

The sobbing voice tailed off. He got up and ran out of the room, and out of the house, and down the drive to the lane. In the village, calm again, he tried to send a telegram to Eve to tell her that he was coming back to her, but the post office was closed.

The train was half an hour late, and he spent the time in the King's Arms, drinking beer and trying to eat bread and cheese, trying to interest himself in the casual evening talk of contented men, trying to prevent the tears coming repeatedly to his eyes.

Chapter 36

ALL night long the train moved beside starlit fields and rumbled through dark tunnels, while on the seat Maddison sprawled, drowsed, and imagined. He saw the dawn through the open window, cold and remote beyond the orient. In the meadows and over streams a white mist was rolled by the winds. At every station the engine stopped, while urns of milk and baskets of dairy produce were clanked and slidden into the vans. He saw the sun rise red and swelled in the early autumnal vapours.

The train arrived at Folkestone at six o'clock. A few sleepy soldiers alighted. A farm cart, laden with vegetables for one of the hotels, rattled down the street, the driver singing as he sat on the shafts. A golden September haze filled the road between the lime-trees as he walked up the avenue towards The Paragon. The street door of the house was not yet unlocked, so he went down to his lodgings to wash and shave.

The young woman in black who usually gave him breakfast was raking ashes from the sitting-room grate when he entered. She said they had been worried about his absence. Maddison wondered if he were the subject of gossip. Colyer—Warbeck—Sandy White—surely all Folkestone must know about it. Hell to Folkestone, anyhow! Wisps of hair were over her face, and a sooty smudge on one cheek.

He replied politely that he had been away on business, and went upstairs to his room. She had cooked two rashers of bacon and a duck's egg for him when he came down. He did not wait to eat it, but hurried to the flat.

The door was still locked so he went for a walk on the Leas, wishing that he had not left the spaniel behind. Yet the dog would be company for his father. Poor Father, how far apart they were. Well, he was glad the beeches were gone. The sooner you ceased to feel things the happier you would be. He must pack up *The Policy of Reconstruction* and send it to a publisher. To Longman's, who had published Jefferies. They would surely accept it at once.

He walked as far as the Grand Hotel, and then returned with faster pace. The front door would be unlocked now. He broke into a run; then compelled himself to walk leisurely.

In The Paragon milk bottles were being laid on the steps of houses. The front door was unlocked. He climbed the stairs.

Someone had arrived before him, for he heard a cough in the drawing-room. It was Sandy White, dressed in flannel trousers and a jacket of Donegal tweed. The boy turned to speak to him, but could say nothing. His eyes were fixed in a wild stare as he sat on the couch.

'Hullo, Sandy. What's the matter with you?'

'Nothing, Captain Maddison.'

He noticed that Sandy's hands were shaking.

'You don't look very well.'

'I feel—I feel——'

'What are you doing here?'

'Nothing, Captain Maddison.'

'Have you seen Mrs. Fairfax?'

'N-no,' he stuttered, 'I think she's still asleep.'

'Have you got more leave, Sandy?'

'I'm not at the R.M.C. any more.'

'Why?'

'I w-was stellenbosched. I say, Willie—I beg your pardon, sir.'

'Call me Willie, you bloody fool!'

'Mary Ogilvie always spoke of you like that, so I'm rather in the habit.'

'What's that book you got there?'

402

'It's for Mi—for Mrs. Fairfax. It's called *Far Away and Long Ago*. It's for her to keep.'

'Why were you stellenbosched, Sandy?'

'I—I couldn't stick the life. I was always ragged by the other chaps, who said I was an outsider, and because I got tight one night to forget ghastly reality they ragged my room and a cad named Formby tore up my photographs. I went for him with a poker and laid him out. Then they scragged me, and made me dance on the table naked with a—a jerry——'

'I know the sort of thing.'

'I didn't care. I swear Formby took one of my photos some time ago. He said he didn't, but someone did.'

'Of your mother?'

'No, just a friend.'

Maddison said, with an effort that made his voice sound curt:

'You shouldn't drink. You're too frail, you know. I get just the same if I drink very much.'

'I'm not really frail, only I get upset, and drink's the only way to forget things.'

'Yes, I know. But it's damned silly, all the same. Why don't you clear off to Canada, or somewhere out of this bloody Europe.'

Sandy White stared on the floor.

'When did you come?'

'Yesterday.'

'Have you told your mother? It will make her sad, and your mother is too sweet a woman to be made sad.'

White gave him a timid look, and said: 'How do you know about my mother?'

'I met her at the Grand Hotel on Peace Night.'

'Oh, yes, she told me she had spoken to a friend—I mean, to someone,' he replied awkwardly.

'I have a high opinion of your mother, Sandy. She is a true woman.'

'Yes. Oh, I must tell you, Willie. M-Mummie is—well, I was terrified for Mrs. Fairfax to see her, because I dreaded what she would think. Once I heard her talking about some-one else, and calling her——' He made an effort, and went on: 'Calling her common. It was like a stab to me. And when Mother came to see me once, at Sandhurst, I knew what the fellows thought, and—and Formby said she was the fat woman out of a booth in a fair.'

'There are cads everywhere, Peter, old man. You ought to get a job, old chap.' He thought: I might be Lionel, talking like this. God, what a hypocrite I am.

'I fought him, but he beat me easily.'

They were interrupted by Martha's face, solemn, expression-less, ugly, looking round the door.

'If you please, Captain Maddison, the missus would like to speak to you.'

'Where is she, Martha?'

'In her room, mister.'

'But I can't go in there. She expects me to wait in the dining-room, perhaps?'

'It's all right, mister. I've took her tea in.'

'I'll be back in a moment, Sandy. I wonder what Lina wants. About having the car decarbonized, I expect. Back in a moment.'

He went into her room, closing the door. She stretched up lace-frilled arms to him, clasping him almost fiercely. He knelt on the Persian praying rug, elbows on her pillow, forming with his hands a nest for her head. Her eyes were dewy with love.

'Billy, is Sandy out there?'

'Yes. He wants to see you.'

'Tell him I cannot see him again. Get rid of him. He plagues me.'

'What shall I say to him?'

'Anything. I won't see him.'

'Shall I give him that message?'

'No. Just say that I meant absolutely what I said yesterday. The boy's mad, following me about. What did he tell you, some rubbish I expect?'

'Nothing. Except that he's been sacked from the R.M.C.'

'Silly kid. Billy, let's swim this morning! Tell him to go; he worries me.'

'Don't worry, dear Eve. Poor little Sandy.'

He laid his head on her shoulder, his arms encircling her. He held his cheek against her cheek, not daring to trust his voice. He left her, and went back to Sandy, who was stuffing a handkerchief into his left sleeve.

'Mrs. Fairfax asked me to tell you, Sandy, that she meant absolutely what she said to you yesterday.'

He saw him wince and shiver, and the dull stare came back to his eyes.

'All right.'

Compelling his voice to be steady, thereby rendering his tone unintentionally formal, Maddison said:

'You must remember that she is a married lady. You should not come near her again, now that she has expressly—asked you not to. Is that clear?'

'Yes,' replied the other. 'I realize that it is—it is—the end. But I don't understand.'

He hid his head in the couch. The elder man waited.

Sandy got up. He took an envelope from his pocket, with a book, and held it out to Maddison, who with back towards him did not see it.

'Willie!'

'Is that for me?'

'Yes. This too, Willie! You do understand, don't you?'

'Yes, Sandy. Life is just hell. I know, old chap, I know.'

Sandy tried to speak. He held out the book.

Overhead Jonquil could be heard jumping on the spring mattress, a thing she was most fond of doing, especially in the early morning, when the sun looked in upon her through the window.

'Willie.'

'Yes?'

'I didn't mean anyone to see that letter. I don't know why I wrote it. Swear you won't read it till this afternoon.'

'Yes. Will you have left Folkestone by then?'

Sandy nodded.

'Tell her I shall never forget her kindness. Won't you?'

'I will.'

'O God, Willie, let me go for a walk with you. I'm so ghastly afraid of being alone. You're so strong. People say I'm weak, but they don't understand. O Christ.' He began to cry.

'Hush, Sandy, old man. We all feel pretty bloody at times. You'll get over it, old chap. I used to be just as miserable as you are over a girl. I don't care a hoot for her now.'

'I—I—haven't even got—my—photo——'

Should he give him the photograph, which was in his breast-pocket? Maddison hesitated. Cruel to be kind? What a swine he was. Better keep it hidden; then Sandy would forget the sooner. God, what a swine he was—he wanted it for himself. That was the truth. O, well. He stood still.

'Won't she say good-bye?' Sandy's voice trembled.

'I'll see.'

'Is it much I've asked you to do?' said Evelyn loudly so that Sandy White could hear. 'Tell him I never want to see him again. Wait. Please return this cigarette-case to him. Tell him he forced it upon me, and that I never wanted it. Thank you, Billy.' And, whispering to him: 'Cruel to be kind.'

'I'll come down with you, Sandy,' he murmured.

At the street Sandy begged him to meet him in the town at Corvano's at twelve o'clock, to bring Lina to say good-bye, for the last time. O, please, would he? Corvano's, at twelve o'clock.

'I swear I'll never trouble her again, I swear I won't. At

twelve. Do ask her. You see, I can't bear to leave—except as friends——'

'I'll tell her. Now, Sandy, you'll feel better when you're away, honestly you will, old chap. Now, you jump on that motor-cycle of yours and go back to your mother. Won't you?'

'Won't you come with me into the town? For God's sake——'

'I can't, really. Now, you do what I say, won't you?'

'Yes, Willie. Tell Mignon—tell her—tell her—Willie, I don't —say to her that beauty is faithfulness, and she must never forget my words.'

'All right. But I don't suppose she'll——'

'And tell her not to worry.'

'Very well.'

'And Willie.'

'Yes?'

'You're the greatest gentleman I know.'

'Don't talk such bloody rot!'

They shook hands. 'Let me know how you get on, Sandy, sometime?'

The boy nodded, and turned away, weeping.

Maddison did not deliver the message, but said: 'I persuaded him to go away. He promised to go this afternoon. Poor Sandy, but his mother will be pleased to see him.'

'I only hope he goes!'

'Your beauty is answerable for a lot of incoherence, Eve.'

'I didn't make myself. I say, Bill, there's a topping show at the Leas Pavilion. A wonderful tenor. He sang the Prize Song from the "Meistersingers". Is that the correct way to pronounce it? My dear, I did long for you to be there—I thought of you all the time. I went with de la Hay and Archie Dodder last night. Did you think of me at all?'

He was thinking of the stolen photograph; of the promise to give the message; but better not reopen the subject again. Poor Sandy.

'You don't seem very pleased to see me.'

What could he reply? He led her into the bedroom, and locked the door. Even so, there was no true relief: his mind could not surrender itself. Nor were her eyes dewy with tenderness. When he went out of the bedroom later he did not speak, but waited for her, unrestfully.

They went down to bathe. By a coincidence, apparently, de la Hay, the actor, went in the sea about four waves after them. He attached himself with easy familiarity to Eve, who, Maddison saw, seemed glad to see him. She swam to a breakwater with de la Hay, and perched beside him in her harlequin bathing dress. Maddison sat beside her, and although he tried to be cheery, his remarks gradually ceased. Evelyn was definitely more interested in de la Hay. De la Hay was not thin like himself; de la Hay was still laughing and talking, and sometimes singing, when Maddison went in, cold and shivering, after the sleepless night and lack of food. He dressed, and lay in the sun; but there was no blessing in the solar beams, because he could not surrender himself. His mind bestrode him like a crab, with its claws in his brain. They remained in the sea for nearly an hour. Unable to bear the sight of Eve diving from de la Hay's shoulders, and realizing that he was not wanted, Maddison went up the path to the Leas.

There he remembered the letter that Sandy had given him. The clock on the bandstand pointed to five minutes to twelve, and he waited till the hour with a sensation of dread and fascination to read what was doubtless a love-letter written to Evelyn. One minute past twelve—it was afternoon.

The letter was written in ink on many sheets of paper, and in parts scarcely to be read. The Hungarian band, looking uncomfortable in the hussar dolmans, and led by the long-haired violinist in Hessian boots, played the opening bars of *Belle Nuit* from Offenbach's *Contes d'Hoffmann*. It was one of the favourite airs of the Folkestone holiday crowd. He began to read.

Chapter 37

So this, then, is the end . . .

The end of everything.

After two hours of silent waiting, with nerves strung up to the highest pitch, my ghastly, ghastly fears have been confirmed. Not confirmed by any actual and conclusive action, but by the feeling in my heart.

It is nearly one o'clock, I know, but I am absolutely indifferent to time or place. At the present moment I am indifferent to life itself. I am callous of the future, and as for the immediate present . . . I have not quite realized it yet. I must write . . . the only outlet for my terrible anguish.

How the stones on the beach outside hiss as each summer wave recedes after its crash. A bluebottle is buzzing about the room. My only dread is that it will settle on my head, and then I am sure I shall scream. My nerves have been on edge for the past two hours.

When I approached your house about a quarter past ten to-night, I noticed that your windows were not lighted up. I concluded that you were either in bed, which at that hour was unlikely, or that you were still out, which was most probable. As I passed, wondering whether I should whistle or go straight in, I heard your laughing voice in the distance. Your laugh has always appeared to me to be joyous . . . although as I think of it now in retrospect it grates on my ear. But that is only to be expected, perhaps, after the emotion my brain has had

409

racing and roaring through it during the last two hours . . .

I saw your white dress in the half-light of the evening, and with you two men friends. I immediately turned round and walked rapidly away. I bent my back as I came under the lamplight, so that you might not recognize me. I tried to hobble along as an old, old tramp might. But apparently my subterfuge was of no avail, for I heard you whistle to me . . . the same whistle that I taught you during the first rapture of our friendship; the whistle that I and my dead brother Herbert used when, so long ago now that it is a blurred and indistinct memory, we used to wander in the woods and fields of Warwickshire.

I heard the whistle. I knew that neither of the men with you would know me, or imagine that anyone was waiting for you.

I crossed the road further down, and hid myself behind one of the lime trees in the Avenue. I heard your voice distinctly; in the calm serenity of the evening it sounded so very clear; I heard you saying good-night to them, and thanking Mr. Dodder for giving you a pleasant evening. Then you ran up the steps and the two figures vanished; the one retraced his steps, the other went around the corner towards your grandfather's house. I walked forward. I saw the light appear in your drawing-room under the roof. I watched you as you drew the yellow curtains across the window, and thought at the time that, if you had wanted me, you would have looked out to me. I am sure you knew that I was down there, watching you, waiting to come up to you. All the evening I had been glancing at my watch, counting the minutes till a quarter to ten, when I would be seeing you. How differently things turned out after all.

The sea is still murmuring; it seems to be sobbing. Perhaps it is my imagination, however, or that my grief and anguish is coming on again. Anyhow, it seems to me that it sobs as it leaves the land behind it. The fly has stopped; he is probably tired, and sleeping as he clings to the wall somewhere.

I stood still on the pavement below. A Ford taxicab rushed past with blazing headlights, and its advent filled the air with a greasy odour of burnt oil and petrol, and little pieces of dust and straw whirled behind it, filling my nostrils and irritating my eyes.

Then, just as I was about to cross the road, I saw you standing at the top of the steps, and I thought you were looking for me. My heart bounded, and just as I started to come to you I saw a dark figure turn the corner rapidly, and leap up to meet you. For a moment I thought that he had been round to your grandfather's, and then I knew. Of course, it was the old trick; I had done it myself. Your parting with the two men was just subterfuge; the elder of the two did not interest you, and therefore you got rid of him in that manner. All arranged beforehand as you and the other man sat alone at dinner, and you probably laughed in his face as you explained the ruse, and the blood flowed slightly faster in his veins at the thought that he, as a man, would naturally think: that you were attracted by him.

For about half an hour I stood near the house, watching the window. I am afraid I was spying again, as you call it, but I do not wish to make any excuse. But why I felt sick at heart, why my brain was numb, and I could not keep still, I cannot tell. Perhaps for the same reason that I was damp with perspiration, and my eyes misted over so that I had to rub them clear again . . .

At the end of a quarter of an hour I suddenly thought I would see the whole thing through. I crossed the road silently, I felt like a tiger stalking in the jungle. Only, instead of the fierce joy of the chase, I experienced that sinking, sickening sensation that one has when very bad news is imminent. Yes, I was apprehensive.

I opened the hall door very silently, and crept into the hall. I paused, and listened, straining my head into the void above to try and hear your voice. I only heard the sound of plates being washed up by the people in the flat below you, and the dull murmur of their voices. I opened the door on the right and entered the empty room, which the decorators are still working on. The light from the street lamps fell on the floor, and I could see the trees through the dirty windows, and a dark patch on the glass of the middle window, where the 'To Let' sign was pasted on. On the floor were brooms, planks, pails of half-dried whitewash, and paintpots, and the sour smell of fresh paint and putty. I glanced round and picked my way carefully over the floor to avoid kicking a pail over and betraying my whereabouts. I finally sat down on the floor opposite the door, in such a position that, with the door half closed, I could see everything that occurred outside. Then I thought that possibly you would turn the light on when you came downstairs with him, and would see me. So I chose a position behind the door and started to wait.

Eleven o'clock struck. I could just hear what the two people in the flat above me were saying. The woman was telling the man about a young girl, a servant girl, I gathered, who had apparently thrown all maidenly reserve to the winds. As usual, they condemned her harshly. The poor girl's ears must have burned, because they tore every shred of character she had possessed completely in shreds. They dealt with her in the usual way the majority of women do when judging, or rather condemning, one of their own sex.

By this time I found that my knees were trembling ever so slightly. My throat was husky, but I dared not clear it, lest the noise brought people down to see who was there.

My cheeks, too, were hot; it may have been all caused through imagination, of course, but then it is very difficult to discriminate between reality and imagination. At any rate, I was very, very nervous, and very, very unhappy. But that is entirely my lookout, of course . . . I heard the clock strike the half hour. Soon the whole house was as silent as the grave. I could hear the metallic tick of the watch on my wrist. The street lamps still threw the weird and grotesque shadow on the floor. Upstairs, in your drawing-room, you were closeted with your friend, talking; I could imagine your having said to the maid: 'Oh, Marty you poor dear, go to bed!' in your gentle voice; perhaps you were being kissed by him; but, still, I must not imagine things. My thoughts are ghastly and tragic enough without imagination to intensify or distort their effect.

One sound came down from above, the sound of cups on a tray being rattled. I wondered how this occurred: did you do it as you rose to get something, or was it caused by his legs as he turned towards you to take you in his arms?

Oh, the torture of that thought. The ghastly, ghastly suspicion that it brings with it in its baneful train; the thought that your deepest words are light as the ashes of a gorse fire settling to the earth, that you give yourself as lightly as bracken to the swaling flames.

Twelve o'clock boomed from the church over the road. Midnight! But I determined to see the whole thing through. About a minute later I caught the sound of a door being opened slowly, and I heard your voice. I could not move. I stood in the doorway. I had it all mapped out, what I should do. I would almost close the door and peer through the space left. If you kissed each other . . . and I even thought he might kiss you hurriedly as a brother might . . . oh, I did not want to believe the worst . . . because I loved you with all that was best in my soul, as well as with the worst in my heart, maybe.

I saw you put the light on, and found I had slipped on to my knees, and was shaking like a leaf. I dared not look. I will not tell you my feelings, although you will never read this letter. My feelings do not concern you at all . . . now . . . and I prefer to leave that aching, reeling feeling of sorrow undescribed, even to myself . . .

You were not worthy of the love I had to offer you; that phrase burnt into my brain as I staggered out towards the sea . . . you were not worthy. You were faithless and insincere . . .

413

you gave me love, and immediately you were tired. If I believed in God, I should pray for you till I died. I cannot understand you. You did love me. In the beginning I loved you because you loved me, and told me so when you suddenly clasped me to your heart and kissed my lips that sweet morning in May down by the Hythe Canal. You loved me, then, although you hid yourself in Devon soon after, but I thought that was because of Phillip Maddison, and because you wanted to think about our love in perfect quiet. It nearly broke my heart with joy that a beautiful poetical girl like yourself could love me. It seemed incredible that you were married. You seemed so intensely mine from the moment you came towards me. I thought you were the one dear, sweet girl I was destined to meet when I grew up . . . and love and cherish in my heart always . . . even after death, when we should wander together in Eternity. I have, of course, told you this before, and how you must have laughed inside you. I know you called me an egoist; I who was always marvelling at the purity of thought and feelings you called up in me and so entranced with it all that I wanted you always to hear about it; how the wind whispered it, and the birds sang it. Ah! How pitilessly I see the shattered ideal, and the feet of clay, as your statue lies in the pitiless white light of fact and reason.

I wandered down to the beach. I wanted the sea to hear my tale; the sea always soothes me so. Perhaps one of these days it will soothe me eternally as my head disappears in its swirling embrace.

The cold moon shone down on the waters, spreading a broad path of silvery spangles as the waves tripped and rippled. Except for the sob of the waves, all was silent. The summer is finished, for this year at least. Perhaps I shall never see another. I have had my springtide of life, and now it is ended.

I was sitting on the beach alone, listening to the wavelets as they sobbed up the land, and dull despair in my heart.

THE BROKEN WEB

The night wind played around my temples, soft was the sob of the sea. I held my head in my hands, and then pressed it into the dark wet pebbles for relief. Far away the lighthouse flashed—down the white path of the moon's radiance on the water a dark fishing boat was going home . . . the beauty of the scene for a moment enraptured my soul, and then I remembered . . . in the moonlight the dark shadowy pools of your eyes were radiantly beautiful . . . your face was sweet, and as the powdered silver of the moonlight drenched you, you looked like an angel . . . and that was gone, false, destroyed, forever and forever and forever.

Mignon! I can see no more; great big tears keep welling up in my eyes. I am utterly, utterly broken . . .

Chapter 38

THE writing sprawled wildly across the page towards the close. It tailed off in visible despair.

The band began to play the National Anthem just as Maddison laid the manuscript down. He stood to attention, cursing silently. As soon as it was over he walked rapidly to the Victoria Hotel, which was a boarding house near the docks, and enquired for Mr. White.

The proprietress, a timid little faded gentlewoman, told him that Mr. White had just gone out on his motor-cycle. He had told her that he was departing that day, but his room was still in occupation, and he had not yet packed his bag. He had, however, burned a quantity of letters in his grate. She asked if he were a brother of Mr. White's, because he resembled him, especially about the eyes and the mouth. Maddison replied that he was no relative but that he was an intimate friend, upon which the proprietress confided her alarm about him.

Mr. White had been out till very late the night before, or she should have said that morning, his return waking up many guests. He ran upstairs in the dark and bumped his head into the door of a resident guest. Then he had been heard walking about in his room for more than two hours, lying on his bed, leaning out of the window, going into the bathroom and filling the basin with water. He left it unused, and went out of the house again. He ate no breakfast, and said that he would not be in for lunch. He had stayed there before, and his behaviour had always been erratic, but he was such a charming boy at times. She feared to say that complaints had been made by the other guests, and she was afraid she would have to ask him not

416

to return there, especially as he had a revolver with him. She had not mentioned the revolver to anyone else, as it would not do to alarm them unnecessarily, besides it would be an unfortunate thing for the hotel if it were generally known. Maddison said he would keep the information to himself.

Mr. White, concluded the landlady after thanking him, had paid his bill by cheque half an hour since, and had gone off on his motor-cycle.

Maddison listened attentively, then replied that Mr. White's eccentric behaviour was probably due to disprized love.

'Disprized love? Oh, it sounds so sad. Poor Mr. White.'

The landlady's face showed sympathetic understanding. Shaking her by the hand, Maddison hastened away.

Remembering that Sandy had said he would be at Corvano's restaurant at twelve o'clock, he ran up the stone steps to the Leas, towards the High Street. It was twenty minutes after twelve by the church clock and Evelyn might have gone there with de la Hay. Hurrying down the side street, out of breath after leaping up the steps, he turned into the High Street. The clock over the Town Hall, facing the meeting of three streets at the bottom of High Street, pointed to twenty-five past twelve as he went into Corvano's restaurant.

He was not there. Corvano said a gentleman of his description had left ten minutes previously, after drinking several double whiskies. Maddison went out into the bright sunlight. He stood still, wondering where Sandy might be. Damn him!

A motor trade-van drew up outside the principal fish shop, where a man was swabbing a marble slab with a cloth. Red lobsters and crabs, oysters and salmon, prawns and soles, lay amid blocks of ice and green parsley, with mullet and cod. His line of sight was upon the fishmonger so energetically swabbing the marble slab, but he was not seeing him, nor did he hear the metallic purr of the Ford trade-van.

The fishmonger ceased to swab the marble, and the regular action being broken, Maddison observed suddenly the peculiar

and fixed expression of his face as he gazed, the swab held
motionless in his uplifted hand, at something in the street
behind him. At the same moment a woman's voice began to
scream, the rough shrillness continuing until broken by a sharp
report and the noise of plunging hoofs. Many people seemed to
be putting hands to faces, and looking down the street he saw
Sandy White behind the motor-van, hatless, and sinking to the
road. A revolver loosened from his right hand as he sank down,
and clattered into the gutter.

Maddison went to him at once and knelt by him, knowing by
the attitude that he might not be dead. Gleams of gold showed
in the red-clotting brown hair of the head lolling on his sleeve,
the lower jaw was askew, the eyes were unfocusing their stare,
the teeth showed between the drooped lips.

'O, Sandy, Sandy! I'll be your friend, Sandy, I'll be your
friend.'

The words fell vain in the sunshine; the dying eyes stared
into his own, as though dimly wondering why the voice was
so far away, why the sun was fading out, and darkness falling
on the earth.

Chapter 39

A VOICE softly singing to the accompaniment of a piano sounded in the drawing-room of the flat as Maddison thrust open the hall door. The wide-brimmed felt hat of Mr. de la Hay was hanging on a peg, his clouded cane and goatskin gloves laid below it on the floor. He was seated at the piano. He nodded to Maddison and continued singing:

> *She is waiting where the willow tree sighs*
> > *My sweet Jeanette*
> *The morn wind passes, the swallow flies*
> > *By my Jeanette*
> *Eyes are cloud-soft, grey as the skies*
> *Lips are tender, good, and wise*
> > *Of my Jeanette*
> *Oh, this London Town's a-swoon*
> *Every hot, vibrating noon*
> *I am coming very soon*
> *To the flowery lanes of June*
> > *And you, Jeanette*

He ceased.

'No, dear lady, I'm not sure whether I ought to finish *falsetto con pianissimo*. And to be quite honest, I'm not sure whether the words will fetch 'em. They're a bit too good, although I suppose I oughtn't to say that as I wrote them myself. However, if I tried to mute the poetical stop a bit, I daresay I shall make rather a hash of it, and merely fall between two stools. It wants more onions in it. But I like it. How do, Maddison, old boy.'

They shook hands. 'Sorry if I interrupted the song, de la Hay.'

'Not a bit! I was trying it out on Lina. They want onions, you know—sob stuff.'

'I thought it rather a nice song.'

'I say, did you really? Thanks very much.'

'Well, Bill, now that you are here at last, we can have lunch. Don't turn away, my dear: it's rude. Do you want to wash?' she asked the man at the piano, who flashed her a smile, and said that he had already done so.

'Then come on. I suppose you can eat grouse?'

'My mouth waters, dear lady.'

He leapt forward, holding the door open for her, and they went into the other room. Maddison remained standing by the window. Martha went in with the dishes, came out again. A masked ex-officer with a barrel-organ stopped in the street below and commenced to play. A breeze came from the sea and filled the primrose-pale curtains, and he saw it ruffle the feathers of a sparrow perched on the gutter above her bedroom window. Buoyantly on the air came a white butterfly, drifting up and down, which the bird pursued and clumsily hawked in mid-air. A starling flew to the chimney-stack opposite, and sang with wings shaking dull colour hues like its song. He dimly realized that he was thirsty but wanted no drink, and then Evelyn with napkin in hand was looking round the door and asking if he had any reason for the display of bad manners other than a childish and spineless jealousy.

'You make me ashamed of you,' she said. 'Why don't you behave like an ordinary decent man? Cannot I meet an acquaintance and invite him to lunch without your insulting him in your hostess's house? Billy, dear, why do you make things so hard for me? What have I done? Oh, you are a damned fool.'

'Please don't bother about me.'

'Why do you stare at me like that? Are you drunk?'

'I'll explain later. Please eat your lunch. Really I'm not hungry.'

'Come on, Billy! Be a man! They are such fine birds and I bought them specially for you. I told him that Naps sent them, but that was poetic licence! Come on, old fellow!'

'Honestly, I'm not hungry. Will de la Hay be stopping long? I rather wanted to speak to you. Soon.'

'Tell me, now.'

'No, not now. Later. Dearest Eve, do trust me. You go and have your lunch. I'll wait here for you. Will he go soon afterwards?'

'You're simply impossible, Billy! You've ruined my lunch.'

'Darling, I'm sorry. Please go and forget me. Eat your poetically-licenced grouse. Dear Evelyn, I won't let *you* down! I'll be your friend!'

'Billy, you *are* drunk! You're maudlin! Your eyes are wet. Be a man, for God's sake. Come in and eat your lunch.'

'Please, I don't want any. I'll tell you something when de la Hay has gone. Do ask him to go, please, after lunch!'

'Do you order me to get rid of him?' she asked quietly, with tightening mouth.

'No, no. I'll tell you later. Please leave me now.'

'You make me exasperated,' she said, with scorn in her voice. 'Thank heaven, all men are not like you. Well, if you won't come, you won't, and certainly I'm not going down on my knees to you.'

She went back to the dining-room. For some minutes the street musician went on grinding, but wearying of playing for nothing, he dragged his wretched organ down the road. Maddison watched him till he disappeared round the corner into the High Street.

Evelyn's desk was open. He took the photograph from his pocket, and put it under the blotting pad. The pad was adorned with various figures of fancy scrawled on the blotting-paper round the edges, beside the large inversions of her quill-pen handwriting. Some of the writing was direct, and seeing the word *Actress*, he peered at it. *Yours, Evelyn de la Poer, the Celebrated Actress*. Then there was *Evelyn Spreycombe*, and below: *Yours sincerely, Evelyn Slepe*. Of course, Spreycombe was the Earl of Slepe's heir. Her fancy included *Evelyn Lorayne*, and, yes, in ancient writing, *Evelyn Maddison*. He clenched his hands and turned away.

When after lunch they came back into the room for coffee, he was still by the window. De la Hay continued to talk livelily in his musical voice. He seemed perfectly at home, lying back on the couch with one leg cocked over his knee, with his effortless and bright man-of-the-world conversation.

Maddison gulped down a cup of coffee; the spoon rattled in the saucer. Noting this, and the expression of his averted face, de la Hay smoothed his nose several times between finger and thumb, sniffed, and looked blandly and with raised eyebrows from the ceiling to Evelyn.

'I'm sorry I'm so rude,' said Maddison, feeling rage and scorn when the other man replied:

'Not at all. Yes, you really must manage to come up to Town for our first night, Lina. It will be awful fun. You must meet Consuelo Fitzroy again. She's an aw-fully nice girl. Getting a hundred a week. Supper on the stage afterwards, don't you know, and a dance. Aw-fully good fun. You really must manage to be up for it.'

'I shall,' declared Evelyn.

The conversation flowed on unheard by the man at the window, except for sentences and laughs that came to him with startling distinctness, only to fade away once more and become blurred with things seen out of the window until he realized that they were going; and when alone he flung himself into a chair and covered his face with his hands. Evelyn found him like this, and stood before him, frowning and with pursed lips, her feet close together, the tips of her spread fingers pressed against her tweed jacket.

He looked up and saw that she was frowning, but her eyes were merry.

'What a conceited bore that man is! How I hate being called "dear lady". I invited him to have a peg and a cigarette last night, after a concert at the Leas Pavilion with Archie Dodder, and he stayed till nearly midnight talking about himself and his lousy old show. I was quite amused, but one knows all about him after half an hour. Well, why do you look at me like that? Don't you believe me?'

'What does it matter?' he replied. 'I've broken faith with one man; I've sent another into the shades. What does it matter, what is truth, what is lies?'

'Whatever do you mean?'

'I mean, that there is no need for you to be other than yourself with me. I realize what you are now. I realize what I am. You once called yourself a wanton; well, you were at least honest.'

'What do you mean?'

'Please don't get upset. I'm trying to—to make friends with you.'

'By insinuating that Aubrey made love to me. Is that it? You think me a wanton—a whore, do you?'

'Listen, Eve——'

'Answer me!'

'Please, darling Eve——'

'Don't you dare to call me "darling"! Answer my question!'

She stood before him in cold bewilderment, a pulse beating in her throat, clenching her hands, opening them again and spreading her fingers.

'It's a hard, a withering word, "whore"——' He looked bleakly at her. 'Yes, if you insist on an answer, I know you are what the world calls a whore. But, Eve——'

'You dare to say that?' she whispered. 'I think I shall kill you. You are the same as all other men! You are! You are! O, God, you are no different, after all! You called me that

terrible name! You, a slinking spy! You, so fine and honourable, to spy on a woman! Bah!'

'You don't need to act with me, Evelyn.'

Her face was pale; her lips were drained of colour. She
stared at him with furious eyes, then leaning forward she
struck him across the face.

'Really, you should go on the stage, Lina.'

She struck him again. 'You sneering beast! Take that!'

'I'm not sneering, really. You'll only hurt yourself, my dear
girl.'

She snatched the rhinoceros-hide whip from the wall and
struck at him; he caught the thin, whippy lash with his hand.
It was torn from his fingers, and she stood over him with upraised arm.

'Oh, you flinch! Coward! Spy! I could cut your
cheek in half with one blow!' Her face was white and
strained.

'You'd only be sorry, Eve. But do it if you want to. I don't
care.'

She flung the sjambok in a corner.

'Well?' she said, looking at him coldly, proudly.

'I have something to tell you.'

'More judgments? More stones to be cast?'

'Eve——'

'Once, once you said I was like a lark that sang for joy. Do
you remember the lark in the deserted aerodrome? Well, your
talons have struck me down. But you won't stamp on me with
your deadly conventional judgment. O God, you think I am a
whore—you, the man I gave love to—for whom I broke the
vows I had made—because I believed you were like Shelley—
like Jesus Christ—yes, yes! I tell you!'

She rocked to and fro on the chair in which she had flung
herself, her hands over her face, weeping. He was pierced
anew by doubt and hope. She was acting, of course. Who
could understand her? No, she was not acting; how selfish his

attitude was, as always. He had damned her merely because he wanted her for himself.

'I have failed you as well,' he cried, beginning to pace the room, clenching and unclenching his hands.

Several motor-cars and taxicabs passed under the window.

'Billy,' she said softly.

'Yes.'

'When I was fourteen I went to work as a kitchen girl in d'Essantville Castle.'

'Dearest Eve——'

'Is that what you mean by whore? A common little prostitute? Well, you're right. I began to be one very early, you see, although I knew as much about things then as Jonquil does now. But you don't believe that, do you? Please will you go away, and never speak to me again? You are a gentleman, and so you will do as I ask.'

'Eve, I beg your pardon,' he cried, thinking that he must remain to protect her against everything very soon. With his love! Had he ever loved as the common man loved, the common man of the masses he had called blind, who in millions had laid down their lives for their brothers?

She looked at him curiously, then went swiftly to him, sobbing, and hid her face on his knees. 'Oh, Billy, I have been a damned swine to you. Do you really think I would let de la Hay make love to me?'

She was beyond his understanding. He did not know what to answer.

'I don't know,' he replied. 'I don't know. What has it to do with me? I am nothing: dishonourable, parasitic, worthless.'

He took from his pocket the letter given him that morning.

'Yet another chapter of "The Policy of Reconstruction"? Oh, Billy!'

'Read it, Eve,' he replied, gently, kneeling by her, and taking her hand. 'Read it, and do not worry. And remember, neither that nor anything else makes any difference. I'm

425

entirely to blame. I broke my word. Remember, I am entirely to blame.'

He left her, wandering about the house, and climbing on to the torrid leaden roof. He sat on the brick coping, wondering what Mr. Fairfax and the hangdog man pulling his bath-chair would think if he were to cast himself down. He saw his father's worn face. *I don't know why you're bullying me like this.* Sandy's white face: *I—I—haven't even got my photo*, and *You're the greatest gentleman I know.* Thrusting his knuckles into his mouth, he bit them to the bone. No, no, he mustn't jump down. He must protect Eve. The frenzy passed. He was calm again, and stronger than before.

Returning through the box-room window some time later he saw upon a tall mahogany wardrobe against the wall a green book that seemed familiar. He fetched a chair to reach it. It was *Far Away and Long Ago*, the copy given him that morning. He saw, too, the beginning of six uncompleted socks, thrown there in the past. Two were in khaki wool, and the steel needles were rusted, and all lay amid dust. The sock of heather-mixture coloured wool she had begun to knit for him was flung among them. They looked so sad, lying there in the dust. No, he must not cry. He must be strong, to protect Eve.

Returning to the drawing-room, he saw her seated on the couch, the manuscript beside her.

'I have read it,' she said. 'It makes my heart ache. Poor Sandy, poor frantic little boy. I didn't know he was outside last night, or I would have asked him up. Fancy him waiting there all the time. Did he give you this this morning?'

He nodded. O God, what was the truth?

'Do you know, when I first met him he was half mad over another girl? And you will, perhaps, hate me for saying it, but his letter is more imagination than pain. To use a vulgar phrase, he was kidding himself when he wrote it. He is very highly strung. Half his letter is a re-hash of what he has unconsciously absorbed from magazine stories. He tried to write some, I know, but they were no good. And, Billy, he mentions hearing what the Smiths, in the flat below, were saying. They've been away for a week! The flat is empty! You see, he is at a period of life when he is neither child nor man; I used to think he was a genius. O, Bill, I hope I haven't done anything to harm him; but I didn't realize his awful capacity for suffering. Do you believe me, Billy?'

He put his arm round her shoulders, telling her not to fret.

'But I can't help it, Billy. Poor Sandy, I wonder if he has really gone. He left his book—poor little Sandy, with his talk of dreams and visions, and poetry. Just like you, only he's a babe—and you, you've grown up since you came to Folkestone. I've put his book upstairs, where it will be safe until he writes for it, as I know he will want to give it to someone else in six months' time. Oh, I know these lads and their broken hearts. Well, what worries you now, my dear frowny-head?'

'Sandy White is dead.'

'Dead?'

'He died this morning.'

'But do you mean it?'

'He is dead, and will suffer no more.'

'Dead? You're lying! Don't joke like that, Billy!'

'Ah, Eve,' he whispered.

'Tell me! Why don't you tell me?'

'He shot himself.'

'Shot himself? But why? Over me?'

'Don't worry, my dear. You are not to blame,' his trembling voice murmured, as he tried to believe that she had never known the dead boy in love, as he held her close. But she struggled free, and he had to repeat a dozen times that he was dead, that he had shot himself, that he was a suicide. With a cry she rushed out of the room. He heard her running down the stairs.

Imagining that she had gone round to her grandfather's house, he waited at the flat, while Jonquil showed him her latest 'comical', which contained an instalment of the adventures of her favourite heroes in fiction, a boy named Freddie Featherhair and his dog Dashatem, among the savage tribes of Bohunkaboo. But his pretence of interest would not hold, so he went into the kitchen and talked with Martha. When he told her about the suicide she stood still and looked at him, while behind the thick lenses of her spectacles the tears dripped slowly from her old eyes.

'Well, mister, he was always a perfect gentleman to me. He took things too much to heart, just the same as you do. The poor dear was young, and 'ow should the young know what us old 'uns know, after suffering?'

'How life beats on us like waves on the stones, wearing them thin. Oh, Martha, I really think it is best to be out of it.'

'Don't you think that, mister.'

The tears fell down her cheeks as she stared at him, leaning his brow against the cold distempered wall.

'You've had no lunch, mister. Let me give you some tomato soup, made with milk.'

'I'm not hungry, Martha.'

'Don't cry, dearie. Here, I'll make you some nice warm soup. O dear, what a mess-up the world's in, to be sure.'

She made him drink the soup, and afterwards put before him some cold game, which he could not eat; he thanked her, and left the sniffing old woman.

Evelyn had been round to Radnor Park Gardens, where Milly had already heard of the suicide, but she had left. Milly showed an hysteria of selfsome pity that made him feel hard and contemptuous to her; then he softened, transferring the contempt to himself, and wondered calmly if he should kill Eve and Quillie and himself, and so end it all.

'What a wicked thing to do. What a selfish thing to do. How unthinking! How sad! He was only just beginning life. That beastly man Warbeck was the real cause of it. He led him into bad habits! Oh, I don't know how I shall ever be able to sing

428

or play again. I used to play while that poor misguided youth sang. Some of his songs are here in this room. Think of it—in this very room! "Now Sleeps the Crimson Petal," "Thou art risen, my Beloved", and that shouting thing he always insisted on singing, "On with the Motley". Poor Sandy, poor silly fellow. Lina is heartbroken, dear gel. And think of the scandal! He may have left some letters to smirch the good name of Fairfax for ever. Oh, I have no patience with him. But I ought not to talk like this. And yet I can't help it! He only thought of himself. Poor Father will hear and be so upset; you know how religious he is, and—oh dear, I hardly know what to do. I might have to go to the inquest. And I haven't a rag to be seen in. What am I saying? Billy, old chap, tell me, what shall I do? Ought I to send his songs on at once to his father, or wait till he writes for them. What would you advise?'

'I shouldn't do anything,' he answered wearily.

'Of course. How calm you are! But I feel so deeply, you know. How I envy you! So cool, calm, and collected! How I manage to control myself I don't know. I wish Margy was here. Hark, what's that? Is it a policeman, do you think?'

'It sounded like the kitchen fire being made up.'

'Yes, I suppose it did. What a blessing Father cannot hear, or he'd start an economy campaign again. What am I saying? I must go and get Father's tea. Do stop, won't you?'

'I ought to find Lina, Milly. She left the flat in great distress.'

'That's so good of you, if you will. Do buck her up. She must not worry. She ought to go away to avoid any scandal. She is not at all blameworthy. Find her and buck her up, old chap. Kiss me.'

He kissed the fluttering woman, and left the house as Mr. Archibald Dodder, his face an agitated purple, entered the gate. Poor fellow, awful, awful; the police are asking for Mrs. Fairfax, he puffed; but Maddison hurried away, searching for Eve. He went on the Leas, hastening through the gay holiday folk by the bandstand, looking at every face. The crowd was thin by the Grand Hotel, and he was about to turn back when an unusual figure caught his attention—an old gentleman dressed entirely in black, wearing on his snow-white hair a hat with an acorn-shaped crown. It was Sir Rudolph Cardew, the veteran actor, walking on the withered grass, swinging his monocle on its black riband, and talking to the audience of himself. Maddison hastened to him to enquire if he had seen Evelyn, and Sir Rudolph paused, screwed the monocle into his eye, and awaited him in an attitude of profound and courtly attention.

'How do you do, Sir Rudolph! My name is Maddison. I met you the other night with Mrs. Fairfax.'

'Ah, yes, well do I remember our little talk by the sea, Maddison. But you are perturbed; may an old man who knows you be allowed to say that you are sadly, ah, sadly, perturbed by the rumours that surround Mrs. d'Arcy Fairfax in connection with the slain youth?'

'Yes, Sir Rudolph, I am trying——'

'It is well for the world, Maddison, that all young men do not feel so keenly. For he has crucified himself! The suicide, the self-slain! Who shall know the thoughts of the young lover distraught? For him the world is dead. That which in the radiance of his lofty dreams is more splendid than life is lost for ever. Time does not exist for him. There is no future. He cannot look ahead. His is too fine a nature to bear the annihilation of its exalted dreams. There is no consolation for him. He has looked upon the loveliest in life, and rather than have the vision blurred, he takes it with him triumphantly to the shades of death. Ah, Maddison, woe unto the man who cannot learn to submit to life as it is, to disassociate aspiration from reality! But who am I that my musings should be of interest to anyone save an old man?'

Sir Rudolph looked earnestly into his face, and saw that the listener was profoundly affected. Accordingly he felt a liking for the young man, whose arm he held above the elbow, an

honour of intimate equality he bestowed upon few men in
Folkestone and Piccadilly. They walked together as far as the
bandstand, where Sir Rudolph turned with an expression of
pain on his handsome face, saying that he had an ear for music.
He swept off his hat, and with a hand-gesture of farewell turned
on his heel and sauntered back the way he had come. Maddison went to The Paragon, but Evelyn had not returned.

For six hours he searched the Leas, the sea-walk, the lower
town, the square, the High Street, the gardens, returning to the
flat many times. Jonquil was crying for her mother, and would
not be comforted. Martha gave him another bowl of soup in
the kitchen, and he continued the search. At the corner of the
High Street he bought a newspaper from a boy shouting
unintelligibly, but the newsbill carried before him like an
apron was plain enough.

SUICIDE

IN

HIGH STREET

LOVE

TRAGEDY

Chapter 40

THE double news-sheet printed on rough greenish paper gave a column to the tragedy, hinting that startling disclosures would possibly be made at the coroner's inquest. Meanwhile it would content itself by stating that a lady locally well known would probably be called to give evidence. The deceased was alleged to be the only surviving son of Councillor G. White, C.B.E., of Birmingham, a magneto manufacturer, and was understood to be a gentleman cadet at the Royal Military College, Sandhurst. He had been staying at the Victoria Hotel. There followed various interviews with various people. He stuffed the sheet into his pocket, and mingled with the crowd on the Leas.

Ahead of him the outline of the bandstand was pricked in silver: roof, spire, pillars, basement. The promenade lights stretched from and beyond it like golden oakapples, decreasing with distance till they were no larger than yellow moth-frecks on the blue foliage of night. People leaned against and sat on the wire fence at the cliff top, smoking, chatting, and observing the passers-by. Below the Leas a vast open-air rink was filled with roller-skating couples, from whom were thrown ragged blends of shadows by the four great arc-lamps at the corners. A rasping blare of waltz music was blown across the rink from the great trumpet of a stertorophone. In the dark the small waves broke like a sweat lather on the beach.

The bandstand became brighter and brighter. A thousand lighted faces were before him. Round the cleared space between the first rows and the stand he walked, searching. Back again among the gaily laughing strollers on the promenade, while the lighthouse over the sea flashed intermittently like the high-shrapnel he had watched above the Bapaume road at night; but there was no war now to which he might go and find peace. Past the dark buildings of the deserted Rest Camp, where rooks sat on the chimney-pots, cawing a last good-night in the afterglow of the sunken sun. Past the bright glowing windows of the Royal Hotel, back again to the illuminated bandstand, along the crowded Leas. Fruitlessly to Corvano's Café Royal, a gulp of coffee while he looked at every table, a return to the flat, to Martha sitting with folded arms in the kitchen, and to hear her dull reply:

'She hasn't been in, mister. A policeman called again just now, mister.'

At ten o'clock he heard in the distance the band playing the National Anthem, and shortly afterwards the blare of the rink stertorophone ceased, and the arc-lamps died out. He was then at the eastern end of the Leas. So fine was the night, so moth-like the moon, that the crowd remained till nearly eleven o'clock, when every other golden oakapple became black on the invisible bough above the promenade, as though blown down by a wind that was arising from the sea. In a few minutes the Leas were deserted, except for solitary male prowlers and affectionate couples.

He continued his quest by the seashore, while the waves pounded the pebbles and flung afar the spray. In the lull of the wind he heard the cries of migrating lapwing. Crests of waves tarnished the silver path of the moon on the waters. He scrambled over the wet wooden breakwaters, trudging on the pebbles which slid and jarred to his steps.

'Yes, Phillip, Lionel, Julian, Pat, Sandy—the guardian female spirit pierced the pre-Adam scar, and grew the rib again, and then was torn away—and we bleed, we bleed, we bleed to death, until we join the rest of our generation.'

He slipped over a breakwater, falling into the backwash of a wave; he stumbled on, heedless of wet clothes or the pain in his knee.

'If only the earth would flare up in space, and crumble to ash to-night!'

Even as he spoke he realized that his despair would not have lessened; the shock of cosmic catastrophe would have seemed puny compared with the shock of realizing that beauty was false to its spirit, to its vowed affection, to its words of love.

Onwards he trudged, the gusts flinging spray on his face, his grief seeming to find answer in the cries of the lapwings in the windy darkness above. He found her just after midnight, sitting on the beach. She did not look up; the noise of his steps was brushed away by the roar of the waves. She lay still, her head bowed and hidden. He took her hand, frigid as the pebbles on which she sat. He spoke her name. She shook her head.

She said tonelessly: 'Why do you come near me?'

'I have been looking for you everywhere.'

'Why?'

'Because I am your friend.'

'My friend? Don't you realize what I am?'

The tone was so flat and dull that he could not answer. He thought of her as a bright-eyed child taking her father his lunch under the hedge, while the youths followed the little girl with their eyes. Men would always pursue her, because she was beautiful, and beauty was only the serf of Life.

'Will'um?'

'Yes, dearest Eve?'

'If only the peasant girl had never left the fields. I learned too early that life was hard and that men were—were—I became arrogant when I realized that I could make men do as I pleased. And now there is a boy who has died for love of me—an unsoiled, gentle boy. I am evil!' she wept, clutching his coat.

'You poor little straying thing,' he whispered, kneeling and taking her in his arms. He murmured into the night, while

434

looking up at the stars and caressing with his hand the uneasy head that would find no rest till joy and sorrow were one with death. He felt his heart grow strong as the earth.

She spoke his name, and he leaned over to hear the small voice.

'What worries you now, dearest Eve?'

'I did let him love me.'

He stroked her head, her restless head. Dear, dear Eva, blaming herself because the poor hungry birds in the wilderness flew to her basket of cherries.

'Billy, only once. I didn't mean to. When he came in such distress into my room one morning after—after wandering about all night, and I was drowsy, I had a terrible and sudden compassion for him, which changed into—into—I couldn't help myself.'

I had a boy something like you, once, Mr. What-do-you-call-it . . . killed, the poor little darling, and only eighteen, too——

'You were compassionate, like a mother, darling Eve. Don't worry your poor head.'

'Billy, I'm what you said' she cried, sobbing again.

'The sun doesn't think so, my dear.'

Listening to the sea he thought of another lying there who in the surge of the past night had heard also the wave-chant of lamentation and despair. A solitary lapwing cried through the dark to the flock it had lost, and the pines on the cliff behind made a wild æolian music as they told of the rain that surely would come with the western wind to heal a land's disverdure.

And when Mother came to see me once they said she was the fat woman out of a booth in a fair—I was always ragged by the other chaps who said I was an outsider.

Ah, Sandy, my darling, when our nation, with its false pride and un-understanding is forgotten—when our earth is ice, and the sun is vanished and black—long after, when the dust of star and planet has ceased to fall on other worlds—the Love which is the spirit of the mother-heart will shine—in the deep, dreadful night——

'Hush, Evie, hush. Poor children, all of you——'

The unheard words were torn out of his mouth by the wind and drowned in the toppling crash of the combers. He spoke to the void above and beyond the moving waters. Her head lay against the great strength in his breast, she was sheltered within the wings of his spirit, she was a poor bird whom the gentle falcon of his love would cherish evermore.

The world of men and women will conquer you, Maddison——

Dear Julian, in vain you breast the bars of brass. Look up at the stars, which have rolled away so much sorrow and hate—crushing the gold of pity—out of darkness.

Eve was asleep.

The stars on the southern horizon became ruddy in the sea vapours, and he watched till they dipped beyond the world. The hourless wind rushed on.

Chapter 41

THE landlady was raking the grate when Maddison returned to his lodging. She made a remark identical with the one she had made to him twenty-four hours previously. Yes, it was a beautiful morning. He smiled, said he did not want any food, and stumbled upstairs to his room, kicking off shoes and lying on the bed. He arose half an hour later, shaved, washed, and went downstairs to breakfast.

Then he went upstairs and wrote a final paragraph to *The Policy of Reconstruction*.

'And thus have I arisen from my dead, my educated, my European self; and I arose completely and finally in that moment in Canterbury Cathedral while God was being thanked for our victory in the war: reading the New Testament during the scale-eyed words from the pulpit, I found a text that brought the tears to my eyes in glory of what I beheld—"My little children, of whom I travail in birth again, until Khristos be formed in you." Therefore shall I live, therefore shall I work until the night cometh, therefore shall I love from everlasting to everlasting.'

'I have to leave to-day, I'm afraid.'

'We shall miss you, sir. I'm sure we couldn't want for a nicer gentleman.'

'Thank you. I've been most comfortable.'

He paid his account and departed, unable to give any reply save a nod of the head to the landlady's hope that he would be coming back very soon.

Jonquil was before the house when he arrived there, stooping over a drain, a string held in her hand. She was bareheaded, dressed in a corduroy jacket and lemon socks with brown shoes. She glanced up at him and smiled.

'Quillie's fishing, Will'um, like your father were, with a little tiny potato.'

'Is Mother in, Quillie?'

'Mummie's just gone away. I say, Will'um, do you think I'll catch a fish? Quillie's glad you comed to see her. You can hold the line if you like! Why, W-W-Will'um, what's the matter?'

'Nothing, Quillie. Was Mother with anyone?'

'Erhum. With Naps.'

'With Naps, Quillie?'

'Y-yes, Will'um. Mummie was crying, and started to go to the trains by herself, but—but Naps came in his moticar. O Will'um dear, why do you look like that?'

She put her arms round his knees, and stared up at him. He bent down and kissed the little face. The love of the linnet-frail girl gave him a poignant longing to fade with her into the sun. How well could he understand now Francis Thompson, the most homeless of poets, whose tiercel spirit for so long having ranged unmated the starry wilderness, evermore was haggard of human love.

'Eve does not want me, even as a friend,' he said, in his immense sadness.

From the mortal world of banished hopes his dream must fly up in the blue-stained air, a white bird that all men should see, and seeing, be comforted. If the haggard tiercel cried its pain, it should fly through the flames of hell until nothing of the mortal hoping frame was left, until the haggard was the phœnix of heaven.

'Will'um, you're not proposen to leave Quillie are you? Don't go.'

Colyer, where was he? Warbeck, Phil, Lionel, Sandy? Why weren't they all there together, being friends for ever and for ever, never changing, never passing away into darkness. He looked down on the pavement worn by the feet of men, and thought of Eve, and said:

'I must go, Quillie.'

'No, you mustn't, Will'um. Quillie loves you so. Honest to God, she does. And so do Marty——'

She dropped her fishing-line.

'Where are you off to, Will'um?'

He looked at a rain cloud travelling from the west, fraught with the light of the sun. Westwards lay the Atlantic, the wide sands, the sea birds crying over the estuary bar. Mary Ogilvie—was she at that moment on the Santon sands, while the waves broke on the bar with a hollow roar? O Mary, she would understand! Or Phillip. Yes, he would walk to London, and find Phillip!

He hurried up the stairs to Martha, giving her the brown paper parcel containing *The Policy of Reconstruction*, asking her to give it to Mrs. Fairfax when she returned. 'Beg her to take great care of it, Marty, won't you? It's very valuable! Ask her to post it to Devon when she's read it.'

'Very well, mister. Going off?'

'Yes, Marty. Good-bye. You've been a friend to me. Good-bye.'

Jonquil was waiting for him in the street.

'Please answer, Will'um. To find Mummie? Or going away for ever?'

He made his answer steady.

'I'm going for ever, Quillie.'

'W-W-Will'um——'

And kissing her on the brow, he turned away, leaving the little child sobbing on the kerbstone, her arm over her eyes.

(*A valediction is overleaf*)

VALEDICTION

Valediction

Now that *The Flax of Dream* is completed, by the addition of this penultimate book of the tetralogy, a small commentary may be permitted.

What happened to Maddison? Readers of the ultimate book, *The Pathway*, know that two or three years later he returned, after working as a labourer on the battlefields of France, to Devonshire, and that he fell in love with Mary Ogilvie, and that the love was never completed in reality. Readers of *The Beautiful Years* know how the child was made to grow the way he grew; and how, in *Dandelion Days*, a system of education was employed to try and make the boy into what was called a useful citizen.

Much has been written about Maddison, which seemed at the time of writing to be relevant to his failings in happiness. Collectively more words have been written about the books than are in the books themselves; the commentaries are like the segments of a circle, or the points of a compass, varying from Mr. J. B. Priestley's declaration, supported by that of Mr. Hugh Walpole, that Maddison is 'half-baked, with all the trappings of a prophet without the prophecy', and that 'there is no evidence that Mr. Williamson is a man of ideas', to Mr. Wilfrid Meynell's belief that the book (*The Pathway*) 'will be read by many to whom, like myself, it will be an experience for which they have been living as a preparation'.

For my own part, if I may now state my opinion, I should be sorry, and guilty, if either of my sons developed into a young man like William Maddison; but in one aspect, or implied hope, I identify myself with him, for like the late D. H. Law-

443

rence (who now that he is dead has more emotional value for some of his friends than when he was living), his thought and utterance were peculiarly directed against those ideas which he believed to despoil human life.

What happened to Evelyn Fairfax? Mrs. Ogilvie is the authority for stating that she divorced Major Fairfax (who was chivalrous about the Divorce Court in the contemporary English manner) three years after Maddison left Folkestone. A year afterwards the Earl of Slepe (as he became on the death of his father) was divorced by his lady wife (Evelyn's name not being mentioned, but that of a professional co-respondent known as 'a woman'), and in due course his companionate union with Evelyn became also a legal marriage, continuing unaffectedly the mutual integrity and harmony of their lives.

Jonquil lived with them, when she was not being taught to behave as a sporting young lady at a school on the cliffs near Brighton. Old Martha became part of the d'Essantville household also; and his Lordship was always a perfect gentleman to her.

And Major Fairfax? He went to Kenya, where he played much tennis and shot big game, and found serenity among his own kind.

As for the Reverend Vernon Fairfax, his grandfather, this old gentleman died on his eighty-eighth birthday, in the hope and belief that the Lost Tribes of Israel would soon be proved to be domiciled in England, which imminent proof would herald the Second Coming of Christ to the British Empire and other countries. Like Maddison, he died without having realized that the intellect cannot understand an emotion.

His daughter Milly, her long filial duty performed in the best Victorian tradition, broke away and became a partner in a Dorsetshire farm for breeding Sealyham terriers, where she worked gaily and wore men's breeches, thus realizing the ambition of a lifetime.

Sir Rudolph Cardew, another Folkestone celebrity, who in

real life was called Sir Squire Bancroft, died shortly before
Mr. Fairfax. He is mentioned here because he remarked to the
author that the fidelity of Maddison to a dead man (Jefferies)
was most pathetic. 'He reminded me of Chatterton,' said Sir
Squire. 'And, at other times, of Hamlet, haunted by the ghost
of ten million murdered men of his generation.'

And Julian Warbeck? His story will be told with that of
Phillip Maddison and the other London cousins.

And Tompkins, the ex-bank clerk, ex-officer of the (now
disbanded) Machine Gun Corps, ex-batman to the 'ace'
Captain Colyer? Probably he went to prison; but it is doubtful
if prison removed his inferiority complex, which was responsible for his poses, and was caused by some unknown mental
anguishes in childhood. I think that Maddison understood
him, although he did not say much, involved as he was in his
own peculiar dreams of escape; with their symbolism and
imagery which in intense moments he believed to be actual, or
immortal. Who shall decide?

And the amiable de la Hay? Of him, at least, something
happy can be reported. He was successful as a *revue* author for
a little while after the War, until the rise into popularity of
Mr. Noel Coward and Mr. Bernard Shaw and other young
men of the transition period. For *The Flax of Dream* is the novel
of the transition; and in this connection perhaps Mr. Frank
Swinnerton will not mind my adapting to Maddison his critical
remark about myself—'I think it is only a question of time
before he is recognized everywhere as an authentic voice of
that generation which is not yet sure of its power.' The power
of my own generation was used almost entirely during the
years 1914-1918; what power remains can only indicate itself
by revealing the past.

Maddison was, as has been stated occasionally in newspapers, a real person, and 'The Policy of Reconstruction, or,
True Resurrection' was written very much in the manner
described in *The Dream of Fair Women*. The manuscript was

445

left behind in the apartment in The Paragon when Evelyn eloped with Lord Spreycombe, and was probably destroyed in the ordinary household elimination of attic rubbish. Maddison wrote one other book, however, 'The Star-born', of which certain people have enquired by letter to Jonathan Cape, Ltd., Publishers, of London. Will it be published? The answer is yes. 'The Star-born' also was composed, and lost, very much in the manner described in *The Pathway*. The extraordinary memory of a friend who heard it read one September night, in a Devon cottage—the night that Maddison lost his life, not by suicide, as Mrs. Ogilvie believed, but indirectly because Mrs. Ogilvie omitted, for reasons she thought expedient, to deliver his message to Mary, who alone would have realized that no salmon boats would be riding up on the swift tide flowing past the mid-estuary gravel-ridge on which Maddison was waiting in the darkness—has been largely responsible for the recovery of many of its authentic scenes and sayings; but otherwise it is inevitably lessened by an inferior hand and mind, namely that of Maddison's biographer. And so farewell.

H.W.

Manhattan Island.
  Fall, 1930.